D0863810

MEMOIR OF A GREEN MOUNTAIN BOY

MEMOIR OF A GREEN MOUNTAIN BOY

A Novel

Raymond J. Rodrigues

iUniverse, Inc.
New York Lincoln Shanghai

MEMOIR OF A GREEN MOUNTAIN BOY

iUniverse books may be ordered through booksellers or by contacting:

iUniverse
2021 Pine Lake Road, Suite 100
Lincoln, NE 68512
www.iuniverse.com
1-800-Authors (1-800-288-4677)

Because of the dynamic nature of the Internet, any Web addresses or links contained in this book may have changed since publication and may no longer be valid.

ISBN: 978-0-595-45205-7 (pbk)
ISBN: 978-0-595-69308-5 (cloth)
ISBN: 978-0-595-89514-4 (ebk)

Printed in the United States of America

Acknowledgments

My wife Dawn could never stop asking me questions, tough questions, but kind, critical questions about what I was trying to say, suggesting improvements, and sparing my feelings as well as anyone could, while also being a firm editor. I'm amazed that she could read my manuscript so many times. My good friend, story teller Ricardo Garcia, read it closely with his writer's eye and helped me tighten up my loose writing. Both of them made this more readable, and for that I am thankful.

I am indebted to many who have written about the American Revolution, but I could not have written this without borrowing heavily from Ethan Allen himself, especially *The Narrative of Colonel Ethan Allen* and *Reason: The Only Oracle of Man*. I could not resist using many of his words and phrases throughout without citation and in contexts that I created, for he could express himself in ways more entertaining and multisyllabic than anything I could have dreamed up myself. Obviously, this is a work of fiction and, as such, it portrays people who really did live in those times as well as people who popped out of my head.

I was also inspired by a real account of what it meant to be a private in the real American Revolution, written with humor and insight, *A Narrative of a Revolutionary Soldier: Some of the Adventures, Dangers, and Sufferings of Joseph Plumb Martin*, the 2001 Signet publication with an introduction by Thomas Fleming

And finally my thanks to those Pownalians whose love of local history and place is both admirable and inspiring, especially the members of the Pownal Historical Society.

—Raymond J. Rodrigues, Carpenter Hill, Pownal, 2007

PROLOGUE

"What good is a revolutionary spirit if nobody gets shot? People need to get shot." Yes, I said that. Once.

If you, my reader, are kind, you probably will try to make me feel good. "Oh, Erastus, that's 'cause you were young."

Being young is no excuse for being wrong.

Do you like heroic stories? Then let me tell mine.

Many years have passed since the tales of glory, Ethan Allen, and the Green Mountain Boys set me to dreaming. Many years have passed since I marched off to Ticonderoga with Ethan Allen and the Boys from Pownal, but only now can I begin to make sense of it all. This is my tale of what happened to me during our Revolution; about the beginnings of the fourteenth original colony of these United States of America—Vermont; about self-serving patriots, sacrificing patriots, and ordinary patriots; about how we set out to fight the Yorkers and ended up defeating the British; and about banshees, witches, scalpers, and profiteers.

You undoubtedly have heard of Ethan Allen, Benedict Arnold, and George Washington. Perhaps you have even heard of Seth Warner and John Stark. But I would bet you have never heard of Cotton Mather Dewey, Theophilus Bates, Pebonkas Kisos, Michael McGinness, Elizabeth Ross, Huntington Hungerford, Ann Story, Jacob Hintersass, and all those the politician John Adams catalogued as "Tories, Landjobbers, Trimmers, Bigots, Canadians, Indians, Negroes, Hanoverians, Hessians, Russians, Irish Roman Catholicks, [and] Scotch Renegadoes . . . . " Well, now you will. I knew them all.

My mother, brothers, sisters, and uncle have been as much a part of my adventures as all those folks, so you'll find them here, too, especially my older twin sisters, Tryphena and Tryphosa. Frankly, some days I would rather not talk about those two, given the ways they have embarrassed me all the days of my life, but I suppose I owe them their due.

Ethan Allen himself charged me to write the history of the Green Mountain Boys, so I am fulfilling my obligation to him. If you are a schoolmaster searching for some theme so you can force your young scholars to memorize that theme and avoid seeing the real story, then this book is not for you. If you are one of those historians who mines remembrances of old soldiers so you can add a footnote to your already too tedious compendium of facts to prove your portentous theory, then you probably should go elsewhere for your primary sources. If you are a dreamer who wants to remember our American Revolution as a mass movement of patriots, all sacrificing for our common vision of a democracy, then you definitely should go find some other cloud to sit on.

I did walk among true patriots—true heroes. You will know them when you meet them here. You will also recognize those who claimed to be patriots, but whose words were braver than their actions, and those whose prejudice against others motivated them more than patriotism. We could fill New York City with all who now claim to have been with Ethan Allen and Benedict Arnold when they took Fort Ticonderoga.

My story begins in 1774 and ends—for the most part and for all the reasons I confess to—in 1777, long before our Revolution ended. Please forgive me for what I reveal here, for I have been, as so many I have known, too, too human.

If you think my story pure unadulterated hogwash, you probably only have the quaint tales of school history books to judge it by. So I end by quoting Ethan Allen, without whose inspiration and exuberance I would never have joined the Green Mountain Boys from Pownal. "The critic will be pleased to excuse any inaccuracies in the performance itself, as the author has unfortunately missed a liberal education."

CHAPTER 1

▼

AFTER A TREE FELL ON MY FATHER

They sputtered saliva on me. Men stood up and shouted at one another. They pounded their fists into their palms. They interrupted one another so no one could finish a sentence. It took Reverend Dewey to restore order. He reminded them that they were still in the house of the Lord, even if it was a town meeting. So, momentarily, they tried respect. Some twitched their faces a bit, gritted their teeth, and pumped up the veins in their foreheads, but they did let the others at least finish their sentences—even if they did not listen.

It was my first town meeting, Monday, May the 2nd, 1774. I expected the meeting to be boring, something of a grown-up version of school, but I was wrong.

"Erastus, up, up, up!" My father woke me early that day and asked me to help him deliver a load of logs down to Pownal Centre and then stay by his side at the town meeting of all the Freemen in Pownal. The Freemen were the male heads of family, those who had settled land granted by Governor Benning Wentworth of New Hampshire. The Grants we called it.

My older sisters, Tryphena and Tryphosa, were each as strong as any man, but my father picked me to help haul logs and attend the meeting.

Town meetings were always held in the old log church in Pownal Centre, our community church where any religious group was free to worship, as long as the

Reverend Dewey, our permanent minister, presided. At a town meeting, anybody was free to speak his mind. Women were not allowed to speak, of course, since they could not own any land, so they could not vote either.

The Reverend Dewey gave a speech about something or other at the beginning. My father nudged me to get me to pay attention.

"I'd just like to see them try to throw me off my land," said Theophilus Bates, a sinewy old man of 40 or so. "That's why we got the Green Mountain Boys. They'll keep them damned Yorkers off'n our land."

My father leaned forward from his end of the pew to look at Mr. Bates, Theophilus, on the other end.

"Them Green Mountain Boys is nothing but a bunch of drunken scoundrels," Beriah Buck said. "They just like fighting and drinking. Any excuse to make trouble. All they're going to do is bring down the army on us, and then what'll we have?"

"Them Green Mountain Boys you speak of has got it right, if you ask me," said Theophilus. "Why I heard Ethan Allen just the other day . . . "

"A braying mule who's gotten too big for his breeches. He's nothing but trouble," replied Mr. Buck, whose large red face became even redder.

I had heard of Ethan Allen from my Uncle Hiram, a Green Mountain Boy himself. Uncle Hiram was no trouble maker. Notwithstanding all this adult talk, I was waking up.

Asa Brown, a little man who kept rubbing his hands together and tapping a heel on the floor, reminded everyone what the governor of New Hampshire, Benning Wentworth, had done. "Wentworth granted this land to folks in Pownal in 1760. We all settled here, fair and square, so we don't owe nothing to New York."

"But the King gave New York the authority over this land," said John-Ernst DeVoet, a tall, sturdy man with a robust jaw. "This is, after all, English land, and he is, after all, our king."

"He don't even know where this land is," said Mr. Bates, saliva running into his beard. "Why I bet he don't know the difference between the Hudson River and the Connecticut River, so how's he going to decide who owns what?"

"Still," said Mr. DeVoet, softly, his ruddy complexion reddening, "New York has the legal right to let us stay or make us go."

The room fell silent for a second as men waited for a response.

That was when my father, normally not a man to join an argument, spoke up. "Thing is, we're all part of the New Hampshire grants here. We own our land because Benning Wentworth granted the land to Pownal, to us. That same

English king who appointed Wentworth governor of New Hampshire also appointed Tryon governor of New York. So they're both acting under the authority of that king over there."

"Our king," Mr. Buck corrected.

And so it went, back and forth, those for fighting the Yorkers and those for letting them do what they wanted. I left that meeting determined to support my father and protect our farm. I left dreaming about the Green Mountain Boys and Ethan Allen, their leader.

Some days after that meeting, a tree fell on my father and he died.

My father had chopped down more trees than any man in Pownal. He had stripped almost all the trees off of our land on top of Carpenter Hill, all the way to "the ledge," the steep cliffs that lead down to the Bennington road. To haul his trees to the sawmill in Pownal, he had cut a road down the side of the hill, alongside the little brook that flowed past our house and turned down the hill. After settling our land in 1760, he and my oldest brothers, Thomas Frederick and Samuel, built retaining walls with boulders they dug from the hillside and shoveled dirt and rocks between the rock walls and the hillside to make the road for my father to drag his logs or carry them on our oxcart. When he could not sell the logs or when too many piled up, he burned them to make potash, selling it to a dealer who came through once a month. My mother would always say it was hard work that killed him, but actually it was the tree that fell on him that killed him.

Thomas Frederick, Samuel, and my older sister Eunice, about to have a baby, had all married and moved onto nearby farms, leaving me, my twin sisters Tryphena and Tryphosa, my older brother Eleazar, and my baby sister Mary to help my mother manage the farm. Eleazar had been sickly since catching the aches and sweats some months ago.

"Stop your dreaming, Erastus. We've more to worry about here on our farm now that your father's gone." My mother kept whacking the blankets while she talked over her shoulder at me, her hard muscles the only meat on her thin arms. "I have to be by Eunice when she delivers her baby. So, against my better judgment, I've asked my brother Hiram to come work the farm with you. Tryphena, Tryphosa, Eleazar, and Mary will go down the hill with me."

No Tryphena and Tryphosa! Freedom! Free to be a man, a Green Mountain Boy.

You see, Uncle Hiram was a Green Mountain Boy. I dreamed of marching side by side with Hiram and the Green Mountain Boys, battling the thieving Yorkers, blasting them off our land, slashing through their ranks. I thought about my father's logic at the town meeting. He would have supported my dream if he were still here.

The next day, when Hiram dropped by for some of my mother's pie, she sat him down, pulled her long, lean body toward his, placed her thin face inches from his, and said, "Hiram, someone has to take care of this farm while I'm with Eunice, and all I have is Erastus." I have since learned that mothers tend to talk of their sons that way.

Hiram looked at her, his soft, round face calm, his eyes half shut. He said nothing, so she continued, "Animals need feeding, and crops need tending. So I ask you to help out, Hiram. I'll leave Erastus up here to work with you."

"Well," said Hiram, holding out his plate for more pie, "I suppose, that is, if you think so." His pudgy cheeks were still full of his first piece.

"Then it's settled." She turned to me. "Erastus, you think you can handle this with your Uncle Hiram?"

"I can sure try," I said, delighted at the idea of living with Hiram and having fun.

"I want you to do more than try," she said. Mothers tend to talk that way, you see.

The next morning, she was more direct with me. "Erastus, I regret your Uncle Hiram's my brother, but we all have to grow crops in whatever soil the good Lord gives us. I won't have you listening to his stories about those rascals who call themselves Green Mountain Boys. They're boys all right. And your uncle! All he loves is going to frolics with his friends in Bennington where the young people dance and sing until late in the night, playing the flute for anyone who has nothing better to do than listen, so I don't expect much of him, but you've got to show him what to do."

"Dad said he was a sincere young man," I said.

"A waste of human flesh is what he is," she said.

"But a good flute player." I did not always think before speaking.

"I don't care," my mother said, clearly bothered by Hiram's having more fun that she ever had, "and I don't care if he hasn't started a family yet, but he wastes his life playing music, and I don't want you thinking it's fun."

In those days I had not yet learned to multisyllabify like Ethan Allen, so I could not argue.

"Giving him this farm to take care of a while'll serve him right," she said. "Help make a man of him." Pronouncement made, she set about her chores.

My mother ignored the best thing about my uncle Hiram, which was, in short, he was a Green Mountain Boy.

Tryphena and Tryphosa, my twin sisters, stopped washing the breakfast dishes. Tryphena waved an iron pot at me, showing off her muscles larger than mine and arms more meaty than my mother's. "Why does Erastus get to stay here?" said Tryphena. "I can farm better than he can any day."

"All he does is get in trouble," said Tryphosa, "and we've got to go get him out of trouble all the time." Their main purpose in life was to make my life miserable.

What really galls me is that, as much as they brag about being stronger than I am, come Sunday they comb out their hair to be straight and silky and dress in their fancy frocks to go to church. Everyone says, "My, aren't they pretty." If only those people could have seen them the way I see them, all snarly-faced and holier-than-thou. Oxen should wish for shoulders like theirs.

"He's a growing boy," said my mother, much to my chagrin. A growing boy indeed! I was going to be a Green Mountain Boy. Fight Yorkers. Then I would show my know-it-all sisters!

Hiram's tales of Ethan Allen had inspired me. They never seemed to end.

In the past year, Hiram claimed Ethan Allen could bite the head off a nail and spit it into a dartboard, hitting the bull's eye every time. Ethan could catch a deer by running it down and catching it by the antlers. He could catch a fish with his bare hands faster than we could get one by shooting it. He once raised up two men who were arguing with him, one in each hand, and banged their heads together to quiet them down. He had knocked out an ox with his fist. Hiram even claimed Ethan could raise a barn all by himself, but I mistrusted that since I had seen what it takes to raise posts and crossbeams.

"You are forgetting," said Hiram, "Ethan is no mere mortal."

"Twaddle," my mother had said that day.

Just a week ago, Hiram, stopping only to put some of my mother's pie in his face, talked about how the Yorker Sheriff Ten Eyck and the Mayor of Albany, a profiteer named Cuyler, marched with over 200 men to force Lieutenant Breakenridge off his farm. "We Green Mountain Boys only had about a hundred men or so, but we knew something of driving deer."

"You never shot a deer in your life," my mother said.

"So," said Hiram, continuing to eat and talk, "when Ten Eyck and Cuyler and the rest of those Yorkers came marching along, we split up into several groups. Forty of us went to the right and stood with our muskets where they could see us." Hiram stood in a crouch and pointed to the right. "Forty of us lined up along the River," he said, pointing from his crouched position to the left, "to show them we weren't about to retreat. And the rest of us gathered just below the hill opposite the Yorkers, where they really couldn't see us. Then Ethan had us raise our hats on top of big sticks," he said, grabbing our broom and my hat and marching in a circle around our table.

"Don't knock my dishes off the table!" my mother said.

"We didn't have enough muskets to go around, you see," said Hiram pumping the broom up and down, "so the Yorkers couldn't see anything but the hats, and we marched back and forth, back and forth, making them think we had hundreds of men just marching into place and getting ready to attack."

"Sounds like Ethan Allen knows how to fight," I said.

"Sounds like more Green Mountain twaddle," said my mother.

Hiram poked more pie in his face. "Then the sheriff ordered an attack on the farm and stepped forward, but only a handful of men followed. The rest were mulling it over, see. Breakenridge, Ethan Allen, and others stepped onto the porch and informed the sheriff it was Bennington land. Told him he'd no jurisdiction there. The sheriff called Breakenridge a squatter. Breakenridge told that Yorker sheriff where he could shove his Yorker nose.

"The sheriff raised his musket," Hiram said, pointing the broom at me. "Then he pointed it at Breakenridge's chest and said he'd show 'em his authority. Then the Green Mountain Boys pointed their muskets at the sheriff." Hiram turned and pointed the broom at my mother. "And then the sheriff said . . . "

"Don't point that thing at me!" said my mother.

Hiram only became more theatrical. "There they all stood, until the sheriff turned to call his men in and, wouldn't you know it, discovered they'd somehow evaporated back into the woods. 'Well, Sheriff,' said Ethan, 'It appears that, if our executioners approach us, they're as likely to fall dead as we, don't you think?' To which the sheriff replied, 'I'll see you in court.' To which Ethan added, 'Or in Hell.'"

"Put my broom down," said my mother, taking the broom away from Hiram.

"Did you shoot anyone?" I asked.

"Ethan taught us to master the Yorker's imaginations," said Hiram, sitting back down in front of the pie.

"I would have shot them," I said. One shot, I imagined, and they would scatter.

I kept a journal to become a master of my imagination. In fact, if I had not kept my journal, you would not be learning where Ethan Allen's words took me, how I grew to admire Benedict Arnold, and why I have little good to say about George Washington. History belongs to those who write it.

"Erastus," said my mother when Hiram left, "you think it's fun and games, this fighting Yorkers, but you should hear what Mrs. Buck thinks. Those Green

Mountain Boys attack the Yorkers, the British soldiers'll come to the Yorkers' defense. Mrs. Buck told me all about those troublemakers in Boston. We're going to start a war with the British if your Ethan Allen has his way. Then where'll we be? We'll all end up without a home and farm."

I knew Mr. and Mrs. Buck were British sympathizers, so why should I care what they thought? Besides, if we did nothing, it might be the Yorkers who took our farm.

When the day arrived for my mother, sisters, and brother to move down the hill, my mother cooked one last breakfast before we all loaded up the oxcart. She said to me, "I don't care if your Uncle Hiram is a Green Mountain Boy, for the Green Mountain Boys only want an excuse to get together and drink and plot ways to keep the Yorkers out of these grants, but all they get done is their drinking and plotting, while their families go hungry, so I don't want you turning into one of them, do you hear me, Erastus, and if I hear that Hiram has any ideas of corrupting you and turning you into a mirror image of him, then I'm going to come back up this hill and drag you down to where you'll learn the value of work and grow up to be the kind of man your father was, and then you'll be sorry, do you hear?"

We loaded our oxcart with the clothes my mother, sisters, and brother would need, most of her pots, her four best dishes ("Why would Hiram need good dishes anyway?" my mother asked, not wanting an answer), and some food. "You won't starve to death, Erastus, for Hiram should know how to cook." Then, walking alongside the ox, they moved down the hill, toward The Ledge. My mother looked back at me. I waited for her to say something sentimental, testing whether I would change my mind and go with them. Instead, she said, "Now that I think on it, Erastus, considering Hiram's inability to do anything, including cooking, you probably *will* starve to death." And having spoken, she turned back down the hill.

I looked around the farm at the two barns, the house with the north room packed with ice and insulated with hay, the pond, and the open fields as far as I could see, except for the sugar maple trees along the rock walls. Our small barn held our pigs on one side, on the other side our chickens. The bigger barn sheltered our cows and the ox, with room to store grains, tools, and the wagon my father used for hauling trees. My mother took the ox and the wagon. I wondered how Uncle Hiram and I would take care of it all without either my father or my mother to tell us what to do, but I figured Hiram would know.

CHAPTER 2

▼

HEROES—MYTHIC, BIBLICAL, AND OTHERWISE

"What should we do now, Erastus?" my Uncle Hiram asked. He dropped his hat, jacket, and pack with, it seems, all his possessions on the floor of the front hallway, between the kitchen and what my parents referred to as the "borning room," where all of their children had been born. Now it served as the only room not a bedroom, the only place in the house not used for cooking and sleeping.

Out of his pack he pulled two sets of clothes—a white linen shirt and plaid pants ("for the frolics") and most nice of all, a fine buckskin jacket, a brown linen hunting shirt, and a homespun pair of woolen breeches.

"My uniform," he explained, "for when the Green Mountain Boys get together." Last, he pulled his flute and pages of sheet music. "Say, Erastus, I ever tell you about the time the town of Durham decided to side with the Yorkers?"

"I am all ears." I listened closely so I could record it in my journal that night.

"Well, Ethan simply told them he and his men would leave the town nothing but ashes and corpses. But a Judge Spencer told the townspeople to stand up to the Green Mountain Boys. Said they didn't have any right to their property. So Ethan and his Boys strode in, grabbed the judge out of bed, and put him on trial."

"If the judge was on trial, who was the judge?"

"Ethan Allen himself," said Hiram. "Not only judge, but prosecutor and jury. And by the end, Judge Spencer had been found guilty of aiding the Yorkers and trying to steal land from his neighbors."

"They hang him?" I asked.

"Nope, just set fire to the roof of his house. But Ethan took pity on him and kindly ordered the roof knocked off. Then he let the judge return home."

"Too easy for the Yorker," I said.

"In hindsight, right, Erastus. Those cowardly Yorkers then went after Remember Baker, Ethan Allen's cousin. They got him and his family out of bed, slashed Remember's hand, broke his wife's arm, and set off with them for Albany. But Remember's neighbors showed them. They took out after the Yorkers, caught up to them, and ran them off into the woods."

"No Ethan Allen?"

"Ethan's spirit again," Hiram explained. "Then, when he heard tell of the Yorker Governor Tryon marching troops to attack us, Ethan gathered farmers and merchants from all over the Grants, went to old Fort Massachusetts in West Hoosick, took a couple of cannons lying there, and got ready to defend our land."

"Then there was a battle, right?"

"Nope, not a thing," he said. "Turns out, Tryon's troops were just marching out to strengthen a fort up north. Truth is, those cannons were so rusty I mistrust we could even have rammed a ball down them, much less fired them."

"So we proved nothing. I cannot wait to fire on an enemy."

"We proved we could gather up our men in a minute if we had to. We proved ourselves in charge of our destinies. Thank Ethan for that."

"So we do not have enough muskets. We have no cannon. What do we have?"

"Words, Erastus, words. Ethan Allen can argue the Devil out of Hell."

"So no one ever gets shot? What good is a revolutionary spirit if nobody gets shot? People need to get shot." Yes, I said that.

Alone on the farm, we walked around our hill, from Thompson's place to the Carpenter farm, while my uncle declaimed about the beauty of the countryside and the magnificence of the Green Mountains to the east, the Taconics to the west, Mt. Anthony to the north, and Mt. Greylock to the south. It was early spring here, "Mud Season." As soon as the weather moves from deep winter to warmer air, the ground starts to thaw. And thaw. All at once. One day we are trying to keep our wagons from skidding off the road, and the next we are up to the axles in mud. Then, at night it freezes all over again. So the best time to move a wagon is after the sun sets and the temperature drops.

We could see the Carpenters and the Thompsons tapping maples to make syrup, this being the right time of year.

"Maybe we should tap our trees, Hiram," I said, knowing my mother would like my initiative.

Hiram did not rise to the work even though the sap was rising.

"My father would want us to cut back this bush growing in our fields," I said, kicking at a sapling.

"Cut back the Yorkers," he said, pushing his hat back on his head. "Stop them from growing."

First, though, we had to go to church on Sunday. We were religious people in Pownal, but not too religious. Sunday preaching was about all most of us could stand, for the rest of the time we had to grow food and live in the reality of the world. If someone coming into our town said he and his family were Baptists, we sent them to Shaftsbury. If another family came in and said they were Separatists, we pointed them straight to Bennington. If they were Romans, we urged them further north, say, to Canada if possible. As I said, we were not unreligious. We simply abhorred disputatious sectarianism (a phrase I was later to learn from Ethan Allen, but which I now use in advantageous hindsight).

The Reverend Cotton M. Dewey did tend to be disputatious, always laying down laws for our behavior. In fact, our nickname for him was "Deuteronomy" Dewey since he usually ladled out a bunch of laws, admonitions, and injunctions, or at least his interpretation of them. His sermons were nothing but a recipe, if you ask me. Begin with a passage from the Bible and then talk about how we would be damned if we would do nothing about it—whatever that Sunday's "it" happened to be—followed by his admonitions on how we should behave.

For example, that Sunday Deuteronomy marched the two steps up to his pulpit dressed in his best Sunday black frocks, his graying hair brushed straight down to his shoulders, and squinted at us over his eyepieces. "My lesson today is taken from Deuteronomy 26: verses 5 to 11." He cleared his throat and paused to be dramatic.

> And the Egyptian's evil entreated us, and afflicted us, and laid upon us hard bondage: And when we cried unto the Lord God of our fathers, the Lord heard our voice, and looked on our affliction, and our labour, and our oppression: And the Lord brought us forth out of Egypt with a mighty hand, and with an outstretched arm, and with great terribleness, and with signs, and with

wonders: And he hath brought us into this place, and hath given us this land, even a land that floweth with milk and honey. Blah, blah, blah.

See, some wearisome listening. Only now, looking back, do I realize he was telling us the Yorkers were like the Egyptians and promising our day and their day would come. But how was I to know it then, with him droning on?

For being a person who preached brother love, Deuteronomy's most common targets were the Dutchies who lived in scattered farms up and down the Hoosic River flowing through Pownal. "They say they're members of the Reformed Dutch Church," Deuteronomy said to my father once, "but they don't even have a church building nearby."

"Perhaps they worship at home, and besides, our church is just a log cabin with a cross on top," said my father, which showed that he spoke before he thought, just as I do.

"Then they do not belong to a church," replied Deuteronomy. "Worse, do you know they claim to have settled here before we did?"

"Then they've got some claim to the land, don't they?" said my father, still not thinking well.

"Do not slip into soft thinking, my friend, for if they worship at home, it explains why they seem to accept anyone else's behavior as long as it doesn't interfere with their lives. Even their wives can own property! Freedom, indeed! Licentiousness, I say."

Even though we called them Dutchies, most of them were not Dutch. Some were Flemish, some Walloons, some Palatines, one was a Norseman, and one called himself a Croat, though I thought that sounded made up. One, I swear, claimed to be English and bragged that Henrik Hudson was English, even though he sailed for the Dutch. But I knew better. Why, once a black African came through with a Dutchie from Albany, speaking both Dutch and English, which proved he was Dutch, too.

"Albany's a festering pool of free will," Deuteronomy proclaimed again and again, his greying locks frazzled from his emotional worries over the righteousness of Albany.

The Dutchies kept a low visibility in Pownal since they were tenant farmers, not owners. They owed their rent to the Manor of Rensselaerwyck, which surrounded Albany and made them a bit suspect in the eyes of folks here in the Green Mountains—Albany being in New York, you see.

"The problem with the Dutch," said Deuteronomy Dewey, squinting at my father once, "is they don't seem to care what religion a person practices."

"Well, seems to me," my father replied, "that practicing any religion and allowing anyone from any nation to settle next to you is the freedom we all want here in the Green Mountains."

"One had better open the door to Satan than allow God to be interpreted any which way one wants. Our Bible's written in English by Englishmen for a reason, so we can speak and understand each other, not have to translate from some foreign tongue." Ethan Allen would call the Reverend Dewey's logic "impeachable."

"Here's the real problem with the Dutchies," Hiram told me as we wandered around our farm. "Most of them are Tories, lovers of the English, not real Green Mountain people."

"Still, they're our friends, our neighbors."

"Erastus," said Hiram, "they can choose whatever they want, long's they chose right. Choosing to be a Tory or choosing to be a Yorker just isn't natural."

My mind was made up—I was choosing to be a Green Mountain Boy. "So what now? When can I join the Green Mountain Boys?"

"Well, Ethan Allen believes in the law, Erastus, so he's formed a committee."

"Boring!" I said, kicking a rock and pulling out a Joe-Pye Weed.

"Never on your life, Erastus. Ethan calls it 'a committee of the whole,' and the whole bunch of us are going to meet soon at Stephen Fay's Tavern to hear what Ethan's got to say. What do you say, Erastus? Join me there?"

You could not keep me from meeting Ethan if you tied me to oxen and tried to pull me away. Notwithstanding, my stomach was growling, so we ran full drive, Jehu-like, for home and supper, where a full pot of stew awaited us—my mother's way of telling us that we could not manage by ourselves.

By the time we had eaten stew for breakfast the next day, skipped lunch, and supped on what was left of the stew for supper, I realized all Uncle Hiram knew about cooking was how to keep the fire going in the kitchen fireplace.

The next day I woke to find Tryphena and Tryphosa cooking up cornmeal mush and molasses in the kitchen. "Mama sent us up to look after you," said Tryphena.

Tryphosa added, "She figured you and Hiram probably couldn't take care of yourselves since he's not very reliable and you're too likely to do whatever he wants to do even though you know better and should be out working on the farm, but would not know what to do without someone more reliable telling you what to do and that meant us, so here we are." I think Tryphosa took after our mother more than Tryphena did.

"I am perfectly capable of taking care of myself," I said.

"Mama says we 'labor in the Lord,' which is what you should do," said Tryphena, slopping a ladle full of the mush on my plate. I should have figured her to say something like that since my father always asked her to lead the Sunday worship service at home whenever the weather was too harsh for us to make it down to the church. Deuteronomy Dewey still chastised those who had missed any Sunday services regardless of how bad the weather was, but my father said that Tryphena could outworship Deuteronomy any Sunday morning once she set her mind to dredging up the Bible, so we probably learned more at home than in church.

I was embarrassed to see that Tryphosa or Tryphena or both had brought in a big load of firewood for the fireplace since neither Hiram nor I had done so the night before even though we ran out of wood while heating the last of the stew. But I was not prone to thank them since I would probably be filled with more Bible sayings, most likely by Tryphena. No sooner thought than said, "'Why should the work stop while I leave it and come down to you?' sayeth our Lord." I would have quoted her right back from the Bible about Man needing to rest if I could have remembered anything.

All her quoting must have awakened Uncle Hiram, for he walked into the kitchen in his night shirt. "Ah, you're so thoughtful. I'll grab my flute, and repay you with a tune."

Understand, this was not the first time I had been embarrassed by the twins. Once, when Charlie Charters and I were having fun climbing the steepest part of the ledge south of our farm, I got stuck about half way up and did not know how to get down. The rock is sort of crumbly around here and a guy just cannot reach out to grab any rock sticking out. Anyway, Charlie was going to work his way over to me to help me figure out how to get down or up, and then I would have managed it myself. But no, I look up, and what do I see but both Tryphena and Tryphosa climbing down to help me. My mother had sent the twins out to watch out for me, just in case I needed the help. Just because they are a year older than I am, they figured they could act like a mother around me, tell me what to do, and worse yet, take care of me. Like I said, it was embarrassing.

I have been keeping a journal to record my adventures ever since I graduated from a horn book to a copy book, but what am I to write when my twin sisters keep sticking their faces into my adventures? "Today Tryphena and Tryphosa rescued me from plunging headlong down a cliff to my death." "Today my twin sisters rescued me from drowning when I went swimming in the Tubs." The Tubs is a place where the water falls and creates potholes in the rock that must be all of three feet deep. They had not kept me from drowning: they kept me from swimming. As a consequence not inconsequential, I determined to escape their unbearable surveillance, and Uncle Hiram was going to help me be my own man—a Green Mountain Boy.

Unfortunately, Uncle Hiram proceeded to tootle away on his flute while my twin sisters grabbed our plates and scrubbed them in a pot of hot water. They made me sore discomfited. I mean, how would you like it if you were trying to be a militiaman and your two sisters came tritter-trotting along behind you with warm milk and quotations from the Bible? Unseemly.

When the twins left with a promise to come back and check on us, I pleaded with Uncle Hiram, "We have got to do the chores ourselves and cook our own food and make sure they stop coming around making fools out of us."

"Erastus, Erastus, Erastus," he said, arranging his shirt. "We do men's work. Let them cook for us. That's what women are supposed to do for men. Then we men fight for our land and protect the women."

Fighting for our land and protecting women is just what I wanted to do, but we needed practice. "For Lord's sake, Hiram," I said, "we cannot let the women cut and stack firewood and cook our food for us. It is unbecoming our manliness, Hiram!" I was sure my mother sent Tryphena and Tryphosa up to teach us how incompetent we were, but, if so, Uncle Hiram had not yet paid any attention to the teacher.

I did, however, proceed to feed the chickens, pigs, and cows.

I fed the chickens. "Let me tell you about the time Ethan strangled a bear with his bare hands," said Hiram sitting on a barrel.

I fed the pigs. "Then there was the time he lifted a whole tree trunk and loaded it on a wagon."

I fed the cows. "Why you know, Erastus, Ethan could single-handedly tap and boil enough maple syrup to feed a town for a year!" Of course, having helped my father tap trees and boil the sap down, I thought Hiram's tale too watery, but, since other stories were probably true, I could not wait to meet Ethan Allen.

CHAPTER 3

▼

ETHAN ALLEN AND THE GREEN MOUNTAIN BOYS!

The day I finally met Ethan Allen and his Green Mountain Boys soon arrived. We borrowed a ride in a neighbor's wagon to bounce in the evening light toward Bennington and my future.

I had never been in Mr. Fay's Tavern, for my father would not stop there on the way to market in Bennington, but having ridden by it many times, I was very familiar with its outside, a two and one-half story building, plain brown. Compared to some of the mansions on the street nearby, it was unremarkable, but did have one noteworthy identifying feature. A stuffed catamount stood on the upstairs porch, a Green Mountain lion, glaring in the direction of New York. I had always wanted to get up close to the catamount, and as we walked toward the door, I finally saw it clearly. Had it been alive, though, it could not have seen me, for both its eyes were empty sockets. And its fur was pulling out in tufts. No matter, for it symbolized our strength and vision to be free.

Inside, a short hallway led us past a room off to the right and another to the left. The doorway at the end of the hallway opened into a large room where many men were gathered. Mixed with smoke from the fireplace, the smoke from their pipes burned my eyes, and I could scarcely see to the other side of the room. Men sat around tables, listening to somebody speaking. Every so often, innkeeper Fay would walk over to a table, set down a pitcher, and plunge a red-hot poker into the contents. The air smelled something of burnt maple syrup and cider.

"That drink's called flip," my uncle whispered to me, naming a brew I had never tasted, nor would my mother allow me a sip even if I were dying of thirst. Some others poured gills of rum (so my uncle told me) into Fay's brew of beer. "Stonewalls," said my uncle. Men who could not find a place to sit leaned against the beams that supported the second floor or leaned over the tables reaching with their mugs for some flip. Some leaned against each other for support. "Yep, they're stonewalled," Hiram whispered.

More men than I had ever seen had gathered in one room. Reverend Dewey would yearn for such a crowd. Most wore the same homespun or leather as we wore. A few, who I figured to be leaders in Bennington, wore fancy dress coats. Regular Macaronis they were. A few looked unusual to me, like a young man in a corner, dark in complexion, with shiny black hair. Another stranger with equally black hair, but pale-faced and freckled, stood just in front of us.

Through the smoke, I could make out, in the center of the room, a man— large, with muscular features, yet overall a handsome man. He wore a homespun jacket with gold braided epaulets on his shoulders. I knew at a glance this was Ethan Allen himself. I strained to hear his words.

"Boys, you know that I am a lover of reason and truth." All there spoke their agreement. "And I am a lover of liberty and property, as are we all!" This time I joined everyone as we all shouted our agreement. "But I tell you, Boys of the Green Mountains, these Yorkers do stretch my ability to reason and risk the displeasure of us all!"

Ethan swept his arm around the room. "We're all gentlemen here in these New Hampshire Grants." Considering the stories of his Boys confronting the Yorkers, I thought that funny, but no one laughed. "But our gentleness is mightily strained when the Yorkers act as ruffians and barbarians, lording it over us as though we be mere peasants on their land, as though, in fact, they own this land. Well, we all know the rightful owners of these grants. The Yorkers are mercenary, intriguing, monopolizing men, an infamous fraternity of diabolical plotters." He paused and sipped his flip. His deep voice and words filled me with awe.

Ethan put down his mug. "Can we ever forgive what they did to my uncle Remember Baker and his family! Ruthlessly, they invaded his home, tore his wife and children from his arms, breaking her arm in the process, and sliced off his finger! Think of him then, his blood flowing forth onto the white snow, his wife and children sobbing and clinging to each other for support. Oh, the lamentations, the grief, the misery those avaricious intriguers caused to burst forth!" A few of the men wiped their eyes as they listened, barely able to stand, though I think not from what they heard. My eyes teared, too, but I think it was the smoke.

Stephen Fay, owner of this tavern called the Catamount Inn, went from table to table, filling the mugs with flip and tallying how much each man owed on a piece of slate attached to his belt.

Ethan invoked God and other deities I had never heard as he built our patriotic fervor. "God Almighty frowns upon those Yorker devils. The mighty Jehovah weeps at their deprivations. Yahweh stands at our side, urging us forward! Zeus arms his thunderbolts! The Muhikan Menutto smiles upon our quest." Until then, I thought there was but one god. The dark-skinned man smiled when Ethan Allen spoke of Menutto. "Dare we let the great Deity lose his faith in us?" asked Ethan.

"Key-Ryst, no!" someone yelled.

"Him, too," said Mr. Allen, and all of us laughed, applauded, and jumped up and down. Most held their mugs and bowls aloft in toast and drank. What young man would not want to be part of all this?

Ethan continued, his words spoken with the assurance of the most practiced entertainer at one of our roving fairs—or the most assured reverend aloft in his pulpit.

"When governments suppress their people and seek to impose their will upon them, the good of society requires that we resist and depose those governments. Governments should protect our property and our communities, not seek to thrust us from them."

We cheered again, and I tried to cheer louder than all.

Ethan raised his hand to quiet us. "Men, I want to quote the good Reverend Nathan Niles, who, in his wisdom, has written, 'It is for the good of the community alone that laws are either to be made or executed.' Reverend Niles teaches us, and I quote, 'Perfect liberty and perfect government are perfectly harmonious, while tyranny and licentiousness are inconsistent with both. Remove good government and you remove liberty. Abridge the former and you abridge the latter. Let good government increase and you increase liberty.'" What a wonderful memory Ethan Allen had, to be able to quote someone else's words at will! Then, while we tried to make sense of what Reverend Niles had written, Ethan continued.

"Those malevolent Yorkers seek to impose their will upon us with the blessing of the King, but the British tyrant knows not what he has wrought. They have no true laws. They have only the empty appearance of Law."

I thought then and there that I should learn to use words that Ethan Allen used. Malevolent. Deprivations. Avaricious. I tried saying them over and over to myself to memorize them and be able to use them with the great ease and felicity of Ethan Allen. Listening and thinking at the same time is no easy task.

"I tell you," Ethan continued, "New York is Britain's favorite government. Yorkers are Toretical kissers of George the Third's royal butt!" The crowd hissed. Some made the sounds of pigs.

"Yes, pigs!" said Ethan. "And sheep! The British love their sheep and have pulled the wool from the thieving, skulking Yorkers, herding them into their archaic legal pens. But we are not sheep in these Green Mountains! We are men. And we can govern ourselves!"

My uncle and I clapped and stomped our feet. We whistled and cheered along with the rest who, by this time, were standing and stumbling forward in their fervor. "Stonewalled and glad of it," my uncle noted.

Mr. Fay was yelling, "More flip for all!" The faster he poured the drinks and plunged his hot pokers, the faster he checked his slate tally. For us Green Mountain Boys (for now I considered myself one), it was all together a profitable evening, and for Mr. Stephen Fay, all the more so.

Afterward, the Green Mountain Boys from Pownal drifted toward their wagons, inspired.

"It's our security we're talking about," Luke Van Arnem said.

"We need to organize our own militia group," Samuel Poppleton added.

"Let's bring our muskets and get us started. What say we meet in Pownal Centre tomorrow," Theophilus Bates suggested with the authority of a French and Indian War veteran.

We all agreed to his suggestion.

"Hiram," I said, "I can bring my father's musket."

"You bet, Erastus. I'll take my musket, too . . . and my flute."

Later that night, alone in my room with my candle and pen, I began to write in my journal the beginning of the story of my life with Ethan by describing him:

"Dark-haired and black-eyed, full-boned and ruddy skinned, he stood—I should say loomed—full six feet six if he was an inch. His clothes were humble clothes: woven tight and earth brown, they identified him as a man of our frontier and were filled out by a muscular structure that resembled that of our family's ox. Yes, he was an ox of a man: big-armed and full-faced, he occupied the center of the room and the center of our hearts. He was absolutely inspiring." I was inspired and, I thought, eloquent.

The next morning, after using more of the wood my twin sisters had brought in and fixing a breakfast of eggs, Hiram and I walked the three miles to Pownal Centre, carrying our muskets. Along the way, Hiram tried to teach me some songs he said were favorites of the Green Mountain Boys. I was too excited to learn anything, so he just fluted our way down the hill.

By the time we got to Pownal Centre's one street, quite a few men had gathered. They had elected Theophilus Bates as drill master. Theo Bates had served in the French and Indian War, had been wounded in a British attack on Fort Carillon, and now was a crusty old man over forty years old.

We sat on a fallen log in the middle of the plot set aside for a cemetery and waited along with the other men who showed up. Shortly, Theophilus called us all out onto the street. I noted that Theophilus had trimmed his beard, cropped his graying hair short to his ears, and even cleaned his fingernails. He stood at attention. "All right. I want you to line up, from the tallest to the shortest."

"I'm taller than you are," Hiram said to John.

"That's 'cause you got high boots," John snapped.

"You stand next to me 'cause you're shorter," said Samuel to Luke.

"You only look taller 'cause you comb your hair up like a rooster," grumbled Luke to Samuel.

"You wish you had my hair!"

"Rooster!"

"All right! Just, just, just line up and just stand tall!" Theophilus finally commanded after listening to the mounting chorus of individual negotiations.

Then he held up in his hands a crumpled pamphlet.

"Now, this here's called *The '64*," he informed us, "*The Manual of Arms Exercise Book*. After the French and Indian War I fought in, the British bastards put it out in 1764 for their troops. Now, we're going to work our way through these exercises until we learn to behave like soldiers."

The exercises sounded like fun to me until he explained, "There's about thirty-five exercises we got to master."

I tell you, this manual was about the most excessively bothersome folderol I could have imagined. Of course, now I know that folderols tend to be many in the military.

"First," shouted Theophilus Bates, "we'll learn to poise our firelocks!" A firelock is a musket, you see, and not every one of us had a musket. Samuel Perrigo ran over to a nearby porch and grabbed a broom out of Mrs. Joanna Perrigo's hands, while others broke off some straight branches from the trees and shrubs around the cemetery plot. Then, while Theophilus stood shaking his head, we all lined up again.

Theophilus had evidently memorized *The '64*. "First," he said, "seize the firelock with your right hand, and turn the lock outwards, keeping the firelock perpendicular." That took a bit of muttering while we shifted from holding the muskets, broom, and sticks over our shoulders or raised them off the ground, but soon we got our muskets, broom, and sticks in order.

"Now," he shouted, "bring up the firelock with a quick motion from the shoulder, and seize it with the left hand just above the lock. Make sure the little finger rests upon the spring and the thumb lies upon the stock. The firelock must not be held too far from the body, and the left hand must be of an equal height with the eyes." When he realized fifteen of us had fifteen different interpretations of firelock positions, Theophilus went from man to man, making sure each understood what he said. By now, I was tired of all this drill, but Theophilus was just starting.

He made us cock our firelocks, present our firelocks, fire our firelocks, and all this with no powder or balls in them. Then we had to half cock our firelocks, all together, and handle our cartridges, which none of us had since we mostly carried powder horns, at least those of us with muskets. "Just pretend!" Theophilus ordered. The next step, priming, was easy for each of us to pretend, and do so seriously, but when he ordered us to "shut your pans," well, that pretty much destroyed whatever order he had managed to create.

By now all the ladies and girls of Pownal Centre had come out to admire us. They whispered and giggled. I stood tall until I spotted Tryphena and Tryphosa looking around the corner of the town store. They were giggling, too. With some embarrassment, I realized, even now, in this most serious ceremony of manhood, our mother had sent them to look after me here. But I told myself that I was a soldier now, and this would give me practice at putting up with privations. I tried to imagine them as Yorkers skulking in the woods. Somehow, by the time the drill practice ended, they had slipped away. Those two could be masters at staying hidden while they spied on me.

Theophilus ordered us to go home and practice before we met a week from now, but I mistrusted I would even remember all we were supposed to learn. I was happy about one thing, though. None of us had actually loaded our muskets with powder and ball, for had we done so, we probably would have saved the Yorkers the trouble of having to shoot us.

On the way back up Carpenter Hill to home, Hiram said, "You know what we really need?"

"More practice?"

"A drummer is what. I've got a flute, so think what we could do with a drummer." I was too tired to comment, but thought I'd rather beat on him than on a drum at this point. He fluted and sang, fluted and sang: "The Death of General Wolfe," "Whisky in the Jar," "The Girl I Left behind Me," "Yankee Doodle"—a bumpy tune that made little sense—and his personal favorite, "The British Grenadiers."

"We'll rename it 'The Pownal Musketeers,' don't you think, Erastus."

By the time we reached the top of the hill and our farm, he had twisted and warped the original words to the "British Grenadiers" tune until he had created what was truly an anthem to the greatness of the Green Mountain Boys of Pownal:

> *We fought the bloody Yorkers and proved how much we're brave,*
> *We marched on them and routed them*
> *And sent them to their grave.*
> *Cause of all the world's great heroes,*
> *There's none that can compare—*
> *With a ho ho ho and away we go—*
> *To the Pownal Musketeers!*

He even had a verse for Theophilus Bates:

> *He drilled us in the grave yard, he drilled us on the street,*
> *He drilled us hard and drilled us dead . . .*

By the time we reached home, he was trying to fit the name of everyone who had drilled that day into the tune, which by then I was sick of.

> *There's Carpenter and Woodward and Gardner and the Wrights,*
> *There's Dunning, Jewett, Vosburgh . . .*

"Oh, wait," said Hiram, "I forgot Sam Perrigo"

> *There's Perrigo and Woodward and Carpenter and Wright,*
> *Dunning, Gardner, Poppleton,*
> *All looking for a fight . . .*

That night, when I tried writing in my journal, all I could hear in my head was that tune, over and over. So, rather than fight it, I recorded it. I bet Ethan Allen never had to put up with drilling and singing.

As we ate breakfast the next day, I wondered why I did not see many men from Pownal. We have three Pownals in our area—Pownal Centre to the north, Pownal to the south, and North Pownal, west of Carpenter Hill. "I thought for sure more would show up. Mr. DeVoet was not there nor Mr. Buck nor the Dutchies."

"Well, you know those Dutchies—nothing but Yorkers speaking gibberish," Hiram remarked, his mouth full of eggs.

"But not just them. No Andersons, no Larabees, no Deals, none of the French family. Half of Pownal missing."

"Nothing but a mess of Tories, Erastus. They do love their English king, just like the Yorkers. Pass the bread, would you."

"But you and I go to church with many of them. I mean, they are our friends, Hiram."

"You worry too much, Erastus. We Green Mountain Boys'll settle things soon enough, and it'll all be back to normal. Hmm, looks like we're out of eggs."

Before my days as a Green Mountain Boy ended and life returned to normal, I had filled out four full journals.

Chapter 4

▼

Step, Suck, Step, Suck

Once our war began, it began well, aside from the mud.

Before Theophilus drilled us again, Uncle Hiram and I both practiced, I with my musket, he with his flute. I worried about whether I could hold my own against the other militiamen, who, I figured, being real Green Mountain Boys, were also practicing their musket drill. Hiram worried about whether we could ever find a drummer. He also continued to add verses to his anthem, "The Pownal Musketeers." When I went out to feed the chickens, he serenaded us with

He fed the feath'ry chickens and searched for all their eggs,
He . . .

Well, I will not subject you more to the musicalities of my uncle. The hens kept laying.

Once Tryphena and Tryphosa reported back to my mother after the drill, she too was worried, so much so that she marched up the hill and established her values in front of both Uncle Hiram and me. "Since when," she said, "does strutting and primping in front of the whole town with a bunch of overgrown boys make you any more of the man than your father would expect you to be when he worked himself to death to build this farm for us and establish a way for us to survive in these so-called Grants or whatever they may be called by all those glory-seeking, lazy, so-called Green Mountain Boys who are nothing more than just that, boys?" I had lost the logic of her question somewhere back around the second or third clause, but I did get the gist of it.

Uncle Hiram tucked his flute under a pillow the moment she burst in the door, and he managed to look appropriately chagrined.

"And you, Hiram, if you have nothing to do but drink with your friends and play music and corrupt my son so he does not even bother to feed the pigs, which, I imagine, if I looked in on them, they would be looking poorly because you have not even lifted a finger, if I am correct, and I think I am, to help around here, ought to be ashamed of yourself."

I had fed the pigs, so I felt smug, but it occurred to me, if I did go off with the Green Mountain Boys to fight the Yorkers, I would have to let my mother know and someone would have to move back on the farm to take care of everything. My older brother was too sickly to work and my younger sister too young, so that left Tryphena and Tryphosa. Well, I thought, I finally get even with them for treating me like a little kid. Notwithstanding, I was feeling guilty.

"Tomorrow we go to church," my mother announced, turned, and left.

Uncle Hiram, as chastised as he might get, volunteered to build the fire for supper.

The next day, we walked down to the Pownal Centre church, meeting my mother, sisters, and brother who had walked by the lower road. The Pownalians stood in separate groups outside the church. Those for fighting the Yorkers gathered on one side—the Carpenters and Nobles, Gardners and Wrights, and Theophilus, wearing his French and Indian War coat. Those opposed clustered on the other side, including DeVoet with his wife, their two sons, the Bucks, the Larabees, and, with them, another Gardner.

Neither side moved into the church first, despite the efforts of wives and mothers to lead their husbands and sons forward. Neither side looked at the other, aside from an occasional glare.

Deuteronomy Dewey stepped out on the porch of his church and said, "The house of the Lord welcomes you in peace and fellowship, my friends."

That was all my mother needed, so she grabbed Hiram by the elbow, evidently pinching him hard by the look on his face, and marched him in. My sisters, brother, and I followed. Mr. Buck then led his family in, glaring back at us and then sitting on the opposite side of the aisle. So everyone followed, supporters of the Green Mountain Boys on one side, Tories and Yorker-lovers on the other. My mother, as you now know, was not a supporter of the Green Mountain Boys, but being associated with Hiram and me had tainted her.

For his text, Deuteronomy chose Psalm 92: "The righteous shall flourish like the palm tree: he shall grow like a cedar in Lebanon. Those that be planted in the house of the Lord shall flourish in the courts of our God." I think Deuteronomy was trying to bring us all back together, but, in truth, I think each side assumed themselves to be cedars and palm trees, while the others were just weeds.

Leaving, each of us thanked Deuteronomy for his thoughtful words, secure in our righteousness, generous in our willingness to smile at the others, and left, heads high.

My mother invited us to eat dinner after the service and, since Hiram and I had prepared nothing, we accepted. Unfortunately, my mother asked Tryphena to say the blessing, which gave her the opportunity to tell us what she thought. After giving thanks for all we had, she ended with, "And if the blind shall lead the blind, they shall fall in the ditch," smiled at Hiram and me, and said, "Amen."

My mother fed my guilt, too. During the meal she talked about what had to be done on the farm and said she knew I could get the crops planted, feed and care for the animals, and keep the house in good order. I knew I wanted to join Ethan's Boys, but I didn't know how to tell her we probably would leave to confront the Yorkers soon. I wondered if she knew and if all this talk of taking care of the farm was her way of trying to change my mind.

That night I tossed and turned and could not get to sleep no matter how hard I tried. I got up once, lit a candle, and tried to write in my journal, but nothing came. All I could think about was my intent to desert my mother, leave the farm, leave the animals, and not put crops in. How would my family make it through the year?

Well, I figured, we will simply go off for a few days, beat the Yorkers about their heads, drive them out of the Grants, and come home. What would a few days matter, anyway? All I need do is make sure someone feeds the animals. Self-assured, I finally fell asleep.

Early the next day, Theophilus came riding up. "It's war, boys!" he shouted.

"The Yorkers?"

"No, the British. Just received word we fought 'em at Concord, Massachusetts, and beat 'em, by God! Ethan wants all of us to put our affairs in order and prepare to attack the British. He'll send word when."

Off Theophilus went, and I turned to Hiram. "The British, Hiram! Mrs. Buck got it right. I thought we were going to fight the Yorkers?"

"Remember Ethan's words, Erastus. The Yorkers are just the pawns of the British king. Now we know they're one and the same."

I was not sure whether I was excited or scared, but one thing I was sure of: this was going to take more than a few days, and, once she found out, my mother was likely to kill me before the British ever got a chance.

I did not even know where Concord was, much less how long it would take us to get there.

Hiram and I started packing that afternoon, extra clothes, a blanket each, powder and balls for our muskets, and flour and dried meat to cook along the way until we were able to get more food.

That night I slept less than the night before, trying to figure out how I would tell my mother and still be able to leave. I could just sneak into her kitchen, leave a note on the table telling her what I was doing, and leave before she found out. Sneaking would be cowardly, unseemly for a Green Mountain Boy. I could walk up and bluster like a man. "Mother, the people of the Grants need me!" I did not think her response would be quite so brief. I could send Hiram to tell her. No, bad idea. I could ask Theophilus. No, he would think little of me then. One thing was certain—I was in deep trouble.

Two days later, Bennington filled with people, including me, horses, wagons, oxen, men like me walking around with muskets and their packs, militia groups like the Boys from Pownal marching in from the countryside, even some women walking next to their men, helping to load wagons with supplies, and supporting the effort however they could.

Including my mother.

As it turned out, I did not have to tell her at all, sneakily leave a note, or ask someone else to tell her for me. I forgot how village news spreads from fireside to fireside faster than broadsides could be printed and distributed.

The next morning, as soon as I had risen after a mostly sleepless night, I opened our door, and there strode my mother, leading the ox who was pulling the wagon carrying my brother, three sisters, and some supplies in it. The sun had not even come up yet.

"I should've known you two wouldn't have the common decency to stroll down the hill, knock on our door like civilized human beings, fall on your knees to ask my everlasting forgiveness for your thoughtlessness at not considering the welfare of your poor mother and suffering sisters and brother, swear you would not go off with that madman Ethan Allen and his equally misguided minion Theophilus Bates to get yourselves killed or worse maimed for life, so I realized we were going to have to take care of you ourselves if you are to stand any chance of surviving this foolishness."

She was going to let me go! I was joyous. My guilt at not having found the courage to tell her disappeared immediately.

"Your sister Eunice delivered a beautiful baby boy two days ago," she explained, "You were not there I noted." More guilt planted.

"Answer not a fool according to his folly, lest thou also be like unto him," said Tryphena. I did not know what she meant by that, but it ended my joy.

My mother directed my sisters in going through my pack and various accoutrements, much to my continued chagrin. (I learned "accoutrements" from Ethan, by the way.) They pulled out my one pair of socks and cackled disgustedly at the holes in them. So, while each darned a sock, my mother checked my food and placed some small cornmeal cakes in both Hiram's and my packs. She gave me one of my father's vests to wear, which made me very proud. Tryphena tucked her small pocket Bible in the side pocket of the pack. I was about to protest when Hiram whispered, "We may need paper to wrap around our musket balls. Count this a blessing."

"Your gift is a blessing, Tryphena," I said and then, smiling, added, "As are you."

The real blessing was that my sisters and brother would look after the farm while I was gone.

Thus I found myself in Bennington amid a real army, with townspeople and my mother helping us. I wished we had uniforms, but Theophilus simply said, "Soon enough."

Shortly a rider rode in, a tall, thin, gangly person of no particular good looks. In fact, he looked pale and sickly, but a few others cheered him when they saw him. This was Seth Warner, a relative of Ethan Allen. I did not write about him in my journal the way I wrote about Ethan Allen, but I should have.

Seth Warner rode among us, checking to see whether we were each packed and armed, whether the wagons were loaded, and whether we could move out. He did not give a speech, and I noted how he paid attention to detail, even checking whether each of us had a good flint in our muskets, which I had. But he noticed my lack of cooking equipment and told me to get an iron pot out of a nearby wagon.

My mother hugged me and kissed me, which I thought not the thing that soldiers ought to allow, but then I saw others hugging and kissing, too. I looked forward to the learning the art of soldiering.

Tryphena and Tryphosa, dressed in heavy farm breeches and my father's shirts, heaved large bundles of equipment up on the wagons. If I did not know they were my sisters, I would have thought those two muscular workers were men.

We did not march, but, strolled out of town. We were heading down the hill toward the West, toward the Hoosic and Walloomsac Rivers. Concord, I knew, lay in the other direction. Next to me slouched the freckle-faced, black-haired man I had seen at Stephen Fay's Tavern, so I asked him if he knew where we were going. "Ah, m'boy," said he in a strange accent, shaking my hand, "I've not a doubt someone knows, one of those bloody officers you see up ahead. As for us, our lot is to follow along and wait. Michael McGinnis I am." I asked him his home, and he answered, "Cork."

"Cork?" I asked. "Up above Arlington or out east by the Connecticut River?"

His freckles accentuated his grin. "Sure, 'tis out east beyond the Connecticut. Ireland, in fact, but now I'm one of you." His accent was a bit musical.

Did I say "stroll"? The worst of mud season may have been behind us, but mud still slowed us. Our boots and shoes sank into the mud and had to be pulled up to free them for the next step. We were near the rear, and all the feet of those ahead had turned the road to a soupy muck. "Step, suck, step, suck, step, suck," said Michael McGinnis, "such is the soldier's lot."

Michael, I was to learn, was short on inches, but tall in complaints. He grabbed my arm and pulled me across a stone wall into the field where the grass kept us from sinking into the mud. Behind us others followed, and soon all the Boys from Pownal and those from Bennington had spread out on both sides of the road, strolling along.

Our noise announced us to the countryside. Pots of all shapes hung from everyone's belt or pack and clanked with every step. The wagon wheels creaked, and the wagons groaned. Horses puffed. Men complained. Whenever fields gave way to woods, we stumbled back onto the road, and McGinnis again picked up his step, suck, step, suck rhythm. Soon, others picked up the rhythm, and it became "squish, suck, squish, suck." Hiram made it a tune: "Squish, suck, squish, suck—our feet are sinking in the muck."

By evening, we had reached the town of Hoosick Falls, and my legs were killing me. Seth Warner ordered us each to get half of a tent from one of the wagons. Theophilus showed us how to put the tents together and had us build fires to cook food, which cheered us up quite a bit.

After we had eaten, Seth Warner, his long pale face calm, gathered us around and told us our goal was to capture Fort Carillon—or Fort Ticonderoga as the British called it. "We'll liberate the fort from the British, men. As Ethan says it, they'll go to sleep in New York and wake up in the Grants."

"Ticonderoga?" asked Samuel Poppleton. "Why Ticonderoga? The fighting's in the other direction."

"Whoever controls Fort Ticonderoga," answered Seth comfortably, "might control Lake Champlain. If we can control Lake Champlain, we can block the British from controlling everything from Canada to Albany, maybe even down to New York."

"I think I got it," said Samuel.

"If we wait," said Seth, "the British will soon realize how important that fort is and reinforce it so much we'll never be able to take it. At least not without a good deal of blood. Now, let's all get some sleep."

I had wanted to fight Yorkers, but this was much bigger. And closer than Concord. I could hardly sleep.

I awoke early, drinking good hot coffee and eating the cakes my mother had given Hiram and me. Theophilus taught us to tie our tent halves on our packs and put out the fires. Our march began again. In short time, the creaking, groaning, puffing, and complaining filled my ears. Hiram fluted for a few steps before falling in the mud. The road grew muddier. "Erastus, m'boy," said McGinnis, slouching off into a nearby field, "tomorrow we start early, get out in front, and make the mud for others to enjoy."

By noon we had reached the town of Cambridge, which, like Bennington, had houses lined along its street. Unlike most houses in Pownal, all had porches. As young ladies appeared on the porches to cheer us on, we marched a little taller. Theophilus moved among us and taught us how to hold our muskets while marching. We appreciated the lesson, for it made us look more soldierly. McGinnis waved to the girls and grinned through his freckles. "Wait for me, darlings!" Some laughed. Some mothers pulled their daughters inside. And, at some homes, the porches stood empty.

"Tories," said Hiram. Another town divided.

By late afternoon, my legs ached. Our line of march stretched out over a mile as each of us struggled with the mud. Again the rain began. Our boots sank deeper. Seth Warner rode back and forth along the line of march and encouraged us. We clutched our muskets tight to our bodies to keep the firing mechanisms dry. I wondered if the British had the same problems as we had and thought they probably had, through long experience, solved the problems of mud and rain. McGinnis answered, "A soldier's life is a bastard thing regardless of the color of your jacket." If he meant to cheer me up, he did not, especially when he added, "Step, suck, step, suck."

The officers decided to stop before it got too dark, but no matter where we tried to put up our tents, the ground oozed water. We could not build fires because the wood was wet. Our hats were wet. Our jackets were wet. Our shoes were wet. My cakes were gone. Samuel Poppleton gave Hiram some stale bread, softened by the rain. To save setting up our tents, McGinnis led me under a wagon with about ten others. McGinnis had much to teach me. We lay on our tent halves, our heads and backs dry, and I scribbled a little in my journal before it got totally dark. I slept well.

No one rushed us in the morning, and, along with the coffee, some men had cooked several large pots of hot cereal, which filled us all up. The dark-skinned fellow I had seen first at Fay's Tavern introduced himself. "Peter Keyes, late of Boston, though my family's mostly northwest of here." His accent puzzled me a bit, so clearly did he speak, not like the musical Cork way that Michael spoke. After we had eaten and packed up, Seth Warner gathered us, saying we would rendezvous with Ethan Allen and other Green Mountain Boys in Hubbarton before heading out to Fort Ticonderoga.

I soon appreciated the extra sleep Seth Warner allowed us to have, for he then proceeded to march us and march us all the way to Hubbarton. By noon, the constant jibber-jabbering among us had pretty well worn out, except for Mike McGinnis, who complained about officers driving men, complained about the weather, complained about his shoes, complained about the heavy cast-iron pot he had to carry, and even complained about the ducks and geese flying overhead. "I do believe that in a former life all those ducks and geese were officers in some army. While we get to throw ourselves upon the breastworks, bleeding our lives away, they get to ride back and forth on their horses, flashing their swords, and cheering us on. There's glory for you. Sure, like officers they glide over us while we slip deeper into the earth, preparing ourselves for the final slip into the earth."

The sky had cleared, but McGinnis created a constant cloud. "My feet are sore." "I think I'm going to be sick." "Who decided this route, anyway?" "Step, suck!"

Not wanting dreariness on such a beautiful day, I dropped back to walk beside Peter Keyes. He stood tall and straight, though so dark in the skin. "So, Erastus," he said, "tell me about yourself." I told him of our farm in Pownal.

"Have you been in the army before, Peter?"

"No, no, I've been a school boy most of my life, I fear."

"Where was that? Pittsfield? West Hoosick?"

"Stockbridge."

"I've never been there. Is it like Bennington or Pownal?"

"More like Bennington wants to be than Bennington actually is. But I was then sent to Boston for more of my education. So, you've never been to Stockbridge?"

"Hardly ever into Massachusetts. What was school like in Stockbridge?"

"Run by missionaries, somewhat strict."

"Your parents were missionaries?"

"Not at all. We were, Erastus, those who were missionaried."

I did not understand.

"We were taught how to be Christians, Erastus. Oh, we were taught how to read and write and calculate numbers, but mostly we learned how to be Christians."

"In Pownal, we go to church to learn to be good Christians. In school, we just study reading and writing and ciphering. Of course, I am done with schooling now."

Peter laughed, "But you see, Erastus, you were born a Christian. All you had to learn was how to be a good one. As for us, we had to start from scratch."

I feared, despite his good humor, Peter might start Bible School on the march. Deuteronomy's boring sermons and Tryphena's snide proverbs had soured me on Bible lessons.

We stopped to rest. Early spring flowers were blooming. I pointed them out to Peter, and he told me their names, even their Latin names.

"You learn all that in Stockbridge?" I asked.

"No, Erastus, Boston. Remember, in Stockbridge I was learning to be a Christian. I proved a willing learner, and so they sent me to Boston."

"What for?"

"To be schooled like a white person, to learn to act like a European."

"How does one act like a European?" I asked. "Either you are one or you are not."

"Erastus, you act like a person from Pownal."

"I do not act!" I said.

"When you walk, you walk like this," said Peter, dragging his feet along the ground and slouching with his hands in his pocket.

"I do not."

"And when you talk, you sound like a sheep," said Michael, who had joined us.

"And when you eat . . . " said Peter.

"All right, you have made your point. Now, tell me how a European acts."

"First, one must learn to turn one's nose up at Indians."

"Makes sense to me," said Michael.

"And second, one must turn one's nose up at people from Pownal."

"Another excellent idea," said Michael.

"But most of all, one must never associate with Irishmen, not even to turn one's nose up at them."

"May banshees visit you all the nights of your life," said Michael.

"But Boston's another story, Erastus. For all the high learning going on there, the low-living makes Boston what it is. Taverns, many taverns. Peddlers hawking everything from fine dishes sent from China to other temptations. And the town smells, Erastus. Much too big with too many people and not enough outhouses. Cow trails they call roads. Those who came first mock those who've come after them. Everyone's out to make money. Even school masters sell themselves to students who can afford them."

"I bet the British soldiers make it worse."

"They're poor people just like you Green Mountain Boys. Most sold themselves into the army to eat. Many had to choose between the army and going to prison for some crime they committed. I doubt many want to be soldiers, and I'd wager most would trade places with you in a second if they could."

Thinking of British soldiers as human made them less of an enemy, so I tried not to think. Eventually we joined forces with Ethan Allen and more Green Mountain Boys near a small tavern in Hubbarton. Ethan towered over us.

We slogged up a mountainside—McGinnis complaining to the top. At sunset we flopped down in a large open clearing. Though my feet and legs ached, I sat on the ground enjoying the view and feeling very good about myself. Trying to describe the view in my journal, I sensed someone over my shoulder. I moved to hide my writing and looked up.

There stood Ethan Allen himself! "Keeping a journal, are you?"

"Oh, yes sir," said I, a bit embarrassed that this master of the language might read my poor attempts at writing.

"And your name?"

"Erastus, sir."

"Good, Erastus," he said, "You shall put your writing to good use."

"Sir?"

Ethan knelt down by my side and said, softly, "History remembers us for the words we write about our actions, not for our actions alone. So, you write for our future, Erastus. Write on, on to our future! Our words are for posterity!"

"Yes, sir."

"And tomorrow, Erastus, we attain a noble victory, for tomorrow we capture Fort Ticonderoga and whatever cannon there. Before they can turn them against us." I could not speak. Ethan Allen had talked with me about my writing.

"Speaking of words," said Ethan, "I think it's time to rally the men, don't you?" He stood and strode off to a rise where all could see him. I hurried to alert the men from Pownal, but what with everyone else going from group to group, we were somewhat discombobulated.

Theophilus ordered us to line up, but no one listened. Ethan said in a low voice, "History and the future of the Grants gaze benevolently upon our venture . . . " Oh, it was going to be a stirring Ethan Allen speech. I loved to hear him pronounce upon how we would "stir the earth and stars," as he once said and moved closer to hear what he called "elucidation." Though I was now out of line, no one noticed since everyone had gotten out of line to get nearer Ethan Allen's words. We Boys from Pownal and Bennington did enjoy a stirring discourse. We stood on our toes, leaned on each other's shoulders, and strained our necks to see our leader.

Ethan—for I now feel comfortable enough calling him that—spoke of how the British occupation of Fort Ticonderoga "needs rectification. We are rightly fitted and abilitated to take back what is judiciously ours." Oh, if only I had my pen and journal to capture his words, I thought. "Our efforts shall shine upon this terraquaceous ball!" I said the words over and over to remember them, to be able to talk like Ethan.

Michael McGinnis leaned over toward me. "I'd surely like to abilitate their rum supply and shine upon my alcoholaceous ball—what d'ya think, Erastus?" he said, poking me in my ribs.

Later, after my heart had stopped beating so hard from actually talking to the great Ethan Allen, I finally fell asleep gazing at the stars and dreamt of the noble victory Ethan promised us at Ticonderoga. A "noble victory," I now know, results from how we write of it—not from how we achieve it.

Chapter 5

We Capture Fort Ticonderoga

This is the high point of my story. It is all downhill from here.

"What's this place?" said Michael McGinnis.

"Hands Cove," said Theophilus Bates, "On the shore of Lake Champlain." In the middle of the night, we had been awakened and marched there, grumbling all the way.

"Can't see a damnable thing," said Michael, "and I'm cold." Clouds hid the moon and the stars. We could hear water lapping the shore.

"Ethan ordered no fires," said Theophilus. "Too close to the fort. They might see us."

"The fort? Where?" I wondered aloud.

"Hold your tongues!" ordered Theophilus. "Sound carries far over water."

"Hold your water, Theophilus," a voice in the dark said.

"I'm not holding mine," said another, moving toward the trees.

I could hardly contain myself, so excited was I to take part in our attack on the British. But after hurrying up to reach the place where our attack would begin, we waited in the dark.

We blew our breath into our hands or kept moving to keep warm, some joking, others grumbling. Off to the side I heard a group mumbling and made out a few faces.

"You say you got a haircut?" old Caleb Morgan asked.

"Haircuts lead to good conversations," answered an officer named Noah.

"In the fort, you say?"

"Yesterday Ethan, he told me to go on up to the fort on some business or other, find out what I could, so I got me a little boat, rowed across down below, and walked right up, saying I needed a shave."

"So which is it?" asked Caleb, "A shave or a haircut?"

"Both, but I learned ample enough. Actually, you'd like them British guards. We nattered about life in the fort while I waited and while they gave me a shave—and a haircut. They sit on their butts most of the day, hate officers, hate the food, hate keeping their weapons clean, you know, like us."

"They hang spies, you know," said Michael, who had walked up behind me.

"I weren't no spy," said Noah, "just a friendly visitor in for a chat. Got about the nicest shave I ever got."

"I could use a good shave," said Caleb.

"Anyway," said Noah, "I asked them whether they thought the damnable Yankees were a threat, and they just laughed at me. Said their head general in Boston, Gage, would squash any uprising before it got started."

"Guess they ain't heard of Concord or Lexington yet," said Caleb, reminding me that blood was spilling even now.

"What about their defenses?" Luke Van Arnem asked.

"Don't seem much. Big hole in the outer wall that ain't been plugged. The door built into the main gate, the wicket door, it's open all the time. Got a bunch of cannons, though, but only a few guards up and about. Most hate the place. Just there to wave the colors, so to speak, not to attack anything. Still, if they find out about us, they could make things difficult for us."

"Many soldiers?" a voice asked from the darkness.

"I don't know, about 40 or 50, I'd say. Plus women and children."

"What about the rum?" asked someone.

I wandered off and shortly walked up against Ethan Allen himself, talking kind of low for him, but awful mad.

"What do you mean we don't have any boats? We need to get us across to the fort! I sent Sam Herrick to Skenesboro to steal ol' Skene's boats. Now where are they?"

"Easy, Ethan," a soft voice said. Now I could make out Seth Warner.

"This tries my soul," said Ethan. "I've got 300 men here all ready to go, morning's not too far off, and these hill farmers aren't about to swim across."

"Be patient, Ethan," said Seth Warner. I could not see their expressions, it was so dark. I determined the word for Seth Warner was "imperturbable." Tall, gangly, and imperturbable.

"If God were patient, he'd still be waiting for Adam to grow a rib," Ethan replied.

By now, the light in the east had started. "Look over there, Erastus," whispered Theophilus. "There's the fort." I could barely see a grey mass across the water.

Turning away, I saw a stranger to the Green Mountain Boys marching straight up to Ethan as though he were in charge. I could make out a splendid uniform, although I could not make out the details, but I noticed he had wrapped himself in a cape and wore a tricornered hat, so maybe he was on our side. Still, this was no Green Mountain Boy. His uniform, which none of us had, not even Ethan, aside from his epaulets tacked on his jacket, was dramatic. I tried to see it more closely. I could swear it was red. For all I knew he might have been a British officer.

"Damned me if he don't look like a lobsterback," whispered Mike McGinnis.

Behind him walked another man, tall, thin, just like Seth Warner, but with an awfully good posture, not like Seth. Later we learned he was a "valet du chambre," which, it seems, meant he carried his leader's baggage, cleaned his uniforms, fixed his meals, and made sure his weapon was cleaned and loaded. I would not want to be what Caleb called a "valley do chamber" under any circumstances, but I thought it might be nice to have one.

New militia appeared out of the woods behind those two.

A close look at this uniformed stranger revealed a short fellow, a little on the well-fed side compared to the stringy boys from the Grants who gawked at him. He did not look at us, but faced Ethan and announced to all of us, "I am Colonel Benedict Arnold, and I carry with me a commission from the Cambridge Committee of Safety to lead you against Fort Ticonderoga."

I could not believe what I saw, for Ethan just looked down at this little man with a commanding voice and seemed unable to bring forth a word. For a brief moment, I almost lost faith in Ethan, but he soon took a deep breath and said, "Did I hear aright?!"

"I believe so," said Benedict Arnold, turning now his broad face toward us.

"Well, now," said Ethan, tilting his head and leaning down into Benedict Arnold's face, "I believe you speak with some temerity, sir." Ethan had found his multisyllabic voice.

"I have my commission," answered Benedict Arnold, holding out a piece of paper.

"And I have the Green Mountain Boys, sir. By what authority do you mean to usurp our mission? Did you say some Commission of Safety, sir?"

"We heard of you assembling this force—and for that I and the Continental Congress are grateful. The Cambridge Commission of Safety has delegated the leadership of this attack to me."

"I am sorry, sir, but isn't Cambridge some place near Boston?"

"Correct."

"And isn't Boston located some miles from here, in the Massachusetts Bay Colony, in fact?" He did not give Colonel Arnold a chance to answer. "And do you not know this free soil you stand upon has been occupied by the brave men of the Grants, not some weak-willed Colony of the British tyrant?" Ethan still did not wait for Colonel Arnold's answer and began speaking directly to his audience—us. "And do you not know these are the Green Mountain Boys, and I am their leader, working under the authority of the Hartford Committee of Correspondence, directed by our Council of War, and solely responsible to these valiant men who voluntarily stand before you and who have undertaken to seek freedom and overthrow the occupation of the English usurpation?"

"All these committees, councils, and commissions will be the death of us," Michael muttered to me. "War by discussion."

"Perhaps we should ask the soldiers in the fort to vote whether they want to surrender to us," added Peter.

I inched forward to get a good look at this Colonel Arnold. In the still dim light, his eyes looked directly at me, I swear. Piercing eyes and a set to his jaw showed me a man not accustomed to taking orders.

"Well, Colonel Arnold, you see before you the men of the Grants, sir," said Ethan Allen, still talking to us and not facing Colonel Arnold. "And, sir, in the Grants democracy holds sway. We do not recognize inherited authority or authority given by some governmental body of a foreign nation, such as the Massachusetts Bay Colony."

Colonel Arnold's posture straightened even more. He folded his arms across his chest and looked at us rather than at Ethan. Ethan continued. "And in the Grants leaders are elected by the populace—and unelected. I, sir, am elected. You, sir, are not."

"If this little strutter's another damned flatlander come to tell us what to do, I say we go home now!" someone near Ethan commented. I started to clap. Everyone around me grumbled their agreement. Well, that is, we all grumbled at a whisper. For the British were near. And besides, it was getting lighter by the second.

"We chose Ethan to lead us," said Seth Warner.

"Well, men, fair's fair. We could hold another election right now," suggested Ethan. Ethan always did what was right.

Colonel Benedict Arnold, it turns out, was a wise man and not inclined to argue with all 300 or so of us, so he said nothing.

We waited. They waited. The sky grew lighter.

Ethan realized Colonel Arnold undoubtedly possessed some military expertise that might come in handy and said, "Colonel, I welcome your commitment to our cause and see in you someone who may indeed value the same outcome as we, and so, allow me to offer this." And then, turning to all of us, Ethan said, "Men of the Green Mountains, we are honored to have with us tonight one whose heart is aligned with ours, who has as his purpose what we have as our purpose, to attain that fort across the lake, to breach its fortifications, and to show the English bullies what we free men are made of. Therefore, I propose that we allow Colonel Arnold to stand by me at the head of our attack, as a brother in arms, and that, before he turns back, he enjoy the victory before us."

To which Michael McGinnis added, "Ah, officers are brothers of officers. It has always been thus."

The clouds continued to glow more on the horizon.

A few grumbled. Ethan said, "All in favor signify by saying 'Aye.'" Silence. "Gentleman, I said, 'Signify with an aye.'" We all so signified. "You may bear witness to your Commission of Safety, Colonel: Green Mountain Democracy in action."

Colonel Arnold paused and, reconsidering his situation, reached out to shake Ethan's hand, and said, "I believe such an arrangement would be suitable."

Just then, Asa Douglas and several others sent to find boats for our crossing came running up. "Ethan, we've secured two boats good enough to hold about eighty men."

Ethan, still upset that Samuel Herrick had not returned from his raid on Skenesboro, answered, "Eighty! We've got four times that number, Asa."

"I'm sorry, Ethan, but that's all we could rent."

"Rent!" said Colonel Benedict Arnold. "Why could you not have just confiscated them? I've never heard of an army renting equipment. Next, I suppose we'll be renting soldiers and then renting a government with a rented set of laws?"

Asa clearly did not know who just spoke to him, so responded to Ethan, "We didn't think the gentlemen at Crown Point'd allow us to purloin their boats, especially to use them attacking Ticonderoga."

"Crown Point? Isn't that still a British garrison?" asked Colonel Arnold.

"Yep, up north a ways," said Asa. "The common soldiers there can use a little money, so we thought we'd help them out by renting their boats." Ethan smiled. The valet du chambre also smiled, while maintaining a fine posture.

Colonel Arnold scrunched up his face and turned away, clearly impressed with the creativity of the Green Mountain leaders. "It's a bit on the uncommon side," he said. "To transact business with the enemy is . . . well, I mean, to rent the military equipment with which to attack that very enemy . . . quite creative." I swear he, too, smiled, if only briefly.

"Now you're thinking like one of us, Colonel," said Ethan. He took off his hat, scratched his head a moment, slapped Benedict Arnold on the back, and said, "Yes! Let's get doubly creative! We've got about 300 men. Room in the bateaux for only about 80 to attack Ticonderoga. That fort up at Crown Point's just sitting there. Well, why not? Seth! Step here a moment, would you?"

Seth Warner ambled over, his hands in his pockets. "What's your pleasure, Ethan?"

"My pleasure's also my displeasure. Seems we've not enough bateaux to transport our keen militia to their glorious destiny across the Lake. So I'm asking you and your men not to attend this meeting with us."

Seth's lower lip pushed out. Any Green Mountain Boy would be disappointed if he had been disinvited to a party. But Ethan soon brightened his outlook. "Seth, the proprietors of the boats at Crown Point have overcharged us for the use of their bateaux, and so I suggest you return there with a bunch of us to request a refund of, say, perhaps the entire garrison."

Seth spoke fewer words than Ethan. (Of course, almost everyone spoke fewer words than Ethan.) "You men," he said, separating a group off from us, "Follow me! We're off to capture Crown Point!"

Michael McGinnis was caught up in Seth's impromptu recruitment and mumbled, "They better have some rum to rent."

Peter Keyes mimicked an Irish accent. "Sure an' we'll miss you, m'boy."

Ethan then turned to the rest of us. "Men of the Grants! The time is upon us. Your spirit and commitment are the motivation we need to unleash the . . . "

Seth stopped, turned, and interrupted Ethan. "Ethan, the sun's coming up."

Everyone from Pownal all rushed the nearest boat and shoved our way aboard—Caleb, Josiah Dunning, Jededia Jewett, Mikel Diel, Isaiah Carpenter, my Uncle Hiram with his flute, Reverend Dewey, Samuel Poppleton, even Obadiah Dunham, who usually tried to maintain some decorum—all of us. "Paddle softly" Ethan instructed us.

Trying to get our oars in the water, we banged them against the boat and probably woke up the ducks. "Damn," I heard someone say, "you just poked me in the eye with your elbow!"

"Then move over. Give me room to sit!"

"Get your foot off my back, you clodpole!"

"Pull, you idiot!"

"How can I pull with your stomach taking up all the room!"

"Quiet!" ordered Sergeant Theophilus. We fell silent, sure we had betrayed our attack to the British. I heard a duck quack.

Pownal folks are not sailors. Our oars dug too deep in the water and lost the rhythm. Our oars skimmed the top of the water and splashed us in the barge. Our barge went first one way and then another. Despite our utter incompetence as sailors, the guards in the fort did not hear us. In the east, the light grew brighter and brighter.

When we reached the shore beneath the fort, dripping and shivering, Ethan issued a simple order, "Let's go!" With that, he started walking at a fast pace. Colonel Arnold started walking faster. As we approached the fort, each took off at a trot, each with his sword raised, each trying to move ahead of the other, stumbling in the early light and panting. Behind them, we all rushed, also stumbling, breathing heavily, and cursing in loud whispers. Ethan, with his legs so much longer than Colonel Arnold's, managed to move ahead as we approached the main gate. Colonel Arnold stayed right near him, though.

We crashed through the brush, snapping twigs. A branch snapped back from the man in front and whipped into my face. I yelled in pain. Around me men tripped, knocked others over. One fell in front of me. I leapt over him. We must have sounded like a herd of bears being chased through the woods. I feared the guns of the fort would open up and destroy us at any moment.

The small wicket door stood wide open. The guard there turned toward Ethan and Colonel Arnold as they ran toward him. "Who's there?" he shouted. "Halt!" he ordered. Upon seeing figures racing toward him in the dim light, he pointed his Brown Bess in our general direction and pulled the trigger. It misfired. We kept rushing toward him. He whirled and ran back through the gate. "Attack! Attack! To arms!"

Ethan and Colonel Arnold reached the gate at the same moment. Each struggled to push through before the other. Colonel Arnold strained to shove his shoulder in front of Ethan. Ethan elbowed him back.

Ethan freed himself first, stumbled, and rose.

Suddenly, another guard charged out of the darkness, and Ethan whacked him on the side of the head with his sword. "Villain!" he shouted. The guard fell. I was amazed his head did not roll away. "Charge on, men!" shouted Ethan. "Rectification!"

We improvised and individualized war cries to terrorize the British and be recalled in years to come over many a drink of flip and stonewalls. Some shouted, "No quarter! Kill them all!" Some yelled the way they had been told Abenakis and Mohawks yell when they go into battle. Some just screamed sounds that, when children, they imagined ghosts to scream. Most were out of breath, their lungs heaving ugly rasps. Reverend Dewey appeared at my side. "Praise God!" he shouted over and over. Thankfully, Ethan was too busy to hear him, or Ethan would have stopped the attack then and there and lectured us on the false logic of organized religions.

Just then, a third guard appeared, and again Ethan whacked him on the side of the head. He too fell to his knees. Ethan yanked the solder to his feet and demanded he take them to the fort's commander. The soldier led them up a short flight of stairs to a door, and Ethan charged up, with Colonel Arnold right behind him. I ran up after them.

Ethan banged on the door with the hilt of his sword. "Come out of there, you damned British rat!" he shouted. And "Get your bare-tailed ass down here!" And "Come out of there, you goddamned old rat!"

We could see a lantern's light showing through the door's window, and soon it opened to show a tall British officer in his nightshirt, holding his pants and jacket over his arm. "Who dares invade this fort?" he demanded. "And by what authority?"

"We're the Green Mountain Boys!" shouted Ethan. "We need no more authority! Sent here to turn your world upside down, you mangy flea-bitten . . . !"

Colonel Arnold stepped forward. "Colonel Benedict Arnold at your service, sir."

Ethan ignored him. "So, Captain Delaplace, you red-backed and bare-legged troglodyte, we demand you surrender this fort immediately, or we shall flay you and every one of your servile soldiers!"

Colonel Arnold pulled a paper from inside his coat jacket. "Sir, by the authority of the Cambridge Committee of Safety and . . . "

But Ethan persisted, "So, Delaplace, you've no choice but to surrender."

"Sir," said the officer, "I do not know who you are, but I am not . . . "

"Not surrendering?" continued Ethan. "Either you tell your men to surrender immediately, or we'll burn them in their barracks." By this time, British soldiers had begun to rush out of their barracks, but halted when they saw us pointing our muskets at them.

"I'm trying to tell you, sir, whoever you may be, that I'm not . . . "

"Don't feign courage, you scrawny rooster-legged occupier! Tell your men to stack their arms, Captain," Ethan ordered.

"Mr. Allen," said Colonel Arnold, "If you'll notice this gentleman's rank . . . "

"I'm not Captain Delaplace, sir. I am Lieutenant Joselyn Feltham, his second in command."

"So," said Ethan, "the goddamned British rat cowers behind the naked legs of a subordinate, does he? Well, then, tell your men to stack their arms and back off, Lieutenant. I'll drag the sniveling rat from under his bed and give him what for myself."

At that point, another tall officer appeared in the doorway, apparently the real Captain Delaplace. Unlike Lieutenant Feltham, he had taken the time to dress fully. He said nothing, but stared with wide eyes at Ethan and Colonel Arnold. Ethan continued as though nothing had gone on before this. "So there you are, you damned British rat!" said Ethan, finally confronting his rat.

And that is how we captured Fort Ticonderoga. If you like grand stories of patriotic victories, you may want to stop reading here.

CHAPTER 6

▼

MY PLATO TO ETHAN'S SOCRATES

Samuel Poppleton ripped his green shirt off his back, climbed up to the fort's flagpole, ran down the British union ensign, and ran his shirt up the pole. "The colors of the Green Mountain Boys!" he shouted to our cheers and laughter.

We jailed all the British soldiers in their barracks, put the Captain and his Lieutenant under arrest in their quarters, with a guard to stand over them, and told their wives and children to go find someplace to rest. Their conquest complete, the Green Mountain Boys went in search of whatever their hosts had to offer.

Naturally, they located the rum first. And shortly after that, Colonel Arnold protested to Ethan, "Mr. Allen, you must contain your soldiery. Their behavior is most unfitting and threatens our very security in holding this fort."

"And who threatens us, Colonel?" Ethan answered. "The British lion sleeps soundly in Canada, his kits in the forts near us know nothing of what we have done, so don't you think our boys deserve a little celebrating?"

The truth is, the fort was more like a tumble-down barn than a fort. The English had done nothing to repair the walls after the French had tried to destroy it when they abandoned it years ago.

Colonel Arnold turned and walked away, clearly miffed. His valet du chambre followed, continuing to move with decorum.

The next morning, most of the Green Mountain Boys still slept, with the British officers and soldiers locked in their rooms. I was awakened by someone shaking my shoulder and saw Ethan Allen himself leaning over me. "Are you feeling well, Erastus? Good, get up and follow me."

Ethan led me outside the gate of the fort and off some distance where we could not be heard. "Erastus," he said, "Once before I observed you writing in a journal, so I assume you've had an education and can write well, am I right?" I could not bring myself to claim great literacy, but I did admit I could write.

"Of course you can," Ethan said. "Erastus, you've witnessed and participated in one of the most glorious events in our young nation's history." My heart beat faster at his calling us a nation. The Green Mountain Grants a nation! "It's essential that children in generations hence learn of our deeds here and equally essential that this place become a hallowed monument to Democracy and Freedom." As he spoke the words, they capitalized themselves.

"Sir," I said, "I do not know if I can offer anything."

"Erastus, I need a scribe, a Cicero as it were, one who can record the events we have brought about so generations to come remember them as they ought to be remembered. A Plato to my Socrates. Yes, as generations hence expect of me, I shall write my autobiography someday, and school children will undoubtedly read it as part of their history lessons, but some will doubt my words—some will claim it's only my attempt to aggrandize my accomplishments. No, do not deny it, Erastus, for there are those among us even today who would seek to overarch their accomplishments and denigrate those of us who act without fear of failure."

I did not know what to say. I am not sure I even knew what he was saying, although I assumed he meant Colonel Arnold when he spoke of those who overarch.

"Erastus, I hope you have a way with words, for I seek your advice as an objective audience."

"I will do what I can, sir."

Ethan stretched out on the ground and motioned to me to sit next to him. "Erastus, do you remember what I said when I rapped upon Captain Delaplace's door last night?"

"Sure do! You called him a damned old British rat, sir."

"Well, that may be what you may have heard, and, indeed, Erastus, it may indeed be what I may have said, but it was not what I meant, and it most certainly is not fit for generations hence to recall. Remember, Erastus, history must remember not merely our accomplishments, but also our intentions. And our intentions are noble ones, are they not?"

"Indeed, sir," said I, eager to learn at his civic knee.

"Indeed, they are, Erastus, indeed they are, and now our intentions and actions must be translated into words that are equally noble. Erastus, what might you remember about what I replied when asked by what authority I had attacked and occupied this fort?"

"Something about being Green Mountain Boys and his being a mangy flea-bitten son of a bitch, sir."

"Well, yes, that was true in the passion of the moment. But you see, Erastus, if history remembers us that way, it will not remember us for the noble act we committed as much as it may remember us as a band of ruffians. So, Erastus, I need your help in remembering the noble words that our noble actions intended. Can you help?"

"I will try, sir."

"Good. Now, what if, when asked by what authority we had attacked this fort, I had replied, 'By the authority of the people of the Grants, that's who!'"?

"That would be true, sir."

"Factually true, Erastus, but not appropriately true. It needs to ring with the grandeur of the moment. Remember that the Yorkers do not recognize our rights in the Grants, and others believe the overreaching Yorkers have legal justification, no matter how misguided their belief." He paused to think a while. "How does this sound? 'I am authorized by God and the people of the Green Mountains.'"

"Stronger, sir."

"But people will know that Ethan Allen does not go around claiming this God fellow or any other deity guides him, much less even exists. No, we must find something more noble and equally authentic."

"How about," I offered, "By the authority of the Great Jehovah?"

"Oh, that has a more sonorous sound to it. But it needs the authority of the people, not merely some spiritual blessing."

"Well, there is the Council of War."

"Hmm. 'By the authority of the Great Jehovah and the Council of War!'" He paused to test its resonance in his mind and heart. "No, that sounds like some upstart group of revolutionary spiritualists."

I actually did think that the Council of War was truly an upstart group of revolutionaries, but I did not think it circumspect to say so. "Then, sir, how about 'By the authority of the Great Jehovah and the Committee of Safety?'"

Ethan scrunched up his already weathered face. "That Benedict Arnold fellow might approve, but the Committee of Safety is not of the Green Mountains, nor is it of our nation-to-be. No, we need something both quotable and politically astute."

He paused, and then sat up, waving his index finger in the air. "I have it, Erastus. Listen. 'By the authority of the Great Jehovah and the Continental Congress!' Yes, I like that. It will appeal to the likes of both those who suffer from Christianity and the politicians who tinker with our future. That, indeed, must be what I must have said. Or, at least, what I must have intended to have said had I time to manufacture verbal remembrances suitable for posterity."

"That sounds very good, sir."

"Noble and sonorous, do you not think?"

"Yes, sir."

He leaned toward me, speaking softly. "You and I both know how that wine-and-glory-besotted Continental Congress shows us no respect. Bloated in Philadelphia, they would rather debate the number of committees they need than deal with the reality of our claims. In truth, I should not honor them in our victory. 'Tis offensive to reason and to common sense, is it not?" I nodded my agreement. "Nevertheless, Erastus, despite what we may desire, they shall bask in our victory and claim it theirs, anyway, so we might as well throw them a bit of an historic bone, should we not? Perhaps then they'll recognize the Grants as the fourteenth colony."

I nodded at his wisdom, thrilled to think of the Grants as the fourteenth colony.

"Well done, Erastus. You shall record the history of our campaigns so those in Pownal and in our nation shall remember us as they should."

And so I began another glorious venture, serving as the historian of Ethan Allen and the Green Mountain Boys.

That morning, Samuel Herrick and his men finally returned, sailing boisterously up in a sloop. Sent by Ethan to find boats to use in attacking Fort Ti, they had attacked Skene's town and captured this sloop, much too late for my pleasure. I would much rather have ridden the sloop across the lake at night than an old barge of a bateau.

Ethan met them, boarded the sloop, walked to its bow and faced those of us gathered nearby. "Conquerors of Fort Ticonderoga," he declared, "I hereby christen this noble vessel 'The Liberty.'"

Then, amid our cheers, he stepped off the sloop and shook the hand of Samuel Herrick as well as those of the men who had accompanied Herrick.

"Colonel Allen!"

Ethan turned to see before him Captain Delaplace, guarded by Green Mountain Boys. His uniform seemed to be as clean and pressed as it was when we captured him. "Colonel, I must protest your men drinking all of my rum." The captain's aristocratic face burned with indignation.

"Your rum, Captain?"

"It is my personal property, Colonel, over 90 gallons of it."

"Erastus!"

I looked up at Colonel Allen. "Erastus, take up your pen and your paper so I may dictate a receipt for Captain Delaplace."

As I recall, I wrote, "To Captain Delaplace for liquors supplied the garrison and for the refreshment of the fatigued soldiery, 90 gallons rum. The Continental Congress will reimburse his expenses upon cessation of hostilities by the King of England." Or something like that.

When I finished, when Ethan had signed it, and after listening to Captain Delaplace protest that we had overstepped military propriety, Ethan thanked the Captain for his opinion and ordered him locked back up.

"Ah, Erastus," said Ethan, "we are become a nation of shopkeepers, even as we enjoy our illustrious victory. Yesterday we rented boats from our enemy, and today we purchase refreshments from him. Tomorrow I will undoubtedly be selling him property in the Grants."

After conducting this business, I observed Colonel Arnold, accompanied by his valet du chambre and some of our soldiers, going from one end of the fort to the other, counting just about everything—cannons, howitzers, mortars, barrels of flour, barrels of powder, stores of clothing, muskets, bayonets—everything. He appeared to be a very conscientious person, making an inventory of all we had captured. Although I considered him uninspired compared to Ethan Allen, I did begin to wonder whether there might be more to soldiering than just attacking the enemy and winning victories. An inventory! Ethan was right—we were a nation of shopkeepers.

I helped gather up the muskets lying scattered across the parade ground, leaning against walls, dropped in the dirt, tossed aside as the Green Mountain Boys celebrated their victory, or stacked by the British soldiers when they surrendered.

I felt both guilt and fear because our attack had shed no blood, while Michael McGinnis may have been wounded or worse when his group attacked Crown Point. So I was relieved when he returned from the raid and stomped up to me. To my joyful welcome, he growled.

"Michael, what happened? You're back so soon. Did something go wrong?"

"Wrong, Erastus? What could possibly have gone wrong, other than having to march against the wind the whole way, brambles ripping our clothes, stumbling over rocks, shivering our bones, our legs aching and arms breaking under the weight of our muskets, damned officers yelling at us to move faster. A miserable time, Erastus. While you all loll about back here basking in the sun, we poor sodden souls suffered mightily, and for what, I ask you, for what?"

I feared our first defeat in battle. "Were they ready for you, Michael? Were their defenses strong? Was it a vicious battle?"

"Vicious? If having to climb over a pile of rubble and skin your knees and scrape your hands is vicious, then it was vicious. If having to search high and low to find someone to attack while your head aches and your skin is scraped and sore—if all that may be called vicious—then it was vicious. If finally finding one drunken sergeant and eight sick, broken down British soldiers more miserable than we may be called vicious, then, yes, it was vicious."

"That was it? No defense?"

"It! That bastard sergeant had drunk the last bottle of rum they possessed! It! The fort had fallen down long before St. Patrick scared the snakes away. It! I come all the way to this God-forsaken wilderness to fight the lobsterbacks and all I get is whipped out and an empty bottle of rum. Their soldiers welcomed us! They asked us if we had any extra food and jackets to keep them warm, they were so miserable."

"But we did capture the fort, right?"

"Sure and now we have to haul 50 cannon out of there, through the mud and the cold, not to mention having to baby those poor wretches we call our enemy. I tell you, Erastus, there's no rest for the weary!"

By now, word had begun to spread around the countryside of our great victory, and farmers, merchants, women, children, and a handful of Abenakis had begun to enter the fort. In a few hours, hundreds of people had joined us, setting up shop to sell whatever they could and luring our men away from their assignments. I saw two ladies who did not appear to be farm wives leading two into an empty room of the fort. One man held four small jugs of something he was trying to auction off to the highest bidder. An Abenaki and one of our Boys from Pownal were haggling over how many furs were worth one Brown Bess. One man leading an old ox with ribs poking out was trying to trade him to a man who had an even older-looking horse whose back swayed close to snapping. A farm wife with a basket full of kittens was trying to trade them for whatever food she could get from other farm wives. Two young boys were struggling with a bench they had found, trying to sneak it out the gate. Another woman was trying to convince any soldier whose head still hurt from the night before that her special willow bark powder would cure his headache. Even I laughed at her. A fiddler stood on a box, and Uncle Hiram had joined him with his flute. Men and women jigged, clapping their hands to the music, and laughing uproariously.

Uncle Hiram played something called "The Soldier and the Maid." Theophilus sang the words.

"A lewd song," said Deuteronomy Dewey, shaking his finger at my uncle. I did not record the words.

We invented games. One of my favorite games was "toss the pan." We didn't have any balls to kick, but we did have our iron fry pans with handles we could grab. We players would each grab the fry pan by the handle and see who could throw it the farthest. If that got boring, we'd find a small opening in the fort walls and try the throw the fry pan through it. Once, we chose up teams, found two openings to serve as goals on opposite sides of the parade ground and then tried to throw the fry pan through the other team's goal. With no other rules and only two teams, we usually wrestled, tumbling into a heap of men as each tried to grab the pan, break free of the pile, and toss it through the goal.

Colonel Benedict Arnold fumed. Followed by his valet du chambre, he went from soldier to soldier, trying to order them to return to work. "We got your damned fort, didn't we?" said one. Arnold ordered the fiddler and Uncle Hiram to stop playing. He told the ox and horse owners that they would have to clean up after their animals and leave. He stepped on the tail of a hound one farmer had by his side and almost was bitten. All he got for his efforts were laughs, except from the owner of the hound, who demanded he be paid for the injury to his dog.

When he approached a group of soldiers who were gathered around a sutler selling home brew and ordered them to return to their posts, one of them actually fired his musket at him. "You tell me what I can and cannot do one more time and I'll blow your bloody head off, you prissy prig," said the soldier, spittle rolling onto his unshaved chin.

"Who is that?" I whispered to Theophilus, who was standing beside me.

"Hunt Hungerford," he said. "We fought together in the French and Indian War. Sorry to say he's a sergeant, too. Mean. Stay away from him."

"I will," I promised, but I would later break my promise and not because I wanted to. "Do you think Hungerford really wanted to kill Colonel Arnold?"

"Wouldn't surprise me a bit," said Theophilus. "Since none of us can hit anything we aim at, hard to tell. But I'm telling you, Erastus, Hungerford'll kill any man if it'll profit him."

Colonel Arnold stared at Hungerford, raised himself up to his full height, turned on his heel, and strode over to Ethan Allen, who stood bartering with a little old lady for a nice shawl. I followed closely.

"Colonel Allen," Colonel Arnold said, his face turning red, "your men have gotten completely out of control. We cannot abide such behavior. I agreed to your leading the attack on this fort, but now it's under our control, so I demand you turn command over to me, for I have the authority of the government to uphold."

"Oh, Colonel, really," replied Ethan, smiling and placing his hand on Colonel Arnold's shoulder. "Boys will be boys, you know. They're just letting their breeches out a little."

"You will continue to abide their insubordination?" A vein pulsed in the middle of Colonel Arnold's forehead.

"I haven't given them any orders, Colonel, so they can't quite be insubordinate, now can they? And furthermore, your presumption of authority is irksome."

"Irksome!"

"Exasperating, tiresome, tedious, and, may I say, bothersome."

"You take umbrage, sir?"

"You do give me a most prodigious pique, I might add."

"A prodigious pique?!" Colonel Arnold's face turned a grander red.

"Had I a tooth bothering me as much as you, sir, I would insist it be pulled. I would hook a string up to my tooth from that skeletal ox out there and slap the beast so hard the ache would fly straight through the gate." You can see why I gleefully copied down Ethan's words.

Colonel Benedict Arnold glared at Colonel Ethan Allen, scrunched up his eyes, pulled on his lower lip, cleared his throat, and said, most diplomatically, "Sir, I grant you your Green Mountain Boys have shown great fortitude in attacking this fort and did so with resistless fury, albeit unopposed. And I grant you no finer group of patriots exists on this continent's soil, at least none that I'm aware of lately. But surely you realize Governor Carlton of Canada will exert himself to retake this fort as soon as he learns we have captured it. I am apprehensive of a sudden and quick attack. We must be vigilant."

"I am aware," said Ethan, picking the wax out of one of his ears.

"And despite the grandiose offerings this local populace tenders us—oxen and horses strong enough to pull cannon from here to Boston, magical powders of willow bark that can invigorate the most sickly of men, home comforts only a dark room can reveal, and music to charm the most violent of souls—still, we really are in want of almost every necessity, excepting, of course, the courage of your soldiery, and so we must write to the Committees of Correspondence urging their support by sending us the supplies we need. We must, likewise, regroup our men so they may resume their march toward a grand and glorious destiny." It was a wonderfully moving speech, spoken in a manner my mother would have praised. In fact, I wondered whether she and Benedict Arnold had studied their rhetoric from the same primer. In short, Ethan was moved.

"Your eloquence touches me, Colonel," said Ethan. "So much so that I agree we need to post sentries in the event the British deign to counter-attack."

"Thank you, Colonel," said Colonel Arnold.

"Your obedient servant, sir," said Colonel Allen, taking off his hat and sweeping it in a grand bow.

Throughout the afternoon, Colonel Arnold gathered up, with the blessing of Ethan of course, all the soldiers who could stand and then marched us around the fort to spots where he had identified good sentry posts. Ticonderoga sat on a small rise jutting into the lake, surrounded on three sides by water. Our job as sentries was to go on duty every two hours and challenge anyone who approached. If we thought we were being attacked, we were to sound the alarm by firing off our muskets. And yelling.

Benedict Arnold gathered us around him and gave us our posts, times, and instructions. His first and last instruction was, "If you should fall asleep or desert your posts, you shall be court-martialed for desertion, which is a crime punishable by death."

"Sir?" said one of the Green Mountain Boys.

"I shall have you shot." Colonel Arnold's concise response made staying awake and alert an easy rule to follow.

The first night, we were given the countersign that would change every night. This night it was "Victory or Death." I thought that a noble countersign. "Stay Awake or Death" would have suited the situation more, but it would not have been nearly as noble.

My post lay way out on the point of land facing the south. We each drew the times we would be on sentry duty, and I unfortunately drew the 2 a.m. to 4 a.m. time. I tried sleeping, but kept waking up for fear I would miss my turn as sentry. Soon enough, the corporal in charge of the night watch woke me up, and off I went to relieve the sentry at my post.

The night was awfully quiet out there, with the stars twinkling in the sky, and after walking around in a circle for a while, holding my musket at the ready, I sat down, leaned against a boulder, and gazed at the heavens. As you can guess, the quiet and peace soon worked their will on me, so I nodded off. When I woke up, I did not know whether I had overslept and not been relieved or whether I had slept for only a minute. Nevertheless, I was thankful I had not been shot by Colonel Arnold.

Just to be sure, I decided to walk over to where the next sentry on the east was posted to see if he knew the time. When I got close, I whispered, "Psst, do you know what time it is?"

"Who goes there?" he shouted. "Stand and give the countersign!"

"I just want to know the time," I said, forgetting that even guards should give the countersign to each other.

Wham, he fired off his musket and shouted, "Enemy in the camp! Enemy in the camp!" He must have learned that as a young boy playing war games.

I turned to step back, tripped over a root and fell. I could hear shouts coming from the fort and hightailed it limping back to my post. I arrived at the same time as the corporal, who asked me if I had seen anything. I answered, "Only the alarm shot and yell at the next post." Given the darkness, I had answered him truthfully, of course.

I will say this about what I started: it proved how ready we were to encounter the enemy, for the entire fort woke up and charged to their posts. First the corporal of the guard and then the sergeant in charge of him and finally Ethan Allen and Benedict Arnold themselves questioned the sentry whom I had frightened. All the poor man could say was, "I swear someone was there and did not answer my challenge."

Happily for him, they believed him and went from post to post, warning us all to be on the alert. "Don't fall asleep," they cautioned us. Fall asleep? My heart was beating like a drum. I could not fall asleep if I tried.

The next day, the Colonels Arnold and Allen directed a handful of Pittsfield men under Abiatha Angell to march the captured officers out of the fort "as a present for Governor Trumbull of Connecticut," Ethan told us. He read us the message he sent along with them: "I make you a present of a Captain and two Lieutenants of the regular establishment of George the Third."

I located a good deal of ink and paper in the fort, so I spent my time, whenever I was not on duty, trying to write for posterity.

Posterity did not inspire me easily. My journal shows me scribbling lists of whatever I saw around me: barrels of food, barrels of powder, piles of the rock from the walls, muskets now stacked together in pyramids, Green Mountain Boys sleeping against walls or sleeping in the captured barracks, men turned into cooks and cooking the meals, Boys from Pownal still playing "toss the pan" when

Colonel Arnold was not around, the valet du chambre polishing Colonel Arnold's boots and belts, Ethan sending out messengers with his letters.

When I ran out of things to list, I started trying to make mental maps of what had happened and drawing arrows between the events, but all I ended up with were arrows crossing arrows and not much sense to the results. All in all, I did not think this the stuff of history. I knew written history has a neatness about it, a purposeful direction. Everything I tried to write was too messy to be read by future generations.

Ethan had called me his Plato, after the Plato who wrote what Socrates said.

I began to suspect that even Plato must have made things up when he was trying to capture Socrates' ideas.

CHAPTER 7

▼

ONE EMBARRASSMENT AFTER ANOTHER

The longer I knew him, the more Colonel Arnold resembled my mother.

It was not just that he counted every cannon in the fort, working or out of action, on its caisson or sunk in the mud. It was not that he systematically set out sentries around the outskirts of the fort and on the walls, or at least what was left of them. No, just like my mother expecting a visit from her mother, making sure her hearth is swept, setting the family pewter neatly out on the table, selecting only her best candles, ordering her poor son to chop wood and have it all neatly stacked by the fireplace, pounding clean the best—the only, actually—family coverlet for the visitor's bed, just like my mother, Colonel Benedict Arnold set about straightening up the entire fort.

He ordered the area just outside the wicket gate to be set aside for the traders who brought in goods or entertainment and would not allow them to even talk to the soldiers inside the fort. He posted an order to use the parade grounds only for drill and practice or for passing from one area of the fort to another. He hand-picked teams of foragers to go out into the countryside to buy or requisition food for the fort. He only picked those who could stand straight without swaying.

Seeing me writing in my journal one day, Colonel Arnold made a request. "Write this, Erastus: The Green Mountain Boys know how to fight for freedom, but having won the fight, they assume liberty allows them to do anything."

As for Colonel Allen, he was busy writing letters to Congress in Philadelphia. He was busy writing letters to friends in Bennington, bragging of our exploits. He was busy writing to his brothers, evidently giving them instructions to put together more militia.

When reinforcements came from the Massachusetts Bay Colony, Colonel Arnold immediately assigned them to guard the inside of the fort. This did not bother the Green Mountain Boys, for they would much rather walk around outside the fort than inside. But what did bother them was when Colonel Arnold had the Massachusetts newcomers gather up all remaining rum and lock it in one of the cells near where we kept the British soldiers.

"Massachusetts Bay is drowning in Puritans," observed Michael as the rum was locked away.

"And accountants," added Peter, watching Colonel Arnold's valet du chambre counting the rum jugs.

When the Green Mountain Boys complained to Ethan about the rum, he immediately went to Colonel Arnold, and we could see from a distance they were not of one mind about the rum. Ethan looked sternly down at Colonel Arnold, but Colonel Arnold only looked sternly up at Ethan. Ethan gesticulated, and Colonel Arnold gesticulated. All of us knew what the outcome would be and were very happy. When Ethan returned, he explained that Colonel Arnold had relented, but conceded not enough rum remained for "the steady consumption that befits men of your stature." So a gill of rum would be rationed out every evening, except to men standing guard, but they could have their gill after they had served their duty. "Well," the men said, "if there really is so little . . . . " And many volunteered for foraging duty or to stand guard more than once a night.

Colonel Arnold also spent what seemed like an extraordinary amount of time attending to the boats pulled up on the shore of the lake. He had men gather up and boil buckets of tar stored by the English. When the tar was soft, they proceeded to paint the insides of the bateaux. They soon ran out of the tar, so then he sent them inland and set them about peeling bark off the elm trees. This they pounded on rocks until they had a sort of elm bark mush. They heated the elm mush like the tar, and when it was warm, used it to paint the insides of the bateaux. Being the fussy person that he was, Colonel Arnold insisted upon inspecting every inch of the bateaux to see whether they had been coated to his satisfaction.

"The little man doesn't want to get his boots wet," scoffed Michael.

The next day, Colonel Arnold took his men out on the lake, testing the seaworthiness of their boats.

"Look at him," said Ethan. "It's not enough to be a general commanding an army on land—now he must be an admiral."

For two days more the naval exercises continued as Colonel Arnold had his men row their bateaux across the lake and back, row up the lake and down. They practiced jumping in the bateaux, grabbing their oars, and rowing rapidly away. They practiced driving the bows of their bateaux onto the shore and leaping off to attack an imaginary enemy. They practiced loading and unloading their bateaux. And they practiced rowing some more.

And then, one morning, we awoke to the commanding voice of Ethan Allen who, red-faced and angry, yelled across the parade ground, "He's taken the boats! Stolen our sloop!"

"Gentlemen," he said, once he calmed down, "Colonel Arnold has usurped his rightful authority and has acted with deceitful arrogance. I have been apprised that, in the dark of the night, he abandoned our mutual responsibility by leaving for St. John, where, our intelligence has indicated, the English have a sloop. He intends to capture that sloop himself and control this entire lake with both sloops—without us!"

We all nodded as though we understood his concern.

"Where is St. John?" I asked Peter.

"Up north in Canada, near the end of this lake. Whoever occupies it controls the entrance to Canada."

Ethan issued orders to load the two remaining bateaux with supplies for the trip up the lake. That is, for me it was "up" since we would be going north, but it seems the inhabitants of this area call it "down" since the water exits out of the north and they think of boating down to the outlet. So we were headed "down lake," which still strikes me as very peculiar.

Peter, Michael, and I were among those who were volunteered to load the boat while the others gathered up muskets, tents, and food. The muskets we laid in the bottoms of the bateaux. Then we piled bags of flour on top of them and tent fabric on top of the flour. Colonel Arnold had not caulked these two bateaux. Water seeped through the seams, so we had to unload them and reload them in reverse order: the fabric on the bottom, flour in the middle, and muskets on top. We had no time to fix the leaks, so Ethan directed us to gather up pitchers and mugs to bail the water out if we needed. Now I understood why Colonel Arnold had his crews spend so much time coating the insides of their bateaux with the tar and elm bark mush. I have since learned he had been a sea captain before the war and thus had an unfair advantage over the rest of us. Still, I began to develop a respect for the man, even though he did not possess Ethan's use of words.

By mid-morning, satisfied all was ready, Ethan ordered us into the bateaux, where we stumbled our way to our seats on either side. The piles of tent fabric, food, and muskets, on top of which we had piled whatever we had on our backs, made it impossible to walk on the bottoms of the bateaux, which would have been covered with water anyway. So we had to either step on the seats or on the packs of goods. And when we did find seats, most of us had no place to put our legs out in front of us, which interfered with the person sitting on the seat ahead of us, so we knelt or sat cross-legged.

We had chosen a beautiful day to row up the lake, with clear blue skies and the sun shining warmly. That is, *down* the lake.

Ethan commanded one boat. Our sergeant, Theophilus, our boat. He ordered us to take up the oars, which turned out to be longer and larger than I remembered from our nighttime crossing to attack the fort. I tried fitting my oar into the pegs on the side of the boat, but Michael, who was behind me, yelled at me to get it off his oar. So I lifted it up and put it on top of the oar of Peter, who was sitting in front of me.

"All together now," Theophilus commanded. "Oars up, out of the water." We pushed down on the handles and all the oars came up.

"Don't we look military!" said Michael.

"All together now," said Theophilus. "Row!" Down our oars went, into the water. Only mine went down forward-like, and Peter's oar went down backward-like, on top of mine. Michael had tangled his oar with that of the person in back of him. All around us, men cursed and laughed.

Not only did we not move forward, but we tangled our oars with those from the other boat. "Everybody lift the end of his oar out of the water!" commanded Theophilus. "Now push the handles away from you." We got that correct. "Now put the blades in the water." Correct again. "Now pull!" In one sweep, we all managed to move our bateau forward. Easy, I thought.

"Now, do it again," said Theophilus. Doing this together a second time proved difficult. We all had the motion down, but some of us moved faster than others, and soon our oars were tangled again. "Stop! You bunch of Yorker heads! Now, again, and slowly this time. Oars up!" We got it right again. "I'll count. Forward, down, pull, up. Forward, down, pull, up." And so he did. And so we did. And so we became sailors. Notwithstanding our newfound skill, and with

Sergeant Theophilus concentrating on our rowing and not looking where our boat was going, we rammed the other boat when it turned in front of us.

"Hey, Theo," shouted Luke. "Does your Manual of '64 cover naval maneuvers?"

Nonetheless, we did get the hang of the rhythm, as did the men in Ethan's boat, and off we rowed up the lake. Down the lake, that is.

My hands began to develop blisters. The joking soon ended, and what was a new and happy experience soon developed into just plain hard work. Even worse, the wind blew against us from in front, pushing waves against the bow. When we stopped to rest, the wind pushed us backward, so we had to pull in toward shore where the land and trees would block the wind.

Later, the dark clouds blew in, and soon it began to rain. It poured. In short time, we were all drenched, with water dripping down our faces and off our noses. Now, not only did the bateaux leak, but they began to fill with the water from the skies.

Theophilus directed every other person to bring his oar in and start bailing. I had a one liter mug. The water level was approaching the bags of flour. Lightning started to flash around us. I feared that our voyage down lake really was to become a voyage down into the lake.

Some of us bailed faster and faster, while the others rowed, but the water level stayed ahead of us. From the other boat, Ethan yelled an order to pull in to shore. We pulled into a little stream and sat under the trees, everyone bailing now. I did not know whether I wanted to be struck by lightning out in the middle of the lake or here under the trees. I recall my father having said that standing under a tree in a lightning storm was inviting the Lord's retribution. I trusted Ethan knew better, floating us underneath many trees. Whatever his wisdom, we did get ahead on our bailing.

We ate whatsoever we could from our packs. Soon the storm passed, and accordingly we set off again. Well, that is, we had to back all our bateaux out of the little stream, which meant we had to reverse our rowing method, not so easy a task when one sits wet and listening to Michael's lamentations.

Once we commenced going forward, our oars seemed to catch the water weeds that grew in the shallows near shore. Even Theophilus cursed. My hands, having been wet and cold, began to cramp. I tried rowing with one hand while stretching the fingers of the other hand, but ended up banging oars with either Peter or Michael. So I stretched one finger at a time while keeping both hands on the oar.

My blisters broke.

Trying to ignore my burning blisters, I imagined how I would record our voyage to St. John, our overtaking Colonel Arnold, our capturing the sloop, and our returning in victory to Fort Ticonderoga. A gust of wind caught my hat and blew it into the lake beside the boat. Instinctively, I released my grip on my oar and reached for my hat. I was successful in grabbing it, but I was also successful in tipping myself into the lake, where I was immediately struck by the tip of Michael's oar.

"Man overboard!" shouted Theophilus.

"Helblub," I said, or something like that, as I sank under the water.

I have never been able to swim. My sisters Tryphena and Tryphosa could swim and lie afloat for hours. Perhaps women have more air in them than men. Whenever I try to float, I simply end up with water in my ears and my arms flapping wildly.

Which was what happened to me there in the lake, flapping and sinking, rising and flapping, coughing from the water in my lungs and certain my life had now gone "down lake."

To my great relief, two from Ethan's bateau behind us jumped into the lake, swam to where I was sinking, and towed me by the arms back to my bateau. They pushed me up against the side of the bateau, and the men inside hauled me up. I was coughing too much to thank them, and by the time I began to recover, my rescuers had returned to their bateau.

As for my hat, it dripped in my hand.

I tried apologizing to my bateau-mates for having been so clumsy as to fall overboard, but suddenly I began to shiver and shake. I do not know if it was from the cold of the lake or the realization that I might have drowned, but I could not control myself. Peter began pulling off my shirt, and I tried to fight him. "You're wet, Erastus, and need warm clothes."

Hiram dragged out a tent half and threw it around my shoulders. Michael reached into his pack and pulled out a small jug of rum that he had picked up in Hubbarton and poured some down my throat. It was my first drink of rum and burned mightily. I began coughing. "Lie down by your seat," someone said. I did. I kept coughing. I was very embarrassed, but too tired to complain. I knew I was recovering when I began to wonder about how I would record this sorrowful event in my journal which, happily, lay dry in my pack on the seat.

Later that evening, after we had rowed some more, after we pulled ashore on a small island in the lake, after my bateau-mates built several fires to cook their meals and keep warm, after my clothes were hung on sticks by the flames to dry out, and after I had time to think about what I would write, I did not, I confess, write of my unfortunate slipping beneath the waves. Truthfully, I could not explain why my hat mattered so much to me and, besides, I was recording the history of the Green Mountain Boys, especially the Boys from Pownal, not of Erastus alone. Only now, reading that record to hark back to those days, am I reminded by the blots caused by water dripping on the page.

But my near drowning was nothing compared to the next day's misadventure.

Chapter 8

▼

Nothing Is as It Seems

The next day I woke up sick. My nose was dripping down the back of my throat, my lungs were filling up with gunk, and my head hurt. Not that anyone else really cared. Theophilus woke us up by kicking us in the shoulder or whatever other part of our anatomy presented itself. You may look back upon this time and call us patriots, but being a militiaman is not all it is glorified up to be. At least my mother would rub skunk oil on my chest when I was sick and could not breathe. Not that I liked the smell of skunk oil. And it could be embarrassing. In school, you could always tell who was sick by the way other students leaned away from that person. Skunk oil may simply be one way a mother shows her love, but it is not socially beneficial.

We had to quench our fires and load our bateaux immediately. I did not even have a chance to start my internal fires with a warm meal. My mother would not have allowed that. Urgently rushing to catch Colonel Arnold, we could not pause, other than stopping in the woods to relieve ourselves. But such, as I have said before, is the lot of a militiaman. If I were not sick, my journal entry might have been more noble and sonorous.

Michael, as you might know, grumbled. Had my head not ached so, I would have told him it was unbecoming a Green Mountain Boy. Peter, packed and alert, was a model of orderliness, which my mother would have praised. Hiram was too tired to pull out his flute. Walking among us while we bent our backs to load tents, food, and muskets, including his, only Deuteronomy Dewey seemed

- 63 -

to have the spirit needed to move us. Of course, as he reminded us, his spirit came with a capital letter S. He seemed intent upon deepening my momentary despair by quoting some sermon I once had to read and recite in school rather than instilling me with spirit, capital letter S or not.

"Let us pray us on our righteous quest and find our inner strength, for 'He that stands or walks on slippery ground needs nothing but his own weight to throw him down.' Remember, brothers, the English and Yorkers are our enemies. 'That the reason why they are not fallen already, and do not fall now, is only that God's appointed time is not come.' Let us speed them toward their appointed time and bear our burdens with humbleness . . . . "

"As you burden us with your humility," mumbled Michael.

"'For it is said,'" continued Deuteronomy, "that 'when that due time, or appointed time comes, *their foot shall slide.* Then they shall be left to fall, as they are inclined by their own weight. God will not hold them up in these slippery places any longer, but will let them go; and then at that very instant, they shall fall into destruction; as he that stands on such slippery declining ground, on the edge of a pit, he cannot stand alone, when he is let go he immediately falls and is lost.' May the Lord speed us on our way and speed the English and Yorkers into their pit! Amen."

And so, armed with these words, we slunk onto the boats and onto our seats, most silently, I observed. Still sick, my head hurt, my blisters made it painful to grasp my oar, but still, I realized, another adventure lay ahead.

Now that we were experienced mariners, we plied our oars with much more dexterity than we had the day before, and so our voyage began auspiciously. The sun had just begun to rise, the wind was calm, and the fog hung low on the lake, wrapping around us in a most ghostly manner.

Michael was the first to remark upon the fog. "'Tis said mermaids and banshees settle in the rivers and pools and rise in weather like this."

"Do not say such things, Michael."

"Ah, if you listen closely, you can hear their keening call."

"All I hear is the sound of our oars and our breathing."

"C'mere, it means someone's about to die."

I tried listening, but still only heard the wooden creaking of the oars and the breathing of the rowers.

"She appears out of the fog in a huge grey dress, holding a winding sheet that she throws upon her victims and then sucks the breath out of them."

"Enough," Sergeant Theophilus said.

"Some have said she's a washerwoman who has washed the bloody sheets of her victims and who uses them to capture her next victims."

Just then, the man beside me turned and said, "Oh, my God!" I turned, looked, and there, rising above the fog a large grey sheet pointed toward the sky, held up by the hand and arm of a banshee. All of us stopped rowing and stared. The crew in the other boat had seen this apparition as well, and they too ceased their rowing.

No manual of '64 prepared a militiaman for such a horror.

"Ooooooo!" said the banshee.

"Ohhhh!" said Hiram.

"Oooooo!" said the banshee.

"She's coming for us," said Michael.

"We trust in the arms of the Lord," said Deuteronomy.

"Alloooooooo!" said the banshee.

"What?" said Peter.

"Helloooooo ahead!" said the banshee.

"She wants my head!" said Hiram.

Then, before the winding sheet held up by the banshee could fall upon us, out of the fog came the prow of a boat. A single-masted boat, a sloop.

"Helloooooo there!" shouted a soldier standing at the bow of the sloop.

"Identify yourself or prepare to be boarded," shouted Ethan, although the sloop rode awfully high in the water for us to board her easily.

"Board at your pleasure, Colonel Allen!" shouted Benedict Arnold, and the men behind him in the sloop laughed and cheered.

The sloop, it turns out, did not have enough wind to move, and rode peacefully on the lake. Our bateaux each pulled up to her sides. Now we could see that the sloop was towing a line of bateaux, each with two or three men in it. The rest of the men who had left with Benedict Arnold were standing on the deck of the sloop, and behind them I saw piled boxes they must have captured along with the sloop. Soon, far behind, we saw the sloop "The Liberty."

"Now we're a bloody navy," remarked Michael.

By now, Ethan, standing in the bateau next to mine, realized that Colonel Arnold had beaten him up the lake, had raided St. John, and had captured the sloop and whatever else they were carrying in the boxes. Ethan pondered his next words.

I understood now why Colonel Arnold had caulked his boats and practiced so much.

"You didn't have to bother yourself on my account," said Colonel Arnold. "We slipped in upon them while they slept, captured two men they had left to guard this sloop, and loaded up their munitions before they even knew what was happening. In all, it was a very successful attack."

"Indeed, I congratulate you, Colonel. I and my Boys were on our way to reinforce your occupation of St. John's, which I see is unnecessary since you appear to be here, and St. John appears to still lie there," said Ethan, pointing toward the north. "Unoccupied."

"Occupy St. John, Colonel? Why, that would appear somewhat presumptuous, don't you think?"

"Presumptuous, Colonel? Why, I would describe it as quite effectual," said Ethan, trading multisyllabification for multisyllabification.

"Surely you do not presume to attack Canada, Colonel?"

"Presume? Most definitively not, Colonel. I *intend* to attack Canada. And I intend to occupy it, upon which occurrence the inhabitants will flock to our side."

Attack Canada? Why had Ethan not told us?

"While you were engaged in maritime theatrics, Colonel Arnold, my Boys and I were ascertaining the situation, acquiring munitions, and establishing our supply line."

"My feet are wet," said Hiram.

"My nose is still running," said I, wiping my arm across my face.

"Had I any intention of attacking Canada, Colonel Allen, I should rather attack the heart of that land, Quebec, not some little wart by the name of St. John."

"Ah, you misthink yourself, Colonel Arnold. The moment the people of Canada realize we're coming to their aid, they'll flock to our side. They desire freedom as much as we. Quebec will surrender without a shot, and we shall have a feast of thanksgiving. Why attack Quebec with force when you can woo them with words?"

"Our feet are wet, our noses are running, and these gentlemen are debating who misthinks worse than the other!" said Michael.

"And my head hurts," said I.

"We appear to be drifting toward shore," said Peter.

"My spies have given me a map up the Kennebec River," said Colonel Arnold. "The English will never expect us from that direction."

"Yes, the shore is definitely closer," said Peter.

By now, everyone realized we had indeed drifted to the shore. The sloop began to push the bateaux until ours began to tip dangerously. Men stood up and pushed their oars against the bottom of the lake to move the bateaux out of the way. Benedict Arnold ordered the anchor dropped, and, after much jockeying and arranging of bateaux, we had manufactured a bridge of bateaux from the sloop to the shore. Colonel Arnold called it "rafting up." Although it was not yet late, both commanders agreed upon a rest, and we made camp there.

The two colonels made "The Liberty" their headquarters. Amid the sounds of much harrumphing and table-pounding coming from the sloop, Peter and I built our shelter, and I fell asleep.

When Peter woke me for supper, the only sounds coming from the sloop were loud snores, two sets.

A hunting party had acquired several rabbits, and we all shared a delicious stew. My headache was gone, though my nose still dripped. Hiram entertained us with his flute. Michael made up words to some of the tunes that I will not record here because they might give the reader the impression that our efforts were not quite as patriotic as, I assure you, they were.

That evening, after recording the day's events in my journal, I asked Peter to tell me about himself. "If I did not know better," I said, "I would think you are an Indian, that is, by the looks of you, your skin being darker than most of us, though I would guess you have been outdoors more than most of us, that is, if you understand what I mean." I did not want to offend him by implying that he looked like an Indian, but no matter what I said, I seemed to dig myself in deeper. "I mean, I have never known an Indian, and I have heard some are really quite friendly, so if you are an Indian I would not mind it, really, and I consider you my friend, so I hope you will understand my curiosity." I hoped he would relieve my anxiety by assuring me he was an Italian or perhaps a Black Irishman, though he and Michael would surely have realized that shortly after they met. Even worse, he might be a Spanish or a Portagee Arab, though, now that I think about it, even they would not be likely to live around here. The people in the Grants, you see, were generally and predominantly exceedingly white, especially the Dutchies, most of whom were whiter than the English. So maybe being white was not the most important aspect of a person.

I wished mightily for Hiram to interrupt me with his flute or Deuteronomy would call us all to prayer.

"Would it make you feel any better, Erastus, if I told you there is no such thing as an Indian?

"Well, of course it would, but, unlike banshees, Indians are real."

"You call us Indians, Erastus, but in fact we're Abenakis and Hurons and Lenapes and Mohawks and Muhikanuhs."

"Us?" I realized my mistake.

"Consider this. You people from Pownal are English and Dutch and Irish and Norwegian. What if everyone called you Europeans and considered you Europeans, regardless of where you came from?"

"So, you are an Indian? I mean, you are whatever you are? I honestly do not mind, you know." Nothing I said was right. "I mean, to me you are Peter, and that is all that matters."

"Would it bother you to know that I am not Peter?"

Nothing was what it seemed. The trip to overtake Benedict Arnold had become something else. Up the lake was down. The banshee was a sloop. My latest adventure had given me a cold rather than uplifting my spirit. And now Peter was not Peter, but an Indian, but not even an Indian, but something else. I recall my headache returning.

"My true name is Pebonkas Kisas, which is an Abenaki name meaning, roughly, 'Coldest Moon.' I'm the son of Mzatonas Kisas, whose Abenaki name means 'First Moon.' My father married Catherine, the daughter of Eunice Oliver and Raniaten, who was born and raised in Kahnawake in Canada. Eunice had been captured by the French and Kahnawake Maquas from a village in the Massachusetts Bay Colony. Raniaten was a Maqua who grew up among the Abenaki. He fled the wars north of here to join the Maquas with other refugees at the town of Kahnawake. His Abenaki name was Awan, but the French priests who converted his parents to their religion christened him Antoine. The Maquas welcomed him into their community by giving him the Maqua name Raniaten. Raniaten's father, in turn, was a Maqua chieftain who was awarded the name Hiawatha who was the son of Atawenta who was the son of Konansase who was the son of Adriaen Van der Kronck, a Dutchman who visited the Maqua many years ago. And so that you understand more about who I am, Konansase's wife was a Muhikanuh, Atawenta's wife was an Unami, daughter of Teedyuscung, and Hiawatha had taken a French woman as his wife. And that is just the male side of my family. Now, let me start describing the other branches . . ."

"Lord," said Michael from where I thought he slept. "And people doubt me banshees."

"My mother made me memorize it," said Peter.

"Let me get this straight," I said. "You are part French and part English and part Dutch and part Indian, right?"

"Wrong. I'm part French and part English and part Dutch and part Mohawk—or Maqua—and part Mohican—or Muhikanuh—and part Abenaki and part Lenape."

"I just said that."

"But I'm not simply an 'Indian.' Generally speaking," said Peter or Petrucus or Probonkas, "I am Iroquois, Algonquin, and European."

"Even more mixed," said I.

"And you are?"

"I am by heritage English, pure and simple," I said, "but now I am a Boy from Pownal, a Green Mountain Boy."

"Let me see if I've got this straight. You're telling me you're pure English, which makes you part French from when the Normans invaded, and now you have a German king, and your ancestors were also Celts, who are now the Irish, Welsh, and Scots—is that right? And if you have any Pilgrim blood, you may also have some Dutch in you, and you know what a mess their blood lines are. And if any of your grandmothers were living along the Irish coast when the Armada was sunk, you might also have some Spanish blood. And if I go back far enough, you had a Roman or two in your blood mix, and they had some relatives who were Greeks and Goths and Visigoths, not to mention Carthaginians or Egyptians, who were Africans."

"Listen, Peter or Probonkas or whatever your name is, if I could remember back beyond my grandparents, I am certain I could prove you wrong."

"Pebonkas, but you may call me Peter."

"I will call you Pebonkas," I said.

"Thank you," he said.

Michael McGinnis looked up from where he lay nearby. "My mother was an O'Neil from Monaghan, and she told me she was descended from the great Niall Ui Neill, but I don't know all the folks in between. And my father was a McGinnis, she told me, but that's all I know." He then lay his head back down and went back to sleep. We did not know what he would remember later.

The next morning, we all woke up, ate fried bread and coffee, and heard Ethan announce, "Boys of the Green Mountains, we are off to conquer Canada!"

My nose was still running.

CHAPTER 9

▼

WE INVADE CANADA THE FIRST TIME

My journal entry from that day reads: "Weather warm. I am sick and miserable, so I ride on the sloop. Col. Arnold headed back to Ft. Ti with captured sloop. Ethan took sloop 'The Liberty' and us north to invade Canada. Col. Arnold calls target 'San Zong.' We call it Saint John. Easy day sailing and pulling bateaux. Some sail in sloop. Trade off sometimes." As you can tell, my sickness did not allow me to employ the multisyllabification I had been practicing after being in the presence of Ethan.

At the end of the first day's sail, we set up camp on an island in the middle of Lake Champlain where the Green Mountain Boys still maintained their ration of one gill of rum. Ethan called it Isle La Motte. The site of an old French fort, nothing was left but some holes in the ground and a stone foundation. We did not post a guard, so quiet it was. Around sunset we spotted some Indians in a dugout canoe paddling by. Pebonkas informed me they were Abenakis, but I still could not tell the difference between Abenakis, Maquas, or Muhikanuhs. They all wore clothes just as we did.

Michael had me drink some rum because, he said, it would help fight my cold. It was the second time I had ever tasted rum, and I knew he was right about fighting the cold because it tasted like medicine and burned. My mother would not have approved, and Tryphena would have tried to shame me with a quote from the Bible. Thus you will not find this in my journal.

On the second day I felt better, so I could help with sailing the ship. Some of us had sailed down the lake with Colonel Arnold and had learned how to handle a sloop. I learned about the mainsail, jib, and topsail, which I was informed was pronounced "topsul" and mainsail pronounced "mainsul." Ropes were "lines." Theophilus now had new terms to use in ordering us around. "Hoist the anchor!" "Haul the mainsul!" "Secure the lines!" I felt somewhat guilty because I was having great fun, so I maintained a serious demeanor while "on board."

Soon the lake narrowed, and we entered a broad river. At this time we were all quite relaxed, and the Green Mountain Boys broke out the rum again, even though it was not evening and they did not use a gill measure.

Ethan directed us to the mouth of the Sorel River, where we set up camp before attacking St. John. After sailing in the warm sun and after the men finished off all the rum, they were quite tired and most fell immediately asleep, including Michael and Hiram. But first Michael began to sing "The Girl I Left behind Me," and shortly Hiram joined him on his flute:

> *I'm lonesome since I crossed the hill,*
> *And o'er the moorland sedgy*
> *Such heavy thoughts my heart do fill*
> *Since parting with my Betsey . . .*

They then went on to invent their own words that, as before, I did not record for fear my mother would read my journal. Lucky for them Deuteronomy Dewey was not near.

Happily they soon fell asleep, so Pebonkas and I had plenty of time to talk. "You have a very confusing set of ancestors," I said. "I know that I cannot remember all of your grandparents' and great-grandparents' names. It is all very much like the begets and begots of the Bible that the Reverend Deuteronomy has read to us, but nobody actually pays any attention."

"But those are merely words on the pages of the Bible, whereas my ancestors are quite real."

"Some would call that blasphemy. At least I can consider you an Abenaki, and that makes it much simpler for me."

"But, Erastus, it is not that simple. I call myself an Abenaki because it is easier for me to talk with the English and you Yankees using a word that you know. But, in fact, I am more properly a Sokoki."

"You are not Abenaki?" Surely he was, as Michael might say, "Pulling my potatoes."

"Sokoki are Abenaki, Erastus, only we live on the west of your Green Mountains, that is, those of us who are left. The English once called us Tarateen, but that was never us. Many Abenaki have the blood of the Pennacook, Pocumtucs, and Nipmucs flowing through them, for those people sought refuge among the Abenaki from the English."

"So you are an Abenaki."

"As much as you want, but, as I have told you, I have much Maqua blood in me, the blood of the Mohawk."

"So what do I call you, aside from your name, Pebonkas?"

"Others have called us by many names. To the Iroquois, we have been Skacewanilom or Anagonges. To the Mohawk we have been Gannongagehronnon. Some Kahnawake have called us Natsagana. Hurons have called us Aquannaque. Your English have called us the St. Francis Indians."

"Just tell me what to call you."

"Anything but 'Indian.'"

"Good. I will call you Pebonkas the Abenaki."

"And I will call you Erastus the Pownalian."

"That's not really correct, you know, since I am a Green Mountain Boy and an inhabitant of the Hampshire Grants."

"So, if I have this straight, you are all three—Pownalian, Green Mountaineer, and Grantsman—depending upon who is looking at you, and that ignores what you told me earlier, that your blood is English."

"Anything but 'English.'"

"We understand one another then," said Pebonkas. To my amazement, I think I finally did.

I said I would think on that and sleep on it, so we lay down to sleep.

"And you two complain of banshees and mermaids," said Michael from nearby. "You'll be haunted by the spirits of your ancestors all your days as they fight over your souls."

"Let me sleep, Michael."

"Actually," said Pebonkas, "we call ourselves 'Alnanbai,' the people."

"Good night, Pebonkas."

"It is very much like 'Lenni Lenape,' which, to those you call 'The Delaware,' means . . . "

"You are giving me," I said, as I rolled over to face away from Pebonkas, "a headache."

I looked very much forward to sleeping all the night, for I did not have to go on sentry duty because, in fact, no one went on sentry duty. We were all, you understand, quite tired. We intended to be exceedingly rested by the time we attacked the enemy.

Wump! Something hit the ground near me and woke me. It was black out. Another wump! And cannon blasts. Someone was shooting at us! A cannon ball thuded just beyond our campsite.

"Everyone up! Everyone up!"

"Attack! Attack!"

I grabbed my musket and jumped up, too fast, for I suddenly became dizzy and fell to my knees. Two people grabbed me by my arms and forced me to run, stumbling and tripping away from the cannon fire.

"Who . . . ?"

"The English. Keep running."

My head soon cleared, so I tore myself free from those propelling me and pulled ahead of them. Shortly I neared the shore where Ethan was standing, rallying us. "We're safe here. Gather and form a line."

Theophilus was shouting. "Make ready! Poise your firelocks!" He was back in the French and Indian War, and I wished I were back in Pownal Centre.

I could not remember where I put my powder!

Just then a cannon ball came rolling down the hill toward us. Theophilus put out his foot and stopped it. Another came rolling slowly after it, and several of us ran to see who could get to it first.

"We're safe, men!" said Ethan, "They can't reach us here. And by the time they can move their cannon forward, we'll be safe in our boats. Now, then, into the bateaux and the sloop."

As I turned to go, Ethan looked down at me, observing, "What do you think, Erastus? Is not the music of their guns both terrible and delightful?"

I hoped he could not see the look on my face.

Back at the fort, several very finely tailored gentlemen walked down to greet Ethan. Fancy buckles topped their shoes, though splattered with mud. I do believe their noses must have been exceedingly offended as we stepped out of the bateaux and jumped down from the sloop, for we were as unpleasant a group as any might meet, not only having not bathed since beginning the attack on Canada, but also, for most of us, not having bathed since we marched out of Bennington to attack Fort Ti. I had seen Pebonkas wade into the lake regularly while we were at Fort Ti, which I might have attributed to some savage ritual. I should not properly say "savage," for he was somewhat more civilized than the Boys from

Pownal. That is, if bathing is a sign of civilization. I dare not say "Indian." I dare not say "savage." Education constrains one mightily.

The gentlemen who greeted Ethan bowed their neat little bows when they shook Ethan's hand. They seemed more English than Green Mountain.

Benedict Arnold did not waste any words greeting Ethan. "Well, didn't I tell you your invasion would be a wild, impractical, expensive scheme that would ultimately be of no consequence?"

The leader of the delegation, whose name I did not get, or if I heard it I failed to record it in my journal, suggested that, rather than argue in public, they withdraw inside the fort to continue their "discussion."

After helping to unload the bateaux and sloop, I slipped over by the commander's quarters that Ethan and Colonel Arnold had occupied. Though the door was closed, the windows were open since our initial exuberance upon occupying the fort had broken most of them.

I heard the gentlemen's leader say, "You understand, Colonel Allen, that by your precipitous attack upon Canada, you're liable to have antagonized the English. Surely you can perceive how this may be conceived as an act of war."

"Do I hear aright?! Surely you jest," said Ethan. "An act of war? What would you call our attack upon the English at Concord and Lexington? A mere snit? And recently we received orders to send all the cannon from here to Boston so that we can besiege the English. Is this a mere mock show, a pantomime, a theatricality?"

"Despite this unpleasantness, Colonel Allen, we have high hopes the English will recognize the rightfulness of our claims and accede to our demands that they drop the hateful taxation and recognize our right to govern ourselves—under our king, of course."

"You befuddle the senses, gentlemen."

"So we'll send a messenger to the Canadians apologizing for our intrusion into their space and asking their indulgence."

Here Ethan uttered an oath—well, several oaths I did not enter into my journal. But they referred to God and to perdition. He unabashedly wished the gentlemen and the Congress would cohabit with Satan. Also, he made reference to animal breeding.

"Now, as for our second set of instructions," another voice joined in. "We recognize there's been some question of the authority under which this fort is held."

"Under the authority of the Great Jehovah and the Continental Congress. I have affirmed that. And the Green Mountain Boys."

"Well, sir, that's just it. Some jurisdictional issues apply here," I heard the second voice say.

"Jurisdictional! The Hampshire Grants have jurisdiction, if Congress is so timorous as to fear retribution from the English."

"Until that issue can be resolved then, Congress desires Fort Ticonderoga to fall within the jurisdiction of the colony of New York," said the second voice.

The clatter of pewter and pottery hitting the walls and floor signaled Ethan's response.

"Really, Colonel Allen. This is most unbecoming," shouted their leader. "Colonel Arnold, we're to await a peace settlement from England before proceeding in any direction. For now, you are to simply secure the fort and await more definitive instructions."

"Am I not the commander?!" roared Ethan. By now, many Green Mountain Boys had gathered around, savoring the debate in progress.

"For now, Colonel Allen, you are the commander of your militia. Colonel Arnold is to command the fort. We commend your amicable relations. For the good of the colonies, that is."

"What is a commander if he have not authority to act in time of war?" argued Ethan. "Are we not in a state of war? Does Congress presume to debate the movement of troops on the ground?"

"We've yet to declare a war."

I knew Ethan would slip into his easy multisyllabification, his ultimate weapon in such circumstances. "You venerate the haughtiness of kingships, obviously."

"We still owe our allegiance to the king. Clearly his advisors and counselors have kept him from realizing the truth about the conditions in which we live. They're self-serving puppeteers whose main purpose is to feather their own nests. They are extremists. And, should we give them the right excuse, they'd urge him to send his armies against us as well. They know they can profit from a war with us. We know they're eager to strengthen their grip upon our king by labeling us rebels. We trust that the king's a rationale human being, but one who simply does not have access to the truth."

"Gentlemen, your counsel is, quite simply, naive. Now, can I prevail upon you to indulge yourselves in our Green Mountain hospitality before returning to Congress with our rejection of your well-intentioned but misguided counsel?"

Again their leader attempted to change Ethan's mind. "Really, Colonel Allen, we do not simply offer you advice. We offer you the considered judgment of our delegates in Philadelphia. Our militias have surrounded Boston and may provoke the British to attack them at any time. We still have time to avoid a major confrontation. It's the middle of May. Summer's almost upon us. With summer the British navy can reinforce their armies. We have little time to restore the former harmony."

"Won't you try some beef confiscated from the Tories?" said Ethan.

"Colonel Arnold," they turned toward Benedict Arnold. "Surely you can prevail upon Colonel Allen."

"I fear, gentlemen," said Colonel Arnold, "I have never prevailed upon Colonel Allen for anything unless it suited his purposes."

I had by now crept up to the window to look in. I thought I saw Ethan wink at Seth Warner. Or perhaps a gnat had flown into his eye.

"But you, Colonel Arnold, have the authority to order these men . . . "

"Gentlemen, what the good Colonel Arnold is suggesting is that we allow the Green Mountain Boys to vote upon any matter of such import," said Ethan.

"An army is not a democracy, Colonel Allen," said one.

"And politicians know nothing of military matters," Ethan replied.

"Sir!"

"We're an army of freedom fighters, sir, and no remonstrance on your part will dissuade us from our beliefs. We Green Mountaineers are of our own mind, not given to following shifts in the current of political thought. I cannot lead without their consent."

By now many of us had gathered to look in at the windows and enjoy the heat of the arguments. The well-dressed gentlemen looked around at us and, if they saw what I saw, they saw men dressed in every kind of clothes imaginable. Some had taken parts of English uniforms. Most of us still wore the clothes we left home with. We had not yet learned to stand like English soldiers, and I mistrusted we ever would.

"May we then accept your offer of a meal before returning to Philadelphia, Colonels?"

That night we stood guard as before, especially since we did not want the couriers from Philadelphia to think us not an army, regardless of what we looked like. But around the fires that night, many talked about returning home.

I thought it weakness. Pebonkas explained they were not indentured, so had no legal commitment to stay. I was most distraught when Hiram said he, too, would be returning to the Grants, returning to Pownal and to Carpenter Hill.

"Erastus, we came to take this fort. We've done it. Now Congress has given it to the Yorkers, so why stay? Besides, your mother'll want us to return to the farm, for the growing season's about to begin."

"What do you know about growing, Hiram? You only farmed when directed to, not because you wanted to."

"It's Spring, Erastus. Do you not smell the earth? Do the new flowers thrusting heavenward not call to you?"

I could not believe what I was hearing.

"We are, after all, farmers, Erastus, and growing food's our way of contributing to our country," said Hiram.

"If you yearn to spread manure on the ground as you spread manure in my ears, then may you slip and trip in it all the way home."

"Well said, Erastus," said Michael. "Sure you'll be a good Irishman someday."

As soon as the delegates from the Continental Congress rode out to return to Philadelphia and to Congress, Ethan rowed up to Crown Point, where he inspected our militia, and then he rowed back. He then began writing letters to French Canadians and sending them off with couriers to their little villages. Since most said the same thing, Ethan had me copy them to save time.

One of the couriers, Ezekial Bates, upon his return, told me about the reaction the Canadians had to the letter he carried from Ethan. "They said that trusting us was like trusting a bed of vipers to climb in bed with you and keep you safe. The priest in charge of the village vowed they would never trust a New Englander more than an Englishman. In fact, they said that they'd rather marry their daughters to the English than to us."

"That's low, 'tis," said Michael.

On one occasion, Ethan asked Pebonkas for his opinion about a letter he had drafted to send to the Kahnawake town. Pebonkas told me, "Your friend Ethan wrote that he always loved Indians and that he'd often fought with them. He said the Green Mountain Boys fight just like Indians. He invited them to send their warriors to Crown Point and Ticonderoga to fight the English Regulars."

"You think it wrong?"

"He offers them the same things Europeans have always offered: tomahawks, blankets, guns, and ammunition."

"Why is that wrong?"

"He would buy the loyalty of the Kahnawakes. If he can buy them, so can the English. It's all the same, one or another. If they come to fight with us, they'll have to contend with the English. The Kahnawakes need food, not more ways to kill each other."

"Did he say anything right?" I asked.

"Even if they did not come to fight, we'd always be friends and brothers."

"Good."

"And then he proceeded to offer them rum."

"Didn't you try to correct him?" asked Michael.

"Easier to correct a statue of King George. Yes, I tried. I suggested he not lump them all together as Indians."

"I'm betting that did much good," said Michael.

"He stared at me as though I were crazy. I told him he shouldn't offer them rum. He thanked me for my opinion and dismissed me."

"All leaders," said Michael, "believe they know what's best for us. Sure you don't expect this one to be listening to a contrary opinion."

"Ethan is not like other leaders," I said.

"One mountain may be very different from every other mountain," Pebonkas concluded, "but it's still a mountain."

That night, as I stood sentry duty, I heard much arguing coming from the fort.

Later Hiram told how Benedict Arnold had gathered the soldiers not on duty and told them he was now in command.

"Says who?" said they. "We've not voted on that."

"It's not your decision to make," said he.

"I say we vote!" said one, and they all shouted their agreement.

At that moment, Ethan strode up to us. "Colonel Arnold's right," he said. "Congress has asked Colonel Arnold to be in charge."

Hiram said everyone was shocked. "Time to go home," they said.

Pebonkas picked up the story.

"This is mutiny," said Arnold.

Then Major Sam Elmore stood up to Colonel Arnold, looked him in the face, and said, "You ain't in charge here." Colonel Arnold responded by striking Major Elmore on the head with a musket. Elmore went down. Arnold kicked him in the gut.

Your friend Ethan stepped in between. "What's all the ruckus here?"

Colonel Arnold, as calm as can be, explained, "I've taken the liberty of breaking his head. In fact, I kicked him most heartily." Thereupon, Colonel Arnold announced, "Now my work is done here. I'm off to Massachusetts."

"Your friend Ethan," said Pebonkas, "told Colonel Arnold we needed his leadership and then threw his arm over the shoulders of Benedict Arnold and walked him into the commanders' quarters."

"I'll wager Ethan boxed his ears off," said Michael.

"More likely he talked his ears off," said Pebonkas.

"Either way," I quipped, "Colonel Arnold's ears will be sorely taxed."

Most of the Boys from Pownal and the other Grants packed to return home. Even Theophilus, who said, "I'm tired. Yell if you need me." And Deuteronomy Dewey, although he insisted upon saying a prayer before he left.

Hiram, too, packed to go. "I'll put in a good word to your mother." I knew her words would far outweigh his.

I still could not believe Hiram was leaving. "Hiram, you bragged of being a Green Mountain Boy. I came because of you."

"And we had fun, didn't we? Just like I promised. But the fun's over. Just plain work now."

"I believed in you, Hiram."

"No, Erastus, you believed in Ethan Allen. He won. We won. What more do you want?"

Ethan did not argue against their going, but, rather, wished them well upon their way and wished them good crops, adding, "Sooner than not we'll be in arms again, and I know I can count on you."

Hunt Hungerford, the rascal who had shot at Benedict Arnold, sneered at the remarks, turned, and marched out of the fort with several of his followers.

Hiram's stories brought me here, but stories could not sustain us. "What now?" I asked Michael and Pebonkas.

"Ah, yes," sighed Michael. "Now we'll be pulling even more sentry duty."

Pebonkas added, "I've heard it said by you Americans and the English that the peoples of this land—we Abenakis, Maqua, and Muhikanuhs—that we strike without warning and then slip like devils back into the forests. It seems you Green Mountain Boys have learned to attack your enemy and then slip into the forest just as we do. Only now you know the truth—we fight when we need to and return to our villages to provide food for our families. That's the work of sensible men, not forest devils."

Later that day, Ethan and Seth Warner called Pebonkas, Michael, and me together. "Seth and I have noticed how you three've banded together, so now we'd like to invite you to accompany us on a journey."

"You'll have a great time," added Seth.

"Swim into my net, said the fisherman to the cod," said Michael.

"We are off for Philadelphia, men, what do you say? We need an escort in case we're tempted by the luxuries of Tory life—or an English patrol."

Pebonkas said one city was as good as any other. "Boston, Philadelphia, it's all the same to me."

"We're off to turn the heads of Congress," said Ethan. "'Twill be glorious."

"Who will be in charge if you leave?" I asked. But I did not need an answer, for Benedict Arnold strode among the remaining militia, issuing orders, followed by his valet du chambre. I must have looked aghast.

"You think I've put the fox in charge of the hen house, right, Erastus?" said Ethan. "We'll have to await the judgment of History, for I put my trust in some higher authority than some Committee appointed by the Congress."

Seth Warner smiled his crooked smile and explained, "It's a mark of Ethan's genius. By putting Arnold in charge, he's assuring this fort will be here when he returns. Though Colonel Arnold may strut and swagger like a rooster, he's still our rooster, and he'll not allow the fox in."

Ethan had put Arnold in charge. Congress had taken the side of the English. The French Canadians preferred the English over anyone from New England. Now Ethan was trusting an Abenaki-Mohawk-Mohican, an Irishman, and a Green Mountain Boy from Pownal to safely escort him and Seth Warner to Philadelphia. On top of all, we had to await the judgment of History. I did not think I had enough time to sort any of this out, much less grow old and decrepit waiting for Lady History to make up her mind.

CHAPTER 10

▼

RUMINATIONS ACROSS NEW JERSEY

This time I did not have to walk up hill and down, for Ethan secured us horses to ride to the Hudson River. Several Massachusetts militiamen rode alongside us to take the horses back to the fort. This was the first time I had ever ridden a horse. I had ridden our ox at home, but we did not own a horse.

The ox provided a smooth, steady ride. My horse, however, could use some fattening, for his backbone poked up into the old, thin saddle, jabbing me between my legs as I rode. I tried standing in the stirrups, which helped, but then my legs became stiff, and I had to sit down. The pains in my legs returned, and now my backside hurt. So it went—stand, sit, stand, sit. Tire the legs. Damage the backside. I had been a soldier, then a sailor, and now a cavalryman. In all, being a cavalryman pained me, being a sailor made me seasick, so I concluded I was destined to be a soldier. Life's choices are seldom fair. (That last sentence came straight out of the mouth of my mother. I could not believe myself. Next I would be saying things like, "You'll be sorry when I'm gone," and "I work and slave my fingers to the bone, and this is the thanks I get." At least I had not taken to quoting scripture like Tryphena.)

When we reached the Hudson River, a small sloop awaited us. I had not known the difference between a schooner and a sloop, so I had chosen to call all boats with sails "sloops." Now I learned a sloop has one mast and a schooner two. One of Ethan's many letters must have arranged for the sloop.

Albany amazed me. The mostly brick houses had very steep roofs, the ends of the roofs looked like steps, and tall, narrow windows reflected the river. Ethan called them typical Dutch houses, though nothing like the Dutch houses in Pownal. But the people! All sorts of people worked and walked along the docks, speaking strange languages. Seth Warner said he heard a lot of Dutch. Michael claimed another spoke French. Pebonkas noted the Maqua tongue. Of course, people spoke English. That, at least, seemed normal. Most strange of all, they seemed to be getting along, working together, talking together. Michael observed, "Making money makes for strange bedfellows, m'boy."

Ethan swept his arm across the waterfront and said, "Behold, gentlemen, the new America." I wondered what kind of country it would be if we all spoke something other than English. In Pownal we at least speak English, that is, except for the Dutch people, but then, of course, they are Dutch.

"Easy now," cautioned Seth Warner, "English soldiers." Three soldiers strolled along the docks north of us, so they could not see us amid all the other people. Nevertheless, "Shall we continue on?" Seth suggested.

I wished we had additional time in Albany, for I would like to have learned more. But we had to rush off from our sloop and on to the strangest craft I had yet seen. The man in charge called himself "captain," and when I asked what he called his vessel, he told me it was a "pettiauger." Michael remarked how this long, flat boat did not seem to know which way to go, for its front looked like its back, and its two sails pointed in opposite directions. Pebonkas said it was a "metaphor for the colonies." If that was true, whatever it meant, I prayed there were not many more metaphors in my future.

The captain, a large fellow with a beard that reached his breeches, bragged how his metaphor "is a great boat for maneuvering across the river or along it."

The trip down the Hudson in the metaphor was uneventful although Ethan cautioned us to keep our muskets at the ready in case we encountered an English ship. Relaxing while others sailed the boat gave me more time to talk with Pebonkas and Michael.

Leaning against the mast, I watched the river and the mountains as we sailed past. The steep mountains falling down to the water's edge captivated me. I thought someone should paint the scenes someday, though my Pownal rearing considered that frivolous.

"Sailing with Ethan, off to see Congress—pretty good, huh?" I had not anticipated Pebonkas's reply.

"Don't think it unkind, Erastus, but your Ethan and Green Mountain Boys aren't fighting for my people, the Sokokis and Maquas. Given a choice, I'd prefer to fight with the French."

"How can you say that?"

Pebonkas's dark eyes seemed to pierce mine. "History's not as simple as you'd like."

"But the French are our enemies."

"No, Erastus, the French are your enemies, not mine. Your people've fought us as much as against the French. Your Rogers Rangers massacred my people. Why shouldn't I feel this way? You killed us. You occupied our lands. You and your Pownal settlers may be able to show the land being sold to you by the Muhikanuh, but what choice did they have?"

"No, Pebonkas, you are wrong. The land was given to us by the governor of New Hampshire."

"Only because we no longer lived there."

"And the Dutch are renting from Rensselaer."

" . . . whose representatives bought the land from the Muhikanuh. I know. Well, nothing we can do about that now, eh." He leaned back against the side and stared off into the mountains.

"Yet you fight alongside us Green Mountain Boys. If you prefer the French to us, why are you here with us?"

"Anyone's better than the English."

"Amen," said Michael, gazing out from beneath the brim of his hat. "Irish, Indians, none of us matters to the English."

"I thought you were my friends."

"As the good folks say," said Michael, "hold your friends close and your enemy's clothing."

I recorded Michael's silly saying in my journal to remember it someday and confuse someone else with it.

When we set foot in New Jersey, we had to climb a long, steep cliff before we reached flat land. On top, we met three New Jersey militia who would escort us across the colony. They were, by any description I could manage, spindly and gaunt. Moreover, as I soon discovered, they were all, each of them, Irish. As I recall, their names were Evan McCard, Kincaid, and Callaghan. This was the first I had ever seen more than one, but before I gave up soldiering, they appeared in just about every militia group I encountered.

The militia had brought horses for us, and once again my misfortune sat me upon one whose backbone stuck up through his hide.

Michael laughed to meet his countrymen, but grew somber later as they talked of their homes in Ireland. The militia rode along with us as a guard. We cut across New Jersey through Morristown and Vealtown, camping near friendly homes in the evenings. Our hosts in New Jersey were very cordial, but, like Pownal, the towns divided themselves between those who sympathized with the American desire for freedom from England and those who believed we owed perpetual allegiance to England and King George. We stayed only at night at the safe houses so that we did not arouse the suspicions of the Tories. To my surprise, no one recognized Ethan Allen.

Outside Vealtown, our escorts met a rider who would guide us to William Alexander's place. I had begun to think of those fighting the English as poor. Mr. Alexander's property proved me wrong as we rode a curved dirt lane past very formal gardens laid out on both sides of the road. A few small apple and peach trees marked the beginning of an orchard. Near the house, a cobbled lane began, leading up to and around the house. If I say "house," I do it an injustice. A large mansion with tall square columns in front, it had not yet been completed. A shiny turret graced the roof, but the top floor had only openings for windows. Although I had seen some mansions in the distance along the Hudson, I had never been this close to one. I looked forward to sleeping in such a building, windows or no. Instead, our guide led us around and behind the house where several large barns stood. "Here's where you can rest," he said.

I was very disappointed at not being able to sleep in the mansion until our guide pushed open the doors of the nearest barn. Compared to this, our Pownal barn was a mere lean-to. A mansion itself, with a smooth brick floor, polished wood walls, copper door handles and hinges, and high ceilings, horses and cows could live in luxury here. "This is Lord Stirling's carriage house," he announced. Two fine carriages sat in the carriage house. "I think you'll be able to sleep in these, and no one will know you're here except for the servants. We'll not say anything."

One carriage looked like a baby's cradle on wheels. Larger, of course. Black on top with two shining lamps in front, green on the bottom, and wheels painted yellow. "Two of you ought to be able to sleep in here," said our guide, who introduced himself as James Potter. "Next to it is Lord Stirling's Beekman Coach." Even grander than the other, it was painted entirely yellow and had a coat of arms painted on its doors. Two of us could sleep inside it and one on the coach driver's seat, covered itself with a comfortable cushion.

"I thought we were at William Alexander's home," asked Seth.

"Yes, sure," said our guide. "Lord Stirling."

"A Lord in American?" asked Ethan. "A Tory?"

"Well, sir, Lord Stirling does have his roots in the English peerage, you know. And though he lives a life most genteel, he is indeed one of us."

I could not image a genteel lord sitting down to eat any meal with our guide, who dressed as meanly as we did.

"Lord Stirling rides around his estate in this coach, and he visits the towns in this coach as well. When the weather's bad, he rides in the other," pointing to the black and green carriage that would have set anyone who owned it far above the people of Pownal. "Please, make yourself comfortable, and I'll arrange for your dinner."

When he left, Ethan said, "I see our William Alexander has aristocratic pretensions. If many more of these fashion-conscious folks inhabit New Jersey, we'll have a difficult time persuading them of our cause. I fear he may be a bit dyspeptic for our tastes."

I imagined William Alexander, the Lord Stirling, riding about Pownal, waiving a lace hanky at those of us in the mud.

"I wonder where this rich bastard keeps his gout cushion," said Michael, looking around inside the coach.

A man-servant entered the barn, carrying a large tray, followed by another carrying a similar tray. On it were fine pewter dishes and food. Oh, what food! Pieces of fresh pork, warm carrots, warm bread. And several bottles of wine, as well as a pitcher of fresh milk.

"Put it there," said one.

"Don't boss me around," said the other.

They put the trays on the ground and left, not even looking at us.

"'Tis," Michael noted, "a feast fit for a king."

"Or a lord," added Pebonkas.

"If the Boys from Pownal ever see how these people in New Jersey live, they will abandon Pownal in the wink of an eye," I said.

"See you the workers' houses?" asked Michael. "Your Pownal folks would trade for them anyday."

Our militia guides rolled their blankets out on the hay in a nearby stall. I do not think a horse ever lived there. If so, they must have had their own privies outside.

That night I slept well. Have you ever slept in a coach that rides on springs? It swings gently as you move, and soon you are, as I was, lulled to sleep.

I woke to hear Lord Stirling's servants arguing. "I said I'm sick of the English and their holier-than-thou attitudes."

"And who'd butter your toast? Where'd we be without them?"

"Me? I'd be free. I'd have me a drink, a woman, and a bed."

"A bed in the poor house no doubt."

"Poor and free beats bowing to lords and masters."

"You've no sense at all. Look at us—free meals, work a little for it, clothes, work a little more. What'd'ya wanna change that for?"

"I'd become a delegate to our Congress, I would. I'd live in a big house that I could mess up when I wanted. And I wouldn't have to feed a bunch of beggars from New England, you can bet."

"Shabby lot, aren't they? Didn't their mothers teach them to bathe?"

"Mercy, I do believe he's talking of us," said Michael.

I could not wait until we arrived in Philadelphia, where I knew the discussions of the delegates to the Continental Congress would be more elevated.

The two servants, tall silky "Call me Clarence" and squat woolen "Call me Douglas," laid our meal on the floor in front of us and left arguing, something about whose job it was to polish the silver that morning. The morning meal was, like our supper, "fit for a Lord," better than anything we had eaten since leaving Bennington.

Though neither Clarence nor Douglas argued us out the door, we set out once again, wondering if we would encounter more Lord Stirlings along the way and whether all the people in New Jersey charmed strangers as much as Clarence and Douglas.

"They did take care of us nicely, though, didn't they?" said Pebonkas.

When we reached Larger Cross Road, a town only a bit more substantial than its neighbor to the east, Lesser Cross Road, I asked wondered why the Irish had joined our militia.

"Did you not hear what Pebonkas has tried to tell you? If you've ever been to Ireland, you'd be shocked by what you saw. My family lived in a house that pigs would refuse to live in. The pigs live better than we do. Our dwellings stink of slop. Our children live on roots. Our roads tear the soles from your boots. You're wealthy if you own any animal to pull your plow."

"How did you Irish end up that way?" I asked.

"The English. Always the English. Worse. The English church, the Protestants, they took over our country with the blessing of the English army. Catholics are forbidden from just about everything. We cannot own land. We cannot be leaders in our own towns. The Protestants control the laws, and the laws control us. The English treat us like savages."

"I beg your pardon?" said Pebonkas.

"You know well what I'm meaning," said Michael.

"Unfortunately."

I did not want my friends falling apart over regrettable words. "So you have come here to fight with us," I said to Michael.

"No. I'm here to fight the English. 'Tis what all these New Jersey militia are here for. Here's a better place for a man to live, but I doubt I'd stay with them as hates Catholics."

First Pebonkas and now Michael thought little of my people in the Grants. "I do not think we hate the Catholics!" I said.

"Are there Catholics in your Pownal, Erastus?"

"There could be, if they wanted to live there. I mean, it seems to me."

"So long as it seems, 'tis not as you dream it, Erastus," growled Michael. Then, grinning, "But look at me now. I've got me new set of clothes, though it smells of Pownal. I'm up on a horse, and me tummy is full."

Their words always set me to thinking. Pebonkas and Michael did not fight on our side just to free us. They fought because we were the least of evils and because they hated the English king more than us, though barely, it seemed. Many of the Green Mountain Boys fought solely to own land. Would such motivations help us prevail over the English, free to govern ourselves? Would we all end up a like Albany, speaking different languages and allowing different religions? What kind of world would that be?

Ethan said our goal was to ride straight across New Jersey to the Delaware River, where we would hire a boat to take us to Philadelphia and the Congress. When one of the militia riding ahead returned to warn us of English soldiers ahead, we returned to Lesser Crossroads where a Dutch family, the Jacobus Vanderveers, welcomed us for the night.

These Dutch lived very well, though I did not want to admit it to myself, their homes as nice as many in Bennington. Well, to be honest, nicer. Many were leaders of their community, which surprised me. That night we ate with others from the community. My journal contains the names Mattias Lane, Nevius, Voorhees, and Samuel Sutphen. Could the Dutch in Pownal someday be like these wealthy New Jersey Dutch?

The next morning, we met our guide, a black man. I had never spoken to a black man before, though I had seen several as we rode across New Jersey. I rode beside him as he led us south. One of Mr. Vanderveer's guests, Mr. Bogert, introduced this man as Samuel Sutphen. I wondered if he could be related to the Samuel Sutphen we had just met, a white man. I asked this Samuel Sutphen how he came to be here.

"My owner lives here," is all he said. Extremely courteous, Samuel pointed out the home of a wealthy farmer.

"Your owner?"

"I'm a slave, sir," answered Samuel. Aside from his light brown skin, he looked like several of the Dutch we had met.

Since he was so friendly, I asked him if the Samuel Sutphen we had met in Lesser Crossroads was his owner.

"No more. He sold me to Guisbert Bogert."

The Dutch not only owned fine homes and farms, but they also owned slaves. This was indeed a new world, this New Jersey.

"So, Erastus," said Michael as we rode along, "how're you feeling now, fighting for these people to own Samuel here?" I did not know how to answer. "Seems, though, these slaves live better than the Irish."

Samuel and I found much to talk about. I learned he was about my age and had learned to read and write in the Dutch Reformed Church, not in a school. I told Samuel I would have to remember all this to record it in my journal, and then I discovered happily that he, too, kept a journal. I said I would like to read it someday.

"And I yours," he said. "You should read the journals of these farmers. Monday, Warmer today. Fed the cows. Tuesday, Feels like snow. Mrs. Smith sick. They seriously lack your imagination."

"How do you know what they write? Do they tell you?"

Samuel laughed. "I'm a slave. No one sees us. You'd be surprised at all I can get away with."

But I did not get the chance to read Samuel's journal, for when we reached the home of Derrick Van Veghten, Samuel said that he would have to turn back. I was sad to see him go, for I truly wanted to read his journal and hoped he would read mine. But I supposed that being a slave was not the same thing as being from Vermont. "Stay with us tonight, Samuel," said Mr. Van Veghten. "I'm sure Mr. Bogert will not mind."

Van Veghten. Another Dutchman. At dinner, he introduced us to Jacob Hardenburgh, a Dutch Reformed Church minister and John Hardenburgh, his son. Two young men named Ten Eyck and Van Arsdalen then joined us. They were constructed like Ethan, tall, broad-shouldered, and muscular. They too were on our side even though they were Dutch. In Pownal the Dutch were Tories. Well, we assumed they were, for they did not join our militia. I wondered if these men were secretly Tories, but realized they must be different from the

Dutch in Pownal. Not all Dutch thought alike, I realized. Then I realized that we folks in Pownal seldom agree on things ourselves.

I do not think Deuteronomy Dewey would like my befriending these Dutch Reformed folks. Of course, Deuteronomy blamed the ills of the world on all other religions. "The Dutch Reformed church preaches acceptance of all differences. Licentiousness. Profligacy. What's left to believe in?"

He found something wrong with all other religions. "Presbyterians and Congregationalists do little but create discord in our world. They think too much and read scripture too little."

If you let him run on, he began to stammer. "And, and, and as for Quakers, you go sit in what they call a church, and you'll soon learn they believe in nothing. They seldom speak, and if they do, they say what they will. Call that a religion? It's a quilting bee!"

At supper, Mr. Van Veghten asked us all about how we had conquered Fort Ticonderoga. Seth Warner and I were quiet, as were Michael and Pebonkas, but Ethan was, as he might say, "exceedingly voluble." "Massachusetts," he said, "sent me a most experienced colonel as my assistant. Benedict Arnold. He learns quickly and, I'm sure, will make a name for himself someday. Very systematic. Exceedingly efficient. A competent accountant to keep track of all those details that tend to bog us down. He does pinch those shillings." Samuel, the Hardenburghs, Ten Eyck, and Van Arsdalen sat enthralled by his tale. I felt certain I knew what Samuel would put in his journal.

At supper they talked about how the British taxes on things like paper and paint had raised their business costs, how the British wanted us to pay for their standing army even though the army did little to protect us, how we had to house and feed British troops whenever they demanded, and how unfair it was the Britain could determine laws without consulting us. They talked of British abuses against women. For me, it was an education. I began to understand why we were fighting the British. They were even worse than the Yorkers.

Mrs. Van Veghten served us apple pie after we had eaten potato soup and a dark bread. She was as good a cook as my mother. It was the first pie I had eaten since becoming a Green Mountain Boy. She told us she stored apples in their cellar. "Now they're only good for pies and apple sauce." That suited me just fine.

Mrs. Van Veghten had hired a neighbor's daughter to help her care for the house. Trintje Becker. She was very fair. I mean, she had a pleasant smile. Well, she smiled at me when we met. I noted her name in my journal and put an arrow in the margin pointing to the name. You can think what you want about my doing so, but it was neither licentiousness nor profligacy, regardless of what Deuteronomy Dewey may have thought.

After supper, while Ethan, Seth, Mr. Van Veghten, and the Hardenburghs talked around the fire, Pebonkas, Michael, Samuel, and I sat outside. The nights were getting warmer. Samuel spoke about how the people of Lesser Crossroads were all talking about the coming war with England. People from New Jersey seemed to read news from Boston and New York and Philadelphia. Not so in Pownal. What news trickled our way usually came from Deuteronomy's lips on Sundays.

Samuel said he had been on the road one day when John Adams had actually passed him in a carriage.

"Who is John Adams?" I asked.

"A representative to our colonial congress," Samuel informed us. "He's from Boston. There's also a Samuel Adams from there who complains of being a slave to the British. Wonder what he'd say if he were in my position?"

His comment made me uncomfortable. I decided to change the subject. "Have you learned anything about Congress?"

"Politicians, you know, rising to give long speeches. Then they give speeches against the long speeches. They agree to disagree. They call each other 'the loyal opposition' or 'my colleague from Virginia.' I doubt they can decide anything. They don't even agree about whether we're English or not."

"They told us to apologize to Canada," said Michael.

"That's politicians for you," said Samuel. "They tell others how to behave. Bunch of told-you-so's."

"Huh?"

"Told-you-so's. You made a mistake. Not me. I wouldn't have done it that way: Told you so. Though, of course, they hadn't."

"Hadn't what?"

"Told you so. Even if they had, they'd deny it."

"Politicians spout the same old blather no matter what side they're on," said Michael. "For me, freedom's a land without politicians. Wouldn't that be grand?"

"If there's a war, politicians will run it. English, French, or American, it's all the same," said Pebonkas.

"I think I would want Ethan to be a politician," I said. "He would do things right."

"The words 'politician' and 'right' don't fit in the same sentence, Erastus," said Pebonkas.

"Yes, yes, they do. At least when Ethan is in charge they will. It will be . . . " I sought the best word, the word Ethan might choose. "It will be . . . enlightened."

"It must be nice to be free to disagree," said Samuel. "Someday I'll be able to disagree. I'll say, 'Erastus, you cannot write your way out of a cistern.' And 'Michael, you Irish are a bunch of ignorant peasants.' And 'Pebonkas, you think like a savage.' Yes, that's my idea of freedom."

"Samuel," said Pebonkas, "you're my idea of a politician."

"Thank you," said Samuel.

"Tell me," asked Michael, "Do you know this fellow Lord Stirling?"

"Oh, yes, we see him now and then."

"Well," said Michael, "as a politician, what do you think of him?"

"As a politician, I would call him an esteemed colleague."

"And as yourself, what would you say about him?"

"I would say I'm not at liberty to say," said Samuel, smiling at him.

"Ah, my poor Samuel, you're truly and sadly a politician."

I wondered about Samuel's feelings toward our fighting the British. "Samuel," I asked, "if the war comes here, will you fight? Will other slaves fight?"

"I'm not sure," said Samuel. "I don't expect our owners to let us go off and fight. After all, we might not come back."

"But you would fight on our side if you could, right?" I wanted to learn whether his attitude was similar to those of Michael and Pebonkas, who seemed only to choose our side as the lesser of evils.

"You know something, Erastus?" answered Samuel. "I've heard the British have offered to free us slaves if we fight you rebels. You know many people shiver in their beds fearing what we might do?" I shook my head. "Slaves outnumber their owners in the southern colonies. Already the British have offered us our freedom there. Now, if you were a slave and someone offered you your freedom, would you take it?"

"Well," I struggled to understand my own reaction, "I suppose. But surely you will fight with us when the time comes."

"Just as you fight for freedom, if I have to fight for freedom, I'll fight with whatever group offers me that freedom."

"But freedom under the British does not make sense.'

"I see," said Samuel. "Why should I give up all I have now for British freedom?"

"Don't tie me up with words," I said.

"As though words don't tie me up?" Samuel said.

Trintje stepped out the door, and I welcomed the interruption. Not because her golden hair hung down in a braid, you understand, but because my notions of freedom had just been ambiguated. Trintje had finished her chores. She said nothing, but smiled at me when I looked at her, the second time. That was a new experience for me.

After waking to a meal of cheese and warm milk to start the day, we climbed on our horses. I worried Michael would refer to our hosts as cheese-heads or butter bellies. In fact, Michael happily gorged himself on the cheese, milk, and butter they had shared with us. I would need to observe in my journal how food brings people together. Then I realized, with all our talk of politicians and slaves, I had forgotten to share my journal with Samuel, and I did not get to read his. "I hope I see you on the way back," I said, "and that I can read your journal."

"Don't you fear meeting yourself in my journal, Erastus?" he remarked as we parted.

"Ah, yes," said Michael. "If we should see each other through another's eyes, how blurry we might appear."

I saw Trintje looking at us through a window and waived at her as we left. I wished I had taken some time to talk with her. At least I knew where she lived.

Jacob and John Hardenburgh rode further south with us. When we reached New Brunswick, we stopped for lunch in a tavern that sat on a hill overlooking the river. The young men in the tavern seemed very serious, studying leather-bound books. Jacob Hardenburgh surprised me saying it was a college. He called it "Queen's College" and said it prepared Dutch Reformed ministers. The young men were all the students in the college. I had not realized until then that a person had to study to become a minister. I thought one just memorized the Bible and acquired what Deuteronomy Dewey said was "a calling."

Only about ten young men or so attended Queen's College. Since we were in a tavern, I observed that it must be fun to be able to drink beer in college. Michael said he might consider converting from being a Catholic to being Dutch Reformed. "I'd drink up that old religion, by God!"

They lived and studied in the tavern, but said they only drank beer because the water tasted muddy much of the year. "Even so, we dare not drink much. If we do not study hard," said one, "we have to drink Raritan water."

"Raritan?"

"We're on the banks of the old Raritan, my boy, where this college stands," said he, pointing at the river.

Michael reconsidered his conversion. "Well, as the good people say, drink is the curse of the land. It makes you fight with your wife. It makes you shoot at your landlord. And it makes you miss him."

Some college, I thought. It had fewer students than our school on Carpenter Hill. Perhaps we should call our school a college, too, and I could go there. But that meant I would have to return to school, and the teachers would probably be ministers like Reverend Hardenburgh. I did not look forward to having Deuteronomy Dewey as my teacher. All study, and no beer.

The Hardenburghs pointed us west, saying the Delaware River lay a long day's ride. So off we went again. By now, my legs had grown accustomed to being sore, though the backbone of my horse continued to jab me with each step. The road, however, was a well-traveled turnpike, and we met many travelers, including one lone British soldier who declared himself lost. Though seeing our militia shook him a bit, he asked if we knew the way to Princeton.

"That way," said Michael, pointing behind us.

"No, I think it's up there," said Pebonkas, pointing to the north.

"We are just passing through," I added, "but I think it is just south of here."

The soldier gave us a perplexed look and hurried on his way. Michael, noting how thin the soldier was, said, "The breath is only just in and out of him, and the grass doesn't know of him walking over it. He's not fit to keep the mice out of the cheese."

When we came to Griggstown, we waved down an itinerant butcher to buy some meat for our supper. Poking out from a leather apron, his short muscular arms guided his cart along the road. He stopped and opened a lid to show his wares.

"Where are you headed?" asked John Honeyman, for that was the man's name.

"We're on a trading mission," replied Ethan.

"And traders need soldiers to accompany you?" Did I hear right? Did he say "traitors" or "traders"? What would we do if this man told the British about us?

"We've hired them as protection against road agents and other brigands."

"We're all good citizens here," Honeyman replied, "and loyal to the Crown. We have no robbers and thieves, for this is New Jersey." He smiled a broad grin in an equally broad face.

"Good to hear," said Ethan.

"So tell me," said John Honeyman, "why are you here?" For a tradesman he asked too many questions I thought.

"To fatten your wallet," replied Ethan. "To buy your beef and to give you the wherewithal to pay your good king's taxes. Or don't you want our money?"

"Oh, I'll take your money, sir. And I'll wish you well on your way."

As we rode away, I rode up beside Ethan and asked, "Do you think we should trust the butcher Honeyman—a Tory?"

"I would not be certain of that," said Ethan. "Few of us are exactly what we seem. Our avowed friends may actually be Tories, and avowed Tories may be our friends. Few dare commit themselves as fully as we, so let us content ourselves for now, Erastus. You look somewhat puzzled. These days, most folks ride the fence, Erastus, until they know from which side the bull is charging toward them."

We rode up on a hill and saw an outpost occupied by British and Hessian soldiers, whereupon our militia said they could not go any farther. Michael, who had ridden with them for most of our journey across New Jersey, said he was sorry to see them go. Being with those Irish made him seem happier. As they turned to leave, Michael said to them, "May the crows never pick your potatoes."

"May the leaves of your cabbage always be free from worms," replied the one called McCard.

"May you go to Heaven or to Hell," said Michael, "but even if you go to Heaven, may your lack of friends not worry you."

"Well, if you go to Hell," said Kincaid, "you'll be so busy drinking with your friends that you won't have time to worry."

"May God turn the ankles of our enemies so that we may recognize them limping down the road," said Michael.

"May we please, please be on our way?" said Seth Warner, though even gangly Seth was smiling. I think I would always like to be around Irishmen when they say goodbye to one another. In fact, I told Michael I thought the Irish more fun than the Green Mountain Boys.

"More fun, perhaps," he said, "but poor sods still." A drop of Irish blood could spoil the freshest milk.

Before I left my horse with the militia, I said goodbye to him and wished him as much grain as he could eat so his next rider did not suffer as much as I had.

The walking pleased me, the sky blue, the weather warmer, and the roads not mud. We curved north of Trenton and soon arrived at the Delaware River, broad like the Hudson at Albany, and looked to hire a boat to take us to Philadelphia.

In time we hailed one floating by. Its master agreed to take us to Philadelphia since that was his destination. I may have called it a boat, but it looked more like a large raft with a small mast, low sides, and a blunt bow on either end. The crewmen sat on bales of wool. "I know this is not a sloop nor a schooner nor a petti-auger," I said to the master.

"So you are a cataloguer of boats, are you? Well, we call this a Durham boat." The boat's master steered the boat with the current, so we did not need a sail, but I noted long oars stored on the bottom.

Seth asked why the strange design. "You'll see," said the boat's master. When the Delaware River became very shallow, the Durham boat started to scrape along the bottom, and no sooner did it scrape than the crewmen jumped into the water, which was only a little over their knees. They grabbed the sides, pushed, and the boat slipped by the shallows. "Now you see what it's good for," said the master.

The squat houses of Trenton did not look like the tall homes of Albany. Like Albany, warehouses lined the shore. Unlike Albany, soldiers, dressed in green, watched us float by.

"Not British," I said to Ethan.

"Brunswickers, Hessian hired soldiers," he said. "I fear we'll see more of them before we're free."

Floating down the Delaware, I made a list in my journal of so much new I had seen in New Jersey, so much to think about: coaches fit for a lord, argumentative inhabitants, slaves free to ride the countryside who might yet fight against us, Dutch who owned beautiful homes, scholars studying to be ministers in a tavern, good meals, the Durham boat we were riding in, a skinny English soldier, the stocky butcher Honeyman, and, most recently, Brunswickers. I thought of writing about Trintje, but thought better of it when I considered that my mother might ask to read my journal. I did not need something else for Tryphena and Tryphosa to rub my face in. Instead I wrote her name and where she lived in the bottom margin of the page, upside down.

CHAPTER 11

▼

THE CONTINENTAL DIVIDE

Philadelphia was more than I could ever have dreamed.

I saw Quakers for the first time, not at all the severe people we hear of. Some were quite drab, but then, so were we. Others dressed quite prettily, with broad-brimmed hats, well-trimmed vests, jackets of the finest material, albeit earth-colored. Most we met were business men, intent upon making a living. They called themselves "Friends," but I observed that they would gladly make money off a stranger as off a friend.

Take Jacob Cook, for example. We did not go looking for him, but he came looking for us the moment we stepped up on the wharf where our Durham boat captain had left us. "What can I do for you gentlemen? Have you a place to stay? Are you hungry, looking for good food? Do you require transportation?" All these questions. I thought he was most solicitous, but Michael said he was "hustling us," though he seemed to take his time. Ethan accepted him immediately, telling him we all needed lodging.

"Yes, my friends, right this way." He led us into the town over more cobble-stoned streets than I have ever seen in my life, up past warehouses and taverns, past small brick homes with small front steps. In Elfreth's Alley, a narrow, clean smelling street swept free of dirt, he knocked on various doors. "Have you a room for my friends?" He tried many houses to find a room here and a room there. Of course, he also accepted a payment from Ethan for finding us rooms. Ethan and Seth were given a room in the first house, though Seth said he would accompany us to know where we were all staying, "Ethan or I will get you later for dinner, but we should rest until then." Michael and Pebonkas secured a place in another home, and then Jacob Cook introduced me to the Widow Lithgow.

Widow Lithgow's husband must have been happy to have died and become free of her, for she was a gruff person who would tolerate no small talk. "Nice town, Philadelphia," I said.

"Mmmm," she nodded, or some such sound.

She had the most severe look, even for an old woman.

"Follow me." "Don't dally." "Here's my home. Please wipe your feet."

After sitting me down in the entryway of her skinny house ("Sit," she said, pointing to the bench), she took off her cape and knocked on a door in the hallway. A young woman answered. She was renting that part of the house and running an upholstery business out of it with her husband. Mrs. Elizabeth Ross smiled, much more pleasant than the Widow Lithgow, and led me up to her small attic room. After nodding off, I woke to Mrs. Ross telling me, "The tall, thin gentlemen came for you, but I told him they should let you sleep. So, are you hungry?"

Darkness had fallen, so I crept down the stairs, behind Mrs. Ross. Her husband heard me and invited me into their kitchen, "Come. Eat." Mrs. Ross had a pot of stew on, and her husband ladled some onto a plate for me.

"We hear you are all Green Mountain Boys, the ones who captured Fort Ticonderoga." Her soft face, ringed with curls, reflected her easy manner.

I told them how Ethan had charged bravely into the fort and how Colonel Arnold had trotted alongside him. "It was easy, really." I hope I was not bragging. I told them of all the weapons we captured and how we were planning to send them to Boston to help our militia there. I did not tell them of our attack on St. John or of all the rum that our men consumed, for I knew I was talking about history, and no one wants to know anything scruffy about history. Suddenly, I worried they might be Tories.

"It's great good news," said Mr. Ross and told me that he was serving in a local Philadelphia militia. He, too, had a soft face and smiled like his wife.

"It's so dangerous," said Mrs. Ross.

"Mostly, we just guard some munitions we've stored. Nothing as brave or perilous as your attack on Fort Ticonderoga. Betsy just worries too much." Taking her hand, he told her not to worry, "Nothing will happen."

Changing the subject, I said, "So, you are both upholsterers? What do you make?"

"Oh, just curtains and clothes, things like that. Betsy's an excellent seamstress."

"So are you, John."

"Why, did you know our Continental Congress sent a delegation to her for help?"

"I wouldn't call it a 'delegation,' John dear. They called themselves 'a committee.' Can you imagine? A committee to talk to a seamstress?"

"What did they want?" I asked.

"They asked whether we could sew uniforms for them. Of course, I was honored, but a bit scared some Tories might find out. Although, an order of uniforms would help our business greatly."

"And . . . ," prompted John Ross.

"And they asked if I had ever sewed a flag. Of course I said I had not."

"But you could."

"And they asked if I knew how to make stars."

"And of course you said . . . ," prompted John again.

"I asked if they wanted stars with four points, five points, or six?"

"And then?" I figured John Ross had prompted his wife to tell this story many times. I have observed how husbands and wives often have their own stories and how one serves as the motivator to drive the other's story along. My mother, for example, knew how to lead my father to talk of the times he had almost been struck by lightning, and my father loved to have her talk about the time a cow fell in love with a Moose.

"And then this committee fell into a terrible argument. Two liked four stars and two liked five and two liked six. I think they forgot I was in the same room with them. I do hope they don't disagree so when they meet as a Congress."

"I would not think so," I said to reassure her. "But five points on a star is odd."

"That's a cute pun," she said.

"Huh?" I did not get it.

"Just think," said John, "my wife may make a flag for the Continental Congress."

"Well, I'm not so sure, John. They said they'd need to consider it, so I don't know if I'll ever see them again."

Mrs. Ross then poured me some warm milk. "They also asked me if I had any thoughts about what design I'd use for the constellation on the flag."

"Constellation?"

"The way the stars are laid out in the design. Well, I should have learned my lesson from the discussion about the number of star points, but I hadn't, so I told them we could lay them out in rows or in lines or in a cross or in a circle. And that started them arguing again. Then, trying to help, I asked them how many stars they wanted, and, do you know, they did not know. On that they were agreed. I think I just confused them too much with all my questions, but goodness, how else can I know what to do?"

Yawning, I thanked the Rosses for their kind meal and excused myself. I actually did not think anything would ever come of the flag business, given what Mrs. Ross described, but I hoped they would get a uniform order.

In the morning, Mrs. Ross had prepared a warm porridge and milk for me. Mr. Ross was in their shop in the front room talking to a lady who wanted curtains.

Mrs. Ross asked me if I was a church-goer, and I confessed that back home I did, but only because my parents made me go.

"I think going to church holds a family together," she said.

"What church do you go to?" I asked.

Tears came into her eyes. I had not meant to hurt her. I have observed many ladies weep at the very least provocation. My mother did not. My sisters Tryphena and Tryphosa seemed to delight in causing me to cry. But I have seen girls in school and in church often break out in tears. Whenever Deuteronomy Dewey saw a girl cry in church, he announced, "She is taken by the spirit, praise God."

"Forgive me, Erastus. It's just . . . Well, I was raised a Quaker, and John was raised an Episcopalian. And when my father found out, he refused to consent to John's courting me."

"What did you do?" I thought it terrible that religions could divide people so, even if Deuteronomy Dewey did have strong opinions about other religions. I did not recall hearing him complain about Episcopalians, though. I wondered then if they only existed in Philadelphia.

"We ran away." I must have looked shocked. "And we have been happy ever since." Well, then, I thought, perhaps I should tell her story to Tryphena and Tryphosa, so maybe they would take the hint, grab some stranger, and run away.

Seth Warner showed up around then and took me to the others. Ethan, Pebonkas, and Michael met us a few blocks away, and we walked to the Pennsylvania State House.

"You don't know what you missed last night, Erastus," said Michael, "getting your beauty rest and all."

"The Rosses invited me to dinner."

"Pebonkas and I found a tavern fit for your everlasting journal," he said. "It's named 'The Rising Sun.' We met true humans there, mechanics and artisans, not a bunch of high born-rich folks."

I shrugged as if to say, "So?"

"So, Erastus, you need to know this. They've sworn to fight to free the slaves we see all around us." I looked around. Many black people walked the streets.

"Are they all slaves?" I whispered.

"Apparently not all, Erastus, but with a Congress arguing about freedom, I'd bet they don't have in mind the freedom of the slaves," said Michael. "Anyway," he continued, "it seems your colonists are not all pure Christians and not above serving themselves. Darling lads, those mechanics, salt of the earth. Not your sugary leaders."

If you have never been to Philadelphia, you probably have never seen the Pennsylvania State House, but my heart leapt when I saw it. A simple, large building with a high central bell tower, sharp red brick, and white painted trim. Not one building in all the Hampshire Grants resembled it, though I wager Pownal will have such a building one day for its town hall.

Once inside the State House, we entered a large room where groups of men were gathered around desks and tables, most of them trying to talk all at once, or so it seemed at first. We were guided by an attendant, another black man, who asked us to line up along the back wall until we could be recognized. Ethan handed him a piece of paper with our names on it and his intentions, which the man, whose name I later learned was Solomon Brown, handed to a tall man in front. The tall, aristocratic-looking man with a sharp chin appeared to be in charge, or at least his seat was central to everything going on. Solomon Brown returned to whisper that his name was John Hancock.

As the group settled down to what appeared to be their business, Solomon would whisper the names of the men who were speaking. "John Dickinson, Pennsylvania," he said as one rose.

Dickinson, a thin, severe man, pointed toward a corpulent man leaning back in his chair with his arms behind his head. "Do you not care for our mother country, Mr. Franklin? Would you abandon her at the least disgruntlement, Ben?"

"Ah, John, our militias have bitten the British at Concord and Lexington and now nip at their heels outside Boston. Our mother country may choke us on a chain if we stop snarling. Don't you think I wish they would love us as a mother her children?"

Mr. Dickinson then launched into so long a response that I lost the words, but it had to do with "excessive exuberance" and "misguided values." A short, chubby man yawned as soon as Mr. Dickinson began to speak, rose, and left in the middle of the speech.

Solomon nodded at him and whispered, "John Adams, Massachusetts."

Seeking support for his position, Dickinson turned to a fragile man beside him. "So, James, don't just sit there. Tell them what you think."

"James Wilson, also Pennsylvania," said Solomon.

Wilson sat, a troubled look on his face. He ran his hand through his thin hair and murmured something like, "Well, John, I truly have no firm opinion one way or another about independence, if that's where you're leading."

"No opinion? No opinion!" Dickinson had turned a bright red color. "What do you want to be remembered as? A judge who could issue no opinion? Come now. Tell our colleagues here how misguided they are."

"What I think at the moment hardly matters, John."

"But you do think something! Tell them!"

"Well, gentlemen," said Wilson, rising slowly, "what I wonder is, what will happen to us should we fail? This is no small undertaking, nothing to be taken lightly. But if we should fail . . . "

"If we fail, we fail, but let us fail in a glorious quest!" shouted someone from a back desk.

"Please, Patrick, let the man speak," said John Hancock.

"Well I say," shouted Patrick, "I say, give me liberty or . . . "

"Yes, yes, Patrick, you have said that before. I'm sure we're all quite aware of what you say," replied Dickinson. Now it was Patrick's turn to turn red.

Dickinson continued, "This is no small step we are contemplating. But surely we must all realize it's treasonous to oppose our king and, as I say quite proudly, our mother country." Mr. Wilson had slipped back down during this exchange, and I would say he looked quite relieved not to be noticed.

"Mr. Wilson," said someone near the back. Mr. Wilson twitched at hearing his name. "James, did you not recently write that you believed all men are created equal?" Mr. Wilson continued to look uncomfortable. "Well, then why do you not now support our efforts?"

The question went unanswered as another asked, "May I speak?"

"I yield to my colleague Samuel Chase," said Dickinson.

"Maryland," said Solomon.

Samuel Chase rose, a smile creasing his triangular face. "I concur with my colleague, John Dickinson." Dickinson smiled broadly. "Though I suppose treason is in the eye of the beholder."

"The beholder is the king," said Dickinson, his sharp eyebrows narrowing and pointing toward his long nose. "Not to mention General Gates and the entire English army."

"As I was trying to say," continued Chase, "treason does. But I have to consider what our colleague Wilson has said." Mr. Wilson looked very uncomfortable at having his name invoked again and slid down into his chair even more. "He wonders what will happen should we challenge the mightiest army on earth, the most highly trained, the best-equipped, the masters of tactics and strategy . . . "

"Yes, yes," said Benjamin Franklin, leaning back in his chair, his thumbs tucked in a broad waistcoat, "but remember, he that by the plow would thrive, himself must either hold or drive."

"May the good Lord save us from your aphorisms, Ben."

"Well," said Ben, "One today is worth two tomorrows."

"As I was trying to say . . . " interrupted Samuel Chase.

"You have the floor," said Hancock.

"As I was trying to say, fighting for our rights when we are in the right need not be considered treason. But fighting for our rights and losing, well, we must be certain of our ability to finish what we begin. An ill-conceived war may end all our hopes for the future. If I may quote our aphoristic colleague Franklin, 'for want of a nail the shoe was lost; for want of the shoe the horse was lost; and for want of a horse the rider was lost.'"

"Oh, well said, Samuel," said Ben.

"And so on. The point is," said Chase, "I've no proof we even have a nail to fit the shoes of our army, should we even be able to raise an army."

I noticed many heads turn to look at a large expressionless gentlemen in a military uniform who was sitting in the back and so far had said nothing.

"George Washington, from Virginia," whispered Solomon.

George Washington continued to sit and say nothing.

"A military man," said Solomon, "and as such does not speak when he might contradict someone else in public."

George Washington did not seem to be made of the same cloth as Ethan, who then stepped forward, raised his hand, and asked, "May I speak to the assembly?"

John Hancock replied, "In due course, we will recognize you when we have 'other business,' sir. Do be patient."

Much to my surprise, Ethan was patient, unlike any other time I could think of.

Samuel Chase continued, the effect of his speech having been blunted by the interruptions of his colleagues, "Well, I think I have said my piece. Do not start what we cannot finish."

One of the delegates began to cough violently, and I thought that he would die of apoplexy so badly did he cough. He seemed to have coughed all the air from his lungs and was desperately trying to regain his breath.

"Caesar Rodney, Delaware," whispered Solomon. Another delegate, whom Solomon told me was Thomas McKean, a colleague also from Delaware, very solicitously helped the weak Mr. Rodney from his seat and guided him toward a door. I noticed that John Adams had returned to the room, looking very sour.

I asked Solomon to point out the Yorkers in the room, for I was anxious to hear whether these delegates burned in their fervor like us Green Mountain Boys or whether they served here to justify stealing our land. He pointed to a group who sat silently.

"They will probably say nothing," predicted Solomon, "for they've not received any instructions from their provincial government."

John Adams pushed himself up to be recognized. "Now that my colleague Dickinson has finally finished . . . "

"President Hancock!" Dickinson jumped from his seat. "I will not stand by and be insulted by this radical from Massachusetts! We've seen where liberal-thinkers from that colony will lead us. We've heard how they brag of the attacks on the English troops by their unfettered militia. These people from Massachusetts think to speak for all of us, when, in fact, we all have the love of our people at heart. But they have, they have . . . " He seemed to struggle for something to say.

"Not looked before they leapt," offered Ben Franklin.

"Well, yes, that. But, to use your own words, Mr. Franklin, 'Great estates should venture more, but little boats should stay near shore.'" Dickinson looked pleased with himself.

At that point, John Hancock declared a recess for one hour and came over to Ethan.

"Colonel Allen, it is so good of you to join us. We look forward to hearing of your exploits."

"Well, I . . . "

"Won't you and your colleagues join us for lunch?"

"Colleagues, are we?" whispered Michael. "Aren't we becoming the dandies? I say, my fine colleague Pebonkas, won't you join me? And you, my dear Erastus, surely you will sup with us."

Seth Warner trailed along behind us all, saying nothing.

John Hancock led us to a modest tavern with shining pewter where several men rose and greeted us. I recognized Patrick Henry, but had not known Richard Henry Lee. After introductions all around, we sat down to order our meals.

"I think I'll order the tea cakes," said Mr. Henry, taking his small brown wig off his mostly bald head.

"They're really not very good here," said Mr. Lee, a thin man whose sharp cheekbones threw shadows across his face. He, too, was balding.

"But I prefer tea cakes."

"Well, if that's what you're willing to settle for."

"Richard, I say, give me tea cakes or . . . "

"Patrick, if I hear that one more time . . . ," said Mr. Hancock.

"I was simply saying I prefer either tea cakes or scones."

"I'm sorry."

"Easy enough for you to say."

"I said I'm sorry."

Mr. Lee attempted to change the conversation. "John—and I think Mr. Allen and his colleagues will appreciate this—I've been working on a draft of a proposal."

"Please, tell us."

"I'm thinking the time is now to assert our sovereignty as free colonies."

"Do you really think it has come to that, Richard?" asked Mr. Hancock.

"Well, what do you think I've been trying to tell you people all along?" said Mr. Henry. John Hancock simply gave him a cold stare. "It's bad enough you won't allow me to order tea cakes, but now to plagiarize my idea."

"If you gentlemen will forgive me," said Ethan, "I hope you have a title that will inspire our people and send fear through the bones of the English."

"What do you suggest?" asked Mr. Lee.

"Liberty or Death," offered Mr. Henry.

"Well, of course," said Ethan, "I'm just thinking off the top of my head, but something firm, like 'A Proposition: toward Self-Determination.' That's not quite it, mind you, but something like that."

"A Proposal for Self-Government?" asked Mr. Hancock.

"It must be eloquent, yet simple," said Ethan, "direct, yet grand."

"A Proclamation of Freedom," said Mr. Hancock.

"Yes, I think that's what we want," said Mr. Lee.

To this day I do not know what came over me, for I blurted out, "How about a 'Declaration of Independence'?" Sudden silence. I drew back, trying to lose myself in my chair so embarrassed was I at my presumptuousness. They were all looking at me.

"By God!" said Patrick Henry.

"A Declaration of Independence," said Mr. Hancock. "Yes, that may be it."

"It has a catchy rhythm to it," said Mr. Henry.

"'Tis both sonorous and noble, Erastus," said Ethan. "You have learned your multisyllabifications well. I am proud of you."

"Waitress!" shouted Mr. Henry, "I'd like some tea cakes! And please bring a charger full for my young friend here."

So there you have it. I am certain I blushed. Michael poked me in the ribs. Pebonkas patted me on the back. Seth Warner smiled warmly at me. It would be another year or so before I actually saw what it had grown into, and I did not have any more to do with its writing, but I am proud of my contribution that day. Of course, Deuteronomy Dewey would shake his head and caution me against the sin of pride, but I think we are each of us allowed some small sin once in a while.

We followed the delegates Hancock, Henry, and Lee back to the State House where John Hancock hammered the meeting to order. I noticed the sickly delegate, Mr. Rodney, was missing. Everyone else was present, even John Adams, looking petulant.

"Gentlemen," said John Hancock, "I have the honor to introduce to you our very distinguished guests. May I introduce to you the Green Mountain Boys, those brave men whose prompt action enabled us to capture Fort Ticonderoga and secure our border against an English invasion from Canada. Today, we have with us two of the officers, Ethan Allen and Seth Warner, and three of their men, Peter, Michael, and Erastus."

The delegates all rose to applaud us. Well, that is, they all rose, but not everyone applauded. Still, I felt my face flush.

"Colonel Allen has requested permission to speak to us today, and I trust you will accord him your undivided attention. Colonel Allen?"

Ethan stepped forward and stood beside John Hancock, who sat down.

"Gentlemen, delegates of the Continental Congress," Ethan began. "This morning I was honored to be present in the midst of your debate about the future of our young nation—about our America." At the use of that word, several members began mumbling, but John Hancock stared them down. "And so," continued Ethan, "it is my hope that my humble words to you today may disambiguate your discourse."

I was surprised to see that Ethan had taken out of his pocket a piece of paper upon which he had penned some notes. This was most unusual, but I assumed Ethan did not want to forget any points needed to convince the Congress to support our efforts.

"I don't presume that my considerations will not be your considerations, for you are honorable men. As honorable men, I know that you will validate my expectations. I invite you to think on our brothers to the north in Canada. We cannot believe that the present race of Canadians is so degenerated that they do not possess the same courage and valor—and values—that we do. They would not permit the infamy, disgrace, and pusillanimity of not joining our fight for freedom nor the consequences of it to rest on the backs of their children forever. We are determined to live free or not to live at all."

"Here, here!" shouted Patrick Henry.

"For our parts," continued Ethan, "we are resolved that posterity shall never reproach us with having brought slaves into the world."

I quickly glanced at Solomon Brown, to see his reaction to Ethan's words, but his face was stoic.

"We must show the Canadians we are their friends and not their enemies. They should not allow those who would endeavor to create animosities amongst us to impose upon our brothers in Canada a view that impinges upon us negatively."

I noticed that John Hancock was actually taking notes of what Ethan was saying!

"We are now masters of Lake Champlain and the garrisons depending thereon. The brave Green Mountain Boys risked their lives to take the forts of Ticonderoga and Crown Point, to capture armed vessels upon the lake, out of the need for self-preservation, not because we desire to conquer our friends to the north."

And then Ethan laid out his case to win the support of the Continental Congress, to demonstrate the need to provide arms to liberate the Canadians from the yoke of English oppression, and to recognize his authority in such an endeavor. When he had finished, he received a standing ovation. That is, those who supported liberty applauded, while those who were squeamish to act precipitously remained seated. I looked toward George Washington and noticed that he had risen from his seat and that his applause was polite but moderate.

When the applause ended, John Hancock rose to thank Ethan for his speech. I waited for the enthusiasm that greeted Ethan's words whenever he addressed the men of the Grants. "Do know, Colonel Allen, your words are an encouragement to all of us, whether we agree upon our future course of action or not. I've taken the liberty to capture as many of them as I could—I trust you will allow us to use them in some future communiqués and deliberations."

Ethan looked pleased, until Mr. Hancock continued, "Lest you leave here not understanding our next actions, do know that we shall appoint a committee to consider what you have suggested and to consider how we will address our friends to the north. Their deliberations will be purposeful and reflective, understanding the consequences of any action we may take. For having given us much to ponder, we are in your debt." And with that, he brought down his gavel and announced that the meeting was adjourned.

Ethan's face was stern. I saw Seth lay his hand upon Ethan's back and whisper something in his ear before he approached John Hancock. Then, Ethan rose to his full height and reached for Hancock's hand. Hancock was smiling, and I heard the words "grateful" and "comfortable journey home."

As Ethan turned to go, John Adams came rapidly up to him and took him by the arm. "Do not be discouraged by our response," he said. "In Virginia, all geese are swans, and in Massachusetts, John Hancock, like the rest of us, may look like a goose, but he'll swim like a swan." Only a New Englander might put it that way. "Colonel Allen, we have much work ahead of us if we are to succeed. Many will consider me obnoxious, but, like you, I am resolute. We need to make friends with France to secure their support. We need to begin issuing our own currency. We need to build powder mills in every colony and make every effort to manufacture salt petre. We need mines to produce lead and mills to melt it down. We'll need sulfur. And, I fear, we'll need to establish taxes." I saw Ethan flinch, ever so slightly. John Adams saw that, too, and continued, "These taxes will not be for trivial matters, like sugar or tea, and they'll not be imposed upon us by a government far across the ocean, but by our own government, a government you and your men are making possible. For that, we are all grateful." Ethan's posture and expressions softened, and he thanked Adams for his encouragement.

Back at the tavern we had visited before, Ethan, voluble once more, proposed that we "move the flowing bowl." For the record, and in case my mother would read my journal as I hoped she might, I note I did not imbibe.

Michael too had only one mug, for, as he said, "I'm thinking I'll need to recover from all that Congressional hubbub."

Ethan was solemn. "A committee! A committee! If we had given the taking of Ticonderoga to a committee, we would still be in Bennington debating the matter while that little Arnold pulled it all off himself. What kind of a world gives matters of import to a committee? Can you tell me?"

"Ah, sir," said Michael, "as for committees, people like to hide in each other's shadow."

"If I had to lift my cow, I'd rather do it with my neighbor than by myself," commented Seth.

One way or another, we needed our strength, for as we finished the meal, Ethan, who had been fairly quiet, said, "Get some rest, men, for tomorrow we leave for the New York Provincial Assembly." When we looked surprised, he added, "Well, after all, New York City is on our way."

CHAPTER 12

NEW YORK CITY IS NOT NEW JERSEY, NOT THE PROVINCE OF NEW YORK, NOT PHILADELPHIA, AND DEFINITELY NOT VERMONT.

If I never have to set foot in New York City again, I will live the rest of my days in bliss. New York City is not Philadelphia. It is not even New Jersey, bad as that is. It is too big, too noisy, too confusing, and the people delight in abusing one another.

Just before leaving Philadelphia, a messenger from Congress came to Ethan with uplifting news. "We're successful," said Ethan. "They're allowing us to keep Forts Ticonderoga and Crown Point, deeming it frivolous to return them to the English."

Ethan held out a packet of documents he had been given. "Moreover," he said, "they've voted to allow us to raise a regiment in the Grants to attack Canada, and they've authorized New York to provide the funds we need. An official letter will follow. Our exertions here have resulted in a beneficent conclusion. As long as our militias continue to hold the British at bay in Boston, Canada will soon be ours."

We left Philadelphia by buying passage on another Durham boat, this one captained by a man from New Jersey named William Rustinghouse. The boat had two sails on it and, thanks to what the captain called "a good following wind," we were able to sail and row our way back north in fair fashion.

Captain Rustinghouse employed two crewmen, a young boy my age named Zarubabel Bostwick and an elderly man named Lemuel Canfield. Lemuel wore a brown fearnothing jacket that looked fifty years old. Both wore breeches well-tarred. Their cargo was a mixture of sugar and various pieces of furniture. Lemuel told us over his toothless gums that he had been a New Jersey Ranger during the French and Indian war, but the closest he got to Pownal was when they marched north to join the fighting. "The roads was so bad and the weather was so bad we bogged down and never did make it. We never did get paid, neither. So I took my musket and the hatchet they'd issued me, kept my breeches and jacket they'd issued me, and come on home."

Zarubabel said that he wanted to be a tombstone carver. "My pa was a tombstone carver, but he up and died of the wandering feet, my ma used to say. My ma died, too, only of dropsy." His sad, drooping face reflected his mourning.

"Yessir," said Lemuel through his toothless gums. "I have fought for the King, and now I'm ready to fight against the King, that's if they'll pay me this time."

"My ma swelled up in the legs something awful, and the next thing she was dead."

"I ain't fighting without no contract first, no more promises of officers, no sir. I want it signed official and sealed complete."

"Me and my sister had to bury Ma out behind the house, without no one to help," said Zarubabel.

"Captain Rustinghouse here, he don't give me no contract neither, but he be an honest man," said Lemuel, "not no army officer."

"We didn't even have a tombstone to put up over her grave, and my father a tombstone carver. Sure is funny, don't you think?" observed Zaruabel.

"'Course, he ain't no lawyer, for sure. I bet my lieutenant in the French and Indian War was a lawyer, and I bet the captain, too, and the major as well," said Lemuel.

"My sister married the first man who come along, and they settled up on the Watchung Mountains, last I heard."

"So I ain't got no trust in no lawyers."

"So I will apprentice myself to a tombstone carver and learn that trade."

So the conversation went the entire trip back up the Delaware River, with the Captain of the Durham boat staying as far away from those two as he could, except when we ran aground and he had to tell them to get out and push.

"Soon's I learn to carve tombstones," said Zarubabel, "I'll carve one for my mother and put it up over her grave."

"Soon's I get paid, I'll settle me down in Pennsylvania," said Lemuel.

"As soon as I get me off this boat, I will unplug my ears," said Michael.

"That is, if I ever can remember where we lived," said Lemuel.

"On a farm by the Schuykill sounds like the spot to me," said Zarubabel.

North of Trenton, we paid the captain, thanked him, and said goodbye to Zarubabel and Lemuel, who each continued the conversation with himself. Ethan found a livery attached to an inn, where he hired horses and a man to return them when we reached the Hudson, and we set off. No bony backbone on my mare! I thought about becoming a cavalryman, but all I had to practice on at home was my mother's ox.

Since we knew our way across New Jersey, we made better time. Once more, on the road from Trenton to Griggstown, we encountered the burly butcher Honeyman, who must have been able to show up anywhere. He tested us again with questions about our purpose and destination. "Get anything done on your trip?" "You should visit Trenton, you know, for a man can learn a lot there." "Where you headed now?" As the first time we had met him, Ethan thanked him and paid him for the meat we bought. "Your silence is golden, my friends, but your money is copper." As we rode away, Honeyman shouted after us, "If you have a good beef, you can never go wrong!"

"I prefer to eat red meat!" Ethan shouted back.

"So do we all!" shouted Honeyman.

"What do you make of him?" I asked.

"More than one would think," replied Ethan, and confused me once more. Ethan sees things in people that the rest of us never see.

The first night, after a long ride, we reached the home of the Van Veghtens, who were as hospitable as before. Happily, I had a chance to talk to Trintje, who had unbraided her hair. I told her all about the Continental Congress. She talked about carding wool. I told her all about the Ross family. She told me how she learned to make dyes for the wool using local plants. I told her all about the Green Mountain Boys. She told me all about the Dutch Reformed service. I told her all about attacking Canada. She described how she prepared cows for milking. My sisters never described so well. If the two of us got a job on Captain Rustinghouse's Durham boat, we could converse just like the captain's crew members, Lemuel and Zarubabel.

That night I thought about Trintje and forgot to write in my journal.

The next day, as I parted from Trintje, I advised her to start a journal. I do not know why I said such a silly thing. She gave me a piece of paper with her post address on it. If she was willing to pay to receive my letter, I thought, I would gladly write. Then she flipped her blond hair away from her big, brown eyes and smiled at me again.

"Erastus, you're grinning," said Michael about a mile from the Van Veghtens. I ignored him.

By that night we were in Lord Stirling's carriage house again, treated to the Lord's hospitality by his servants, Clarence and Douglas, now dressed in their blue and red livery clothes. Clarence told Douglas, "It's not my responsibility to wait hand and foot on every patriot Tom, Dick, and Harry who happens to beg a room off Lord Stirling's generosity."

Douglas told Clarence, "If you'd trouble yourself to serve anyone at all, that would be a miracle."

Clarence pointed out, "It's your turn to climb up on the roof and polish the copper cupola roof."

Douglas said, "Whenever you decide to take your turn at washing the floors in Stirling's house, I'd gladly go up on the roof and polish the cupola roof."

Most people in New Jersey must be born with a litigious nature, and they well deserve one another. The winters in Pownal are so bad and so long that people use all their energy just trying to stay warm and so do not have the energy to punish one another as they do in New Jersey. In New Jersey, the winters are just bad enough to annoy people, but then winter goes away, and the people come out of their groundhog holes all annoyed and anxious to combat anyone who says anything. Deuteronomy Dewey would say I am being unkind, but I do not think the Bible says anything anywhere about people from New Jersey, so how would he know?

Which brings me to New York, sad to say. As we approached the Hudson River, we encountered the same group of militia who had guided us across New Jersey when we first crossed. They recommended we not take our muskets into New York, saying New York swarmed with English sympathizers. "They see your musket and they'll slit your throats." So we stored them in a barn in Weehawken. Then we found a ferryman to row us across the Hudson River, for the Hudson is very broad at this point, more like a bay than a river and the water very choppy. I think the choppiness comes from being so close to New Jersey.

However, compared to the city of New York, New Jersey is a land of angels whispering the glory of everything in our ears. New York stretches out about a mile across its top and a mile from its southern tip where the wreck of a Dutch fort lies crumbling. Beyond the city, rich green farmland stretches north. No sooner had we gotten off the ferry at the wharf and started to walk up Wall Street, a narrow path with houses closing in on you, than a mob came howling up the street. Fearing for our skin, we ducked into a little alley to avoid being trampled. They seemed to be running for their lives, but scared so much they paid us no attention. A young lady had gotten caught up in the rush, and she stumbled just as they were passing our alley. Seth pulled her out of the way of the mob and into our alley.

She could barely breathe, but thanked us for saving her.

We stepped out into the street after they passed and immediately saw another mob running up the same street toward us. These were rougher looking than the first mob, carrying heavy sticks and stones and yelling some awful things. Two men carried a long pole between them from which dangled several stuffed bags put together in the shape of a man and wearing what had once been very fancy clothes.

"Who are these thugs?" Ethan asked her.

"They call themselves 'Sons of Liberty,' sir."

"Well, then," Ethan said, with a bit of puzzled look on his face, "Let's follow them."

Seth said, "You're crazy." Only Seth could talk to Ethan that way.

But Ethan was our leader, we his followers. Soon we came to an open square where the two mobs had both stopped, so we stood back behind the second mob. They taunted one another. The first mob did not have anything to arm themselves with, and the second mob was hurling their stones at them. They were even trying to pry up the cobble stones to throw, but the few they were able to loosen were so heavy they fell far short of the first mob. The first mob tried to protect themselves, so they picked up the rocks and stones that the second mob had hurled at them and began hurling them back. So it went, with several people having to be carried away with bleeding heads.

At first I could not understand anything they were saying, but I soon realized the second mob, the rougher looking one, hurled epithets like "Tories!" and "Lobsterback Lovers!" and "Dirty Loyalists" and "Boot-licking Bastards!" This second mob was on our mob!

Immediately I concluded that the young lady we had saved must be a Tory. Our enemy.

"Ah, aren't they an earthy group," said Michael.

"The spirit of liberty," said Ethan.

"Salt of the earth," said Michael.

We sat on a door stoop to observe the proceedings, safe from the missiles each hurled at the other. "That one has a good arm," observed Michael. "And that one a fine voice."

"We may have some recruits," noted Seth, quietly, so the young lady could not hear.

In a little while, members of the mobs on both sides grew bored with the proceedings and drifted away. When the square had cleared of all but stones and broken cobbles, Ethan announced it time to find lodging for the night.

"I know an inn just off this square," offered the young lady. "The Sons of Liberty will not bother you there."

Ethan seemed pleased with that, and though I thought better of staying at an inn where Tories were safe, he did not seem worried. "May we escort you to your door?" he asked the young lady. She only lived a few blocks away.

Pebonkas asked her how she happened to be part of the group being chased by the Sons of Liberty.

"We'd been to see a play, down at the New Theatre on Nassau Street, and we were walking together afterward when we were caught up in the awful rush."

"Oh, what play did you see?" What play? The lady had just escaped being trampled and Pebonkas wants to talk about plays?

"*The Beggar's Opera*," she replied, "by Mr. Gay."

"Ah, a delightful satire."

"You've seen it?"

"No, but I had the pleasure of reading it. Have you seen other plays?"

"Last year my father took me to see *The Recruiting Officer*, by Mr. Farquhar. It's a very old play, but quite funny."

"'There's a pleasure sure, in being mad, which none but mad-men know.'" Pebonkas said.

"You know the play, sir!"

"Well, again, only from its reading."

"Sometimes reading may be the best way to enjoy a play, I think," she said, "for the theatre draws all sorts of people. Do you know, many of them spit in the stove as they pass, those who chew tobacco? And some bring their dogs to warm their feet. Some of the women there are actually business ladies. My father frowns upon my going to plays without him, for he says they incite unpatriotic thoughts."

"Well," said Pebonkas, "rest assured, we're all patriots here."

When we arrived at her home, an imposing structure, Pebonkas introduced himself as Peter Keyes. She replied with hers, "Mary Cunningham."

Ethan looked at her and said, "Cunningham, Cunningham, would we have heard that name? I fear we're new to New York."

"My father is William Cunningham," she answered. "I'm sure he'd want to thank you gentlemen for your assisting me. May I know your names?"

"Durhams, from Pennsylvania," said Ethan before any of us could reply. "We're simply passing through, but happy to assist you." Then, not giving her a chance to ask more, he ushered her to her door and led us away. As I said, Ethan sees things in people I do not.

"Who is William Cunningham?" I asked when we were out of sight of her home.

"If he's the William Cunningham I've heard tell of, he's the grey eminence behind the Tory violence in this city. Though there may be other William Cunninghams, I thought it prudent we not find out."

"Into the lion's den," added Seth.

"Where we shall find warmth and sustenance," responded Ethan, "provided we allow the lion to sleep undisturbed."

"You don't mind playing with lionesses, do you Pebonkas old boy?" said Michael.

"Well, I found her to be a very erudite young lady," said Pebonkas.

"Ah, Peter, my boy," said Michael, "you are a wonder."

That night, safe in the inn, I described my amazement at Ethan Allen's optimism. He had to share the victory at Ticonderoga with Benedict Arnold, Colonel Arnold had beaten him to St. John's, our victory at St. John's had been thwarted, Congress had once wanted to apologize to the English for Ethan's capturing Fort Ticonderoga, we had stumbled into a band of Tories here in New York, and still he continued as though victorious throughout.

The next day being Sunday, we would not be able to address the Provincial Assembly. Over our first meal, Ethan fell into a lengthy disquisition on the observance of the Sabbath. "The very institution of a Sabbath was itself a quite arbitrary decision of Moses, for reason dictates that one day is much like another. For our civil governments to institute pecuniary damages for breach of the Sabbath does not fit within natural reason from which all moral laws flow." I imagined the vehemence of Deuteronomy Dewey's sermon should he ever hear such words.

Seth Warner smiled politely during all of this and continued eating his meal. "Ezekial effectually repealed the statute of Moses in consequence whereof the administration of justice became disencumbered of the embarrassments under which it had labored for centuries. Thus it appears those laws denominated the laws of God are not infallible, but may be dispensed with." I had never heard anyone speak that way, at least not in Pownal Centre, which was, as I am sure you have discerned, my center of the universe.

Pebonkas said, "Colonel Allen, people will label you a Deist."

"What of it? The Christian believes the gospel to be true and of divine authority. The Deist believes it's not true and not of divine authority. So the Deist and the Christian are both true believers—and as their Christian Bible would have it, true believers will be saved. So the Deist is in the right if he should call a Christian an infidel, just as a Christian would accuse the Deist of being an infidel. It's impossible for us to believe other than that which we understand to be true, whether we are rightly informed or not. So, in both camps there are honest men and true who, because of the strength of their beliefs, both deserve to gain the Salvation of God."

If I followed his logic, my head was spinning. I had almost forgotten we were stuck in a hotbed of Toryism and at risk of having our heads bashed in. Yet here was Ethan Allen, passionate in debating the authority of the Bible! Perhaps the preachers will bash our heads in before the Tories have a chance.

"You should write down your thoughts, sir," said Pebonkas.

"Ah. I do intend to do so. In fact, I have scribbled some preliminary drafts toward such an end. My working title I call *Reason: The Only Salvation of Mankind*. Do you like it?"

"Yet," said Pebonkas. "Yet, I wonder if anyone will ever publish it."

"That's why we're here, fighting for freedom of the press, just as we fight for freedom to own our own land. How can a man pretend to be free if he cannot speak his own mind, if he dare not question the authority of his government, and if the government should punish him for his beliefs?"

This was exhilarating stuff, though I feared I could not accurately remember it. I feared writing it in my journal, for we would be at great risk should it fall into the wrong hands. Well, I would personally be at great risk if Tryphena and Tryphosa should ever read it. As it turned out, many years later Ethan did publish his tome on natural reason, so I have used it to remember what he had said that day.

As we walked the streets of New York, all sorts of people were peddling an unbelievable assortment of goods. Fresh fish I had never tasted in Pownal. Carrots and radishes growing here long before they would grow in Pownal. Hard candy and soft. Bread and cheese. Hats made of fur. Gloves. Scarves. All out on the streets. A multitude of smells accompanied our walk, not just those of the people. The stores were closed for the Sabbath, but these vendors did not seem phased by that. At times it seemed to me as though everyone in New York was out to make a shilling.

And the people! New York seemed to have attracted every type of person imaginable. We encountered many Dutch and English here, of course, but others spoke languages I had never heard. Pebonkas, who was turning out to be a veritable schoolhouse, identified French and Spanish, German and even Portuguese, which to me sounded much like French and Spanish combined. Black men and women walked the streets along with white. The very wealthy walked alongside the ragged poor. Sailors walked among civilians who walked among English soldiers. Ethan called it a "cornucopia of humanity."

We walked down to the river on the east, for New York is actually an island, and then down to the point where we had landed. Out in the bay was a large English warship. I could see how easily one large ship like that could threaten a town with bombardment.

"That rough bunch we saw last night, Miss Cunningham called them the Sons of Liberty. Are they really on our side?" I had to ask this, for the mob action did worry me.

"Well, first, Erastus," said Ethan, "whether they were Sons of Liberty or not, they appear to be on our side. Whereas the Loyalists . . . "

"Tories," said Michael.

"Exactly my point, Michael. Tories to us, Loyalists to them, but either way they're the same. The Loyalists or Tories call any group that opposes them Sons of Liberty these days. So I don't know if they really were an organized group of patriots opposing English oppression or whether they just happened to get together to chase a group of Tories."

"A city of fun," added Pebonkas.

All around New York we walked. At the wharves we observed some of the toughest looking people in the city, many of them sailors off the boats and ships in the harbor. Not knowing which side any of them might be on (Michael argued each stood on his own side), we did not try to befriend any. I tried looking away from them. One tough took that as an affront. "What've we here? Some country ladies from up north, I'd bet. Come to entertain yourself observing the natives, eh?"

We kept walking, but he fell in behind us. "What's the matter, folks? Scared to talk to us? Think you're too good for us, eh?"

I began to worry for our safety, especially after Michael turned to him and said, "Shove it, you tar head, or I'll shove it for you."

"Oh, aren't we the tough one, now? Sounds like you're a Mick, huh? Potato digger, fresh from the ol' sod, now, huh?"

"Try me," said Michael.

"Let's keep moving," Ethan advised.

"Tea sippers! Free Thinkers! Macaronis!" the man continued to taunt us, but we moved on. In time he fell behind, and we lost him.

Later we worked our way up to some of the nicest mansions in the city, and then Ethan stopped at one on Duke Street.

"I think this is what I've been looking for." To our puzzled looks, he said that he had been given instructions by the messenger from Congress to go to the house of Phillip Livingston, one of the wealthiest supporters of our cause. "Mr. Livingston was a member of the Committee of Fifty-One, and then that became the Committee of Sixty. Now I think it is the Committee of One Hundred. In any event, that is the group I need to address, and I'm to receive instructions here."

"Another bleeding manor lord," observed Michael.

"We need the support of Yorkers, even if they suffer the burden of wealth. We need to annihilate the old quarrel with New York and swallow it up in the general conflict for liberty," Ethan told him.

We knocked and were met by a servant in clothes much like those of Clarence and Douglas at Lord Stirling's estate. I hoped this one held fewer opinions and complaints. Ethan introduced himself as "a Grantsman," evidently a code name he'd been given in Philadelphia.

The ceilings in my home rise barely six feet high, a reasonable height since fuel needs to be conserved to make it through the winter up until April. These were twenty feet high! Think of the wood needed to heat this house. Obviously the owners thought of that, for all the rooms off the hallway stood shut. The servant led us upstairs to the second floor. Twelve foot ceilings. He knocked and entered a bedroom where a man stood by the fireplace, which blasted heat. Thick rugs cushioned our soles.

When he turned to face us, I think I gasped in shock. He laughed, "Is there something wrong?" Before me stood the sailor who had just taunted us a short while ago. New Yorkers do not smile—they smirk, as he did.

"Sorry to have worried you a bit earlier, but Mr. Livingston assigned me to work the docks, among other tasks. I didn't recognize you gentlemen, but even if I had, I probably would have behaved the same way." To our general consternation he explained, "We each have special assignments. Geyser here has infiltrated the Cunningham gangs. I stick to the Sears gangs." He held out his hand.

"I'm John Smith. Actually, my name's Johannes Schmidt. I grew up on Mr. Livingston's manor below Albany, but people prefer talking to an Englishman rather than a German. You've been introduced to Geyser Landtmann?" pulling the servant toward him. "Geyser's no servant either, but his pose as one insures him entry into a variety of groups. Holding a higher station in life is not the safest of behaviors, as I hope I convinced you earlier."

Geyser nodded and smiled, but said nothing.

"I understand you wish to speak to the Provincial Assembly, or what is more correctly the Committee of One Hundred. True?" Ethan nodded. "We'll have you on the agenda tomorrow. Please, sit down."

"Thank you," said Ethan. "Tell us about all these gangs."

"William Cunningham controls those sympathetic to the Tories. He stands to profit from his continuing business with the English trade, so having gangs to keep the Patriot sympathizers in check serves him well."

"I think we were introduced to his daughter," said Pebonkas.

"Ah, yes, a charming lady. Not fully aware of all her father's dealings. But still, not one to trust, if only because she might unwittingly let her father know things he shouldn't know."

"And the Sears' gangs?"

"They're ours. Or more rightly, they're sympathetic toward any side that opposes the English. Sears is like Cunningham, not one to be trusted, prone to violent actions, but on our side at least."

"We Dutch call them 'bosses,'" said Landtmann, speaking for the first time.

"Does Mr. Livingston work closely with Mr. Sears?" I asked.

"No, no, Mr. Livingston would never be seen associating with Boss Sears. He has other go-betweens who deal with Sears. They work together when it seems appropriate, but otherwise each approaches our efforts to free ourselves from England in totally separate ways."

"But at least they trust one another?" asked Seth.

"Not a bit. No, Mr. Livingston knows that, if we're successful in our efforts to free ourselves from English oppression, the next obstacle here in New York will be Sears and other bosses like him. Sears wields a lot of power, control over the mechanics in town, the dock workers, and other laborers. All he needs to do is give the word, and they'll start a fight or close down an area of town with little effort."

"And this Cunningham?"

"Well, he, too, controls his own people, mostly the poor who don't have any work and who don't trust anyone with power or money, such as Mr. Livingston. He's installed a system to provide food and clothing for them when they need it, and in turn they're loyal to him."

Geyser had left the room, returning with some tea and food. He sat down with us and said, "Our success here in New York depends in part upon your success up north, so Mr. Livingston welcomes your addressing the Committee."

"Of One Hundred?" said Pebonkas, sampling the food.

"Well, not all one hundred'll be there tomorrow. We need such a Committee to control Cunningham and Sears, for they have the real power over the people."

"Surely Mr. Livingston has power over the people," Pebonkas said.

"Not really. At least, not direct or immediate power the way the Bosses Sears and Cunningham have. His power's the power of birth and money, the power to influence those who also have money and a good station in life. With money they can find ways to keep the gangs in check."

"By buying off the poor," said Michael, and I could see him beginning to fume.

"If that's what it takes, yes," said Schmidt. "You know that as well as I."

"Damned if I like it. 'Twas the same in Ireland. Damned if I want it to be the same here."

"What matters," said Geyser, "is achieving freedom. The price of freedom is often paid under the table."

"And once we achieve that, then everyone'll profit," said Schmidt.

"The promises of the elite and the manor lords are only to keep the poor in check. After that . . . "

Ethan reached out and touched Michael's knee, "Freedom in the Grants won't be that way, Michael. We're all a free and resolute people, all of us having to pull ourselves up. We'll be a model for the rest of the country."

"It's only a matter of time before the British occupy this city. Our militia outside Boston won't be able to stop them. Then we'll need all the gangs on our side," said Landtmann.

Schmidt leaned toward Michael, looked him in the eye, and said, "When I taunted you down by the docks, you had a chance to smack me, but you didn't, did you? You might even be able to beat me badly, though I doubt it. So, self-control served you well then, and it'll have to serve you for a long time into the future, I fear."

"Wise bastard, aren't you?" said Michael.

"Yes, yes I am, and so are you. So must we all be."

"We shall chagrin the enemy prodigiously," said Ethan, using his multisyllab-ificatory skill to calm the meeting. "They shall be mystified by our ability to materialize out of the atmosphere and dematerialize just as abruptly. Our new friends Geyser and Johannes enchant the streets of New York as only they know best. We astonish our enemies in our own fashion in our own realm. The Cunninghams and Sears of the world may frighten us, but remember, Jack-with-a-lantern gives a frightful appearance to some people, but is after all little more than a pumpkin with a short light. These men have instructed us well in their techniques, and for that we are grateful. Ultimately, all our lives will become rectified."

I left our meeting mystified that the patriots in New York used the terror of gangs to achieve their ends. Michael was probably assured his cynicism regarding those in power had been justified conclusively. But Ethan, it seems, was willing to try anything to secure the right of the Grants to govern themselves. As for Pebonkas, well, he had already declared Americans and English as pretty much the same to him, so I mistrusted his being upset by what he had heard. As for Seth Warner, a good soldier who would do what his leaders asked, I do not know what he thought, but wondered what I would do were I in his position.

That night I wrote in my journal about how we had met certain patriots, but I did not want to include their names in case someone from the Cunningham gang should acquire my journal. I did reflect upon ends and means, though, and wondered about how much power we really wanted to invest our leaders with. Would we really surrender our freedom to be secure? Ashamedly, I wondered whether Tryphena could come up with a biblical quote to address my apprehension.

The next morning, being allowed in to talk to the Provincial Assembly proved another obstacle. When we knocked on the door to enter, we were met by a burly gentleman who described himself as the "sergeant at arms," though he did not wear a uniform. "Hold your water," he said bluntly and shut the door in our faces.

They kept us waiting for one hour. I feared we had stepped into a Yorker trap, waiting while they plotted to spring it. I kept looking down the street in case another gang showed up. We needed an escape route.

I was wrong again.

But had you dropped me into that room unannounced, I would have thought I had been dropped into a gathering of gangs. Wall to wall people. Smoking, chewing, spitting, cursing, joking, punching each other in jest. Eating street food from sausages to cheeses. They sweated in the summer heat. Perfumes worn to cover up the lack of bathing nearly gagged me. Those who wore wigs had slapped them on their heads and hadn't washed them in years. Many simply had their heads shaved.

This was the Committee of One Hundred.

If the Second Continental Congress could not agree upon anything, at least they were polite enough to not speak all at once and to give each person a chance to express his different perspective without being interrupted. Except for Patrick Henry. But everyone knew what he was going to say anyway. The Committee of One Hundred behaved like New Yorkers. They spat on their stove, cold in the summer heat, and a dark stain grew beneath the stove. Just like the theatre-goers Miss Cunningham had described. Happily, they turned out not to be "Yorkers," but, instead, "New" Yorkers. Half a step ahead of Yorkers. Rude Yorkers might be a more accurate term.

Everyone spoke at the same time. They all waived their arms in the air and pointed at each other and gesticulated constantly. No secretary could ever capture what they said or what they proposed and most certainly what they concluded. The benefit of their procedures, of course, is that no enemy could ever capture the minutes and then hang the Committee members for what they said. A Tory judge might accuse them of treason, only to have them respond, in typical New Yorker fashion, "Yeah, prove it!" which of course the judge and prosecutors could not.

So there stood Ethan, in the middle, standing head and shoulders over most of them I noted, trying to start a speech. "Siddown!" yelled the chair, banging his pewter mug on the stove pipe. Only those nearby heard his order, and only half of them had chairs. So as they scrambled to see who could get a seat while seats still remained, those in back continued to yell at each other about whatever they were talking about until they realized those in front were sitting, and so they too scrambled for seats.

"This here's Ethan Allen. Ticonderoga Allen," said the chair. Cheers, whistles, stamping on the floor. "All right, knock it off!" said the chair, whose name I did not catch.

"It gives me great honor to be able to address such outstanding citizens," Ethan said. Cheers. "I come to you as the denominated leader of the Green Mountain Boys." More cheers. "Designing men have imposed on our credulity by obtruding false consequences from our impetus toward freedom." Lots of cheers, although I mistrusted they had the slightest idea what he meant. Even I puzzled over his multisyllabification.

Ethan proclaimed, "The Second Continental Congress stands unified in supporting the capture of Fort Ticonderoga and Crown Point." They cheered. He said, "Canada will rapidly come over to our side if we but ask." They whistled. He said, "My dream is to live in a unified continent, one nation united under one government." They stamped on the floor. He said, "I dream of the day when the people of the Green Mountains may govern themselves." They looked at their neighbors and mumbled. Unfazed, he concluded, "We are proud to be in your magnificent city and proud to have met patriots such as you." Cheers, whistles, and stamping.

When he finished, they voted in favor of all he had said. They did not even debate a word, which, for a New Yorker, must be a prodigious strain. Those nearest him stood and clapped him on the back, shook his hand, offered him puffs on their pipes, and waived to their friends in the back of the room. Then, much to my astonishment, they voted to support the recommendation of the Continental Congress to raise funds to create the regiment Congress had authorized.

We left the Committee meeting feeling elated, but the moment we stepped out in the street, we were greeted by a crowd with sullen stares and sticks in their hands. I asked Michael, "Is this a Cunningham gang or a Sears gang?" for neither Johannes Schmidt nor Geyser Landtmann had given us any kind of code word to use to test which side they were loyal to. Staring in silence, they did not help us any. We huddled together, whispering whether we should make a run for it or retreat back into the Committee room, when Johannes the sailor stepped forward out of the crowd and spoke to us.

"Well, now, what have we here, a bunch of rich lords or just some squarmy toad kissers?"

None of us knew how to respond, but we realized he was trying to help us. "Better to kiss a toad," said Pebonkas, "than to kiss to boots of that German King."

"Well said, you shaking sod eater," said Johannes. Then, turning back to the crowd, he shouted, "Just a bunch of shivering Sons of Liberty, boys, just like us," allowing us to walk past them safely. As we passed, Johannes waived his stick at us and shouted, "Glad to see you've learned your lesson! Now get along, if you know what's good for you." He even shifted his dialect from his educated upper Hudson sound to the New York sound, "Gedalong, 'fya know wass gud f'ya."

He may have been our friend, but I for one was very anxious to leave New York and its mystifying mixture of people whose way to show friendship was to yell at you. Besides, the fourth of July heat rose from the cobbles and bounced off the walls.

We found a boat and boatman to row us back to New Jersey to pick up our muskets, rowing right under the bow of the English ship of war and all its cannons. "Study how it's constructed, men," said Ethan, "for we may need to know some day."

"Built like a tub," said Henry the boatman. "Stinks of rot, stinks of sweat, stinks of piss, stinks of sour food, stinks of the English, just plain stinks."

"How do you know?" I asked.

"Served on one once. Below decks the whole time. Anchored here. Abandoned ship. Been keeping my head low since."

Pulling on the oars stronger than anyone from Pownal ever could, Henry landed us back in Weehawken, just south of King's Bluff, the cliff the boatman called "The Palisades." The Palisades rise about 150 feet above the Hudson River and, Seth observed, would make a good fortress wall to guard New Jersey against an attack from the English. Personally, I thought the best way to defeat an English army would be to put it between any two natives of New Jersey and force them to listen.

Finding the barn where we had hidden our muskets, we identified ourselves to the militiaman smoking a pipe, guarding the place. Barrels of gunpowder lay beneath a thin cover of straw, along with our muskets. The militiaman turned out to be Evan McCard, one of the three who guided us across New Jersey to the Delaware.

"Have you ever been to New York?" I asked Evan.

"No, never go there, too far, too much trouble, too loud, too busy, too big, too many people, too many troublemakers."

"But you took us all the way across New Jersey."

"New Jersey is not New York."

Down near where the Weehawken Creek empties into the Hudson, we found a sloop unloading potash and its captain planning to head back north to Albany. So, we paid our fare and sailed back to Albany, far, happily, far away from New York, the city.

CHAPTER 13

▼

A FEW CONTRARIETIES TO MILITARY RECTITUDE

Betrayed by our own Continental Congress, Ethan and Benedict Arnold both stormed up and down the parade ground of Fort Ticonderoga, one on one side, one on the other. Between them, Colonel Timothy Hinman stood in the middle of the parade ground, holding the orders he had brought with him from Philadelphia, and looking sorely perplexed as to what he should do. Pebonkas, Michael, and I huddled against a far wall, watching shocked as Ethan's plans disintegrated.

"I have been balked by those politicians!" shouted Ethan, who assumed that the Continental Congress's support for his plan to invade Canada was also support for his being the sole commander of Fort Ticonderoga.

"This is an absurd set of instructions," shouted Benedict Arnold, who assumed that he would be recognized as the commander.

"What kind of rectitude is this?" asked Ethan.

"We have everything in order, inventories, stores, and boats," said Arnold.

"This is a contrariety to military rectitude!"

"We have prepared our boats to invade Canada at the least notice, if need be," said Arnold.

"I've a good mind to take these boats to Canada and turn them over to the British," said Ethan.

Arnold yelled, "They assured us this fort would remain in our control, and now they send you to take it out of our hands!"

"It's absurd!" concluded Ethan.

"Absurd!" Arnold agreed.

"Sirs," said poor Colonel Hinman, "This wasn't my idea. I did not ask to be in command of this fort and the territory between here and Canada. I'm merely carrying out the orders of Congress."

"Are you prepared to lead these men to Canada or not?" asked Ethan.

"Well, sir, that's not in my orders."

"And what, explicitly, are their expectations?" asked Benedict Arnold.

"More rightly, how can you explain these political machinations?" asked Ethan.

"My responsibility, gentlemen, is to carry out the orders of the Continental Congress. Those orders say I'm to take charge here." Colonel Hinman had treated Ethan and Benedict Arnold politely at first, but now he held up his orders and pounded them with his finger. He did not smile.

"Blind obedience to a government without forethought or, in your case, even hindthought is an abomination to free thought," said Ethan, smiling.

"I asked you a question, Colonel Hinman," said Benedict Arnold, stepping up to Colonel Hinman and staring him in the face. "What are their expectations?"

"More pertinently, what're their motivations?" asked Ethan, stepping in front of Benedict Arnold.

"Answer my question first," said Benedict Arnold, elbowing Ethan aside, his first chance since the had crashed through the wicket gate when we attacked the fort.

"But my question has a superordinate priority, sir!" said Ethan, pushing aside Benedict Arnold's arm.

"Are you gentlemen truly co-commanders here?" asked Colonel Hinman. "The wisdom of the Congress appears to be self-evident."

"You insult my friend here," said Ethan, throwing an arm across Benedict Arnold's shoulders.

"And my friend also," said Colonel Arnold, looking up into Ethan's eyes.

"Your declaration of friendship touches me to the soul," said Ethan.

"And your recognition of my coequal position of command does my heart good," said Colonel Arnold.

The two commanders shook each other's hand vigorously, grasping the other's shoulder with the opposite hand. Sitting nearby, I saw Ethan bend to whisper in

Colonel Arnold's ear, "Benedict, my friend, I did not exactly go that far." At that, the two turned to walk away from Colonel Hinman.

"Then you agree to my assuming command?" said Colonel Hinman as they turned to walk away.

"Colonel," said Ethan, stopping and turning toward Colonel Hinman, "look around you. What do you see? A pile of rubble. A symbolic exclamation point that smolders on the maps of the English. In a short while, someone will arrive to haul all the cannon to Boston. Then what'll you have? A pile of rubble that's no longer an exclamation point."

Benedict Arnold added, "This fort will always be a symbol of the military genius of the colonies. It, or at least the pile of rocks you see before you, will be a place that our descendants will visit to remind themselves of the beginning of our revolution. They'll think back upon the accomplishment of the brave men you see around us and remember all our sacrifices. That's the gratitude we accept with all humility."

"Benedict, you've learned to speak almost as well as I," said Ethan.

"May God forgive me," said Colonel Arnold.

That evening, Colonel Arnold wrote to the Continental Congress, resigning his command of the fort. Ethan wrote to the leadership of the Grants back in Bennington and in Dorset telling them he was returning to assume command of the Green Mountain Boys there.

Pebonkas, Michael, and I sat together over our evening meal to discuss the turn of events. Most of the Green Mountain Boys had already gone home by now, so there was no point in thinking we would stay simply to be with them. Michael had seen Benedict Arnold ride out with a large number of Massachusetts and Connecticut militia. Timothy Hinman remained with the soldiers who had accompanied him from Philadelphia and a small number of us who had not left.

"Everyone else from Pownal may have gone home, but we are still Green Mountain Boys," I said, "and as such our duty is to follow Ethan."

"That sounds like blind obedience," said Pebonkas.

"Just what I think," said Michael. "The officers do what they want and to hell with the rest of us."

"There's this, though," said Pebonkas. "If we stay here, we have to do what officers want anyway. If we go with Ethan Allen, we know what he's about. And Benedict Arnold will take care of himself no matter what."

"Why did they not leave Ethan in charge here?" I asked. "What is it I do not understand? If it were not for Ethan, the Continental Congress would not have this fort."

"Politics," was Michael's explanation, picking a tick off himself. "Officers and politicians decide what to do with our lives. Then they make brave speeches about our sacrifice and how much our country owes us. Meanwhile, they keep all their money and power. Politics and power. That's all it is. Leaving us with the fleas, ticks, and rats."

I looked to Pebonkas for his argument against Michael's bitterness. He had none.

"Your Ethan Allen is a bit of a puffer, Erastus."

"Without him we would not have captured Ticonderoga, Pebonkas."

"And now what? We've had our momentary glory. Now comes the hard, long slog."

"Well, as for me, I am decided. My loyalty is to the Grants. Ethan's loyalty is to the Grants. So I am with him." I hoped I was right.

"I suppose that decides it, eh, Michael?" Pebonkas said.

"I can die following him or I can die following someone I don't know," said Michael. "Potatoes have choices, too: rot in the ground or be eaten."

And so I became a leader. Well, for one brief shining moment anyway.

Ethan led Seth, Michael, Pebonkas and me out of Fort Ticonderoga and into Hubbarton, where we stopped at the tavern. The tavern owner grinned, his arms open.

"I recognize you," he said to Michael. "You're the rascal who cheated me out of my good rum."

"I may have cheated you out of rum, but it wasn't good rum, my friend. And as I recall, you took my shillings."

"Probably counterfeit," the tavern owner said, "but I've passed them to the next thief."

"Whose side are you on?" asked Seth.

"Whoever has the shillings, my friend," said the tavern owner.

"And if we were English with shillings, you would be on our side?" said Michael.

"Why be in business if you don't do business?"

"But if I tell you that we are Green Mountain Boys?"

"Then I am on your side."

I was momentarily puzzled by the tavern owner's preference for making money over being patriotic, but then I remembered the ferryman Jan Rough, whose only reason for supporting us was to assure his ability to make money. Why fight for freedom when the end result would be people who were free to choose money over country?

It dawned on me: Ethan was now vexed more with raising money than with leading soldiers. It was my first lesson in the economics of patriotism. If we could not afford muskets and powder, then we could not afford to fight for what we believed in. I know now that such economic thinking seems perfectly natural, but in those days I was severely troubled by what seemed to me to be false priorities. Money first. Then patriotism. Now, looking back on all those years, I say, if you want to study the history of the American Revolution, you will need to study the history of money, how it was raised, how it was used, and how it commanded the attention of politicians and generals more than lofty ideas. Enjoy my lecture for the moment. You may see it as an intrusion, but it intruded sorely upon my brain in those days, so suffer along with me.

Which brings me—and us—to Dorset, where the leadership of Vermont was meeting. "You can rely on the leaders of Vermont." said Ethan. "My old friends know how critical our work has been to the future of Vermont. It'll be good to be back among friends. They'll support us with all their heart." His enthusiasm had returned.

Towns from Hubbarton to Dorset continued much as when we marched from Bennington to Fort Ticonderoga. People either welcomed us with open arms or closed their doors in our faces. No matter how I looked at it, and I think I looked with more understanding now than before, we were a deeply divided people, and I wondered how we would ever come back together once this was all over. If this strikes you as overly morbid or cynical, so be it. I hope our country is nevermore so divided.

The people in the town of Dorset all welcomed us openly, perhaps because the entire leadership of the western side of the Grants had come to town to convene as a government. Or perhaps because only Green Mountain Boys paraded the streets with their muskets. Still, I liked believing everyone agreed with us.

Dorset has a long oval green in the middle, overall quite pretty. A large inn sits at one end of the green on the side, a store sits across the green from it, and large white houses take up all the other spaces. By contrast, Pownal Centre seemed homely, but Pownal Centre was my home notwithstanding.

Compared to the Continental Congress in Philadelphia and the New York Provincial Assembly, dealing with the leadership of the Grants, our Committee of Safety, should be a simple matter, I thought. They would reaffirm Ethan as leader of the Green Mountain Boys and send out a call for men to join him in his plan to bring Canada on to our side.

I was, of course, again, wrong.

The room in Mr. Cephas Kent's home where the leadership met was too small to allow anyone but Seth and Ethan in, so Michael, Pebonkas, and I had to sit outside, waiting for Ethan to come out and confirm the good news. I imagined him walking out, a giant among men, supporters clapping him on the back and eager to be near him.

What seemed like hours passed before he finally emerged. By himself. His face had a haggard, unusual look to it. Only Seth followed. Only Ethan spoke. "I am beside myself with dismay! These old men have decided not to accept me as the leader of the Green Mountain Boys. Can you imagine?" He stomped up and down the porch before us, waiving his hat in the air and muttering to himself. Pebonkas, Michael and I held to our seats in silence. "Seth! They chose you, Seth!" I wished I had not been there. I wished I could disappear.

Seth Warner stood to the side, his eyes downcast. "How can you accept their appointment, Seth?" said Ethan. "I thought you were my friend."

"What would you have me do, Ethan?" said Seth. "I didn't come here looking to be the leader of the Boys." I looked at Pebonkas and Michael. They had chosen Seth over Ethan!

"Ethan," said Seth, "you frighten them. You heard them. They're afraid you'd attack the entire English army in Canada if they put you in charge. They're proud you took Fort Ticonderoga, but they're afraid the next time might be a disaster."

"You can turn them down," said Ethan.

"And then who'd lead the Boys? You proposed Remember and Peleg and Robert and Gideon as officers, and they turned them all down. If I'd turned them down, they'd've picked someone you'll truly regret."

"If this be retribution, it be ill-conceived," said Ethan, "for I am the one who saved them from the encroachments of New York."

"True," said Seth.

"And I'm the one who led the capture of Ticonderoga. And I'm the one who convinced the Congress to support our efforts. And I'm the one who convinced the New York Provincial Assembly to support us."

"True, true, and true."

"Perhaps I should return to Bennington and raise my own militia. I could lead them anywhere," said Ethan.

"That's what they're afraid of." Seth put his hand on Ethan's arm.

"Perhaps I should go to Connecticut and join forces with Benedict."

"You cannot abide him."

"Perhaps I should ride to Boston and help drive the English out. John Adams was very supportive, you remember."

"But then you'd have to contend with Sam Adams, and he's just like you," said Seth, smiling.

"Then, perhaps I should return to Philadelphia and convince Congress to raise a force so I could head west and drive the English out of Pennsylvania."

"Ethan," said Seth, moving in front of Ethan to face him, "you believe they'll stand behind their pledge this time?"

"Then perhaps I should return to New York City and remind the Provincial Assembly of their pledge to raise funds for a force to invade Canada."

"Yes, that's true. I'm sure they love the unfunded mandates Congress shoves down their throats," observed Seth, pausing. The rest of us clamped our mouths shut.

"Well," said Ethan, straightening his back and grinning, "I am satisfied with their democratic decision."

Seth looked surprised.

"You are, after all, just the right person to follow their orders," said Ethan.

Seth, though his jaws clenched and eyes narrowed, said nothing. He sat in a chair, crossed his legs, and looked away toward nothing in particular.

"And I am, after all, Ethan Allen. Think of it, gentlemen," he said, turning to us, "Ethan Allen a free agent, free to go where he will. The English will shake in trepidation, not knowing where I'll strike next." Michael, Pebonkas, and I nodded silently. Seth looked at us and winked. The Dorset leaders did not know what they had unleashed.

Ethan grabbed my arm and took me aside for a private conversation. "Erastus, I have charged you with being the recorder of our history. You are still at it, are you not?"

"Yes, sir."

"Then do not hesitate to record this moment, for we must let our descendants know what truly happened in our quest for freedom."

"Do you want me to write of how the political leaders at Dorset turned you down?"

"I would have it no other way, Erastus, for leaders everywhere have had to overcome adversity and are, on occasion, not recognized for their accomplishments. My life shall not be that of a tragic hero, but of one who placed his country first. Please note that."

"Yes, sir."

"Yes, yes, well, Seth can lead the Green Mountain Boys, but we . . . " He paused, while we waited, and then pulled Pebonkas, Michael, and me over to him. Softly, he said, "Boys, we all need a respite from the turmoil of our struggle. I suggest we all take a few days off, return to our families if we have them, and be prepared to resume our quest in the near future. Canada still beckons."

"Easily said," said Michael. "We've not been paid, and my family's too far to visit."

"You're absolutely right, Michael, and paid you shall be. Seth!" Ethan looked down at Seth, who continued staring away at nothing. "Seth, see that these men are paid for their time with us. We're all going to rest for a while and regroup in the near future." Seth raised an eyebrow. "Our Committee of Safety, right behind those doors, Seth, they have the responsibility for raising the funds to support our efforts. You're in charge, Seth, so I leave all to you."

The task assigned, Ethan turned and strode toward the livery behind the inn. Seth shook his head and looked at us. "Look, my house is down the road. You can all stay with me until we sort all this out."

"My family is but a few miles beyond," I said, "so I think I will return to them."

"Good, Erastus, they're probably worried about you, as my wife must be for me. Pebonkas, Michael, what do you say, will you accept my meager hospitality?"

Pebonkas and Michael readily agreed, and all of us then borrowed some horses from the militia guarding the Committee of Safety, with Seth promising to return them tomorrow. On the way south to Seth's home, we encountered a wagon headed toward Bennington, so I changed from the horse to the wagon, road into Bennington, and then walked to our farm up on Carpenter Hill.

It was nighttime by the time I arrived. My sisters, brother Eleazar, and Hiram were all in bed, but my mother was still up, sewing a few things. She grabbed me and hugged me and kissed me and called to the others to come greet me. And then she said, "It is about time you returned here, for we were worried to death about your safety, and what with the other Pownal men returning from that dreadful fort I feared I had lost you, and you know I could not live if you were not to return, so where in the world have you been, and why didn't you write, and where was your consideration for your poor mother, sisters and brother?" My sisters Tryphena and Tryphosa both greeted me, smiles on their faces, hugging me together. They looked very healthy, tan from working out in the fields I assumed, and very strong. My brother Eleazar looked a bit peaked. Hiram finally staggered down in his nightshirt, saying, "Oh, Erastus, it's you. Has your mother told you it's about time? I tried to defend you, but, well, you know."

The next two hours we talked about my adventures. I read some of my journal aloud, but did not read anything that might displease my mother. Tryphena and Tryphosa asked all sorts of questions. I was amazed at their insight and ability to ask just the right things. When I described our decision not to capture St. John, leaving out the surprise attack by the British, they asked, "Is that all? You haven't left out anything?" I wondered why they asked, but figured they were just being difficult. Hiram just grinned.

"Since he returned, the Reverend Dewey has used a great many of the events in his sermons," my mother said. "He's spoken of the depravity of war and how some men lose their sense of direction when they're far from the comforts of families and church."

"We feared you might have fallen away, brother," said Tryphosa.

"Ignorance of Scripture is ignorance of Christ," said Tryphena. "Have you kept up with the Scriptures?"

"If I left my bucket back home and was dying of thirst, would I die?" I said.

"I'm not sure what you mean, Erastus, but it sounds blasphemous to me. Have you become a blasphemer?"

"I am going to bed," I told Tryphena. "Here I have risked my life for freedom, and you accuse me of doing things I have not had time to do. But I shall tell you this: if I have another chance, I will."

Tryphena picked up my pack and started upstairs. "Well, just so you know, Mr. Green Mountain Boy, all the beds in this house are taken, but we'll make a place for you on the floor, because we forgive you."

I began to wish I had drunk all the rum I had shunned and had learned to curse and swear like the other Green Mountain Boys. I struggled to find something to set them back on their holy seats. So I rebutted them with religion lesson Ethan taught us in New York. "And by the way, you two holier-than-thou cows, what do you know about natural reason, the only salvation of Man?" There, I had them.

"Erastus," my mother said, "they're just funning you. No need to make up blasphemous thoughts to shock them. Now, you two girls go upstairs and find a bed for Erastus. Give him Hiram's. You don't mind, do you, dear Hiram?"

So I did not run away. Instead, I unloaded on my journal. "It would serve them right! They will be sorry when I am gone."

Michael once told me the difference between a Protestant and a Catholic: "Priests versus printers, Erastus. We Irish Catholics depend upon our priests to give us the Word. Priests and a fat serving of ritual. Besides, few of us could read even if we could afford a Bible. You Protestants have to put everything in your

Bibles, building them into gigantic books too heavy to carry. Explains why your ministers need such big pulpits." Well, I decided then and there that my two sisters, like our Bible, were way too heavy to carry and would probably waste away as Bible-quoting spinsters. Serve them right.

The next day, Sunday morning, Tryphena and Tryphosa walked me around our farm. It looked wonderful. The wheat grew firmly. The corn reached my waist. The pigs had grown fat. My sisters had worked very hard while I marched with Ethan, and I felt bad for all the unkind thoughts I had written in my journal. I may not have possessed a Godly amount of scripture, but I certainly possessed a goodly amount of guilt.

From working the farm, the twins' arms seemed even more muscular, their skin a deep tan, and they seemed to have boundless energy.

Then we went to church, where Deuteronomy began, as always, with a Biblical quote and finished us off with a batch of admonitions.

Afterward, as families gathered outside, they spoke of anything but the war, of how their crops grew, of repairs they needed to make on their homes, of what a nice day it was. Soldiers were off fighting for them, and they spoke of ordinary matters!

Hiram collected around him young boys and girls. They listened, rapt, to his story of a Ticonderoga victory unlike any I had experienced.

"We Green Mountain Boys marched into our boats in the dead of night, took up our oars, and rowed silently toward the looming guns of Fort Ticonderoga . . . .

"Silently and stealthily we crawled toward the wicket gate, and then, with perfect military precision we rose as one and charged! Ethan Allen led the way. The guards fired on us, but the Lord protected us. Ethan rushed to the left, smote a guard, and rushed to the right, smiting more guards. The British came tumbling out of their barracks, fear on their faces, throwing down their weapons . . . .

"The British commander fell to his knees and begged for his life . . . .

"'In the name of the Great Jehovah and the Continental Congress!' he proclaimed, holding his sword aloft . . . .

"As the sun rose, it rose upon a conquered fortress and a free nation, and we Green Mountain Boys stood, our eyes toward the rising sun, firm, resolute, a military to strike fear in the hearts of all who oppose us."

Ethan had gotten it right: history belongs to those who tell it. Or, as I now began to realize, those who believe the stories of those who tell it.

CHAPTER 14

▼

FREE ENTERPRISE AND FREE CHOICE

My interlude from reality ended when Pebonkas and Michael rode up to tell me Ethan wanted us to join him in Albany. My mother did not think kindly of the notion. "So," she said, "you cannot stay home but must go off with a bunch of Indians and Irish. I don't know which is worse, pagans or heathens."

I unleashed my multisyllabifications upon them. "I do not intend to exacerbate your trepidation and apprehension . . . "

"Oh, do speak English, Erastus, really. Now, would your friends like some food? Shall I pack a meal for you? Come, boys, sit down. You look starved."

I do not understand mothers, especially mine. Chastise you first and then comfort you. Forbid you to do something and then help you on your way. Tryphena and Tryphosa smiled and spoke gently around Michael and Pebonkas, an amazing transformation from their usual scolding natures.

We had only two horses, but I was glad to share a horse just to be free of my sisters. Our route took us down into North Pownal and along the Hoosic River, past the Rensselaerwyck farms. A couple homes owned by Tory sympathizers stood abandoned.

"Ethan sent orders to us at Seth's house," said Pebonkas. "Told us to join him at a Mr. Schuyler's home. Your friend Ethan has a notion to raise up another army, even though Seth's been given charge of the Green Mountain Boys."

"Well," I replied, "there does not need to be only one group of Green Mountain Boys, does there?"

Michael stretched in the saddle and scratched. "Sure and we'll be the Green Mountain Fleas, for we damned well have enough of them."

At a cluster of houses called Hoosack a wagon met us with three other Green Mountain Boys—Epheram Blackmon, Azriel Blanchard, and Jack something or other. Jack took the two horses to take back to Bennington. Later we slept at old man Holmes' place, a farmer we trusted, and the next day we rode into Albany.

"So tell me why you're so itching to do this," Michael said, still scratching.

"We are Green Mountain Boys," I answered.

"I seem to see only five of us," said Michael. "Count us: one, two, three, four, and five. We seem to be missing a few."

"Four," said Azriel. "I'm just your royal coachman and have to take this wagon back. Besides, Seth Warner needs me and the others."

"More will join us, you will see," I said. "I bet Ethan has already gathered a militia in Albany. Anyway, my sisters tell me I have to have faith, and I do, in Ethan."

"Hiram's exaggerations and your faith are nothing next to these damned fleas," Michael said, reaching down his shirt. "Except perhaps Ethan Allen's fantasies."

"Not fantasy, Michael. Vision."

"Fleas. Fantasies. 'Tis much the same. Their bite leaves an itch. Me, I've a vision of banshees," Michael concluded.

Across from Albany, Azriel dropped us off so he could return to Bennington, Seth Warner, and those who were now Seth's Green Mountain Boys. We found a ferry owned by a Jan Rough and paid our way across.

"Fighters for freedom?" said Jan Rough, a barrel-chested man with a hat too small for his head. He raised the small sail and pushed off the bank with a long pole.

"Yes, sir," I replied, proud.

"Well, freedom is what it's all about, ain't it, boys? Take me. I can't wait to be free of English rules and regulations. Free enterprise! Yes, sir, when we're free of the King's regulations and taxes, we'll be rich. That's what freedom's all about, the freedom to become rich on your own terms."

"Think so?" I asked.

"Think so? I know so, boy. Those who can't make money when they're free are free to be slaves and work for those of us who can. It's a dog-eat-dog world, and I intend to be one of the top dogs."

"A politician?" asked Michael.

"What! And feed at the public trough? No, no, not me, boys. I will be the one who tells the politicians what to do. It's all about money, see? You make a lot of money, and politicians come flocking to your door, bowing their heads, smiling at your stupid jokes, and doing what you want them to do. No, sir. Now you just go out there and beat those English enemies of free enterprise, and I'll sing your praises all the way to my mansion."

"Will slaves be free in your world?" asked Pebonkas. I was ashamed that he had thought of Solomon and Samuel, while I had not.

"They'll be free to buy themselves out of slavery just like some low Irishman's free to buy himself out of his indenture."

"And that'll take years, if ever," said Michael.

"So be it. The world's not equal for all people, my friend. Some have the skill to rise up in the world . . . "

"And birth," said Michael.

"And luck," said Pebonkas.

"Well, that's what freedom's all about. Them as can't make money remain slaves, stay indentured forever, not able to buy their education, and make the mistake of staying to support their poor families when they could go out in the world and make it on their own. Freedom means making choices, ain't that right? Some of us choose to be poor. Some choose to be rich. We're all equal to choose. At least when I'm free I can choose whatever path I want. Tell me I'm wrong. No, don't tell me. I know I'm right. Now, you boys take a look at some of the people in Albany. Some are poor, so poor they don't even have jobs, don't even know what to do with themselves. Well, once they're free, my guess is they'll be the same way. But that's their choice, right?"

"You know what I'm thinking?" said Michael. "I'm thinking . . . " Pebonkas put his hand on Michael's arm.

"Look at the choice you made," said Mr. Rough, "choosing to become militia, to fight for freedom. You're my heroes, and I intend to support you all the way. And you know something?" said Mr. Rough, pausing for a breath. "Without the support of those of us who are successful, you're not going to win. I know that. You know that. And I need you to win."

I had made the choice to leave my family back in Pownal, leave my mother to manage without me, leave my sisters and sick brother on their own. Was I fighting for Mr. Rough's freedom?

"Everyone free!" said Mr. Rough, taking off his hat and waving it in a circle. "Just think of it! It's a dream for the ages!"

I turned away from Mr. Rough, trying not to think of the Rough definition of freedom. Albany filled my senses. The riverfront where we landed smelled something awful. Breweries, slaughterhouses, butchers, taverns, all dumped their garbage into the river here. Sloops of all sizes had taken all the space at the docks, so we could not land there. Instead, Mr. Rough landed us on a mudflat since the river was low at the time, and we had to walk through all manner of slop, broken pottery, and rotting boards to gain a firm footing on land.

"Watch your step, boys!" yelled Mr. Rough. "Don't get stuck before you get my freedom for me!" I hoped my shoes would dry so the gunk would fall off before we reached Ethan. Well-dressed businessmen and their ladies kept a wide distance when they smelled us.

Since we were not carrying muskets or bayonets and since we looked like ordinary people—from the Grants, that is—we could pass unnoticed into the town, unnoticed except for the way the mud smelled on our shoes. The truth is, people tried their best not to notice us. A passing merchant told us just to follow the river south until we saw a large house on a hill. That would be Schuyler's place. We could not miss it, a large mansion that dominated the high ground over the city. "Another Lord Stirling, I'm betting," Michael remarked.

"Isn't Schuyler a Yorker?" Pebonkas asked.

"They have seen the light," I said.

"The only light they see's the glint of money," said Michael.

"He's Dutch. You better watch out, Erastus." Pebonkas asked.

"The Dutch we met in New Jersey were good folks," I said.

"Trintje was very nice, right Erastus?" said Michael, grinning and poking me in the ribs. I ignored his comment.

We climbed up to the house through a beautiful garden and orchard and knocked on the kitchen door, where a servant escorted us into the house. He asked us to leave our shoes at the door and ushered us into a room where a very beautiful young woman stood. "Mistress Elizabeth Schuyler," he announced.

"Looking good, these Dutch, eh?" Michael whispered, poking me in the ribs again.

"Colonel Allen told us you would be joining him. Please, follow me," she said.

Pebonkas whispered to me, "There's this about being one of your Indians—we don't blush like you."

The hallway ceilings rose high way above our heads. Doors closed the side rooms off, maintaining a comfortable temperature. I figured some rooms were used only for frolics or other public events. At the end of the hallway, Elizabeth Schuyler opened a door and pointed us in. Ethan and Mr. Schuyler sat on couches in what appeared to be the library. Mr. Schuyler stretched his leg out on a stool and said to us, "Please excuse my not rising, for I seem to be afflicted by the gout, I fear. But do take a seat." Books surrounded us. I had never seen so many books.

Ethan introduced us. "Boys, allow me to introduce you to General Schuyler, who recently was given a command second only to George Washington." General Schuyler's piercing eyes gazed at us over his long nose. I do not know what he must have thought of us standing there in our stocking feet. I also had not known whether George Washington was very high in rank or not, but now he was a general.

"George Washington has assumed command in Boston over all colonial troops," said General Schuyler, "where they continue to have the British bottled up." Knowing what I had seen of George Washington, I knew he was no Ethan Allen and no Benedict Arnold, so I feared for our ability to defeat the English army.

Ethan introduced us to another man in the room, General Montgomery. Now I stood next to two generals!

"General Schuyler, General Montgomery, you see before you the magnificent specimens that predominate among the Green Mountain Boys." Ethan meant us! "These are the soldiers whose heartiness and willfulness will overcome all adversity. They stand as evidence of our ability to advance our cause victoriously. Boys, General Schuyler has approved our mounting a force to capture Canada."

"A winter campaign!" said General Montgomery, "Insanity! Preposterous! Posterity will never believe it!"

"General Montgomery has his doubts," said General Schuyler. "But your Ethan Allen has convinced me the Canadians will flock to our cause."

"Should we but ask them," said Ethan.

"You understand, Ethan, that we really do not have enough soldiers to mount a full campaign, so I'm relying upon your ability to recruit." Then, turning to us, he explained, "General Montgomery will be in charge of the campaign and will bring you Green Mountain Boys together with the New York militia."

"The sweeping of the New York streets!" added General Montgomery.

"We hear the British are putting together a fleet of boats at St. John," said General Schuyler. "It will hurt us severely if they should command Lake Champlain. So we have little choice but to stop them."

"We're quite familiar with St. John," said Ethan, but he did not talk about how our familiarity almost cost us our lives. I began to gain an insight into Ethan's use of rhetoric to shape the future.

General Schuyler then called his daughter Elizabeth, who had been outside the door, and asked her to take us to the kitchen to eat, while he, General Montgomery, and Ethan remained in the library to continue planning their campaign. The kitchen, we soon learned, was a building by itself outside the mansion and very hot. But the cook served us a fine meal that we ate on a bench outside the door, the last decent food we would have for many days.

"Now I know why the General suffers from gout," said Pebonkas, stuffing some rolls in his pack.

"Give me gout food all the rest of my life," said Michael, "and I'll die happy."

As we were putting our shoes back on, Ethan ordered us back to Bennington to gather up as many men as we could and to meet him in a few weeks at the lower tip of Lake Champlain. General Schuyler's head servant gave us some money to pay for the ferry back across the Hudson. We hired Mr. Rough again. "This one's on me, gentlemen. An investment in my future."

"The bastard bought us just like he buys everyone else," said Michael after Mr. Rough landed us and turned back. "And we let him."

Since we had no horses and since Azriel had taken the wagon back with him, we were looking at a long walk home. We snagged a ride on a butter wagon heading back to Bennington. Happily, the farmer driving it had no opinions about freedom.

We divided up to recruit more men for Ethan's new militia. Michael traveled north to Arlington, Pebonkas rode beyond him to the Dorset and Poultney areas, and I took Bennington and Pownal. We sent Epheram over the mountain to the east. We agreed to meet at the Lake within two weeks. None of us had considered the impact of Seth Warner having been appointed head of the Green Mountain Boys when we left Dorset, but we soon learned. Seth had enlisted every Boy worth his salt. The rest gave every excuse imaginable. Benedict Arnold had it right: some believe the fight for freedom allows them any liberty they choose.

"Sorry, Erastus. My crops are about to come in, and my wife's about to deliver." Well, that excuse sounded reasonable.

"My bones're aching something fierce. The doctor don't know how long I got." We did not have a doctor in Pownal, unless he was seeing a mid-wife.

"I signed on to take Ticonderoga. We took it. That's enough for me." Some people's stomachs fill up faster than others, evidently.

"'Love is the only force capable of transforming an enemy into friend' sayeth the Bible." The Good Book will be this sniveler's salvation. I thought to have Tryphena check the Bible to see whether this really is there.

"I'll not allow my husband to associate with such people." A coward's wife serves many purposes.

"Someone has to stay here and keep an eye on our Tories." This particular person, I observed, had his eye on his Tory neighbor's daughter.

"The wolves are threatening our sheep, the catamounts are decimating our cows, and the raccoons are wreaking havoc with our corn." I give this an outstanding grade for creativity. Our neighbors had shot every wolf and catamount that dared set foot in Pownal, but the raccoons were indeed too smart for them.

After two solid days of rejection, I turned to Deuteronomy Dewey, and on Sunday he delivered a blistering sermon designed to shame those who would not take up arms against the enemy. He shamed them all right. They slunk so fast out of church we could not hear their excuses. No enlistments there.

My mother said, "Perhaps it's a sign you're not meant for this fighting, Erastus." In the name of love, mothers have a way of making sons feel totally useless.

Tryphena asked, "Is Mr. McGinnis coming back?"

Tryphosa said, "Mr. Peter Keyes is a handsome man, don't you think?" At least they did not throw the Bible at me, but I began to fear for my friends.

During the next week I traveled to Bennington and Walloomscoick and Hoosack, stopping at every farm along the way. I encountered barnyard lawyers enough to clog the courts with their arguments. Notwithstanding, I recruited one of my school friends, Hanry Turner, and four others whose mothers may never speak to my mother ever again.

Michael, Pebonkas, and I rendezvoused at the appointed place. I felt better seeing they had as much success as I. That is, they, too, had failed to recruit many for the thrust into Canada. Epheram returned a few days later with one person.

Ethan reassured us. "Do not despair, for with the fortitude of a few, we shall emerge triumphant. The Quebecois and Kahnawakes shall flock to our banner, and we will be a multitudinous horde when we confront our adversary."

Then we met the Yorkers who had been recruited for the trip. General Montgomery was right. If the New York recruiters had just swept the streets to recruit them, it would have been bad enough, but they must have cleaned out the gutters to find this bunch. Half were sickly city dwellers whose shoes had never seen a barnyard, mountain, or river before now. The other half were toughs who must have agreed to enlist as a condition for being released from prison. I was sure I recognized some who fought in the Sears and Cunningham gangs.

While we sat in camp waiting for the order to move north, we understandably insulted the Yorkers. I listed a number in my journal so I could find out what they meant sometime. In return, the Yorkers threw rocks, sticks, mud, iron pans, anything in reach at us. Ethan and General Montgomery agreed to quarter us far apart from each other, which suited me just fine.

General Schuyler? His gout must have overcome his patriotic ardor, for his doctor would not allow him to take the journey.

CHAPTER 15

▼

WE INVADE CANADA THE SECOND TIME

The Yorkers moaned and groaned so, but not Ethan's Green Mountain Boys, as he still called us. We were stoic, except for Michael, who complained about his fleas, complained about the rain, complained about the sun, complained about packing the boats, and complained about having to be around such complainers as the Yorkers. All in all, quite normal for him. Yes, it had rained all night, and yes, it was still raining, and yes, we all shivered and sneezed, but the lot of a soldier is misery, as I have learned.

General Montgomery ordered us all into the bateaux and boats he had collected from near Fort Ticonderoga and all around Lake George. Then he started us rowing down Lake Champlain. By now I had learned the difference between down and up on that lake, even if it made little sense. I estimate about fifty boats and over one thousand men griped and cursed our way, most of us Yorkers, unfortunately, and few of us the Boys from the Green Mountains.

My bateau consisted mostly of those of us who had rowed down and up the lake with Ethan and Colonel Arnold before, so we knew how to pull an oar. Someone (it had to be Michael) suggested we pull away from those sorry "land lubbers." Yes, those are the words he used. So we made a race of it even though they hardly knew they were in a race. We pulled and pulled and soon were well ahead of the rest. Equally soon my rowing blisters returned, so I was not too happy about our unrecognized victory.

One could distinguish the Yorker boats from the Green Mountain boats by the quantity of blasphemations emanating from them. Those from the city of New York employed a collection that I had never heard before in the Green Mountains. Those I could understand were quite creative. Those I could not understand piqued my curiosity. I asked Michael to explain one of them, and when he did, I am sure I blushed at the answer. If Deuteronomy Dewey had sat in our boat, he would have had great fodder for future sermons.

A strange feeling drew my attention to the Yorker boat near us. There grinning at me was Hunt Hungerford, the man who had shot at Benedict Arnold. He stared at me and grinned, a large, almost toothless grin. Near him slumped the men who had followed him out of Fort Ticonderoga. They sneered as well. I looked away.

In a short while we had pulled away from the Yorker boats, and in no time, the boats all spread out across the Lake in one long line. General Montgomery sailed up in his sloop and ordered us to stop until the others caught up. "If the British catch us like this, we'll all be dead in the water."

"It looks like all you Yorkers are dead in the water anyway," said Michael. General Montgomery, to his credit, said nothing, or perhaps he did not hear Michael's comment.

By the time the last boat reached us, I could see why they were last. Their boat leaked badly, and they were bailing water with hats, shoes, and anything that held water. An officer in one of the Yorker boats told them to pull to shore and leave the boat, just in time. Such a sorry bunch I had not seen, and I felt bad for them, even if they were Yorkers. Well, we were in the same army, you see. But none of the Green Mountain boaters offered to share space with the Yorkers.

When the sun began to set, General Montgomery had us pull in and set up camp. My journal reflects our mocking crowd. I wrote how, in their military ignorance, Yorkers put their muskets on the bottoms of their boats and packed everything else on top. In truth, we had once done the same, but, also in truth, these were still Yorkers, we were still the Boys of the Green Mountains, and this was still a Green Mountain fight. One must keep to one's principles.

That night I dreamed Hunt Hungerford was roasting me in a fireplace.

The next day went much like the first. Somewhat tired, we all stayed together. We made very little progress. The next day, we made even less progress. Michael muttered about "how I did not sign on to be a sailor," and claimed we could walk up the lake faster than we were rowing. By now, everyone slumped on the oars, so the Yorkers did not share creative curses with us, and we did not insult them as befitted those who lived on the wrong side of the Hudson.

Given our slow progress, we soon ran out of whatever food we each brought and had to eat the salted shad General Montgomery provided us. Michael praised it. "Salted sawdust, 'tis what it is, but it fills the gut."

Having tasted the shad, the next night Pebonkas gathered up a bunch of Yorkers and Green Mountain Boys and taught us how to fish the lake. He converted some of the shad bones into fishing hooks. For string he stripped one of the bags used to carry the shad. I learned something about fishing. I do not know what we ate later, but it was delicious. Yorkers ate with us, and we spat out only bones instead of insults. Pebonkas observed how hunger makes for strange brotherhoods. As for me, I hoped folks in Pownal would not learn I had eaten with Yorkers.

Much later that night, after we turned in to sleep, sentinels down the line from us began shouting, and someone far away shouted back. "Lobsterbacks!" yelled one of the Yorkers. In no time at all, we all rose to our feet with our muskets loaded and hammers cocked, waiting for our first chance to engage the enemy. Nothing happened.

"A sad state of affairs," said Michael. "I'm thinking I'll never get me back to sleep now." My heart was still beating wildly, and I wondered if I could sleep, too. Just in case, I lay down with my musket close to me.

"You might want to uncock that thing," said Pebonkas.

"I would have," I replied, "but I wanted to be prepared for any possible attack."

"Thereby saving your enemy the trouble of shooting you," he said."

"Ah, poor Erastus, a bit on the distracted side," said Michael, "having to leave those two fine Dutch caileens, Elizabeth and Trintje. He probably thinks to shoot himself."

"You should talk," I said. "Is a caileen another word for banshee?"

"'Tis Irish for girl," he said. "Now please to point your weapon away from me."

The next day we learned why the sentinels had alerted us that night. Remember Baker's militia had gone north before we set out with the Yorkers. Survivors were straggling back. Baker's group had been attacked by Indians, and Remember had been killed. Rumor spread that they had cut off Remember's head and were taking it back to the British to sell. We were considerably sobered.

We reached Ile aux Noix on September 4th. (I learned some French on my two invasions of Canada, and I can teach you to pronounce the Island's name "Eel oh

Nwah." I cannot explain why the French do not spell French in English as we do.) No sooner did I lay down to rest than Ethan roused our boat crew. "Arise, for we have been awarded a special assignment. Destiny obliges us to ride the torrents of adversity and promulgate the word of freedom throughout the Canadian hinterlands. Our brothers to the north have been subjugated to a state of absolute dependence upon a corrupt monarch, to the great detriment of truth, justice, and morality in the world. So we go forth to enlist them in a mutual accord."

Michael raised his hand to ask a translation, but before he could, Ethan interpreted himself, "We have to recruit troops from the Canadians, Michael."

To Pebonkas he said, "I will need your special interpretive skills among the Kahnawakes and other relatives. I've already found a ready interpreter for the Quebecois we seek to recruit." He turned and called to a gentleman with fine aquiline features, whom Ethan introduced as Christian Doline, "as honest and true a Quebecois as anyone I have met."

We set off, following Ethan into Canada. We did not have to go far before we came to the first small village, St. Valentin. The few inhabitants we met looked at us with great fear and disappeared quickly into their homes. I wondered how I would react if armed strangers had walked into Pownal Centre. Ethan did not hesitate one moment, but strode right into the Catholic church where he soon reappeared leading a small French priest. The priest was followed by a young man almost my age who looked very scared. Ethan said something to the priest, and the priest said something to the young man, who disappeared back into the church.

Soon the church bells began to ring, and as they rang the people slowly emerged from their homes and gathered in the square before the priest. Once a crowd had gathered, the priest yelled back into the door of the church, and the bells stopped ringing. Then he said something in French to the people and looked at Ethan. Ethan called for Christian Doline to interpret while he spoke.

What follows is the best that I could reconstruct of what Ethan said that day, for I was writing rapidly in my journal, jotting down phrases as he spoke, so I may have some of this wrong, but the essence is true.

"Fellow lovers of freedom, my wonderful people of St. Valentin," said Ethan. Christian translated, "Camarade de la liberté, mes personnes merveilleuses de St. Valentin," and some of the people stopped frowning. My French quote is accurate because Christian wrote it in my journal for me that night.

Ethan continued, "I come before you to urge your confederation with your Yankee cousins to the south in our attempts to throw off the yoke of servitude to which we have been subjected." Christian translated and some people nodded.

"We know that you excel in liberality and bravery and that, side by side, we shall behave with fortitude becoming of our hearts. For years, we have expostulated upon the unreasonableness of the British usage of our lives . . . " Christian looked puzzled and put his hand on Ethan's arm.

"Expostulated?" said Christian.

"Complained about," said Ethan, and continued. "But the British, being by nature underwitted . . . "

"Underwitted?" said Christian.

"Stupid," said Ethan, and continued again. "The British, by nature stupid, have continued us in this miserable situation. We have endeavored to touch their humanity, but have found that they have none. In addition to the British, we have been abused by perfidious and overgrown Tories and land-jobbers . . . " Christian had the confused look again. "Those who profit by buying your land cheap and selling high," continued Ethan, "whose only purpose is to profit from our misery."

"Isn't that what Ethan and his brothers do?" Michael whispered to me. I glared at him and continued trying to capture Ethan's words.

" . . . de propriété," said Christian, something about property.

"They will not suffer you to imbibe of freedom. So now, I invite you to take up arms, side-by-side with your cousins, we Yankees, to overthrow these despots. I assure you that, upon our victory, you will be supplied not only with the necessaries and conveniences of life, but also with the grandeurs and superfluities of it." Christian looked concerned, but only for a second, and then translated something clearly more succinct than Ethan's words. Later, he told me he had said, "les bonnes substances de la vie," or "life's good stuff."

Ethan continued, "I implore you to join our ranks as fellow fighters for freedom," and then a look of great enlightenment came upon Ethan's features, "as Quebecois Boys!"

Upon hearing the French word "garçons," many in the crowd laughed. Christian immediately used the word "heroes," which even I could understand. Then they applauded.

"Join us," said Ethan, "and we will provide you with muskets, powder, balls, and bayonets!" They cheered. Ethan smiled. The priest gave the sign of the cross.

Afterward, the priest, who introduced himself as Father Pierre Thibault, invited us into his home for a meal. A large room with a long table in the middle seated all of us. He called out his cook and the young man we had seen before, who turned out to be her son. "Let me introduce you to my housekeeper," he said in excellent English, "and her son. Madam Madeleine d'Entremont and her son Philippe. Madeleine has been with our family ever since she was, how do you say in your quaint English, captivated."

"Captivated?" I asked.

"Do you mean to say she was captured?" asked Pebonkas. "And you criticize Indians for keeping slaves."

"No, no," said Father Thibault, "Madeleine is here of her own accord. That she was captured is unfortunately true, but that she is a slave is far from true."

"When the Indians who raided your Fort Massachusetts were returning to Canada," said Madam d'Entremont, "they stopped for a brief moment on their way north to capture me and take me north. I was but a young girl, but was living a hard life with a hard father. They treated me kindly, and when they reached Montreal, they sold me to the French priest there. He took me in his home, where I met a gentle farmer named Philippe d'Entremont, young Philippe's father. He and his family had escaped from Acadie to avoid being imprisoned by the British. Unfortunately, he died of small pox a few years after we married. So, Father Thibault invited me and young Philippe to join him here. He has been wonderful to us."

"But if you were captured," said one sitting next to me, "surely you want to return to your home."

"Why?" asked Madam d'Entremont, smiling. "I am loved here and cared for here. I even became a Catholic, gladly. These are my people, and my heart is here."

"This is my home," said young Philippe, quietly.

"Well," said Ethan, grandly, "you all shall soon be part of the united colonies, and we shall all be in the same country, our home."

"But surely not to remain a Catholic," said one from Dorset sitting next to me.

"What's wrong with that, you puking Orangie!" shot back Michael.

"Who you calling a puking Orangie?" said the Dorseter, standing up.

"I bet you don't even know what a puking Orangie is," said Michael.

Ethan slammed his fist upon the table, "Gentlemen! We are guests in this House of the Lord, whatever we may think of it. Now, father," he said, lowering his voice to its normal boom, "what advice would you give us to recruit soldiers from your village?"

"Mackerel snapper!" said the Dorseter to Michael.

"Orangie!" said Michael.

"Dirty Mick."

"Syrup slurper!"

Ethan grabbed Michael by the arm. "Leave. Both of you. And Pebonkas, you and Epheram go with them and make sure they don't scare the people of this village."

"I will go, too," I said, concerned that Michael would get in more trouble.

"No, Erastus, you stay. Remember, History needs you to create this event. Now, Father, about recruiting soldiers . . . "

At that point, I thought the more interesting history was probably occurring outside, but I stayed to hear Father Thibault say, "The French have been fighting the English for generations, Mr. Allen, so I do not think you need to convince them of the value of continuing the fight. But what will it mean if we win and if we become part of your colonies, or even part of the Green Mountains? I see what your Green Mountain Boys think of each other, and they have come from the same place. Will we simply replace one master with another?"

"Father Thibault," said Ethan, "the issue is not whether we Yankees will become your masters, for that's not our desire. But the real issue revealed by the behavior we just witnessed is whether all these religions will lead us down false paths. For me, I wish good sense, truth, and virtue may be promoted and flourish in the world, to the detection of delusion, superstition, and false religion."

"And if we each believe our religions to be the true ones?" said the Father.

"Natural reason will show us the way," said Ethan. "Of that I have absolute faith."

"Then let us naturally reason how to defeat the British lobsterbacks," said the priest, much to my surprise.

"Father," said Ethan, "you are a man of my cloth. Did you get all that, Erastus?"

So Ethan recruited a priest who in turn recruited a handful of Quebecois soldiers. Ethan asked them to wait patiently while he recruited others, but he would return in a few days or more with weapons and lead them to Montreal and the British.

In such a manner our recruiting trip continued as we traveled to towns apparently all named after Catholic saints: St. Blaise, St. Luc, St. Philippe, St. Et Cetera. At each town Ethan recruited the local priest to help him, at each town he gave a speech to the people, and at each town the speech became shorter and shorter, easier for Christian Doline to translate. By the end he was usually ahead of Ethan in delivering the word to the people.

Eventually, Ethan's speech went something like this: "People of St. Fill-in-the-saint's-name-here, we're Yankees, and we've come to beat the British out of Canada and welcome you into our arms. Are you with us?" Christian's translations seemed only to grow longer as he added his own flourishes.

Then we came to the village of the Kahnawake, where Pebonkas was critical to our success.

As we approached the village, Ethan said to Pebonkas, "I think we can convince these Mohawks to join us, don't you?"

"Sir," said Pebonkas, "if I may, I'd advise you not to call them Mohawks, for that's a name given them by their enemies. Means flesh eaters or man eaters, not a nice term."

"Many call them Maqua," I offered.

"That's an Iroquois word for Mohawk, meaning 'bear,' and less derogatory, though still not correct," Pebonkas said, "but these people call themselves Kanien'kehaka or 'People of the Flint.' Could we all please say Kanien'kehaka?"

"Kanien'kehaka," we intoned.

We reached the village, which resembled the Quebecois villages we had just been to, with the addition of long houses built of poles and bark. Ethan looked for the church and started off for it immediately, but Pebonkas stopped him. "This priest will be able to bring together Christians, but you may not want just those."

"Are they not all Christians?" I asked.

"The priest would say they are. I say, the more gods we have to help us, the better. Look, it's been a long time since I was last here. I'll know a few people, but I'd like to get a sense of who's who first. Let me go first, alone, and then I'll come back and tell you what I've learned."

Pebonkas went off while we set up camp in view of the town. We laid our muskets in the open where the people of flint could see them, as he suggested. A few Kanien'kehaka children came out to look at us and ran off giggling.

"I don't see what's so funny," said Michael

"You're what's funny looking," said the man who had gotten in a fight with Michael in St. Valentin. His name was Stoddard Rowley and, after visiting all those St. Et Ceteras, had become a mutual cursing mate of Michael.

"Orangie," said Michael.

"Mick," said Stoddard.

The next morning, Pebonkas returned with a Kanien'kehaka as tall as Ethan whom I thought he introduced as the war chief, Roskarakete Kowa. Ethan, Pebonkas, and Roskarakete Kowa sat down around a fire, while Christian Doline and I sat off to the side.

Ethan explained why we had come, while Pebonkas translated. Roskarakete Kowa listened politely until Ethan finished, which, as you know now, took a long time.

When Ethan finished, Roskarakete Kowa waited a while and then said, in surprisingly good English, "Ethan Allen, if you want someone who will say we will join you, you should go look for Thomas Cook, for he will agree to anything you want or anything anyone wants. We know of you and of your Green Mountain Boys. We know you are the leader who captured Fort Ticonderoga. We have heard of the weaponry of your words." Ethan glowed at hearing this.

"For many years, the French sought our help in fighting the British. They even joined us on raids into your colonies. Many of you fought with the British against us. Later, the British sought our help in fighting the French. Then the British sought our help in fighting the rebellious colonies. Now you come to us to help fight the British. In all of this, do you see a pattern? Why should we help you?"

"We offer freedom," said Ethan, whose glowing had ended, "freedom for all."

"Then you'll give us our land back?"

"We'll guarantee your land," said Ethan.

"And how is it, if I visit your Green Mountains, I do not see many of our peoples on it? You have taken all our land from us. Isn't that right?"

"Chief," said Ethan, "in Bennington where I come from and in Pownal where Erastus here comes from, the Muhikanuh sold their land to us. We did not take it by force."

"We sold the right to use the land, not to keep forever." He stiffened, signaling he might break off our talk.

Ethan raised his hand. "We Yankees are very powerful, and we can do much for you if you fight by our side."

Roskarakete Kowa's mouth smiled, though his eyes did not. "I have heard how very powerful you were a short while ago when the British chased you back to Ticonderoga. That does not seem to be very strong."

"We were surprised, then," said Ethan, "but now we're building a mighty force of soldiers to sweep into Canada, including the Quebecois. We offer you the opportunity to be part of our victory."

"A group of your soldiers attacked us just a few days ago," said Roskarakete Kowa, "and they did not leave this land alive." He raised his eyebrows, waiting for Ethan's response.

He was talking about Remember Baker! I looked to see how Ethan would handle this insult to his relative. Instead, he remained silent.

"You do not seem strong enough for us to fight with you," said Roskarakete Kowa.

Ethan's voice was low and solemn. "You've fought with the British, and you've seen what good that's done you. You've hurt us as well, but we can forgive you."

"We are filled with remorse for having hurt you, but still, you are not strong. Your delightful forgiveness will not defeat the British."

Pebonkas then said, "What can we do to show you how strong we are?"

"Win a big victory. Do it without us. Then we will talk."

Ethan stood. Roskarakete Kowa stood. I thought that Ethan would storm out of there. Instead, he reached out to shake Roskarakete Kowa's hand. "You have my promise," he said.

"What will you do?" I asked as we walked away. "They insulted us."

"I'd rather think, Erastus, that they were very politic. Perhaps we can learn from them. In any event, he did listen to us."

We returned to General Montgomery, where Ethan reported that we had "encountered considerable success" and that the Quebecois "await our call to rise up against the British." Pebonkas, Michael, Christian, and I accompanied him to General Montgomery's tent and waited outside where we could easily hear the conversation.

"I need assurance, Ethan, otherwise it will be a risky venture," the General said.

"General," said Ethan, "Montreal can be taken by our force with no substantial resistance. It lies there waiting, if only we will act soon."

How Ethan would know this was beyond me. Our trip to the St. Et Cetera villages had produced few volunteers, and no Kanien'kehakas joined us.

"And the Indians you encounter?" asked General Montgomery. "Will they support us?"

"They need a sign that we can win, General. All we need is a quick victory. They're awaiting some substantiation of our prowess, and their collaboration is assured."

"Very well, Ethan," said General Montgomery, "I trust your judgment. Mind you, I'm not convinced you're correct, but we don't have the time to wait. So, I agree to your plan. But listen to me: You are to recruit as many Quebecois as possible, and if you can recruit from the Indians at Kahnawake, do it. But don't wait for them to deliberate. If they won't join you, keep going. You're to communicate with me regularly and not attack any force unless I approve. You'll need at least 1,000 men to attack Montreal, so don't try it with any less. I will send Major Brown on a parallel route with the same instructions. Do you know him?"

"John served under Colonel Arnold at Ticonderoga."

"Colonel Arnold has apparently proposed his own plan to attack Quebec from a different direction, but I don't yet know whether that's been approved, and, in any event, we can't assume we'll be able to join forces. Or wait to learn more. We must be successful in our own right."

"I understand, General."

"Remember, you're not to attack Montreal or any British force without my approval. You're just to recruit more men, Ethan. You're good at that, so I trust in your being able to succeed. Only with enough men will we be able make Canada our fourteenth colony."

We slipped away before Ethan or General Montgomery discovered we had been listening. Ethan came to us after his meeting and gave us our orders. "Get plenty of rest, for General Montgomery has ordered us to move north tomorrow, recruit the army of Quebecois, and prepare to lay siege to Montreal. He's chosen a brave stroke."

That night, loosened by a bit too much rum, Christian Doline told me what he honestly thought about us going into Canada. "Last year, Britain passed the Quebec Act. Very shrewd of them, Erastus, is it not? It let my people, French Canadiens, keep our French language and be Roman Catholics. What more do Canadiens need now? Most of them will yawn at you. British Canadian citizens are too few and so remain loyal to the king, so they won't embrace you. No, I think you'll have to look elsewhere for your fourteenth colony."

When I read my journal now, I note my doubts about bringing Canada over to our side, doubts about whether Ethan could recruit all the Quebecois he claimed he could, and, I now realize, doubts about Ethan himself. For the first time I began to ask myself what my father would do in this situation. He advised me to be cautious when working in the woods cutting trees. Yet, at the end, he fell, despite his caution. Is caution a sign of weakness? Real leaders do not appear afraid of risking all for their beliefs.

CHAPTER 16

▼

A DAY OF REBUKE

Later that night, as Pebonkas, Michael, Christian, and I sat around our fire, the conversation did not calm my concerns.

"Your Ethan Allen smells much like William Wallace," said Michael, "the hero of the Scots. He also raised an army of common soldiers much like us. They won many battles over the English, so the Scots remember him with a great deal of pride."

"What about him?" asked Pebonkas.

"Ah, well, the English eventually captured him, ripped his guts out of him while he was still alive, cut off his arms and legs, and then, to kill him, cut off his head."

"Your story reminds me of Teedyuscung," said Pebonkas, "the wise Lenape leader who fought to secure his people's land, land they'd been cheated out of. He was very respected by the whites."

"And his end was?" asked Michael.

"Well, he reached a peaceful settlement and land for his people. So some whites burned him to death in his cabin. Oh, yes, and then there was Metacom."

"Another great hero to his people?" said Michael.

"A hundred years ago, the Wampanoags and others in the Massachusetts Bay were being slaughtered by the English settlers. Metacom's brother was killed, so he brought together our peoples from all over and fought a hard war against those settlers."

"Which, of course, resulted in . . . "

"Metacom being betrayed, tracked down, and killed. After which even more of our people were slaughtered."

"I detect a common thread here," said Michael.

Pebonkas rose, walked away from our fire, looked up at the sky, and observed, "At least Metacom has an entire war named after him—King Phillip's War. King Phillip was how the English referred to him."

"Eh bien, let's not forget our great hero, General Montcalm," said Christian.

"A distinguished general who, now that you mention him, captured Fort Ticonderoga from the English, just as we did," said Pebonkas.

"And who fought the English General Wolfe," said Michael.

"Who was attacking Quebec," said Christian.

"Only this time General Wolfe and the English won," added Pebonkas.

"But unfortunately . . . " continued Christian.

"Both Wolfe and Montcalm died at the same battle," finished Michael.

"Thus, my people lost Canada. All of which leads us back to where we are today," concluded Christian, poking the fire with a stick.

"And our new hero charging off into your damned French wilderness," said Michael.

"No, my friend, it's not a damned French wilderness. It's now a damned English wilderness."

"But we'll change that, won't we Christian?" said Michael.

"With luck, we may make this simply a wilderness, neither English nor French, neither damned nor saved," said Pebonkas.

"Then 'twill be a damned Kanien'kehaka wilderness," concluded Michael.

Pebonkas smiled. Christian nodded his head in agreement. Michael threw a rock in the fire.

And I, well, those were very fine history lessons, though deeply depressing. They were not the stories of adventure and glory that Hiram told. They were not the imaginings of Erastus, Green Mountain Boy.

Later that night, Hungerford, Wallace, and King Phillip all gathered around me, laughing. My dream startled me awake. Above, I saw the clear night sky, the stars crisp and clear, the Milky Way a grey path. The reality of the night seemed much more clear than dreams and stories of victory and defeat.

The next morning, Ethan arose in his typical exuberant form, shouting, "Up, up, up!" and "Time to wake Canada!" The reality of the night disappeared with the morning sun of his enthusiasm.

Once again, the first village on our journey was St. Valentin, and once again Father Thibault welcomed us to a meal. Madam d'Entremont fed us well, a stew made of fish and shellfish. I had never eaten shellfish before, so Phillipe showed me how to eat what he called clovisses and huitres. Christian told me they were oysters, clams, mussels, and whelks. They tasted fine in the broth, but I could not look at them, as ugly as they were. I suspected the Quebecois also ate slugs and snails, but I did not ask for fear that they would confirm more of the stew's ingredients.

After the meal, about ten men showed up at Father Thibault's door, having been brought there by Phillipe, who had stepped out while his mother was serving us cakes. Like the stew, her cakes were delicious, especially since they held no mussels or slugs.

A wagon pulled by one horse accompanied us, loaded with the muskets and powder that Ethan had promised, so we distributed them and went on up to the next in a string of St. Et Cetera villages.

Not all the priests welcomed us as Father Thibault had, although I suspect they would have joined forces with Satan if it would have meant being free from the English.

The priest in St. Matthieu was especially irate since we had intruded upon his saint's day celebration. A procession marched around the square, with four men carrying a platform on which stood a statue of their saint. "Sortez d'ici!" he kept shouting at us, hoping we would leave. Christian tried to reason with him in French, but he continued to tell us to sortez, as well as much more that Christian did not have time to translate.

Ethan stood behind Christian and tried to suggest things Christian could say. "We bring freedom to your saint. Try that. Once we beat the English, you can have a parade every day. See if he likes that."

Unfortunately, some of us had joined the procession around the town square, and four of them, happy to assist the affair, grabbed the platform supporting the saint out of the hands of the marchers and started to carry the saint around. Evidently the people preferred carrying their saint themselves, for now all the villagers were shouting at them, little girls in white dresses were crying, and little boys in white shirts were kicking our militia in their shins.

Then the Quebecois we had recruited so far—over 200 of them—came to the defense of the villagers and tore the saint out of the hands of the Green Mountain Boys, giving it back to the villagers. Our soldiers shouted. Villagers shouted. Little girls cried. More little boys ran around kicking our shins. And parents tried to pull them away so we would not shoot them. You realize we would never. Except for the one who kicked my shins, both of them. Hard.

Christian suggested to Ethan that he restore order among our soldiers rather than try to convince the priest we had come in friendship. Ethan strode among his men, knocking those on the head who would not stop shouting. The saint returned to his peace. Little girls stopped crying. Little boys threw rocks at each other instead of us. And we marched out of the village of St. Matthieu without any new recruits.

Not indicating any regret about the St. Matthieu humiliation, that evening Ethan gathered all of us around and told us he was able to dispatch a courier to General Montgomery telling him we now had over 200 recruits. "Why, we can easily raise three times that amount by the time we reach Montreal, so I told him we'd continue the march."

He raised himself to his full height, lifted his chin, and proclaimed, "Men, Quebecois and Boys! We will be powerful enough to take Montreal with hardly a shot being fired. They will scurry before us when we arrive. Our future is unambiguous!"

Later, Christian told Pebonkas, Michael, and me that he had translated it as, "We will continue to march toward Montreal gathering more men as we go. And when we arrive, may God be with us!"

I feared Christian's words were more appropriate. Given all the noise we had made in St. Matthieu, the British must have known we were on the way.

From there, our recruiting yielded few men. People opened their doors to us. They fed us wonderfully well, making our stomachs quite comfortable. We had *oeufs* and *patates,* eggs from their chickens with potatoes that reminded Michael of home, fish pies that were, shall I say, different, and meat pies we all liked. They called the meat pies *cipate,* and Christian told me they were filled with deer meat, rabbit meat, and "maybe a skunk, maybe a raccoon, maybe a squirrel. It depends upon what they are able to shoot at the moment." I wished for an apple pie like my mother baked.

On September 24th, outside of La Prairie, our sentries sounded the alarm, and out of the woods marched a short thin officer followed by a handful of men. They had left General Montgomery's force. The officer was Major John Brown.

"Ethan, my friend," he began and thrust his hand out. "We could have massacred you given your lack of security."

"I sniffed you long before you came into view, Brown."

"Given your nose, Ethan, I imagine you did," said Brown, twitching his neat thin mustache.

At that, Ethan and Brown threw their arms around each other and hugged each other vigorously.

"So tell me, Allen, have you been able to recruit many of these Quebecois, or do you just pick up whatever happens to be lying around?"

"I have over two hundred men just waiting for the word to attack, Brown."

"And I too have over two hundred men just waiting to attack, Allen." I counted his handful on one hand again.

"I can raise three times that amount, Brown."

"I can raise five times that amount, Allen."

"Well, Brown, if I try hard, I can raise ten times, no, twenty times that amount."

"If only we had time," sighed Brown.

"Ah, yes, time is of the essence, Brown," said Ethan, shaking his head and kicking a rock.

"With time fleeting," said Brown, pointing out a farmhouse nearby, "what say you we begin to plan, Allen? Besides, I could use a drink." He slapped the flask on his hip.

Once inside the farmhouse, they pulled up the two chairs and settled by the cold fireplace. Ethan and Major Brown each uncorked their flasks and poured each other a cup of the liquor. The interpreter Christian Doline and I stood to the side. Many of our men looked in the one window, watching history in the making and happy not to have to keep walking for the moment.

"What do you think, Allen?" said Major Brown, screwing up his face after tasting a sip from Ethan's flask.

"I think this is damned good Madeira, Brown. Where'd you get it?"

"I liberated it from a British officer on the outskirts of St. John, Allen, while he was asleep. And this you've served me, what is it?"

"The rum of Ticonderoga, Brown, aged in this fine maple flask, and mixed with a little something the Kahnawakes gave me in gratitude for my having shown them the door to freedom."

"A little something?" said Brown, his lips and nose twisting in distaste. "It's a brave brew you have. Perhaps you intend it to poison the wells of Montreal if they don't surrender."

Ethan leaned toward Major Brown. "How many do you think I need to poison, Brown?"

"My informants tell me there can't be more than thirty British soldiers there, at most, with perhaps an equal number of officers, the rest having embarked to defend St. John."

"If you're correct, Brown, then I do believe that Montreal's ours for the picking."

"Did you receive instructions to attack? Montgomery told me to wait for orders."

Ethan straightened himself up, took a last swallow of the drink, and said, "Montgomery couldn't know how weak Montreal's defenses would be now that they've split their forces to attack him near St. John. We simply don't have time to communicate this to him. He'll forgive us when we hand him Montreal. And thank us, too."

"And your plan, Allen? Seems to me you once said it would take fifteen hundred men to capture Montreal."

Christian, while all this was going on, translated furiously for the Quebecois who listened at the window

"It's Ticonderoga all over again, Brown. They'll just be waking up by the time we attack. They won't even have time to put their trousers on." The memory of Lieutenant Feltham standing at the door in Fort Ticonderoga lived on in the picture Ethan created.

Major Brown looked doubtful, clearly not understanding Ethan's military mind. "It's a city, Allen, with several thousand inhabitants. You really believe our four hundred men can force them to surrender?"

Major Brown clearly did not appreciate Ethan for the man he was, not solely the conqueror of Ticonderoga, but more importantly the vanquisher of the scoundrel Yorkers who coveted our land in the Grants, and, most essentially, the leader of the Green Mountain Boys. That is, Ethan was the inspirational leader, even if Seth Warner had been appointed leader, and most of the Boys were now back in the Green Mountains. I might have felt more comfortable with less inspiration and more of Seth's caution.

"Our reputation will have proceeded us, Brown. They fear our smiting hand."

Brown grunted a sarcastic laugh, leaned toward Ethan, and said, "Montgomery has instructed us both not to attempt an attack on Montreal without his blessing."

"Prognostication is for losers, Brown. The door's open to victory. The British know Montgomery's headed for St. Jean. They'll have dispatched the greater bulk of their forces to defend it. That gives us the opening we need. When we capture Montreal, Montgomery will congratulate us, you'll see."

"So, now what?"

Ethan took a stick and scratched a map on the dirt floor. "Look, here's Montreal. And here's the Saint Lawrence River flowing by. If your forces come from one direction and my forces from the other, we'll have Montreal trapped between us."

"That means crossing the River," Brown pointed out.

"Well, yes, Brown, it does, but once we're across, the way will be clear."

"I suppose we can do that." His voice reflected his doubts.

"Think positively, Brown, you know you can do this. We cross tonight, when it's dark. That gives us enough time to gather up canoes, dugouts, bateaux, whatever the local populace has. Then, before daybreak, you alert us when you're across by giving three loud cheers, and we'll attack together. By breakfast time, we'll be eating *oeufs* at the British General Carlton's table. What say you?"

"Three cheers it is," said Brown softly, took another drink from his flask, and left with his men. I hoped he really did have two hundred men waiting in the woods.

"Ticonderoga all over again, Brown!" shouted Ethan after him.

We began moving toward the River immediately. Shortly after leaving Brown, our scouts in front encountered another force. They turned out to be just four Yankees from the northerly Grants, New Hampshire, and Maine. My stomach fell when I recognized their leader, an older, squinty-eyed, almost toothless man. "I'm Huntington—you can call me Hunt—Hungerford." Hungerford claimed they were commissioned to hunt down any and all British and, he bragged, "dispatch them without prejudice." He eyed Pebonkas with some suspicion. "And savages, too."

"Pick them off, one by one, that's what me and my men do," said Hunt. "And then claim our bounty back home."

"Bounty hunters?" asked Ethan. "I'm not aware of a bounty on British heads. Have you accomplished anything?"

"A straggler here, a straggler there, pretty soon you have a good collection of scalps," answered Hunt, sticking a straw in his mouth and sucking on it.

"You collect scalps?" Pebonkas asked.

"Henry," Hunt turned and said, "bring that bag over here." Then reaching into it, he drew out a fistful of human hair. "What do you think of this, huh? Pretty good, eh?" From his hand hung two or three batches of hair still attached to skin.

"You call that British hair?" asked Pebonkas.

"This?" Hunt said, holding up the piece with long black hair, braided. "Well, sure, it is. At least he seemed to be a British sympathizer. Had a Brown Bess with him. That's English i'n it?"

Ethan stepped in. "We don't allow scalping among our militia."

"Then you never fought in the French and Indian War, did you?" Hunt replied. "Listen, my friend, I was at Fort William Henry, you understand? I saw my friends after they were slaughtered by the French savages, after they'd had their scalps ripped off. I saw a woman brought into the fort after her scalp had been taken. She screamed for hours until she died. I give back to them what they took from me."

"It looks to me that you're giving back to more people than just the British," said Pebonkas. His hand rested on his knife stuck in his belt.

Hungerford and his men grinned, as nasty a set of grins as I have ever seen. "I aim to win, my friend. Anyway, we could use some victuals, if you'd be so kind."

"Our provisions are slim," said Ethan, "but if you and your men will join us, we'll gladly share."

"We are sorely fatigued and could use some rest," said Hunt, slouching off to the right, away from Pebonkas.

"We've no time for rest, Hunt. Do you join us or no?" asked Ethan.

"What's in it for us?" said Hunt, slouching further to the right.

"Thirty coppers a day and a share in the plunder," Ethan replied.

"Done, then. Me and my men will trail along with you, though we'll fight our method, and you can fight yours." Then he called his men over. "Henry, Barber, Bluetooth, we been employed, for a fee, of course."

"Michael," I whispered, "did you hear what Ethan offered them? We are not here for plunder. What is he doing?"

"He needs more men. He knows that. These rascals'll plunder anyway, Erastus, so he's just promising them what they'd take anyway." I understood Michael's logic, but nevertheless, it did not sound right to me. "Besides, I ain't been paid anyway. You?"

We spread out along the river, looking for any kind of vessel that could take us across. The wind blew something fierce, and the waves were building. We managed to scrounge a few boats, including a dugout canoe, and Ethan directed us into them and across to the other side.

The night crossing felt like our attack on Ticonderoga, only worse. The waves slapped up against the sides of the boats and sprayed everyone inside. By the time we reached the other side, we were wet through and through. Then we had to send the boats back for more men. Struggling against the waves and wind, our crossing took all night. Though it was early Fall, we shivered in our wet shirts waiting for everyone to make it across. I volunteered to help row a boat back a couple of times, just to keep warm.

Ethan sent scouts south around Montreal to make contact with Brown's force. By daybreak we still had not heard any shout signaling they were in place to attack. Two scouts returned and reported they had not encountered any sign of Brown. The sun was starting to rise. Ethan called his sergeants and other leaders together "for a confabulation." I looked around for Hunt, but saw neither him nor his men. They had not crossed with us.

"Gentlemen," Ethan said, "we seem to be in a bit of a premunire. It depends on what the forces in Montreal will do, whether they'll threaten us or no. But I don't believe our attack can succeed with so few men. For whatever reason, Major Brown and his men haven't made it across the River. I don't believe we can successfully recross the river without being attacked piece by piece." He was answered by our silence. No one dared say the obvious. Ethan looked more stern than I ever recalled him to be, even when he knocked heads with any who opposed him.

A shout from one of the men watching the city decided things. The gates to the outer walls had opened and out poured a number of men, those in front clearly carrying muskets. Behind them came more and more people, running toward us. Our men began firing at them, but they were too far away.

"Ah," said Ethan, "this will be a day of trouble, if not rebuke."

Both sides continued shooting, but we were too far away from each other to hit anything, except by the wildest happenstance. I saw the enemy's forces spread out in a long line before us, wrapping around us bit by bit. Where were the citizens greeting us as liberators? There, among the British soldiers, carrying guns, pitchforks, and tomahawks.

"Christian!" Ethan called out, "send that group of Quebecois to the right to cover our flank."

Christian turned and ordered men to the right. They grabbed their weapons and ran. Ethan was using the same strategy he had used against the Yorker sheriff Cuyler.

"Tell the others to go to our left flank." Christian issued that order, so they, too, picked up and ran. Only they did not stop running. I turned toward those who had been sent to guard our right flank, but could see them nowhere.

"Rebuke, is it?" said Michael. "Retreat more likely."

By now, a little over thirty of us stood by Ethan—those Green Mountain Boys who had come with him and some of the Quebecois. He looked to the left, looked to the right, looked behind. "I think one trip across the river's all we need," he said. "Let's try it, now!" We rose up and ran full drive for the river. None of us stopped to cavil.

Unfortunately, British solders also ran for the boats and reached them before us.

Ethan ripped off his shirt, tied it to a stick and began waiving it over his head. Surrendering! "Parlay!" he shouted.

A man carrying an officer's saber, one who appeared to be commanding those nearest us, shouted at us to lay down our weapons. Ethan signaled us to do it and stepped forward.

"Do you surrender?" the man said.

"Provided I can be assured good quarter," answered Ethan.

"Granted," said the man.

I lay down my musket and glanced to see where Pebonkas, Michael, and Christian were. Christian was beside me. I could not spot Michael or Pebonkas.

"Identify yourself," said the man whose dress, I could now see, identified him as a gentleman of means.

"Ethan Allen, officer in command," said Ethan, his arms in the air, as were mine.

"Allow me to introduce myself in turn, sir," said the man, "Peter Johnson."

They shook hands. I was flabbergasted. They spoke like old school friends, each motioning the other to sit, watched by British soldiers. By this time, the others who had poured out of Montreal had almost surrounded us. Indians stood among the civilians.

I had been surrendered. I had never had a chance to fire one shot at an enemy since joining Ethan and the Green Mountain Boys. Not once! Not even to miss. And there lay my musket, in the mud. Indeed, a day of rebuke.

Then, while Ethan and Peter Johnson deliberated the terms of our surrender and behaved like wonderful gentlemen, one of the Indians suddenly started shouting and waiving his musket in the air. Johnson turned, looking worried. Ethan stared at the Indian, who had shaved half of his scalp and had eagle feathers sticking out of his hair on the other side. I had seen Ethan stare down the commander of Ticonderoga when we captured it and knew Yorkers cowered in his presence, but I was not be prepared for what followed.

The Indian suddenly raised his musket and pointed it at Ethan. No sooner had he done so than Ethan, quick as a copperhead, leaped behind Johnson, grabbed him by the shoulders and spun him toward the Indian, keeping Johnson between the Indian and himself. Johnson only had time to yell, "Wait!" or "What!" or "Wuh!"

The Indian jumped to his right. Ethan spun Johnson toward him. He jumped to his left. Again Ethan spun Johnson toward him. Jump left, spin right. Jump right, spin left. The Canadians began to laugh and seemed to be enjoying the show. We Yankees stood in shock, fearing for our leader's life and also for ours. The Indian yelled. Ethan yelled. Johnson stared, starting to stagger as he became dizzy from all the spinning. The Canadians kept laughing. And then Ethan started laughing. Johnson, spinning and dizzy, seemed to smile. Then the other Indians started to laugh. The British soldiers started to laugh. And then a big Irish sergeant—a British soldier—grabbed his tomahawk and stepped toward the Indian. "Put the musket down or by Jaysus, I'll split you in two." The laughing stopped. The Indian stopped. And then before anything else could happen, he began to smile. He began to laugh. Everyone began to laugh.

Except for me. Stunned by the events, I staggered backward. Everyone was laughing at Ethan and Johnson, looking at them and not at me.

Suddenly, before I had a chance to act, someone jumped me from behind, slapped a hand over my mouth and drew me backward. Another person grabbed me around the waist. We were being betrayed! They were going to kill us! I shut my eyes and waited for the blow to fall on my head.

No blow fell. Instead they dragged me, struggling to break free, over a nearby embankment and through the brush, out of sight of the soldiers, Montrealers, and Indians. I fell and had the breath knocked out of me. The two who grabbed me pushed me behind a log and said, "Stay put."

Then, before I could get my breath back, I swear I heard one of them say, "Trust in thy mercy. Your heart shall rejoice in thy salvation." I opened my eyes, looked up, and they were gone, the bushes still waiving where they had passed through.

I had heard that self-righteous voice before!

Chapter 17

▼

I Almost Die Twice

After I had been so unceremoniously tossed down the embankment and out of sight of the British, Indians, and citizens of Montreal, I was sore, skin scratched and trousers ripped from tumbling through the brush along the embankment. I lay petrified, breathing heavily and shaking all over. My brain told me to run full drive away, but my knees buckled and my legs cramped up on me. I slapped them, trying to get my blood flowing. In my retrospective years, I have come to appreciate the enormous wisdom of my body: it chose not to run and left me trepidated with the trembles. Had I risen and attempted to run, I surely would have been espied and shot, which would have mortified me somewhat finally.

I slunk low in the brush until I could hear the sounds of voices no more, and then I crept up to the edge of the embankment, slowly lifting my head up behind a bush. I could make out a crowd walking back to Montreal. I was sure Ethan and those who could not escape with me were in the middle of them. So I stayed where I was until the sun began to set and until I could be sure no one was looking for me.

I needed to get back across the river. Happily, all the boats we had used to cross it still bobbed where we left them. I found the smallest one I could, pushed it into the river, climbed into it, and lay down. The wind was blowing from the north across the river, so I just let it drift downstream until the wind finally blew me to the opposite shore. The Saint Lawrence River stretches out a distance, like the Hudson, so it took a long while for the boat to drift ashore, and, in the meantime, it had floated downstream quite a ways to the east. I was lost.

Here's some advice: If you are ever lost, all you have to do is simply start climbing downhill. If you find a stream, follow it in the direction it is flowing, eventually you will come to a bigger stream or a road or a town. Simple. But had I followed my own advice, I would have ended up in Quebec. I aimed to put several miles between me and the Canadians.

I tried to sleep in the brush so no one would find me, but shivered from the cold. I tucked into a hollow spot suited for a fox, the ground matted with last year's leaves. I awoke several times, my face chilled by the night air. I tried curling up like a dog and finally slept soundly. When I awoke, I walked as fast as I could, knowing the brilliant fall colors around me signified colder weather coming and realizing that if I did not find my way out, who knows what might happen, a freak snowstorm, anything.

The Saint Lawrence River flows north past Montreal, so I knew I had to start walking east and south if I hoped to reach safe territory.

After a while I began to think I was safe and so began to hum "The British Grenadiers," one of the songs Hiram had taught me, singing the words in my mind:

> *We fought the bloody Yorkers and proved how much we're brave,*
> *We marched on them and routed them*
> *And sent them to their grave . . .*

Once our school master taught us the word "irony" and asked for examples. I could not think of one then, but that song gave me the perfect example. How I wished I were back in school answering his question.

After walking southeast for a day, I encountered more woods than I expected, so, after sleeping the night in the woods, I turned south. This time I wished my pack contained jerky and not my journal. I could not make as much progress as I desired, so when I came across an abandoned house, I went right in, hoping there would be some food. Inside I found some moldy old cheese and some crusts of hard bread, both of which tasted wonderful. After eating, I lay down on an old blanket in the kitchen and fell asleep. I slept well.

That is, I slept well until I was awakened by a laugh. I shook myself awake, sat up, and through bleary eyes saw people standing over me. Were these the people who saved my hide outside Montreal? The laugh was nasty. "Just call me Hunt," their leader said, grinning his toothless grin. I had escaped capture only to be scalped, my hair bringing them one more bounty.

"Ah, our little Green Mountain Boy," said Hunt, picking at his nose. "You got smart and ran away, just like us, huh?"

"I escaped," I answered, shifting my legs in case I could run.

"Oh, yes, yes, well, so did me and my boys here, just that we escaped first."

"You cowards did not come across with us," I said, immediately thinking that honesty may not be a deadly sin, but it sure could be deadly.

"I'd say we was considerable careful, eh, men? And that's what I'd be, if I was you."

"I shall be going on my way," said I, pulling on my shoes and judging how quickly I could get out the door.

"You'll be going our way, my young friend. We lost our pack horses when a bunch of Abenakis chased us up and down a mountain or two, so we need a new 'horse' to help carry our supplies."

Some salt beef they shared with me I suspected they had liberated from one of the "British soldiers" along with its owner's scalp or maybe even one of our militia escaping from Montreal. I kept my mouth shut. Loaded up with packs, I trudged along with them.

We came across a Quebecois farm. The gang burst in, chasing the husband, wife, and children out the back door.

Hungerford screamed, Henry threw his tomahawk at them, Barber ran after them with his scalping knife, and Bluetooth just moaned outside the door. The family escaped.

"Don't mean no harm," said Hunt. "Just like our privacy's all." They sat down to eat as much as they could of the family's food, stuffed the rest in their packs, and left the farm. I did not eat with them, not wanting to steal food. "You're somewhat stupid, my young friend," said Hunt, "'cause you're going to need your energy if you're to travel with us all loaded up like you are." I soon realized how much I appreciated our family's old ox and swore to treat him more gently if I ever saw him again.

The more we walked, the more they cursed at not finding anyone they could profitably scalp. Hunt bragged to me about Indians they had been able to surprise and kill as they traveled along. "Why not get them to join you?" I asked him.

"Can't make no omelet without breaking eggs," he said. "If we get white men to join us, we'll take Kahnawake someday and just keep at it 'til there ain't no more savages left."

I remembered how we kids tried to keep our teacher from testing us by asking question after question about the day's lesson. Hunt launched into everything from the best scalping techniques to economic philosophy. "We're the independent small businessmen of the forest, is what we are, eh. Why, without our efforts and expertise this place'd be all run over with savages and the British. We clean up the trash and droppings of society, a good service, don't you think?"

"Yes, I agree. Someone needs to clean up the trash and droppings of society." Happily, he did not question my meaning.

"See?" he said, "You share our philosophy. That's good."

"But does it really pay?" I asked.

"Pay? Fifty pounds a head for males! Now them's good earnings. We only been promised about twenty-five for a female, but even then, that ain't bad. Why, during the French and Indian War, they only offered 50 shillings a head. Fighting for our freedom really pays, don't you see." The Albany boatman, Mr. Rough, might agree.

Years later I read that, after 1776, most states only offered about twenty pounds for enlisting, and then soldiers seldom drew any regular pay. I wondered if Hunt had misinterpreted the bounty. If so, those he killed were the real victims of his misinterpretation.

The sun had already set when we climbed up over a hill cleared of trees and found an isolated farmhouse. We could see the family in the kitchen. Hunt's men complained they felt hungry again. Hunt and his men began creeping up on the house. Thinking they might kill first and get supplies second, I decided the best thing I could do was to scare away the family and, at the same time, maybe gain more trust from the Hunt gang. So, before they could move to surround the house or shoot anyone, I said, "Let me try this."

Without giving him a chance say no, I ran in the front door, yelling and screaming. The mother rose and screamed. The father stood and yelled. The young child stared in shock. I screamed, jumped up and down, and waived toward the door. Petrified, they would not move. I screamed more. I made my face as evil as possible. They kept standing still. I motioned toward their back door. Nothing. I grabbed a knife off their table. They began screaming again. I ran toward the door, opened it and kept waving them out. Finally, they surmised my intent and bolted for the woods. As a madman, I needed lessons.

"Oh, dear, dear, dear," said Hunt, coming in behind me. "That ain't no way to do this at all. If you had to survive on hunting, you'd starve to death. From now on, you stay behind us and watch what we do. We'll teach you to be a bounty hunter."

"Thank you," I said. "I am truly sorry for having wanted to capture them myself. I realize my behavior spoiled everything. Please, I respect your experience. I am prepared to learn."

"Let's kill him right here and now," said his man Henry. "He speaks funny."

"He's got a fine hank of hair," said Barber.

Hunt said, "We call him Barber 'cause he's such a neat and careful scalper." He whispered, "Actually, his name's Caryl, but I wouldn't call him that, if you catch my drift."

"Listen to him," said Henry, "the way he speaks, keeping him alive's going to be more trouble than he's worth."

"Hunt, my tooth's killing me," said Blue Tooth, aptly named for his black tooth in front. He had started complaining earlier that day and by now was clearly in pain. "I'm dying. I can't take it no more. I could use something spiritous."

"This happens every month or so," Hunt told me. "It's amazing he's got any teeth left at all. Let's look for something to drink," something strong to knock Blue Tooth out. "I need a stimulator, too," he said. The kitchen had one cupboard in it, and their search turned up nothing. "They must be Baptists or something," observed Hunt, "to have nothing decent to invigorate the bones. Blue Tooth, you just got to make do."

"Does Blue Tooth have a name?" I asked.

"Osborne Fortesque," he said. "But I have rebaptized him."

I noticed a simple crucifix on the wall. "It looks like they are Catholics."

"Catholics? And nothing to drink? Must not be practicing Catholics," said Hunt.

If the family I had scared out the back door ever returned to their home, I want to apologize to them for having eaten their meal, as did Hunt's gang of bounty hunters, for I was sorely hungry that night. So well did we eat that we soon felt very tired and climbed into our blankets. Blue Tooth continued to moan for what seemed like several hours before he finally went to sleep.

Once Blue Tooth fell asleep, I listened very closely to the snoring around me to determine whether they were all asleep. When I thought I could count four different snores—Blue Tooth, Henry, Barber, and Hunt—I carefully eased myself out from under my blanket, slipped on my shoes, and tried to remember where they had put their muskets and powder. Recalling they had each gone to bed with their muskets—uncocked, of course—I slipped on my pack with my journal, eased the back door open, and left.

After I had walked slowly away from the house, careful not to step on broken branches, listening to make sure they were still snoring, I ran out into the field and did not stop until I had reached the woods. I kept running, branches scraping my face in the dark and fallen trees tripping me many times. The sun came up, and I kept moving all that day, aiming generally south. Once, when I saw the smoke from a village to the west, I circled around it for fear British soldiers occupied it. Other than St. Jean, which I assumed General Montgomery was attacking around now, British soldiers probably were not in the villages, but I dared not chance it. My near-capture in Montreal kept me going. Gratefully, I remembered my mysterious rescuers.

By sunset, I was exhausted, so I found myself a big slab of rock angled up from the floor of the woods, crawled under it, and went to sleep. I slept soundly until the light was just beginning to show the next morning. Then I heard, "Hunt, my tooth still hurts." They had found me!

"Damn your tooth, he came this way. I mean to find him." Hunt's voice was faint.

Then Barber's. "Fifty pounds on the hoof. Wait'll I get him." Their voices faded in the distance.

They had tracked me down! For fifty pounds. Well, I thought, the next time Tryphena or Tryphosa tells me I am worthless, I will tell her, I will. Unless the bounty really is fifty shillings.

I lay on my side under the rock listening to their footsteps fade away. After scarcely breathing, I scurried in the opposite direction. Around noon I passed through a cornfield and came out where the ground rose above the level of the corn. I looked back and spotted four men on the other end of the field. If they were Hunt, Henry, Barber, and Blue Tooth, I thought myself worth more than fifty pounds or fifty shillings.

I concede, Huntington Hungerford and gang were truly excellent trackers, and if they had been Green Mountain Boys, I would gladly have apprenticed myself to them to learn tracking skills. I contemplated that notion for a while and giggled at the thought of their opening a tracking school and charging fifty pounds per pupil. They would not have even had to scalp their pupils to get it. But pity the poor student who daydreamed.

So there I was, trying to escape my prospective killers and smiling at my silly speculations, when I came to a fairly good-sized river flowing to the south and west. I followed it downstream all the rest of the day, stopping every once in a while to look back and listen in case the trackers had caught up with me. I could not hear much over the sound of the stream, but I do believe I had a heightened sense of hearing that day.

Eventually I came upon a small boat pulled up on the bank. Though I knew it would be stealing if I took it, I decided I wanted to keep Hunt and gang from earning fifty pounds or fifty shillings, whatever I was worth. So I took it. Someday I will go back and find out who owned it and pay them back.

I found no oars or paddles, so I broke off a large branch and, by pushing at the bank whenever I came near, managed to keep myself from lodging against one side or another. A couple of times the stream widened out, leaving only shallow riffles, so I had to get out and push or pull the boat across the shallow part until it could float again. The sun came out from behind the clouds, it grew nicely warm, and I fell asleep in the bottom of the boat.

When I awoke, the boat had drifted under the overhang of a large oak tree along the bank. The dirt had eroded from the roots of the tree. A person could crawl up under the roots and be protected from the weather or trackers or whatever. I pulled the boat up under the roots of the tree and saw some brush piled up, which I supposed the river had deposited there some time in the past when it was flooding. The brush would hide my boat from anyone passing downstream or on the opposite bank. I was just starting to move the brush onto my boat when what should I discover under the brush pile but a dugout canoe.

I looked around in the fading light and tried to see whether anything else had been left there by the canoe's owner, wondering all the while whether that person was running from someone as well. I crawled back farther underneath the roots of the tree to check for anything or anyone hiding there and discovered a narrow opening leading back into the dirt. I debated the wisdom of crawling back in there, for it could all collapse upon me, burying me forever, keeping me from being scalped, but also keeping me from anything else in life. The thought of possible scalping convinced me that crawling into the hole was the better choice.

It was pitch dark. I had crawled maybe ten yards, my shoulders rubbing against the walls of what now appeared to be a tunnel, when the tunnel opened up into what felt like a room. I pushed myself into the room and was about to try to stand up when the barrel of a musket jabbed me in the neck. I froze. A woman's voice said, "Lie down, flat, or I'll blow your head off!" I had gone from the scalping blade to the musket ball.

I stammered about escaping men trying to kill me, but the voice said, "When I want you to talk, I'll tell you so."

I felt several sets of hands patting me all over and heard a young boy's voice say, "He don't have no weapons."

"Keep laying there," she told me and uncovered a candle she had tucked in a hole covered by a board.

You probably know how a face looks when you hold a candle beneath the level of your chin. I had encountered a witch, ugly, her face flickering in the light. I had escaped the bounty hunters, only to end up underground with a hideous practitioner of the black arts, ministered to by little devils whose hands tested my flesh.

"You look harmless enough," she said.

"Yes, ma'am, very harmless. Simple-minded, to be honest," I said. "I will not tell anyone. I will just back out now, if you will allow me."

"Who are you?" she said.

"My name is Erastus," I said, and then poured it all out. "I am a Green Mountain Boy, one of the Boys from Pownal, and I have been fighting with Ethan Allen, only we were captured by the British outside Montreal, and I escaped only to end up with bounty hunters trying to kill me and take my scalp, so I ran away from them and found a boat and floated down the river and woke up here, and here I am, so I will go quietly if that is, that is, if you will allow me, please."

"You talk a mighty lot."

"Yes, ma'am."

"Ethan Allen, you say?"

"Yes, ma'am. Ethan Allen. Leader of the Green Mountain Boys. He is a patriot who . . . "

"Oh, do be quiet. I know who he is."

"Yes, ma'am."

"You know, you certainly have told me a lot."

"Yes, ma'am."

"I could be a Tory, you know, and I could turn you over to the British to be hanged as a traitor. What do you think of that?"

I could not bring myself to say anything. After trying to escape, I may have blundered into the den of the enemy.

"Of course, I ain't no Tory. And I'll not turn you over to the British." She laid the candle on top of a barrel, and I could now see that she was not ugly as a witch, not even ugly at all. She wore a simple dress, much like my mother's, with a man's pants underneath. Off to the side stood a young boy wearing breeches much too big for him.

"Meet my son Ephraim. I'm Mrs. Story."

I started to relax. "Pleased to meet you, Mrs. Story."

"I mistrust you are, but you will be. Now, stand up and stop pretending to be scared. Ephraim, take Erastus upstairs."

Ephraim took the candle and led the way to the end of what I could now see was a large room carved out of the dirt, with the roots of trees serving as the roof. I almost snorted when I thought of this as a real root cellar. At the end of that room was bedrock and a crevice with stairs built using short split lengths of logs. We walked up the stairs to a trap door. Ephraim pushed it open, and we climbed out into a very small one-room cabin.

Mrs. Story climbed out last, carrying her musket. I now could see Ephraim had a knife strapped to his belt. "Have a seat, Erastus," she pointed to one of two chairs in the room, by a small table. Four mattresses lay along two of the walls and one cot was by the fire. Just then, two young girls came crawling out from under the cot. They wore simple frocks sewn from cloth bags. They held hands and grinned at me.

"This here's Susanna and Hannah," Mrs. Story said. "The boys and I were doing a little work downstairs when you intruded. Hungry?" She pulled out a pot buried in the embers of the fireplace. "I'll bet you're so hungry you could eat the north end of a south-bound skunk." It was the most delicious deer stew I had ever tasted. Of course, I would have said I was hungry as a trapped fox, but I think the skunk covered it better.

She asked me to tell her about Montreal. "I know your Ethan Allen," she said. "He's eaten here, too, you know." I must have looked surprised. "Oh yes, he's got people all across the Grants working with him. We can provide shelter for Green Mountain Boys when they need it, hide them until the British or Tories ain't around, pass messages along when necessary. In fact, that's where my older son Solomon is now, running a message out east."

I heard a noise behind me and turned toward the only window in the cabin, just in time to see a musket barrel being pulled back. Then the door opened and another boy entered, carrying the musket and a rabbit.

"Samuel, meet Erastus," said Mrs. Story. Samuel wore an old hunting shirt, much as we wore in Pownal, with breeches worn open at the knees.

"That is a substantial room you have below," I said. "But Ethan never told us about you."

"Well, I mistrust he'd want to. The fewer people know about us, the better. We only know our contact people east, west, north, and south of here. I suspect they know just those people near them. Just as well we don't know too many people, in case we're ever caught." Maybe Ethan was not all multisyllabication after all.

"So, how did you end up here?" I felt myself flush at my impertinence.

Mrs. Story told me of how her husband and their son Solomon had come up here to clear the land, while she waited back in Connecticut for them to send for her and the others. Her voice fell as she gazed out their one window. "But when Solomon came back to me, he near broke my heart. My Amos had been cutting down trees when one twisted on itself as it was starting to fall and fell on him. Solomon saw the whole thing and ran to town for help, but too late."

"My father died that way," I said, remembering him once more. "I was not there when it happened. I do not know if I could have helped." Then, I felt a sudden swelling in my throat. "Do you miss you husband?" I asked.

"All the time. But we came back here to finish the work he'd started for us. Do you miss your father?"

I guess I had tried not to think about it. "Yes, ma'am."

"Well, that's good. That's what they'd want, wouldn't they? And you're doing the work he'd've wanted you to?"

"I do not know," I said, for I really did not. "I left my mother, sisters, and brother to take care of the farm while I joined the Green Mountain Boys. Seemed the right thing to do." Then my throat closed up, and I could not speak.

"I think you did the right thing, Erastus. I think your father'd be proud of you."

"But I left my mother and family to do the work."

"You'll have plenty of time to make it up to them," she said, reaching out to grasp my arm. "You're doing the right thing. And if folks around Pownal are like folks around here, they'll all pitch in to help your mother."

"I hope so," I said, swearing to myself I would not leave my mother and the farm if I ever made it back.

"Now, let's get you to bed. I'll bet you could use some rest."

"But what about you?" I asked. "How did you come to build that cave? How did you get involved with Ethan?"

"One day, when we were out in the field working, some Indians burned our cabin. They didn't see us, thank God, but afterward I swore we'd be better prepared. Well, we'd been stumbling over that crack in the rocks and storing potatoes up under that tree by the river. All we had to do was dig out a room down below and a way out to the river. We thought we had our canoe hidden, but Ephraim tells me you uncovered it."

"Oh, I would have covered it back up."

"So, if anyone ever does attack us again, we can slip down below the floor and hide. Then, if they want to burn this cabin, let them."

"Smart."

"Well, cautious, let's say. Now, what say you go to bed. Take the cot. No, don't say you won't. The girls can sleep on the floor with us. And Solomon may not be back until tomorrow."

Her little cabin felt like home. "Would it be all right with you if I wrote in my journal for a while? I have kept it ever since I was little."

"If you'll read some of it tomorrow. That is, if it's all right with you." She smiled, and I could see a resemblance to my mother, both of them bone thin, but warm.

That was Mrs. Ann Story. She took me in though she did not have much to share, gave me a place to rest, fed me, and, best of all, listened to me read from my journal.

After a breakfast of simple hot grains, I admitted I was lost. She told me we were in the Salisbury grant, not too far from the town of Middlebury. I could not be more than about two day's walk from home! Somehow, I had managed to find my way out of Canada back into the Grants, and I had not even had to go through New York.

"Are you going home?" she asked me that morning.

"Yes, ma'am. But do you think I should rejoin General Montgomery's forces? I am so torn. What would you do?"

"You can always fight another day," she said, giving me the advice of a mother to her son. "I'd bet your mother's so worried about you she's let her stew boil over on more than one day."

Solomon came back later in the morning. More than a young man, he was older than I was, big like Ethan. Friendly, too. But he talked as much as a turtle. Mrs. Ann Story told me he would guide me for a day, just in case the bounty hunters were still around. "I'd estimate they've gone back north to prey on more innocent people. We're too tight knit here in the Grants. They'd not get away with their murdering ways here."

The next day Solomon took me down the river in my stolen boat. "Two boats here are too hard to hide. Attract too much attention. I'll leave this boat down below when you get out and hike back to the cabin." When we came to a bridge and a road leading south, Solomon left me and returned home.

I did not want Solomon to leave, but I knew his responsibility lay with his family. I figured on at least two days walking ahead, maybe more if Hungerford caught up with me. No matter. Once you decide to go home, the road home is the shortest road there is.

CHAPTER 18

▼

SOUTH TO HOME

South to Pownal, south to Carpenter Hill. That is the course I kept, aiming myself down to Rutland (not much of a town to speak of, just a few farms), through Wallingford, and on down to Bennington. Mrs. Story had filled my pack with plenty of bread to see me on my way, so I did not want for a full stomach.

But my full stomach churned all the same. Every time I came around a rock or passed a clump of trees, I expected Hunt Hungerford and his men to grab me. In a woods overgrown with brambles, my worst fears came alive: a long musket barrel poked its nose out from behind a tree. I dropped to the ground. The musket barrel slowly turned in my direction. I was a dead man.

"Hey, mister," said the voice behind the musket, a very high voice. I said nothing, holding my breath and hearing my heart pound in my head.

"Hey, mister," said the small boy who stepped out into the clear, holding a fowler twice as long as he was high. "You seen any deer or rabbits?"

His name was Bump Brewster, and he was hunting food for his family. His knees poked through his breeches and his elbows through his sleeves. I shared some of my bread, told him I had not seen any game, realized the only game I knew of was me, and wished him well in his hunting. In my heart I thanked him for his gift to me: He called me "mister." I am a man, I thought, a man scared to death like a boy.

After a long walk, I reached Wallingford and begged a ride with a Mr. Evans who was driving a wagon south. "Might's well take you," he said. "You don't look like you weigh more'n a sack of potatoes."

"Have you lived here long?" I said, wanting something to talk about and not knowing whether he was a Tory or a patriot.

"Yep." Mr. Evans' words were as spare as his body. Without his beard, his face would resemble a skull.

"Things going all right for you these days?" I asked.

"Best as I can hope for." He flicked the reins over his horse.

"You drive this road a lot?"

"Substantial." He wrapped the reins over the bar of the wagon.

"Pretty day," I ventured.

He shifted in his seat, but said nothing.

Clearly Mr. Evans believed in our old saying, "Don't talk unless you can improve the silence." With only the sound of the horse's hoofs on the road and the creaking of the wagon wheels, my head drooped, and I gave in to sleep. Once, when the wagon hit a rock, I woke and glanced off to a hill beside the road. There on top stood four men, each carrying a musket, each waving, each smiling, except for one who had a bandage tied around his jaw. Hunt Hungerford and his men? The hair on my neck rose. I reached for my musket and realized I had none. I was again a dead man. I stared straight ahead, hoping they would disappear. Perhaps I saw only farmers hunting their meal. Perhaps.

Mr. Evans followed the Otter Creek down to Danby, where he dropped off his load of corn and picked up boards at a mill.

I offered to help him, meaning to thank him for his ride. "You look like a weak sapling, son. You just set. I can manage." His conversation with the mill owner was as fulsome as his conversation with me—virtually nothing. They appeared to have made this trade before. Then Mr. Evans climbed up in his wagon and turned to look down at me. "Keep your pants clean," he said. I nodded, not wanting to overburden his ears. And feeling the flick of the reins, his horse headed home, saying about as much to me as Mr. Evans had.

The mill owner and his assistant let me sleep in the mill that night. Though not as luxurious as Lord Stirling's barn in New Jersey, the mill harbored no Hunt Hungerford. The next morning, I found another ride with Mr. Lemuel Cook, who had also come to the mill to trade. "Where're you coming from?" he asked.

"Canada," I said.

"I've a son in Canada, named Lemuel just like me," he said. "Went off with them Green Mountain Boys." Was this a test?

So I decided to test him. "You supported him?"

"Seemed right," was his answer. I breathed more easily.

We talked, as Mr. Evans might phrase it, "substantial." Mr. Cook was as bony as Mr. Evans, but his warm eyes made him appear softer. Mr. Cook asked about Canada, how the food was, whether the people were friendly, and whether I had ever met his son.

I told him of our defeat outside Montreal, but then I saw tears in his eyes when he talked of his son. I said I did not know if his son was with us, that maybe he was still with General Montgomery. "The good Lord knows," he said and did not talk for a long while.

In Arlington, Mr. Cook invited me to sleep the night with his family. Rutland, Wallingford, Danby, and now Arlington—the people in these towns seemed to be living as though no war was going on. Because I was not marching with a musket, I saw life going on despite the war. Ethan captured, my friends possibly dead, young men off fighting and dying, and people at home living normally.

The Cooks' little house was as spare as Ann Story's, as simple as the cabins Hunt Hungerford and his bunch—including me, unfortunately—had raided. "Lemuel joined the Green Mountain Boys because he believed in them," Mr. Cook said, "but really I think it was to ease the burden here." Five young children, all very thin, and all with clothes thinner than I could look at proved his statement.

Mrs. Cook looked at me intently, and I remember looking down at my plate, empty now of the little food they were able to share with me. Her dress hung loosely over her thin frame. Her sandy hair was tousled and her voice reedy. "Is the war worth it?" she asked.

The more I thought, the more confused I became. I mean, it had been so simple at first. Fight the Yorkers. Then it became fight the British. But not everyone wanted to fight. Not everyone who fought did it for freedom. "I hope so," I answered, but her look told me that hoping so was no answer.

"You know," Mr. Cook observed, "I cannot say it'll matter who wins, long as our son comes home safely. We don't have much now, under the British. We won't have much after the war, whether we win or not."

"But we will be free from the British," I said, falling into hollow rhetoric.

"Free? To do what?" he continued, "To vote? For what? To keep the hail from destroying my corn? To make sure there's enough rain in the spring to start my crops right? King George don't know we exist, but neither does that Continental Congress. You admire them, Erastus? I hear some own slaves. So much for freedom and equality, huh? Maybe we should volunteer ourselves as slaves. Then maybe we'd be guaranteed a meal. Maybe."

Mrs. Cook understood her husband's anger. "I think Lemuel means to say we have all we can do to live from day to day. Ain't that so, Lemuel? We don't really have much say in anything else. And he don't mean nothing against you, Erastus."

"Like I say, Continental Congress or the King in England, it don't make no difference here," said Mr. Cook and then added, "But you keep on doing what you think's right, son, and maybe you and my son will both be home someday."

I did not have all the answers. Worse, I realized, I did not even have all the questions. I was mightily unsettled. Well, no matter, for I wanted to complete my escape from Canada and from Hunt Hungerford.

From the Cook's home I walked in to Bennington. I did not stop, but headed right out and up Carpenter Hill.

My mother hugged me, my sisters hugged me, even my sickly brother Eleazar hugged me. They had all moved back from below the ledge to keep the farm going. Uncle Hiram, not surprisingly, offered to play a tune, but my mother, most likely sick of his endless tune-playing, sent him down the hill to notify the rest of my family. My mother had changed little. "I have been worried to death about you, Erastus, and you still haven't written me or anything to let me know how you've been, which is a poor way to treat a mother, after all, what with all the work here on the farm and your Uncle Hiram not worth much more'n a barrel of air. I would hear more if I'd given birth to a stone."

Hiram, as by now you know, moved slower than molasses running up hill in January, but, amazingly, by evening, he had somehow gathered all my family. Tryphena prayed our dinner open and did not embarrass me by sneaking in a preachment or two. I repeated the entire account of our attack on Montreal and my escape. Tryphosa asked about Michael and about Pebonkas, or Peter Keyes to her. Hiram asked if I had picked up any tunes from the Quebecois. Tryphena and Tryphosa kept going back to Pebonkas and Michael.

"Do you think whoever saved you could have saved Michael and Peter?" asked Tryphosa, looking into my eye, putting her face just inches from my nose.

"I do not even know if they needed saving."

"Don't you think you could've gone back for them after you were safe?" asked Tryphena. Those sisters still think me a child, I thought, incapable of doing anything without their help. In truth, they asked the very thing that gnawed at me. Still, Bump Brewster had verified that I was now a mister, and a mister does not allow any woman to cow him, especially a sister.

"I was not safe until I met Mrs. Story."

"If they're safe, do you think they'll come back here?" asked Tryphosa.

"Where else would they go if they're safe?" asked Tryphena.

"I do not know."

"Well, what do you think?" asked Tryphosa.

"If I knew, I would tell you."

"Farther into Canada?" asked Tryphena.

"I told you I do not know."

"Back to General Montgomery's army?" asked Tryphosa.

"I do not know, I do not know, and I do not know. And furthermore, if you want to find out, why not go and look for them yourself?"

"We could do that, you know," said Tryphena, while Tryphosa nodded in support.

"Now, girls," said my mother, "leave Erastus be. The poor boy must be exhausted. I'm sure he knows what you could do if you'd a mind to."

"He still knows nothing," grinned Tryphosa, and Tryphena nodded in agreement.

Thomas Frederick, Samuel, and Eunice, except for bringing her baby with her, had all left their families behind, so they departed for home as soon as dinner ended.

I did not sleep well that first night back. Tryphena and Tryphosa's incessant questioning worked me up something awful and brought back my worries about Michael and Pebonkas. The next day, my mother asked me to read them parts of my journal. I excised a few parts and extemporized on others whenever I thought my mother might not approve of what I reported.

Tryphena and Tryphosa questioned the accuracy of my stories. Had I not known better, I would have thought they were actually with me and Ethan. Questions and more questions. Why did Ethan Allen invade Canada? What made him think he could convert the Canadians? Why did he attack Montreal without more men? Do you really still believe in him after all that? My respect for their insights grew.

The farm, I saw, looked truly healthy. My mother, Tryphena, Tryphosa, Eleazar, and, yes, even Hiram had worked very hard to keep it going. Friends on Carpenter Hill had helped, and they, in turn, had helped those friends. They told me of what had happened in the Pownal area since I left. Tories and patriots divided the towns of Pownal, Pownal Centre, and North Pownal, and treated each other worse than before we left for Ticonderoga. The folks of Pownal were holding meetings in their homes to debate what to do about the situation. Neighbors no longer talked to neighbors. Loyalists—for that is what the Tories called themselves—still believed it wrong to oppose England and the king. The rest believed our future lay in being able to manage our own affairs. Our freedom was the freedom to disagree with each other. Notwithstanding all Ethan's self-assurance, my vision of the future continued to cloud up.

Natural reason always lost when butted up against emotional beliefs.

"This," said my mother, "is what we get for listening to stories and such twaddle."

CHAPTER 19

▼

FREEDOM REARS ITS HEAD AND DUCKS

The Reverend Deuteronomy Dewey, who returned to his pulpit long before I returned, attempted, Sunday after Sunday, to bring the town back together again. He employed homily after homily, such as that prodigal son story, which, for the life of me, I could not truly understand. I mean, Hunt Hungerford is my idea of a prodigal son, and what father in his right mind would welcome him back?

Unfortunately, most who attended his sermons were all of one mind, that freedom from New York and from England were natural, right, and just ends in our quest for liberty. To them, Tories were not prodigal sons. (After that particular sermon, one member of the congregation referred to Tories as "prodigious sons—sons o' bitches.") His congregation divided over the issue, with those against the war staying away.

Reverend Dewey undermined his own Sunday attempts to bring us back together when during the week he worked to strengthen our militia and to organize our continuing efforts to separate ourselves from England.

A couple of weeks after I returned, I attended a town meeting at the church, the date having been set so that the farmers could bring in all their late crops before winter set in. I had to suffer a long invocation by the Reverend Dewey in which he lay out all he knew about the deprivations attributed to the British, about their economic despotism, and about their dissolute character. Even Tryphena and Tryphosa, who walked me into Pownal Centre and who were listening at the window of the church, fell asleep from sheer fatigue of the ears. Remember, women could not enter because only male property owners were allowed to attend the town meeting. My family designated me the official property owner, despite Tryphena and Tryphosa's snickers at that decision.

Deuteronomy's concluding "amen" signaled the start of the arguments.

"Reverend Dewey, if you were not one of my fellows in arms at Ticonderoga," said Theophilus Bates, who had himself returned safely, "I'd have to shoot you to put the rest of us out of our misery. You're speechifying's a God-awful drain on one's enthusiasm."

"Thank you, Brother Bates, for your kind thoughts, but if you'd not fought side-by-side with me at Ticonderoga, I'd allow you to shoot me so that I need not abide your military pomposity any longer," responded Deuteronomy.

"It's indeed a miracle that Ticonderoga's in our hands, when I think of the two of you attempting to do anything together," said Tom Parker.

"Let's get on with why we're here," said George Wilcox, whose blonde, closely shaved head glistened through the sunburn. "What're we going to do about the Tory sympathizers? Them not joining us has gone on long enough."

"Get rid of them," said Asa Brown, who had not changed since the first town meeting I attended with my father. "A poor town's got two Tories. A damned poor town's got more." He continued rubbing his hands together.

"We can accidentally let our cows trample their crops," said Parker.

"That'd make us Cow-Boys, just like them Tory bandits we been hearing of," added Wilcox.

Wilcox, Brown, and Parker had not joined the Boys from Pownal, but had remained behind to tend what they called "our interests."

"They've got families just as we do," offered Deuteronomy. "We should consider their welfare, for they're our neighbors. Let's not sink to being Cow-Boys."

"Arrest them, then," said Brown, his nervous eyes blinking and hands twitching.

"Lock them up, load them up on wagons, and ship them out of here," said Weaver. "That'd be the kind and humane thing to do, for all of us."

"We're a quorum of a town meeting. Let's just pass a law here and now making it an offense to consort with the enemy, and of course we know who that is," said Sykes.

"Why don't we ask young Erastus, here?" suggested Deuteronomy, turning toward me. "He's just returned from the terrible battle at Montreal, where we lost

Ethan Allen and so many others. What do you think, Erastus? Any thoughts on what to do?"

A long lifetime had passed since I had last worried about the warring divisions in Pownal, and before I could think more, my words slipped out with all the inspiration of Ethan Allen. "It seems to me the answer lies in natural reason," I said, though I had not thought of what I meant by that. All the eyes turned toward me. I could feel my blood rushing to my head. "How can we fight for liberty, when we take liberty away from those who differ with us? Can we live with the pretense of law without giving those against a law a chance to speak out against it?" There, I knew I had invoked the spirit of Ethan Allen, and I sat up in my seat, proud. I was really a mister, after all.

"Ah, what's he know? He's just a snipper-snap," editorialized Brown.

"But a snipper-snap who risked his life on our behalf, first at Ticonderoga and then at Montreal," Deuteronomy said, coming to my defense. "Go ahead, Erastus."

Emboldened by his words, I continued. "Are we not all fighting for freedom? And does not freedom mean the freedom to speak our own mind and to vote our own mind, even if ours is not the popular will?"

They looked thoughtful, and then Brown, who had called me a snipper-snap, jumped right in. "Provided they speak and vote the way we would. If I wanted to put up with fawning King-lovers, I would've stayed in Rhode Island. Either we're for freedom and against England, or we're against freedom and for England. It's as simple as that. Gentlemen, our lives are linked to those of others. If they won't fight with us, then we shouldn't do anything for them. They're a spot of rottenness in our community, and we all know what happens if you don't cut the rot out of a vegetable—it spreads."

Witton wagged his finger in support. "We got to be vigilant against the Tories and traitors like them among us, not only the king's men. Our security depends on it."

I had not convinced them. Natural reason means nothing to people who fear what they do not really know. It is all, as Michael would say, "blather." Like cats who hear sounds we cannot, they snarled at the unknown. I took a deep breath, let out a long sigh, took another deep breath. "Look," I said, giving up any pretense of wisdom, "Tories are frightened, too. We have to try to talk with them before we kill each other."

"You gets a winning hand when everybody's playing with the same deck of cards," argued Sykes, who had lost an eye in the French and Indian War. I did not argue against him. I did not even understand him. His eye socket twitched as he spoke.

"We're steady, clear-eyed, and patient, but pretty soon we'll have to start displaying scalps," argued Weaver, who never fought in any war. He smirked.

"Should we not love our neighbors as we would have them love us?" asked Deuteronomy.

"Save it for the children, Reverend. No Tory, no one with scruples about rebellion can be my neighbor," was Brigg's reply. "Indeed, we do love our neighbors, for neighbors are those who love what we love. That's freedom."

"Clean out this town. Make it safe for liberty-loving Grantsmen. Understand, you can't negotiate with these folks. No compromise. No middle ground," Brown said.

"Let's be logical," said Whitby, "Would the British people come to our aid, even if they want the same freedoms that we want? Of course not. And here in our own community, the British sympathizers wouldn't fight for those freedoms."

"Now let's not get our bowels in an uproar," argued Deuteronomy. "You know you're not sure of that. And besides, we're not even sure whether the other colonies will support us in our fight for freedom. I read that Pennsylvania's badly divided. South Carolina shows no inclination to join our efforts."

"Excuse me, Reverend, but damn them all and who cares?" Whitby rasped. "We're the men of the Green Mountains. If no other colony supports freedom, we'll be the first. We fought the Yorkers with no support, and we beat them back. We're in a war. And in a war we got to do things we might not do if we weren't in no war."

Once upon a time I might have admired Whitby's or Weaver's certainty, perhaps even looked to them as leaders, but now, I did not know. They had never gone to war. Sykes, who had known war, said nothing, but his eye socket continued to twitch.

Deuteronomy tried again. I felt ashamed for having criticized his sermons. "Erastus here can tell you," he said. "General Montgomery's marching on Canada even now as we sit here, and we don't know what may happen. If he should fail, the entire weight of England could fall upon us."

"What do you think, Erastus?" asked Brown, who stopped rubbing his hands.

Why would people ever ask me what I think? What I thought in those days hardly mattered. Would my thoughts put more food in the Cook's children?

"I think General Montgomery plans well. He might be able to do it," I said. "Moreover, a colonel with a strong will is marching with an army to Canada, at least, so I have heard. His name is Benedict Arnold."

"That's right, a true patriot," observed Deuteronomy.

"Fine," rasped Whitby. "We have two armies marching on Canada. And meanwhile, what about here? What about the Tories here? Get rid of them or not?"

Deuteronomy, recognizing the general opinion against our Tory neighbors, fell back upon his last remaining effort to calm the mood. "I think we've said all we can tonight. Shall we pray for the guidance of Divine Providence?"

Tryphena and Tryphosa, having listened to the entire meeting, walked home with me. "You know what's best, Erastus. You know what fighting's like, something most of them don't," said Tryphosa, trying to encourage me.

"We know what you went through," said Tryphena, but how could she? I did not really know what fighting was like myself, for I had yet to fire a shot. But if being shot at is fighting, then maybe I knew a little. For the first time, I think Tryphena and Tryphosa saw me as more than just their little brother. But their little brother just wanted to go home. All I could say to them was, "I can throw grass and apples, but I cannot bring myself to throw stones."

CHAPTER 20

▼

STONES

For almost two years I threw no stones.

By the end of the month all the crops were in. I had worked side-by-side with my sisters and was impressed by their perseverance. They, in turn, tolerated me, I believe, more than they had before I joined the Green Mountain Boys. Even Hiram worked, albeit somewhat awkwardly. "I am a musician, Erastus, not a farmer."

We traded corn for other vegetables from a tenant farmer down on the Rensselaerwyck properties, Gerretse Van Kouwenhoven, who had moved into one of the abandoned farms. I asked him if he knew why Tories opposed us.

"Or those of us who choose not to take sides?" he asked. "My family and I simply want to be able to work our land, respect our neighbors, and enjoy the freedom to worship whatever way we want. Isn't that what you Green Mountain Boys want? Why hate us for wanting to do the same things you want?"

"And the other Dutch?" I wondered. "Will none fight?"

"Well, first, not all of us renting land here are Dutch. Second, who am I to speak for everyone? And third, those of us who are Dutch have lived here for many generations. We are what you are, all Americans, if I've got the term right. I don't want to be English. I'm happy if all of you don't want to be English. But I also want to be able to own my land, like you. Right?"

"I guess. I joined the Green Mountain Boys to keep the Yorkers away from our land. Only, now we fight the British. All mixed up. If Yorkers side with the

King, then we fight Yorkers. But now Yorkers are fighting with us. If the Dutch will not join us . . . I mean, folks here think you are against us, you Dutch, that is . . . " My disorganized argument showed my ongoing confusion.

Gerretse tried to explain things to me. "Look, we're poor farmers. Tenants. We don't even own our own land. We're locked into paying what little we can scratch out of the ground to our land owners. Now, who are those land owners? They're the ones fighting against the British. If you defeat the British, they'll still own our land, and we'll still be unable to buy our own farms. They'll still own our lives. So why should we join the fight against the British? We'd only be fighting against ourselves."

"I suppose. But still . . . "

"For us, the enemy's the rich and powerful who do whatever they want, patriot or Loyalist. My children have one set of clothes. My wife almost less. I'm sorry that you happen to be with the rich and powerful. But if we join a revolution, it'll be to break free from those land owners, whether they're against the king or not."

I just looked at Gerretse, unsure of what to say.

Gerretse put his hand on my shoulder. "The Pownal Loyalists, those you call Tories, think of what they may be facing. Many are very poor. They're not your enemy. They just want to live their lives, too. And if they think like us, it'll most likely be no different under an American government than it's been under the English king."

I stared across our fields, trying to see something that was not there.

"But at least we're friends," he said, slapping me on my back. "So come visit again soon, huh?"

I decided to set aside my multisyllabic arguments. I would attend no more town meetings. I would be content to work with Tryphena, Tryphosa, and my mother, taking care of our farm.

My mother sent Hiram back down to below the ledge to occupy a small house my father built near Eunice. Hiram did not object since that freed him to go to frolics. "The crows'll turn white by the time he turns useful," said Eleazar. Maybe my brother's humor reflected his growing health. At least I hoped so.

Winter settled in. My mother observed, "The snow is butt-high to a tall cow." Then, sometime in November, it warmed up, and all the roads turned to mud, our pond overflowed, and our basement flooded. Our wagons bogged down and chewed their way down toward the rock, making deeper and deeper tracks in the mud. Then it froze again, causing the mud to freeze and the deep tracks to remain. Hiram returned to say that he had run out of wood and needed to stay with us to keep from freezing to death. "Hiram," said my mother, and then gave up, her words a lost cause with Hiram.

In Pownal winter closes in around you so that you live in darkness more than light. Snow piled up over the window sills. Ice cycles stretched from the kitchen roof to the ground. I had many hours to think, read, and write. Samuel and Trintje in New Jersey entered my mind often. Were they writing in their journals? Worse, were they safe? I decided to write them letters, the first I had ever written. One Sunday, in "deep December" as the hymn says, I handed them to the man who carried the mail out.

Word from Canada arrived long after events happened. One Sunday Deuteronomy announced, "General Montgomery and Benedict Arnold have linked up to attack Quebec." The next Sunday, Deuteronomy announced, "General Montgomery has been killed and the colonial forces defeated." I sat, guilty, my friends lost. Michael. Pebonkas. Benedict Arnold, even if I could not call him a friend. Ethan Allen, who might be still alive and in prison somewhere. He may have been executed or killed in the fighting around Quebec. And what of the poor Quebecois who had joined us? Another Sunday, and Deuteronomy reported, "The British have reinforced Boston with many ships and soldiers." Deep December, 1775. The light of my soul was low.

Spring 1776. Deuteronomy announced that Henry Knox and his men had successfully moved the guns of Ticonderoga all the way across Massachusetts to our forces surrounding Boston. Just south of us. I had missed helping them. Ethan said the guns of Ticonderoga would matter. He had that right.

Spring burst upon us and with it a chance to work hard to get our crops planted. In two weeks, the woods exploded in lush green. Hiram retreated downhill. Tryphena and Tryphosa grew stronger every day, if that is possible. Eleazar, too, grew strong. The last snow had melted. Deuteronomy continued to work at keeping our spirits high. But the hatred of patriot for Tory and Tory for patriot continued to divide us, a rot in our community that grew worse as each Sunday passed.

March, 1776. Deuteronomy reported the British had abandoned Boston, but now no one knew where they were headed. Theophilus used the community announcements time to reorganize a militia in town, but I still could not bring myself to join him.

In May, Deuteronomy reported, "George Washington and the militias have left Boston. That's all we know."

Summer came and with it a drought that threatened all our crops. My mother said, "It's so dry, the trees are chasing the dogs around."

I knew that, if they had survived, Michael and Pebonkas were probably still fighting the British, while I was here with other summer patriots.

Then, Sunday, July 14th, 1776, Deuteronomy rose to the pulpit, dispensed with his opening homily and held up a copy of *The Pennsylvania Packet,* a broadside published just the Monday before. "It got here faster than the cat who attacked the paper wasps' nest." He said he wanted to read what it said and, when he finished reading, he would ask us all to join in a prayer of thanksgiving. Then he announced, "Congress has approved a *Declaration of Independence!*"

I sat back in my pew in utter surprise. Mr. Paine and Mr. Hancock and Mr. Adams and all the rest had actually gotten their act together and written what we had talked about. And they had used my title! Well, I did not tell anyone that, for who would have believed me? Tryphena would have said something like, "When pride comes, then comes disgrace," and would have gloried in her smugness. No, I would not give her the chance, but I would know inside me that it was true.

As if in celebration, the drought suddenly ended when a storm blew in so hard my mother said, "If it ever stops, we're all going to fall down." Our pond, which had shrunk deeply, filled up. Our crops revived, though the corn was a bit stunted.

Sunday upon depressing Sunday Deuteronomy fed us news and rumors. "The British are preparing to attack from Canada . . . . The British have turned the Indians on us . . . . The politicians in Boston and Philadelphia have decided to save themselves and let those of us in the western colonies fend for ourselves." The patriots Wilcox, Brown, Parker, and Sykes talked about developing an evacuation plan. Pownalians stored whatever food they could, food that would not rot if we had to abandon it on short notice. The patriots began to arrest the Tories, those who had not fled, that is. The people on the Dutch properties hunkered down.

We worried about Gerretse and his family. My mother sent me with some old clothes when I visited them to trade for some of their vegetables.

Summer and 1776 began their long fade. Rumors spread that Washington was retreating from the British. Theophilus continued to drill the Pownal militia and to urge me to join them. The outspoken Tories in town had all either fled or been arrested. Gerretse told me he was thinking of leaving with his family. Only the verbally militant patriots attended church now.

Hiram became engaged to a lady from Bennington. "God help her!" said my mother, "for Hiram will not."

Then, one Sunday in October, Deuteronomy rose up into his pulpit with a look he had not had since reading the Declaration of Independence. "Praise be to

God!" he exclaimed, and we all knew something was up. "The British started down Lake Champlain with a large fleet of ships, but they've been driven back outside of Valcour Island by General Benedict Arnold." Arnold now a general! I thanked God that I had known Benedict Arnold and thanked Him for allowing General Arnold to survive Quebec. Having seen George Washington sitting in silence and having served with Benedict Arnold, I wished Congress had put General Arnold in charge of the army instead of George Washington, who, as far as I knew, had not yet won a battle.

Later we learned General Arnold's little fleet had actually suffered greatly under the guns of the British, but the British had retreated back to Canada. I wished Congress would appoint General Arnold as Admiral of the Fleet, too, for I had witnessed his sailing ability down Lake Champlain and back.

Outside of church, I tripped over a stone and kicked it. I kicked it again.

I walked back to Theophilus and told him, "I will join the militia now, if you still want me." I had left Michael, Pebonkas, Ethan, and all the rest of my fellow Green Mountain Boys out there somewhere, and I was determined to act as they would.

Winter came again. George Washington had fled across New Jersey. Samuel, Trintje, the Hardenburghs, even Clarence and Douglas—all filled my prayers.

Christmas. Our army defeated the Hessians at Trenton. Perhaps my prayers were answered. Still, my natural reason tormented me, telling me nothing could be so simple.

Then came 1777, which some jokingly called the "year of the hangman" because the sevens looked like gallows. Our militia did not practice much, but we did gather at the tavern in Pownal to talk about what we would do when the British try to attack again. Hiram said that he was "happily wed" to Hannah and could not abandon his bride "just to go gallivanting off in the wilderness." I thought that, if anyone would know what gallivanting was, Hiram was that person.

Tryphosa observed, "From the look on Hannah's face and the calluses on her hands, I think I know why Hiram calls himself 'happily wed.'"

Tryphena nodded. "There's this about it—at least he does not expect us to split his wood anymore."

My journal entries deteriorated into daily weather reports. I had become like the New Jersey farmers Samuel had described. Spring came, we planted our crops and garden, and our militia practiced maneuvers under the guidance of Theophilus. Summer 1777 came, our crops grew well, and our militia felt pretty good about itself. I only felt guilt. July came and, with it, Deuteronomy's terrible news.

"Our army has abandoned Fort Ticonderoga to the British. They've defeated us at Hubbarton. Our army's fighting to delay the British, but we hear they're coming our way." Refugees from up north flooded into Bennington. Rumors of Indian and British atrocities flooded in with them.

Maybe I was done throwing grass and apples. After almost two years, maybe I was ready to toss a few stones.

CHAPTER 21

▼

A DAY I DID NOT WRITE ABOUT

About this day, my journal is silent.

Hanry Turner from Pownal rode up one morning with word to gather in Bennington in the morning, no matter how we got there. He reported the British and their Hessian soldiers marching in our direction and people from Cambridge reporting Indians moving through the region. We were to prepare to stop them before they could move into our area. My mother nodded her acceptance. My sisters Tryphena and Tryphosa solemnly did all they could to prepare me, melting and casting lead balls in the fire, even offering to clean and oil my musket. I was surprised at how much they had picked up about weapons from watching me. Eleazar stuffed my pack with bread and cheese, filled my canteen, and even offered me one of his extra shirts.

We gathered in Bennington, most of us standing or sitting quietly, unlike when we marched out to take Fort Ticonderoga. Up on the high ground we had stored a good deal of powder along with a large number of horses. The militia understood this supply point was the reason the British forces were coming our way.

I heard an officer on a horse proclaim, "No one takes our freedom away in Vermont, no one!"

Sykes, who had joined us, asked, "Where the hell's Vermont?"

- 193 -

"That's where we live, praise the Lord." It was Deuteronomy Dewey, armed like the rest of us. "Our leaders decided that back in June. If you'd been in church any time this past month, you'd know it. 'Some people are wise, and some people are otherwise' as I have heard say." Sykes' empty eye socket twitched.

Many of the Pownal militia had been at Ticonderoga, though none had been with Ethan at Montreal, but we were united again. We soon realized, however, we were outnumbered by militiamen from New Hampshire who had marched rapidly to our side. Their colonel, John Stark, had become our commander. Militia who had abandoned Ticonderoga and fought at Hubbarton were missing, and we did not yet know their fate.

The Boys from Pownal sat together, waiting for our orders, which soon came when a New Hampshire officer directed us to join others from Bennington under Samuel Herrick's command. Together, that made about 300 of us. Satisfied with the numbers, Herrick marched us out of town toward Walloomscoick along the Walloomsac River. Other militia, ahead of us or behind us, all moved west.

As we drew near the farms of Walloomscoick, word spread down the line that our forward militia had encountered the British. We had not expected this so fast. Our officers riding back and forth along the line told us to keep moving. Shortly, they told us scouts had met up with the lead British soldiers, Hessians. General Stark drew us up behind a low hill south and east of the bridge on the Walloomsac and told us to rest. When we started to hear musket fire, all of us rose and moved forward, but our officers kept telling us to hold our march, to wait for orders.

We Boys from Pownal wanted to see what was going on, so Hanry Turner and I crawled to the top of the hill where we could get a view of the low valley ahead of us. Far in the distance we could see movement of soldiers who appeared to be wearing blue uniforms, too far away to tell much more. Militia dispatched to the front of us became sharpshooters, and we could hear an occasional shot.

We continued to watch movement of our militia and the Hessian soldiers, but received no orders. Every other unit seemed to be moving but us. "Damn," said Theophilus, "we're the reserve forces of the reserve forces of the reserve forces. We'll be the last to do anything." We kept watching as the Hessians occupied a hill far off to our right front and appeared to be digging in. As they did, other enemy began to spread out in the field in front of us along the Walloomsac, and even more moved up a small hill to our left front, then began to dig in. Many of the men in front and to our right appeared dressed just as we were. "Tory bastards," said Sykes, whose eye socket twitched mightily. We were facing our neighbors.

When we finally received orders to move out, we were nervous, but anxious to get into battle. Hanry looked at me with eyes wide open. I imagine my eyes looked the same.

Remembering Montreal, I wondered whether I could do anything. I still had never fired at an enemy, though they had not hesitated to fire at me.

Our anticipation soon turned to frustration when we realized what we were doing. Our one long line of march extended from the top of the hill down the hill to the right, then back behind the hill and up again to the top. We were marching in one continuous circle. Theophilus had a huge grin on his face. "General Stark wants to make it appear we're more than we really are. So we're just going to march up, show ourselves, disappear out of sight, then march up again. That way, they may think we're hundreds more than we are and not dare attack us."

"Why waste energy on this?" Sykes asked.

"Look behind," said Theophilus. "All our militia ain't here yet. We're buying time to build our strength."

So we marched until the sun started to set. Then we settled down to rest and eat. The forces opposite us had done the same. Fires broke out on the hill to our right, across the front, and up to the hill on the left. We ate, told jokes, bragged about what we would do to those Hessians and Tories, and eventually went to sleep, that is, those of us who could sleep. Next day we would test how brave we really were.

But the next morning it started to rain. It poured. It poured and poured all day long. Now the enemy was the water. We did all we could to keep our powder and muskets dry and huddled together, cursing the weather. General Stark rode along the line, giving encouragement to us. It was the first time I had seen him, thin and craggy, but full of energy. "Patience," he told us. "Our time will come."

The next morning, August 16, Sergeant Theophilus woke us while it was still dark. The rain had stopped. Colonel Herrick told us to eat as quickly as possible, not to waste time cooking. I was glad for the bread and cheese Eleazar had given me. Then we started marching to our left behind the hill, all of us Boys from Pownal and Bennington. We passed other militia moving to the top of the hill and off to our right—militia from Massachusetts. We were being pushed pretty fast, and what with trying to get our breath, we spoke very little. We moved along the edge of a field of flax and could make out to the north and east of us a redoubt, its walls thrown up hastily by the Hessians. Militia from Massachusetts and New Hampshire were taking up positions before it.

"Damn me, but we're just running around all the action," Hanry puffed.

We crossed a road, dropped down into a ravine, and reached the Hoosic River, which joined the Walloomsac off to our right. Our officers walked us into the river, our muskets held over our heads. We could hear musket fire from the redoubt up on the hill.

The sun rose behind us. "Time's just right to attack them," said Theophilus, "while they have to stare into the sun."

We halted to rest a while and heard cannon fire open up from far in front of us. None of it came in our direction. Then we were up and jogging across another field and into the woods. Theophilus yelled, "Indians, off to the right." We knelt down and prepared for an attack. But the Indians kept moving back, actually running back, and soon were out of site. "Keep alert for an attack," yelled Colonel Herrick, and we moved out again. Finally we were told to halt and prepare to attack. Cannon fire continued. Colonel Herrick called Theophilus, several other sergeants, and our officers to move forward with him to scout out the enemy's positions.

Theophilus returned, gathered us around, and reported. "We got Tories and Canadians to our front. They're facing across the river toward where we were. Into the sun." I could see the New Hampshire men starting to move down toward them. "The Tories and Canadians have thrown up a breastwork, but they're facing away from us. They still don't know we're here."

Later, he said, "Damn, they got Jaegers among them."

"Jaegers?"

"Light infantry. Riflemen. They can pick us off before we get in range of our muskets."

Firing came from the direction of the redoubt we had just passed, a lot of it. The noise grew. We could barely see anything. Musket smoke filled the air.

"Fix your bayonets," ordered Theophilus. "Wait for the order to charge and then run like Hell. Don't shoot until you know you can hit something." My hands were sweaty.

The firing stopped from the area of the redoubt we had passed. Then, from our left, off the hill where we now knew Hessians had been firing a cannon in our direction, the sounds of more musket fire rattled. Before I knew what was happening, all around me men rose up and started marching forward. The Boys from Pownal were right there with them. Then we began running. No one shouted. We appeared in a field behind the Tories and Canadians before any saw us, but they soon turned and started firing toward us. We kept running, some firing in their direction, though I doubt anyone could have hit anything while moving on the hoof.

Finally, the order came to form a line. The Tories and Canadians were trying to reload. "Fire!" I fired my first shot at an enemy. A few fell. We reloaded. Others were still fixing their bayonets. "Forward!" and we ran.

We all charged up to the breastworks. I think I fired my musket, but I don't know. I was running and yelling and pointing it who knows where. The enemy soldiers were climbing out over the breastworks on the other side. When we reached the breastworks, we all scrambled and jumped up on its walls, some of us shooting over the logs and dirt in the hopes of hitting one of the soldiers opposing us. Smoke filled the air. I cocked my musket and jerked the trigger. My musket misfired.

Suddenly a young boy stood up in front of me. For what seemed like minutes, but probably only seconds, we stared at each other. I swear I thought I was looking at myself in a mirror. My mirror image looked scared, his eyes wide open. I felt myself in a dream, seeing myself.

Before I could act, my mirror image raised his musket, preparing to shoot me in the face. I lunged with my musket, and my bayonet went into his face, into his eye socket. I think I screamed and pulled away. But my bayonet pulled out of my musket and stayed in his face. We screamed. I in utter horror. My mirror image in utter agony.

He fell dead, lying on his back, the bayonet standing straight in the air.

I dropped my musket and stumbled back, heaving everything in me, my stomach, my soul.

All around me, men were wrestling each other to the ground, swinging their muskets at each other, screaming. I was unable to move. A Tory was standing on the breastworks then, pointing his musket at me. I stared at him, frozen. Suddenly someone jerked me backwards and down. "Erastus, take this musket, here!" she shouted. Her! Another person came up behind her, dressed in a militia-style jacket. Them! Tryphena and Tryphosa! "Trust in the Lord, Erastus!" My mother had sent them after me again. Now I knew—they had saved me before. "Don't just stand there, Erastus! Fight!" and then they were gone.

I do not know if I was more shocked at realizing that they had been trailing after me like overbearing older sisters or at realizing I had just killed someone and might be killed any second now. I turned back toward the breastworks and saw fighting on the other side of it. I loaded the musket and climbed up over the breastworks, where I could now see that the New Hampshire men had crossed the bridge over the river and had trapped the Tories and Canadians between us.

Men had fallen on both sides. Though many Tories and Canadians were trying to surrender, our militia continued firing, while officers tried to gather them together and stop the slaughter. I saw some of the enemy running off between us and the hill where the cannon fire had now stopped. An officer yelled at us to follow them, and we began moving off in their direction. Now we came together and were told to form up in a line, which we gradually managed, our drill practice finally coming into play. New Hampshire men, men of Vermont, all of us together.

"Take your time," said Theophilus, his arm bleeding. "We'll need our energy."

We proceeded along the river, picking our way, our eyes sweeping everywhere. Occasionally a shot or a yell would sound, but we began to think we were safe. "We've won, Erastus!" Hanry said.

"It ain't over. Keep your mouth shut," cautioned Theophilus, his arm now covered in more blood.

He was right. We had not gone more than a mile when suddenly shots came at us from the woods. Hessians were moving among the trees, fighting just like us, from cover. We moved in closer to them. Just then, from behind and above them, more Hessians fired down upon us. Our group was cut off from the others. We broke and ran for cover. I ran into the woods, hoping to put some trees between me and those trying to do me in. But I ran into a batch of blackberries, their thorns scratching my face and the branches tangling themselves around my feet. I fell, losing my musket. I was done.

Not only Hessians were trying to kill me. Terror gripped me. Now I heard the fearful screams of Indians and saw several of them running toward me through the woods. I tried to reach my musket, but my arm was caught in the blackberry branches. Lord, I was a dead man. Three screaming Indians charged in my direction, muskets in one hand, tomahawks in the other. I closed my eyes, resigned to die, but they ran right by me. The Hessians had stopped firing and had disappeared. I looked up to see an Indian with long black hair staring down at me. Behind him stood several others. He appeared to be their leader. He stepped toward me. I closed my eyes again.

"Well, if it isn't Erastus! Haven't seen you since Montreal. What've you been up to?" I opened my eyes and stared back. "All this fighting caused you to forget your courtesy? Won't you say hello to an old friend?" It was Pebonkas!

"You've gone over to the British!" I said, trying to stand and willing to be killed by that traitor, my former friend. He reached over, grabbed me by the arm, and pulled the brambles off me.

"Oh, don't be dramatic, Erastus. Save that for the New York theatre. Here," he said, stepping toward me, "give me a hug." And that's what he did, while his Mohawk-Maqua-Kanien'kehaka friends laughed at me. My jaw hung open. My brain whirled.

"Look, Erastus, I don't have time for a celebratory party. You're not the only one who ran at Montreal."

"I did not run."

He smiled at me.

"Why are you fighting us?" I screamed, shocked he had turned against his friends.

"I saw you being pulled over the cliff at Montreal," he answered. "Thought to myself that's a good idea. So I jumped over myself. Tried to find you, but you were gone by then."

I tried to absorb what he said.

Pebonkas continued explaining. "I went back to Kahnawake, tried to convince them to join forces with us. Some did, some didn't. So we infiltrated the British forces, pretended to be allies, and for the past week we've been trying to spread fear among the Kanien'kehaka who allied themselves with the British. We've done a fair job, don't you think? Most Kanien'kehaka all turned for home as soon as they realized they'd lose."

"You really one of us?" I could not think.

"Truly, Erastus. And what about Michael? He with you?" Two of Pebonkas' Kanien'kehaka friends returned to join him.

"I lost him in Quebec," I answered.

"Well, he's tough. Now, you'll forgive me, we've got to keep spreading fear. Keep your head down." And at that, they turned away from me and ran back into the woods. I never saw Pebonkas again.

I walked out of the woods just in time to see more militia moving up. Seth Warner's men had arrived from somewhere. I joined them as fast as I could. One of the men told me they were off to stop Hessian reinforcements from reaching Stark's tired men. They looked haggard enough themselves. I now know they had escaped from Ticonderoga and Mt. Independence, had fought a rear guard action against both the Redcoats and Hessians all the way from Lake Champlain to Hubbarton. They had fought and retreated from Hubbarton, but slowed the British down so they could not trap the Yankees between them and another column of Redcoats. Now, pushed by Warner, they had rushed down here from Manchester and Arlington to help us.

I loaded my musket.

We soon came upon more of our men firing from behind trees across the river at what appeared to be a newly arrived army. After the battle, I learned that this was Breymann's relief column, more Hessians trying to save those we had just defeated. I lay down behind a log, exhausted. I plopped down beside a skeleton of a man who looked at me long and hard and then said, "Well, saints be praised if it in't me old friend Erastus. How've you been, Erastus?" I looked at him, trying to place the face behind the beard.

"Michael? Is that you?"

"Ah, yes, well, let's see, I last saw you near Ethan, didn't I? Looking like you'd seen the banshees. Myself captured too, you know."

"You got away!"

"Yes, well, your old friend Ethan talked so much while they marched us back into Montreal, they got tired of hearing him and yelled at him to shut up, which, of course, being Ethan Allen, he did not." Michael poured powder down his musket barrel. "They gathered around him, threatening to hang him then and there, so mad were they." He stopped to ramrod a wad and ball down his musket.

"Then what?"

"Well, I being so unimportant, I decided to take me away and slipped into a doorway to hide. So proud were they of their victory, they didn't know how many prisoners they had. So here I am," he said, pouring some powder in the flashpan.

"I am sorry I left you Michael." Stupidly, we lifted our heads to look at one another. Musket balls broke limbs over our heads.

"Well, you seem intent on getting me killed now." He fired in the general direction of our antagonists and ducked to reload.

"You know you cannot hit a thing that way," I said. I loaded my musket.

"Oh, Mr. Too-Wise-for-His-Breeches. You'll be telling me how to shoot? Just shoot in the general direction and keep your head down."

I raised my musket up to fire over the top of the log. The pan flashed but nothing happened. "Dump it out," said Michael.

"What?"

"How many times've you loaded it since firing it last?"

I slapped the barrel. Three musket balls and powder slid out the barrel.

"See?" said Michael, "No matter. They stopped shooting for a while. So, how's the family?"

"How can you ask about my family when we are about to die?" Or kill someone else, I thought.

"Have it your way. Where'd you like to be buried?"

His humor made me feel better. "My family is fine, but wait until I tell you about my sisters."

"Still old maids?" asked Michael.

"Worse. Old soldiers," I answered.

"What? What do you mean?" he asked, firing blindly over the log again.

Just then a loud cheer came from the men around us, at least those who had been paying attention to what was happening in the battle. The Hessian force, led by Breymann, was dropping back.

"Let's get them!" someone shouted.

"Hold on, men," an officer ran up. "It's getting late. General Stark wants us to pull back. We don't want to get caught in a trap once it gets dark."

Men swore at the officer, but gave up the battle gladly.

By the time we worked our way back to the field below the Hessian redoubt, the scene was a terrible one. Bodies from both sides were scattered across the fields.

Colonel Stark had given orders to bury the dead. We joined others dragging the bodies of Hessians and Tories to an empty cellar hole used for storing potatoes from a nearby farm. Michael McGinnis and I pulled them by the arms or legs or whatever we could grab. I could not stand holding them by the forearm and feeling their hands rub against me, so I always reached for their legs. We pulled the boots off the bodies to use ourselves, took knives, swords, bayonets, and bullet pouches if they still wore any, though few did, and threw the stuff on any wagons nearby. We left their uniforms on. We dropped them gently into the holes, one on top of another.

Searching for other bodies, I glanced into another cellar hole, and there lay my mirror image, the bayonet still standing in his eye socket.

"Grab that, would you, Erastus?" said Michael. "Hate to waste a bayonet."

I could not. The thought of pulling the bayonet from his poor head filled me with horror, with disgust at myself. I turned and walked away, a pressure in my brain that dizzied me. I aimed myself back toward Bennington.

Michael's voice spoke at my side. "Don't you worry over that, Erastus. There's more of it ahead of us, I fear."

We moved back toward town. Rounding a curve of the river, I spotted a Hessian propped up against a tree up ahead, begging for water. I started to reach for my canteen, but just then one of our militia stepped up to him, looked down on him, and shot him. I yelled to stop him, screamed that he was already down and out of the battle. I screamed.

The shooter turned and looked at me. Looked at me and grinned. Grinned his mostly toothless grin. Hunt Hungerford! He said nothing, but took out his knife and carved a mark on his musket.

I raised my musket to shoot him. This time killing was right. I pressed my finger on the trigger and tried to shoot. I tried.

Hungerford turned to walk away from me, saying, "Enjoy it, Erastus. Grow up." When I think about my lost opportunities in life, this one haunts me still.

I ran up to the Hessian and saw him looking at me with eyes filled with pain. "Michael, we have to help him."

"Let him go, Erastus, we'll never be able to get him help in time."

"Help me, Michael!"

We wrapped our coats around our muskets, making a litter of sorts, and put the Hessian on it, still breathing.

We passed another potato pit, filled with bodies wearing plain clothes, no uniforms. Tories. Many shot in the head.

The road back was filled with the walking wounded and with others being carried in other makeshift litters or on horseback. Many had broken legs and arms. Some horses carried two men hanging over their backs. Men with broken heads, blood still streaming down their faces, walked with determination or walked only with the help of someone else. Captured Tories and Hessians, not wounded or slightly wounded, helped carry their comrades or even their enemies, our men. As we passed scattered houses, women and children came out with water and offers to help. Occasionally a body lay sprawled beside the road, dead.

As we reached the outskirts of Bennington, the houses gradually filled up with the more badly wounded among the patriot soldiers. We were directed toward Elijah Dewey's Tavern, across from the Congregational Church, where the Hessian and Tory prisoners were being kept until we could determine what to do with them.

Wives and children were stopping soldiers as they passed, seeking information about their sons, husbands, and fathers. Wounded Hessians and Tories lay on the ground between the Church and Tavern, guarded by militiamen. I saw Tryphena and Tryphosa moving among the wounded offering them water or whatever little comfort their words might be. They saw me and smiled. I could not be more proud of them.

Tories able to stand were tied in pairs so they could not easily escape and made to stand together. Some townspeople gathered around them, jeered at them, and spat at them. I could not bring myself to hate them. They had fought as bravely as we had, even if they were on the wrong side.

We looked for a doctor for our wounded Hessian before he died. We set him down while Michael went looking for someone who could minister to him. Michael found a surgeon behind the church, so we carried the Hessian there. Dr. Roebuck had his hands full with many wounded, but I would not leave the Hessian until he looked at him.

The Hessian briefly opened his eyes. I bent down and asked him his name. He shook his head that he did not understand. "Wie heissen zie?" said Dr. Roebuck.

"Jacob Hintersass," he whispered.

"I will be back to check on you," I said, but knew he could not understand my English. Dr. Roebuck said he would handle things and told me to go help those I could, so I walked back out in front of the church. More and more Hessian and Tory prisoners were arriving. Those Hessians well enough to walk, their faces showing their fear, were herded into Dewey's Tavern. Tories continued to be tied together and forced to endure the taunts of our people. More wives and children were crying. Our guards pushed back Tory wives from reaching their husbands. Militia not helping the wounded tried to rest.

I searched for Green Mountain Boys from Pownal, Michael, and my twin sisters. I found several Pownal men resting, in no mood to talk or to celebrate. No one knew where Theophilus or Deuteronomy were. Michael had found Tryphena and was helping her care for some of the wounded. A group of the New Hampshire militia offered me bellytimber, their wheat cooked in water. The evening was hot.

A minister from Massachusetts, his shirt covered in blood, was preaching to no one and to everyone in general as he walked down the street. "Did we not put the fear of the Lord in those Hessians? Did we not bring down the thunder of Heaven upon those Tory traitors? Do the British now know the terrible fury of our vengeance? Are the men of Massachusetts not the fighters I said they would be?"

In front of the church, Mary Faye cradled the body of her husband John and sobbed. Two weeks later, she too was dead—of a broken heart. She lies buried by him in the churchyard near where I last saw them.

I do not know if anyone not wounded slept well that night, though many tried. I found a porch near the church and tavern where I squeezed in between several others, but we tossed all night long, listening to the moans and cries of the wounded.

I tell you, even today, so many years later, I do not need my journal to remember that day, August 16, 1777.

By the next day, the wounded had fallen silent, but the morning began hot, and the day became hotter. The sound I remember most was the sound of the flies. They buzzed around open wounds. Behind Elijah Dewey's Tavern, a pile of Hessian bodies lay, those prisoners whose wounds could not be cared for. More flies buzzed. Farmers and their families began to take the wounded away to their homes to care for them, whether they were Hessian or patriot. Tories well enough to walk began to be marched south. Wounded Tories were herded into wagons to ride into imprisonment. How many survived the rides, I cannot tell.

I saw Mr. DeVoet from Pownal among the Tory prisoners and nodded at him. He called me over, tears in his eyes, saying his son George had died after the battle, and asked me to try to find his other son, Abraham. I wondered about the boy I had killed, but would not say anything for fear of adding to his misery. I said I would look for his other son and walked away. I did not see either father or son again.

Militia began gathering the Hessian prisoners together. Hundreds of them, young and old, stood silently. I saw Dr. Roebuck, who spoke German, talking to some of them, along with a Dutchman from Walloomscoick, Heinrich Linker. I asked the doctor about the Hessian Michael and I had carried to him. "He was alive when last I treated him, Erastus. Look for him with the wounded prisoners." And then he commented, "Look at them, Erastus, they don't even know why they're here. These men are almost entirely Braunschweigers, not Hessians. They joined the army so that they could survive. And here they are."

I remembered the Cooks in Arlington and thought of their son. How many who actually fight for our cause or theirs do it just to help their families survive?

Only a few Braunschweigers still wore their blue jackets. All their white pants were dirt-stained, many bloodstained.

Wagons had begun to arrive in town from the farms and villages around us, the three Pownals, Arlington, Shaftsbury, Manchester, Williamstown. I suspect those from down the Walloomsac River helped in their own area. Deuteronomy showed up leading other wagons. He had gone from the battle directly home to gather help from the Pownal folk. Hiram and his wife Hannah drove their wagon in. Later my mother showed up with my brother Eleazar, our ox pulling our wagon along slowly but steadily. They brought ground corn to be shared among the militia.

I checked on Jacob Hintersass and found him lying on the porch of Dewey's Tavern under guard. He had survived, but he was unconscious.

Officers of the New Hampshire militia began to round up their men who could walk and lead them out of town to make room for those who needed help most. I saw Colonel Stark. He complained loudly that some "low, thieving bastard" had stolen his mare and saddle while the battle was going on. "How'm I going to explain that to my wife Molly?"

Two officers were animatedly comparing their wounds. I stopped to listen. "You know those two?" I asked a man who laughed at their stories.

"Joab Stafford, he's the one sitting on the right, and the other's John Orr."

Joab had his bandaged foot raised on a rock and was explaining how he received his wound. "I was leading my men around the Tory redoubt, trying to find a way to attack, but I couldn't see it because we were down in a ravine by the river. Then, soon as I came out of the ravine, saw the top of the redoubt, and ordered a charge, some scoundrel up there shot me here in the foot. My men charged up the hill, and I was left lying in the dirt. Those cowards all ran as soon as we attacked."

"You think you've been mistreated," said John, whose bandaged foot lay near Joab's. "I was leading my men through the flax in front of that redoubt. We were only about fifteen rods from them. We crept along, careful to move toward them before they could see us, when some noisy fellows down in the ravine started shouting. That alerted all in the redoubt, so I stood up to order a charge, and they shot me in the foot, too!"

"Are you telling me that I caused you to be shot!" said Joab.

"Well, we had them all to ourselves before you opened your mouth."

Seeing their amusement in their misery, I felt better. I went back to Dr. Roebuck to ask him what would become of the wounded Hessians. "They'll probably stay here until they're able to be moved and then be sent off to prison somewhere. But I've been told, if they agree and if someone can swear to look after them, they'll be put on parole—free to go, but not to fight, or else put in prison if that's what's needed."

Seth Warner, pale as ever, walked his horse through the wounded and the well, enthusiastic and encouraging. He urged his Rangers and other local militiamen to go home if they could, but be prepared to regroup at a moment's notice. He reached down from his horse to shake the hand of Leazar Edgerton, who, I later learned, had slowed the Hessian advance by burning a bridge over the Sancoick Brook all by himself while being fired at by the enemy. "You bought us time, Mr. Edgerton," Seth said, "and for that I'm thankful." He looked up, saw me, smiled, waved, and rode off.

Michael was about to go with some of the militia from Arlington, but Tryphena asked him to stay with us. "After all," she said, "Erastus will be there, and you two can share stories." I suspected she had other motivations, though.

My mother was tending a wounded man from New Hampshire, her sinewy arms lifting him into a more comfortable position. "There is a wounded soldier I would like us to take home," I said. She just looked at me. "He is a Hessian, well, a Braunschweiger."

"Why would you do this?" she asked, her mouth grim.

"As a favor, please. Because he has been abused by us. One of us shot him even though he was wounded and helpless."

"Isn't he a prisoner?" asked my mother.

"He can be paroled. We have to swear to watch after him."

"Well, Erastus, far be it for me to criticize your judgment now that you have gone off and almost lost your life, but . . . "

"The battle is over, mother," said Tryphena, who overheard.

"It might have been Erastus," added Tryphosa, her hands bloody from helping bandage the wounded.

"I'll care for him," they both added, almost together. Again, my pride in my sisters made me see them through new eyes.

I hugged both. "You have saved more than his life," I said. They looked at me. "But I think I am old enough now so that our mother does not have to send you to look after me whenever I go on an adventure." We laughed. My mother raised her eyebrows.

"If I did not . . . " she started to say.

"I know," I said.

Michael, Tryphena, Tryphosa, and I all carried the Braunschweiger—Hintersass—to our wagon, and our ox carried us all home to Carpenter Hill, where I now had time to write in my journal again.

August 20, 1777

I am done fighting. My heroic story is over.

Many years ago, I asked what good a revolution was if people did not shoot people. I guess I was right—and wrong. Men fight. Men die. Life at home goes on. I am home now, but the fighting and dying will not stop. Where would we be without leaders like Ethan Allen? And with leaders like him, where are we now?

Carpenter Hill is so peaceful. My family comforts me. How lucky I am. If only I did not dream at night.

CHAPTER 22

▼

ONE EPILOGUE AFTER ANOTHER

I would have fought in the Battle of Bemis Heights and helped defeat General Burgoyne outside of Saratoga if a tree had not fallen on me. I would probably have been at the Battle of Yorktown when the war ended if it had not been for that tree.

Well, the tree falling is true. My mother had worked our farm often by herself, what with Eleazar weak, Hiram useless, and Tryphena and Tryphosa off skulking after me, watching after me, and, yes, saving my hide several times. So, I swore to repay her and show my appreciation by cutting wood for the winter. What with winter very rapidly advancing in Vermont, it being August in Vermont, you see, and I being quite strong from all my soldiering, I took up the ax and saw to cut a goodly supply of wood, at which I was doing very well, thank you, when a tree twisted, just as it must have with my father and just as it must have with Ann Story's husband Amos, and fell on me. I was sharp enough to jump out of the way, but not quite far enough, and thus it broke my leg in several places. That is why I did not defeat General Burgoyne.

And well, frankly, I had finally fired my musket at an enemy. Fired it enough. Enough fighting. Enough rhetoric. So I retired from the War to our farm in Pownal.

But you know the truth. The War brought out the best and worst of us, and I, well, I fell somewhere in between. Like most of us, I imagine.

That should be the end of my story, but now everybody in my family thinks they are authors and must have a say in this history, so out of the goodness of my soul I have agreed to allow them to write their stories here as a way of conclusion. Of course, I will have the final say. But first, out of the enormous respect I still have for Ethan Allen, I asked him to write his story, which he did some years ago and which now begins this collection of mini-tales.

Ethan Allen's Story

Erastus is a good lad and has fulfilled all of my expectations of him as the historian of the Green Mountain Boys. Of course, he could not be expected to write about what happened to me after I was captured by the enemy at Montreal, so I have consented to do that here. Most pertinently, if any of you would purchase my excellent treatise on my experiences in captivity, *The Narrative of Colonel Ethan Allen* by Ethan Allen, published in Philadelphia in 1779 and available from your usual book purveyors, you shall be enlightened by reading the fullness of my story. Consequently, since I have put to print all of this in that work, here I will but quote enough of it just as it was printed to flavor your imaginations and enhance your mental appetite for more. I begin immediately following my capture:

> I came to the barrack-yard at Montreal, where I met Gen. Prescott, who asked me my name, which I told him, he then asked me, whether I was that Col. Allen, who took Ticonderoga, I told him I was the very man; he then shook his cane over my head, calling many hard names, among which he frequently used the word rebel, and put himself in a great rage. I told him he would not do well to cane me, for I was not accustomed to it, and shook my fist at him, telling him that that was the beetle of mortality for him, if he offered to strike . . . .
>
> I was after sent with the prisoners taken with me to an armed vessel in the river, which lay off against Quebec, under the command of Capt. M'Cloud of the British, who treated me in a very generous and obliging manner, and according to my rank . . . .
>
> When the prisoners were landed [in England], . . . the majority [in Parliament] argued, that I ought to be executed, and that the opposition was really a rebellion, but that policy obliged them not to do it, inasmuch as the Congress had then most prisoners in their power . . . .

From there I was shipped on board a prison ship to Halifax and was continued in confinement until I was paroled in Long Island, but, in between suffered and witnessed sundry intemperate tortures of the poor prisoners in their custody. It was while still in captivity I learned of the victory of the Green Mountain Boys at Bennington after Seth Warner's brave men delayed the British at Hubbarton. I wrote in my treatise,

> The downfall of general Burgoyne, and surrender of his whole army, dashed the aspiring hopes and expectations of the enemy, and brought low the imperious spirit of an opulent, puissant and haughty nation, and made the tories bite the ground with anguish, exalting the valour of the free-born sons of America, and raised their fame and that of their brave commanders to the clouds . . . .

On the 4th of May, 1778, I was released at Elizabethtown-point

> . . . and, in a transport of joy, landed on liberty ground, and as I advanced into the country, received the acclamations of a grateful people . . . . [In] Valley forge, where I was courteously received by gen. Washington, with peculiar marks of his approbation and esteem, and was introduced to most of the generals and many of the principal officers, of the army, who treated me with respect, and after having offered Gen. Washington my further service, in behalf of my country, as soon as my health (which was very much impaired) would admit, and obtain his license to return home, I took my leave of his excellency . . . and set out for Bennington, the capital of the Green Mountain Boys . . . . Three cannon were fired that evening, and the next morning col. Herrick gave orders, and fourteen more were discharged, welcoming me to Bennington, my usual place of abode; thirteen for the United States, and one for young Vermont."

Michael McGinnis's Story

As you know, we won our revolution against the British, but it took many more years after our battle at Walloomscoick, what people call the Battle of Bennington now.

Recall how Erastus and I were separated at the battle of Montreal, where Ethan Allen not surprisingly miscalculated his ability to defeat the enemy. After I escaped by hiding in a doorway, I made my way to a Quebecois village where they obliged me by rowing me across the St. Lawrence River, in exchange for the remaining rum I carried in my flask, along with the flask itself—the thieving river rats. Then I worked my way south by begging in the St. Et Cetera villages Erastus has written of and found shelter in the home of an Irish family named Ryan in the village of St. George d'Henryville. They fed me potatoes until I cried for the old country.

When word arrived of colonial troops in the neighborhood, I thanked my hosts and strode out to find them. I discovered Seth Warner and his men, most of them from Vermont, and so, with no Ethan Allen to stick my neck in somebody else's noose, I joined Warner's troops, certain anything we did would be well-conceived. We settled near Longueil along the St. Lawrence River while our General Montgomery was laying siege to St. John. At last our side held a strong position. Since Montreal was an island, the British would have to cross the St. Lawrence just as we had done before Allen's disaster there.

Our scouts ranged all up and down the river, keeping their eyes out for the British. When they returned telling us the British were boarding boats, we hid ourselves along the banks and enjoyed the shooting when they tried to land. At last it was their turn to run—or row—for safety. (I think I recognized among them the river rats who had taken my flask of rum, so I sent a packet of curses after them, riding on my lead musket balls.)

Then the river froze, and we prepared to attack Montreal. Again. I had premonitions of more banshees coming at us. Fear is banshee enough. To our relief, the British abandoned Montreal and, like frightened deer, hightailed it for Quebec, so we followed and attacked them there. The banshees did not come to me before that battle, but they should have. General Montgomery found himself unfortunately killed, and later we heard Benedict Arnold, who also attacked Quebec, had either been captured, wounded, or killed. Again we retreated back from Canada.

A plague of disasters befell us. Deceitful villagers claimed they'd guide us toward the British, but deliberately mired us in a swamp. So we mucked our way out of Quebec, slipped down to Deschambault, and then withdrew south to Sorel, where smallpox broke out and decimated us. We left many good Vermont men there. We escaped Canada and settled across from Ticonderoga on Mount Independence.

The British General Burgoyne coughed in our direction, so, to avoid falling sick, we abandoned Ticonderoga and Mount Independence without a fight. Warner led us to Hubbarton where all we could do was stand, shoot, and run, but all our run, turn, shoot, and run slowed the British, allowing us to fight at Walloomscoick with Erastus.

When Erastus took us to his home after the battle, I was assailed by a more persistent enemy, his sister Tryphena. You may not know this, but I am unable to read and write, so Erastus is writing this for me as I tell it. I therefore must tell you this woman Tryphena is the strongest woman I ever met in America, resembling the Irish caileens I used to know. Of course, wisdom compels me to note how beauteous she is. When Erastus stupidly broke his leg chopping down trees, I decided to enlist with Captain Eli Noble. We joined Seth Warner again because we now had General Burgoyne trapped outside Saratoga at Bemis Heights. So impressed was I with Tryphena's qualifications that I decided to take her with me. Truth be told, she told me she was going to Bemis Heights, so nothing I could do would stop her.

Erastus will not admit it, but his sisters are excellent shots, and Tryphena can out-soldier any man I know. She tied up her hair, hid her characteristics in other ways, and fought right alongside me until Burgoyne was forced to surrender. It was the greatest victory of Americans in the Revolution. Even Benedict Arnold showed up again, absorbed a musket ball in his leg, and led us to our victory. When our General Gates would not attack, he did. Arnold is one reason we won.

After the battle, Tryphena decided I was tired of fighting and took me back to Pownal Centre and Carpenter Hill. Tryphena's command of the Bible is undeniable, and she used all her ability at quoting it to try to convert me from Catholicism to her Protestant sect, which, for an Irishman, is blasphemous. Once a Catholic, always a Catholic. But to quiet her incessant quoting of the Bible, I agreed to marry her in the Pownal church. The Reverend Dewey presided. You can check it in the records of the town clerk.

Now I live at the bottom of the ledge with Tryphena and Erastus's mother Rachel, and I invite you to come visit. I am a mere shadow of my former self.

Tryphena's Story

You must have realized by now how naïve and incompetent Erastus was before he went off with the Green Mountain Boys and our Uncle Hiram, as lazy a man as ever existed. So it should not have surprised you to learn that our mother sent Tryphosa and me trailing after him wherever he went. He got in trouble climbing a cliff with that Charles Charters, looked ridiculous learning to drill with Theophilus Bates, and was foolish enough to allow Hiram to take him into Mr. Fay's Tavern, so would you ever expect him to survive on his own? What else were we to do but look after the boy? He would have me capitalize "boy" to designate him as a "Green Mountain Boy," the self-glorifying, self-serving, and self-righteous name of the rascals who had little else to do with their time but play at soldier, but I say to you that he was a small-letter boy if anyone was.

Tryphosa and I walked effortlessly into Fort Ticonderoga since that prideful Ethan Allen allowed entry to anyone who wanted in those first days. Colonel

Arnold would not have done so, and I appreciate Arnold's dismay at Ethan Allen, even though we do not speak well of Benedict Arnold these days. We passed as soldiers easily enough since none of the boys had uniforms. So, with muskets lying here, there, and anywhere shortly after the fort fell, we found two for ourselves before Colonel Arnold conducted his inventory.

When Erastus climbed in a boat to row with Ethan Allen up to Crown Point, and when he so clumsily fell out of it, who do you suppose rescued him? Why, Tryphosa and me. When Ethan Allen irresponsibly put all his soldiers in harm's way outside of St. John and allowed the British to fire upon them with their cannon, who do you suppose rescued Erastus that time? Yes, Tryphosa and me. Then, when that same Ethan Allen rowed across the Saint Lawrence with his men and recklessly managed to get them captured, who was there to rescue Erastus yet one more time? Well, by now you have ascertained the consistency of behavior needed to keep Erastus well and alive. So, it should have come as no surprise to Erastus when we were right behind him at the Battle of what-is-now-called Bennington to keep him from wandering around in a daze and succumbing to an enemy musket ball. But then he went running off after the fleeing enemy, and we lost track of him.

For those of you who do not believe a woman or two could do all that, I say to you, "My strength is made perfect in weakness," and "Therefore all things whatsoever ye would that men should do to you, do ye even so to them."

And how did our mother manage the farm while we were away? Why, neighbors, that's how. The Carpenters, the Thompsons, the Gardners, our older brothers. Farmers help each other out. How else could we all manage?

As for Michael, he truly is a cute little man, even if he alleges to remain a Catholic.

Tryphosa's Story

Actually, I believe that I am stronger than Tryphena except for her spirituality. You should know that, after she married Michael McGinnis, she convinced Reverend Dewey to allow her to be his assistant. She could be the minister herself once he steps down, but our town would never accept a woman as minister, even if she could shoot straighter than any of them and quote the Bible better than any minister. She will lecture me about the folly of pride once she reads what I have written.

I am so grateful Erastus saved Jacob Hintersass. That one act alone convinced Tryphena and me to no longer waste our precious time looking after Erastus.

Once Tryphena left with Michael to fight against General Burgoyne, I was left caring for both Jacob with his nasty chest wound and Erastus with his unfortunately broken leg. Jacob was so nice as he was recovering, but Erastus was a troublesome brew of regret and disappointment, constantly asking me to do this for him and that for him. "Bring me my journal." "Bring me my pen." "Make me more ink." "Go to Bennington and trade more cheese for more paper." Jacob was sugar. Erastus was salt. Jacob asked for nothing. Erastus asked everything. "What has happened to Mr. DeVoet?" As if I knew. "Have any of the Tory sympathizers come back into town?" "How many Dutch are still living here?" He wanted me to find out the answers to all these nosy inquiries so he could write about it all in his journal. "It is part of the history of the Green Mountain Boys," he would explain as his excuse for all his constant writing. My recommendation for any woman who is thinking of marrying a writer is to find herself a good farmer.

We sent our brother Eleazar to find Dr. Roebuck when Jacob started burning with a fever. Poor Dr. Roebuck looked terrible from his constant work helping to save the wounded, both Yankee and Hessian or Braunschweiger. He instructed my mother and me how to clean the wounds Jacob suffered and how to feed him to keep him strong. Erastus was no help whatsoever during this time.

Dr. Roebuck had studied in the Dutch University of Leyden, where he learned the difference between sickness and health to be the balance between acidity and alkalinity. Poor Jacob's body was either one or the other he explained, so he instructed us to let him drink only water drawn from our stream out back, which was difficult to do since it was the end of summer and the stream had just about dried up. He also said we must keep Jacob cool, which, in the heat of summer, was not easy. All I could do was bathe Jacob with water and put him outside in the cool evening air.

With all those treatments, Jacob's acidity and alkalinity became balanced, and he grew stronger. By now, Erastus's leg had healed, so he could start working around the house and the farm again.

When we took Jacob to church, many of the people in Pownal looked with great suspicion upon us, and some, I heard from Mrs. Carpenter up the road, suspicioned we were secretly Tories, which of course was absurd. So, we started to ask in town about what choices Jacob had. I didn't want him to return to being a prisoner, for he was a very handsome man and—I stress this more than his handsomeness—a kind man. Erastus went to Bennington one day to talk to the town's leaders and came back to say Jacob simply had to take an oath of allegiance to Vermont to protect himself from imprisonment. Once he became a citizen of Vermont, he'd be relieved of being on probation.

So we gathered up the proper papers and arranged for Reverend Dewey to announce at a Sunday meeting that Jacob would become a citizen of Vermont and swear his loyalty that afternoon. We figured many people would show up just because they did not like the Dutch, which they considered Jacob to be, even though he was a Braunschweiger. To assuage their feelings, we baked many pies and prepared as much cider as we could, which we allowed to ferment some (based on the recommendation of Michael, who had by now returned with Tryphena from defeating General Burgoyne). Nothing so calms the human heart as good food, especially if some of it is fermented. Jacob swore his loyalty, and everyone shook his hand. I even think some of the ladies admired his tall handsome self. But, as I have said, it was his kindness that attracted me.

Jacob had been raised in a farm family in Braunschweig, near the town of Vienenburg, so he knew much about agriculture. He joined the army because his family was too poor to feed everyone in it. He has been a great help around the farm.

Just to be on the safe side with our neighbors, he changed his name from his original name of Jacob Johann Hintersass to John Henderson, so now I am Mrs. Henderson. We live on a nice little farm in Williamstown, Massachusetts.

(Oh, and just to set the record straight, I believe Erastus wrote I once was interested in a gentleman named Mr. Peter Keyes. Liking a person and loving him are two different kettles of fish. Erastus has also revealed to me that Mr. Peter Keyes was an Indian, of all things, and that his name was Pebonkas Kisos or something equally savage. Erastus insists I not call that man an Indian, for he says Mr. Peter Keyes was part Abenaki, part Mohawk, and part Mohican. That sounds like an Indian to me.)

Jacob Hintersass's Story

When I awoke from my delirium, I saw bending over me a woman of admirable handsomeness. Since I did not know any English, I could not converse with her. She cared for me in a manner that convinced me she hoped this enemy soldier would die. That is, every time I grew warm and comfortable, she would pour cold water on me and put me outside to shiver in the night air.

When I learned some English, I learned her name was Tryphosa, which was a fine Deutsch-sounding name. And strong! She could carry me outside all by herself!

She had a brother named Erastus. As I learned more English, I learned that he was the one who had saved me when I was almost murdered on the battlefield, so I owed him my life. For a while, his leg was badly damaged, and I assumed it was because he, too, had been wounded on the battlefield. Then I learned, instead of being wounded on the field of battle, he had been attacked by a tree. Nevertheless, I thought it inappropriate to laugh at his clumsiness.

Erastus spent much of his time writing in his journal. When I asked if Tryphosa could read it to me, he explained how his journal was for his eyes only, how it was to help him remember details he would otherwise forget, and how, in time, he would translate those details into his remembrances about the group he called the Boys from Pownal. I was, at first, deeply chagrined that our army had been defeated by a group of boys, but then I learned of the American tendency to say things at a slight tangent.

Erastus and I became friends. He said I could help him understand more about how the people around Carpenter Hill and Pownal thought, so he would take me to visit families that had settled on the old Dutch patroonship owned by the Rensselaer family. Erastus said I could talk Dutch to the those speakers and then tell him what they said. I tried to tell him that Dutch is not Deutsch, but he did not seem to care. After we started to visit those people, I tried to tell Erastus that most of them were neither Dutch nor Deutsch and all spoke English, but he said he knew all that. If I went with him, he said, they would be more willing to speak honestly.

I have become friends with one tenant farmer there, Gerretse Van Kouwenhoven. He is trying to organize the farmers on Rensselaerwyck to break free of their landlords.

These Americans are a strange breed, caught between giving liberty and equality to all and making sure only those with the correct last names and correct language and correct skin color receive all the blessings of that liberty and equality. That is why I changed my name to Henderson and learned to speak English. Henderson or Hintersass, I do not have to bow before a king or his officers. But if one sister of Erastus is any indication, I have traded a German king for an American queen. I will take my American queen over my old king any day, for my queen can carry a calf or a pig as far as I can, and that is what any husband needs.

My Final Say

Sergeant Theophilus Bates, veteran of the French and Indian Wars, leader of the Green Mountain Boys of Pownal, never did return from the field after the Battle of Bennington or Walloomscoick, and may still be there today, eternally drilling those who fell alongside him.

I never again encountered my friend Pebonkas Kisos after he led his warriors away from me and the other Yankees at the Battle of Bennington. However, I read a news report after our Revolution ended about a new mayor of Montreal, described in the report as "swarthy" and named Peter Keyes. Not long after, I read that, for service to His Majesty, he was designated Sir Peter Keyes and chosen as a member of the Executive Council of the House of Assembly in Upper Canada's first parliament. Moreover, he had urged reconciliation with "our cousins to the south." Well, I leave it to you to draw your own conclusions. I have drawn mine.

Mr. DeVoet, who had been arrested as a Tory in Pownal, who escaped from that imprisonment, and whom I had seen being led off to prison following the Battle of Bennington, escaped from prison the second time and became a member of the United Empire Loyalists who fled to Canada, along with other former Pownal residents such as Beriah Buck, Conradt DeFoe, Charity French, Joseph Anderson, and Nathan Walker. I hope they are happy in Canada and would welcome them back any day, although I doubt they will come.

Cotton Mather Dewey, "Old Deuteronomy," preaches out his days here, with my sister Tryphena as his assistant. He became substantially less boring after the Battle of Bennington and is actually quite entertaining to hear. Tryphena is so busy assisting him and trying to control her husband, poor Michael, that she has no time for me, which is much to my satisfaction. Deuteronomy's sermons tend to be overly sprinkled with quotations from the Bible now, but that is a slight price to pay for my peaceful existence at home.

Whenever Tryphena or Tryphosa tries to lord it over me, I ask why they did not save me in Montreal, instead of just dumping me over an embankment and leaving me. To this day, they have not answered that to my satisfaction.

The tenant farmers in the Dutch patroonship of Rensselaer are becoming more and more like those of us in Pownal were when the Green Mountain Boys marched off with Ethan. That is to say, they are restless about not being able to purchase their own land and having to work just to pay their rent. I suppose one day they will have their own revolution to throw off the yoke harnessing them to their rent payments. I also believe we citizens of Pownal will come to their assistance and will at last be their friends and allies. Who knows? One day they may be as rich and powerful as the Dutch in New Jersey.

Ethan Allen unfortunately died in 1789, but before that he went north to live and be a landjobber along with his brothers. He finally published his philosophical beliefs in *Reason: The Only Oracle of Man* and was attacked as a Deist. Some say he threatened the U.S. Congress to turn Vermont back over to the British if they did not declare us a State, and some claim he actually began negotiations with the British to do so. I say he simply innovated political methodology. Congress finally collapsed in the face of overwhelming common sense and made Vermont the fourteenth state in 1791. Today, school children are compelled to memorize the phrase "the thirteen colonies" when they learn of our Revolution, but I am convinced they will be taught to memorize "the fourteen colonies" as soon as History recognizes Vermont's contribution to our freedom.

Benedict Arnold, clearly the best commander in the colonial army, led an army across Maine in the worst of winter, suffering mightily with them, until they arrived outside of Quebec and failed in their noble effort. Then Arnold, clearly the best admiral in the colonial navy, built a fleet that stopped the British fleet at Valcour Island in Lake Champlain and thereby held off their invasion for one more year. Michael and Tryphena can tell you how, though wounded, Arnold led our men at Bemis Heights and contributed greatly to the surrender of Burgoyne. Though Tryphena and others may not speak of him these days, I swear I am proud to have known him when I did. I only wish that George Washington and that perpetually disputatious and excessively politic Congress would have been proud of him, too, instead of dredging up and promoting their favorite sons from their barrels of pork. I especially wish Benedict Arnold would have exhibited a bit more patience and perseverance in leading his snail to Jerusalem. We all make choices in our lives, some of which we regret. His choice to go against his former comrades must surely have caused him great regret.

Do you remember the New Jersey butcher I did not trust, the one named John Honeyman? It seems I may have been right in not trusting him, but for the wrong reasons. Honeyman, from what Samuel Sutphen in New Jersey wrote to me, was spying on the Hessians in Trenton and knew they would be celebrating Christmas and not paying much attention to Washington, who by now had been defeated in New York and defeated in White Plains and chased all the way from Boston across New Jersey into Pennsylvania. So Honeyman allowed himself to be captured by Washington's men, gave Washington himself key information about the Hessians in Trenton, and, rumor has it, was allowed to escape when Washington diverted his own soldiers guarding Honeyman by setting a fire in another part of the camp and then cutting a hole in the tent that held Honeyman. Personally, I think this is a story either made up by Washington or made up by Honeyman, each of whom needed to have people think well of him. Trenton was Washington's first victory. I note it took him longer to win his first victory than it took Ethan Allen to win his first.

George Washington, despite his obvious weaknesses, finally defeated the British at Yorktown. But since so many so-called patriots gave up the war, including me, it fell upon the poor, the Irish, and the Deutsch-speakers to fill his army of patriots, not to mention those slaves who did not fight for the British—and boys—not the Boys from Pownal—but young boys, boys such as I once was. After the War, in 1787, Washington presided over the Convention that put together our Constitution and said, as far as I can tell from reading the newspapers, just about nothing—the same old silent George I once saw in Philadelphia. For saying nothing, he was unanimously elected our country's President by the delegates to Congress.

As for me, I am a farmer. I go to town meetings. Some people even care what I think. Sometimes at night, when I cannot sleep, I remember my mirror-image.

I have begun to correspond with a gentleman in Liberty Corner, New Jersey, Samuel Sutphen, who was sold to another owner shortly after I met him; who fought for our militia against the British; who at one point served under, of all people, Lord Stirling; and who, in spite of all that, was not allowed to buy his freedom until well after the War ended. He had been sold and resold and resold, like an old farm wagon, despite fighting for us and being wounded. I have also begun to correspond with a lady in Somerville, New Jersey, named Trintje, whom you will remember, I hope. She began to keep a journal after meeting me, and I am thinking of going back there for a while—just to share our journals, you understand.

978-0-595-45205-7
0-595-45205-1

Lightning Source UK Ltd.
Milton Keynes UK
UKOW051900241011

180846UK00002B/181/A

9 780595 452057